Dream Keepers

by

Celaine Charles

Keepers Series

The Wild Rose Press, Inc.
PO Box 708
Adams Basin, NY 14410-0708
Visit us at www.thewildrosepress.com

Publishing History
First Edition, 2025
Trade Paperback ISBN 978-1-5092-6250-2
Digital ISBN 978-1-5092-6251-9

Keepers Series
Published in the United States of America

Dedication

Dream Keepers is dedicated to those who dare to imagine something more in their lives, so they create it! Of course, I couldn't make a thing without nature's inspiration outside my window, my amazing family, friends, editors, and readers endlessly supporting me, and especially the shining light from above, always steering me onward!

Chapter 1

Breathe

Mason closed his eyes at the manic stir pelting against his rib cage. Every instinct argued for release, so he ground his teeth and fisted his hands. It was impossible to hold his feeble human side in check, not that he had much left. But right now, his dad's life depended on whatever strength he could muster.

Stepdad.

Dad.

Air burst from his lungs.

"Again." Bethesda's voice hitched on a whisper. "Breathe and hold. Gather every painful doubt. Every fear. Every regret."

Mason's diaphragm filled with the sweet air permeating the healer's sanctuary. It was a familiar scent, like rose bushes outside his childhood bedroom window. His mom had planted them long before she died and came back to life.

"Keep holding."

The air in Mason's chest pulsed against his ribs, forcing his eyelids open. His vision burned into the lavender eyes peering back at him, their unique hue softened by age. Tiny creases whittled along Bethesda's cheeks, each one interlacing into the next, vanishing behind lengthy strands of silver hair. How long had she been a healer in the Spiritual Realm?

"Slowly release." Gently, she pushed the air away with her hands. "Let every impulse fade."

Mirroring her, he thrust his palms out, blowing away the reality of his new life far away from his childhood home in Seattle. Air deflated from his chest like a balloon.

"Not working."

A month ago, if someone had told him he'd be cross-legged on the floor with a healer, in an unimaginable realm seeking guidance in meditation, he would have deemed them irrational. For the suggestion of another realm, yes, but when would Mason Deed, attention deficit extraordinaire, have sought meditation?

Bethesda's eyebrow arched. "Meditation may not be warranted. More crucial is *acceptance*. Better to spend time preparing for your first mission as lead."

Hearing the words *mission* and *lead* made him grimace. He doubted his estranged family knew much about his leadership skills. His cast was still new. But Ashton. He dabbed sweat from his forehead, relieved she would be by his side, and he wouldn't lead alone.

Bethesda stared, expecting a response.

"I know you think I'm worthy." Bile threatened to rise, and he swallowed down the names that deserved no voice, Cillian…aka Ian…aka biological, monstrous, finally banished birth father. "I'm trying to be the man everyone thinks I can simply choose to be—"

"The Blessing Council knows who you are."

He runs a hand through matted curls. "I'm sure the council is reconsidering their acceptance offer."

Bethesda's glare softened.

Mason shook his head to scatter the pity veiling her

face. He let his memories wash away into the sun-filled room. He couldn't afford distractions when he stood a chance at reuniting what little might remain of his dysfunctional family. But they ricocheted off the windowpanes and back into his head.

He slapped his hands against the wooden floor, stinging his palms. "I can't keep my head straight. Why make Ashton and me lead? We're too new a cast."

"You must trust your superiors. They hold enough confidence in you and Ashton, regardless of your hesitations or disbelief."

"Ashton, of course. But me? This mission must be a test or punishment for involving my dad—*Max*." He dropped his head into his hands. Using his stepdad's name felt foreign on his tongue.

She rested a hand on his back.

Mason peered up, wide eyed. "Please help me find focus. I can't ask anyone else."

Bethesda moved to stand by a framed painting. He clambered up for a better view. Sunlight continued its steady stream through the tall windows, creating a hazy curtain between him and the art. The weather outside glistened, as always in Toria, the village of northwest keepers. If only he could drink the serenity of his current surroundings. Squinting, he drew closer, and the piece of art took shape. A map.

Mason's jaw dropped. To see the seamless connections of new lands, blended together with familiar continents and oceans, blew his mind. The map reminded him of a tree cookie, with trunk slices that showed all the rings of a tree's age. A dark circle marked the center, with layers of other realms spreading from there.

He recognized the first layer outside the center spot where he and Ashton had grown up. "Human Realm."

He searched for Washington State in the northwest corner. Seattle. *Home*. More spheres looped outside of that, like ripples to an infinite blackness he once believed made up the universe. A pink circle outlined the Human Realm. Labeled in whimsical script were the words *Dream Realm*. The swirling paint reminded Mason of cotton candy. The map didn't stop there. Another layer depicted in lavender brushstrokes marked the Spiritual Realm. Mason knew this to be his current location. Every time he blinked, the colors in the painting blossomed like giant flowers before closing and blooming again.

He rubbed his eyes. "That painting *is* moving, right?"

She smiled.

Mason would have to show Ashton. Her artistic side would overflow using magical paint.

He looked back at the map, which came alive the longer he stared. The largest circle of all encircled the lavender one. This realm was the most spectacular, painted in blues. The depths of hues pulled Mason nearer. The closer he stepped, the deeper the blues swirled. A hum, strumming from each paint stroke, needled through his mind.

"The Heavenly Realm." It wasn't a question, simply everything settled into place.

He exhaled a long-held breath. Only a day ago, he and Ashton had returned from her adopted parents' funeral. An avoidable funeral, if not for—*that*. His head snapped to the center of the map. The dark spot he'd seen as a flat circle in the middle of the painting rolled and thundered like a storm. "The Dark Realm."

Fury superseded his apprehension. Blood boiled under his skin. Mason whirled toward Bethesda. "Where is he now? On the map."

Max wasn't supposed to be involved. His memories should have been wiped, if only he would have stopped snooping.

But Max Deed? He was more stubborn than Mason had already known him to be, bargaining with the demon, Ian, before everything was set!

"Where is Ian's realm?" Mason's voice increased in volume.

Bethesda set a hand on his shoulder. "Hidden. We speculate its location somewhere between the Dark and Human Realms. As you know, he worked alone."

Mason paced the hall. "Every time I think of my dad stuck in there, it feels like I'm going to explode."

"It is good to hear you referring to Max as your dad, proving blood doesn't always bind." She nodded her approval. "Your emotions are understandable. Remember, with Ian's banishment and his realm unknown to others, your dad is surely safe from harm. For now. We are keeping watch at every portal."

Mason stopped pacing. "What if the blessing council can't find a loophole in the contract? Will he be trapped there forever?"

"Have faith, my child." She looped their arms and guided him away from the map. "Let me pour you some tea."

"No." He stormed to the center of the room and sat down to practice breathing. "Tea isn't going to give me control. I can't risk anything going wrong in this mission Shunnar wants *me* to lead. There's no way I'm ready, even if it's supposed to be quick and easy because of Ian's absence." His chest tightened. As of late, nothing had gone to plan. The human confidence he'd once worn like an armor hung just out of reach, leaving him…weak.

The healer gazed with sorrowful eyes. "Mason, you're working against your own soul. Why change who you are?"

Mason blinked at the lavender realm on the map, the place he currently stood in his new world.

There were many reasons he didn't want to fail this mission. But more than proving to his cast or the council he was somehow worthy of his accidental placement as seam keeper, he needed to fix the aftermath of a now-banished demon, especially when it involved the only dad he wanted to claim.

He needed to find control. To meditate. To focus. He sucked in a deep breath.

"Mason, I ask you again." Bethesda's tone clipped his weighing thoughts. "Why change *who* you are?"

His breath released in a huff. "It's not every day someone like me gets a second chance." Although he struggled to remember the exact moment his world changed during his last battle, the memory of his miraculous rebirth shined brightly behind his eyes.

"I can't mess this up." His head bobbed to his chest. "Please, help me find the calm I felt after my healing. It was there. Briefly. I felt it. But now I'm freaking out, and I don't want my team losing faith in the free will they *think* I command."

Bethesda lifted his chin with a finger. "The energy you suppress is the drive you need for guidance." She wiped a dangling curl from his brow. "A blessed trait, not misgiving."

She patted his shoulder and turned toward the teapot. Through the window, Mason studied the bright sky, blue like the Heavenly Realm he'd seen and heard through the painted map. Impulsivity and impatience were never traits he'd been proud of. What was Bethesda talking about…his attention struggles were a blessing? How strange to think of the diagnosis he'd taken medication for as a child might somehow be the edge he needed to lead his team of keepers.

Mason rested on the hard floor and closed his eyes. They wouldn't leave to free Max from Ian's hidden realm until morning.

Breathe.

"I thought I saw you through the window." Ashton's voice startled, and he sprang upright from the sanctuary floor.

"Am I interrupting?" She froze in the doorway, noticing Bethesda.

Mason glanced at the healer, wide-eyed and warm-cheeked.

Bethesda extended an arm to Ashton. "Join us." She spoke over her shoulder, voice fading as she disappeared from the room. "I'll get more tea."

Ashton moved closer, her blue eyes a horizon of concern. "You okay?"

"Of course."

He couldn't tell her the self-assurance he'd felt only days ago had faded. His human days of confidence when he hadn't cared about anything but dragging Ashton to parties at Hicks's house or hiking on forest trails outside Seattle. Those memories all seemed a lifetime ago. Maybe because they were.

Ashton tilted her head to the side. Her long brown hair swooshed across her shoulders, her smile thinned, and her blue eyes glowered until he cracked, caving as usual when it came to her.

"Okay—I'm worried about the two of us leading this mission. Bethesda's helping me meditate." After growing up together, he couldn't get much past her.

She snagged his hand. "It's going to be fine. *We were made for this, remember*?"

He rolled his eyes at his own words used against him. Why couldn't he relax? "The realms believe in *you*."

"Not fair, Mas. You were there when the Blessing Council accepted *you*."

"Gavan doesn't want me here." Mason strode to the sitting area, falling back onto a sofa.

"Gavan's not the only one in charge—"

"He's *my* boss."

"And my—"

He filled in her huffed blank, birth father. But she wouldn't acknowledge that. She hadn't spoken to him since he'd tried to force her from the last battle.

Instead she plopped down next to him, resting her hand on his leg. She was either holding her tongue or realized he was right. As she opened her mouth to respond, Bethesda emerged from the hall offering them a tray of teacups.

"Thanks." He reached for the tea that would never help him feel better.

"Thank you, Bethesda. Mason's telling me about your lessons in meditation." She winked at him.

"I am not sure meditation is in his make-up." When Mason dropped his chin, she grinned. "It will simply take time. Your impulsiveness may be your most useful trait."

Ashton's eyes lit up. "You see—"

"Don't say it," he warned, adjusting his fingers around the warm cup. He didn't care how much his recklessness defined him growing up. He was a new perso—seam keeper. He would find a way to stay in control, lead his cast to free his dad, *prove* he was in charge of his own free will, *and* make it clear he was meant to be paired with Gavan's only daughter.

"Mason, you can do this. You have a chance to get your family back, and we won't let anything stop us. We'll do it together."

"Well said." Bethesda sipped her tea.

He tasted the warm liquid, the fragrant essence smoothing over his jagged thoughts. When had he ever *not* been ready for a fight? A staggered breath escaped because he knew the answer to his question. When it reunited his once believed to be dead mom and forever grieving stepdad. When it might salvage his lonely childhood. And when it involved him and Ashton in charge of a team that had already trained their whole lives to be warriors. The stakes were too high to have everyone relying on his unsharpened leadership skills.

Now he was supposed to have faith in himself.

Mason's stomach rolled as he gulped down more tea…no amount of meditation would calm these stormy seas.

Chapter 2

Reflected Warrior

Ashton stepped into her commander's office. Rory held up a finger without looking up, her red mane, probably half her body weight, spilled atop curved shoulders, as she penned a message onto ivory paper. It was the first time Ashton had been in her office. Their meetings before had been in the makeshift quarters at training camp.

"All done." Rory stood, tipped the feathered end of her pen to the paper, and brushed it from top to bottom. In a tiny burst of ivory haze, the letter vanished. "Have a—"

"What was that?"

Rory placed the white plume in a drawer. "I messaged the Dream Realm. As you know, only shifters have telepathy limited to their assigned casts. No cell phones here." Her gray eyes gleamed in the sunlight pouring through the window behind. She pointed to a chair next to a wall of bookshelves.

Still staring at the residual sparkles, Ashton sat. This new world still surprised her.

"You wanted to see me?" Ashton folded her hands in her lap.

"How are your memories, your gifts…your headaches?"

"They've settled. I know who I am now." She sat up taller. "My human side finally agrees I'm as brave as my keeper side believes." She paused, searching for the right words. "In that last battle, it wasn't two streams of memories filtering through anymore. Just me."

"I can't imagine. No wonder you've suffered headaches. But you've also gripped your human life with both hands." She frowned in sympathy, fiery red curls cascading. "Centennials only happen every hundred years. You're *my* first experience. I hope I haven't pushed too hard."

"Of course not." Ashton pulled her ponytail over her shoulder. Her hair had grown longer in Toria, in a short time. She twisted the chestnut ends around her fingers. She wasn't nervous. Her past anxieties had been quiet since the final battle with Ian. She had no idea if they might resurface and fill her chest with tiny familiar pinpricks, but for now, confidence flowed in rivulets through her veins. "I feel stronger. But I want—" She paused, biting her lip.

"You want more."

It wasn't a question. Rory was right. Her warrior inside, finally dressed in full armor, was empowered. And restless. She wanted to rescue Max. She wanted to slay more demons. She wanted to become the Centennial in every way her birth father, Gavan, had never wanted. Proving him wrong was her new mantra. But she would never say those words aloud, so instead she slumped. "Yes."

"So you shall." Rory beamed. "If we cannot bring Max home because his contract is binding, then we will need you. Your ability to solve complex problems will be imperative. Sometimes brute force isn't always the answer. We need solid strategy."

Ashton clutched the arms of her chair. "But I can't always command it to work. This gift—whatever it is—clicks away at its own pace."

"It rises in need. You've wielded its knowledge before, always in perfect time. Have faith in the process."

"But this is about Max, the only dad Mason's ever known. After thirteen broken years, he can finally reunite his family."

"Years are of little consequence in the Spiritual Realm. Surely you've learned that in your short time here." Rory angled her vision out the window, the sun resting lower in Toria's blue sky.

Ashton *hadn't* realized. Time was tricky in all the realms. But any amount of time alone, without the ones you loved, was a year—day—minute too long. "Will there always be so much at stake?"

"Protecting souls is always high stakes, wouldn't you agree?" Rory's overcast eyes gleamed with the hope of a clear day.

Ashton rubbed the oak leaf charm on her bracelet. "We haven't talked about my new gift. The one that exploded from my palms, stopping the windstorm that breached our borders."

Rory tapped her finger on the desk. "Yes, that was new, and oddly appeared much later than your other abilities. Again, you are my first Centennial. We are still searching for a safe location to practice your newest skill."

Safe? A chill branched from her spine to her shoulders. She had no idea where the force had come from that day, her emotions—on fire—when Ian had set foot in Toria. Maybe just as her gift of unlocking solutions was based on her sense of danger, this new gift of stopping storms was based on rage. She fisted her hands onto her lap.

"Can we run through our regular simulations?"

Rory straightened. "I thought you'd never ask."

"Let's start now." Ashton made way for the door, knowing full well Rory would follow. Ashton had always been first to call it quits with her simulation training, the experience often eerie. Though as much as Rory pushed her, it was never *too* harsh. For such a small frame, her commander carried a strong punch, though she was patient. All those weeks when Ashton's human side was afraid, when her head thumped in pain by the third simulation, Rory waited.

But Ashton was different now.

Maybe it was time to test *how* different.

She and Mason would lead their cast tomorrow. They would bring Max home, return to the Seam, destroy any demons seeking entrance to the Dream Realm, and build their lives together. She wiped the smile from her lips, enamored by the warrior she saw reflected in the window. She wasn't that shy girl from Seattle anymore.

Chapter 3

Mission: Hidden Realm

Sleep hadn't inspired any more confidence in his own leadership abilities, but Mason swallowed his nerves and met his team to brief the mission. The flight arena, brisk in the morning air, still had him wiping sweat from the back of his neck. Long evergreen shadows fell over the wooden launch platforms that surrounded the clearing as he raised an arm, signaling the group.

Ashton and his mom, Mia, hushed their conversation, as did his cast of ten—five shifters and five riders. Shunnar stood ready, watching Mason take charge. Had he nodded his approval to begin, or was the mission already moving too slowly?

Mason pushed his shoulders back to address the teams. "Ashton and I will follow you to the portal, then we'll travel with her gift of transference once you're through." She could only take one person at a time, and he needed a moment to settle his thoughts without everyone staring at him.

Trying to look convincing while averting his eyes from Shunnar, he nodded to his team to initiate the mission. When his shoulders dropped, Ashton leaned into him. Her touch comforted, but still his mind raced with the possibilities that might not end well for his stepdad.

With Ian banished and his realm hidden from all worlds, the council had concluded that Max must be alone or with whoever—whatever—was left inside. The test: getting him out with his contract uncompleted. His stepdad might be unaware Ian was gone. He might still be working on the details of their bargain to publish a book on the truth of demons, release it to humans, and create an excess of fear into the Dream Realm. Mason had learned human souls released their emotions during sleep and, though he'd never seen it himself, could only imagine the ramifications if all those emotions were negative.

He thought of his stepdad hovering over his manuscripts back home, but all Mason had seen was a shut door. Max preferred privacy. What conditions might hang over him now, creating a book of evil in a place that shouldn't exist?

Mia's blonde head was the last of their cast to disappear through the portal. She would then lead them to her property in the Human Realm, where she'd previously discovered the entrance to Ian's secret realm. He ignored the rest that clawed his mind, the part where she'd hidden from him for thirteen years.

"Ready?" Ashton's voice wavered until he held up a thumb. He prepared himself for the swaying that challenged his equilibrium when swept through her magic.

Ashton tightened the elastic band holding her long dark hair, then pulled the silver compact from her pocket. The palm-sized trinket, hinged on one edge, allowed the top to fold over snugly. Open, the tiny holes resembled a saltshaker, too small for her purple petals to fall out. The flower power made Ashton and whoever she touched invisible. Closed, it was round and flat, the face etched with an oak leaf design. Made from blessed iron, the case controlled the energy of the unique flowers, another of Ashton's Centennial gifts.

They clasped hands as he peered into her blue gaze. She was nervous too, but they didn't say a word, staying brave for each other, as always. Ashton thumbed the lid open, and tingles raced up Mason's arms. It was important they be invisible when entering the realm, as Ashton wasn't sure where they might land. Usually, she pictured locations in her mind, but this realm was different—not quite there, but there—so she wanted to be safe.

Ashton gripped his hand, shook off the vibrations from the flowers, then peered into the mirrored top of the compact, using the reflection to pull them through.

Mason stretched out his free arm. His body dissolved into liquid along with hers before melding back together in a matter of seconds. It was one of her more curious gifts, and the fastest way to travel between realms.

Still holding her hand, he rolled his shoulders from his squatted position. "A massage compared to the bone-crushing shift into my hawk."

She smirked, dusting the strange chalky groundcover off her gear pants. "I'm going to ignore that comparison." She pulled him up to stand. "I know this is important. We're leading, but it's also Max." She touched his chin when he started to look away. "You can do this. And Shunnar must agree since he's given you the reins."

Mason huffed. "Us. He's given *us* the reins." He

shook his head. "Part of me hopes nothing happens. I need to bring my dad home. The other part wants to prove we can handle anything."

"I've never seen you this nervous. We could meditate?"

"We'd have to be able to breathe for that to work." He scrunched his nose at the horizon.

Ian's self-created realm was a vast, colorless wasteland. Lifelessness hung in the pale trees, barren branches scratching the ashen sky. The air was thick and heavy to breathe. The light, dim. Everything felt as dead as the now-banished demon prince, just how he wanted to remember his biological father.

Ashton found his gaze. "Should we go in or wait for the others?"

He stood taller. "We're seam keepers. We wait for our team." They would arrive soon, traveling through the portal Mason's mom had shown them.

She squeezed his hand in approval.

Waiting wasn't in Mason's makeup, but it was the keeper thing to do. He needed a distraction though and leaned closer to that soft spot behind her jawline. Faint traces of honey and lavender scents slipped through the hazy environment.

He and Ashton would always be stronger together. Maybe that was why his mom's prayer had been granted, and his life miraculously restored. He'd been given a second chance, no matter the amount of demon blood coursing through his veins. But hadn't that become more to prove? He pushed the thoughts away when Ashton tilted her head for a kiss.

Maybe *this* was all the meditation he needed. How many human years had he been this close to her without realizing she was the one? Ashton reached an arm around his neck.

"Stay alert. They should be close."

Mason and Ashton jumped at Shunnar's voice. Their team stalked from the portal, almost on top of them.

Ashton flipped the lid to her compact, sealing the magic. Mason let go of her hand, and they both materialized into view. Their cast halted, though their shock to Ashton and Mason's sudden appearance was subtle, only a few bugged-out eyes or hands hovering over weapons. Battle ready, their team followed Mason and Ashton behind another cluster of lifeless tree forms.

Shunnar nodded to Mason, his sandy hair perfectly in place, his hazel eyes calm, as if handing off control *wasn't* some kind of test.

Mason took a deep breath, or tried to, before addressing the group. The stale air, along with rattled nerves, caught in his throat. How was his stepdad enduring this strange atmosphere?

Mason's heart rate increased, his shifter gear sweltering. Ashton took a step closer. It was enough to ground him, but when he glanced at her for help, she only winked. And he knew. She was serious about letting him lead this mission. He didn't know if it made him mad or love her more for believing in him.

She whispered, "Consider this a mountain-climbing experience."

He raised a brow, accepting his payback for always pushing her.

"And here I thought you were concerned about my growth," he muttered back.

The entire group stared in wait, and with or without

any clean air for his lungs, he called out the game plan. "The estate is small. The five-story castle stands about three-quarters of a mile that way." He pointed northwest of their location. The tops of stone-gray turrets poked atop the milky gray horizon.

"There are no guards and nothing outside this small forest, from what we know." He addressed Nigel, Bronwyn, Adam, and Hannah from their second line. In a regular cast flight at the Seam, their triangular formation consisted of Ashton and Mason on point, a row of two pairs behind, with a final row of three pairs behind them. "You two cover the front of the house. Adam, you and Hannah cover us outside once we enter from the back. Third line, spread through the surrounding forest. Everyone stays hidden and keeps watch. This place may be a secret from other realms, but there were servants last time Mom—Mia—and I were here. We don't know if they're dangerous. Stay guarded."

His cast nodded as if Mason had always belted orders. Shunnar stood by Mia, newly retrained after her...sabbatical...and invested in retrieving the husband she'd been dead to for the last thirteen years.

"And us?" Shunnar's statuesque form hovered like a blockade.

"Come with us, I guess." He motioned for the two of them to follow Ashton and him toward the back entrance of Ian's estate.

"You guess?" Shunnar crossed his arms.

This *was* a test. Mason's eyebrow twitched. But he put a hand to his forehead, smoothing the tension, and cleared the doubt from his throat.

"The four of us will head to the back-east

entrance." He addressed the rest of the team. "We'll sweep the inside. You all have the perimeter, and since this place isn't supposed to exist, we should be able to retrieve my da—Max—without a hitch. Though be ready for anything."

"What about the contract? Do you foresee any holdups?" Shunnar grilled.

Mason peered at his mom. Mia's amber eyes glossed over, brighter than anything this half-realm had in its smoggy skies. She wanted her husband to be safe. He would make that happen.

"Let's hope the conditions of the contract died with Ian's expulsion." He nodded toward the estate. "Only one way to find out. Let's go."

The teams moved out in opposite directions. None of them expected a dangerous battle as they would have if Ian was alive, but they were in a demon-created space, unknown even to the Dark Realm. There was no telling what might happen.

With Shunnar's keen eyes scrutinizing, Mason led his group of four to a side entrance of the fortress. His second line dispersed to their posts outside the estate. His six members of the third line stretched along the gray tree line. Sound traveled strangely in this place, or rather, lack of it. Shunnar and Mia followed behind Mason and Ashton as they crept toward the back of the property, staying as far back from the windows as possible.

Mason studied their route. He'd been in this spot before, and even then, it seemed surreal. How did this place exist? He could hardly think through the murky surroundings, the strange atmosphere blending into the stones on the house.

Shunnar approached on his left, his stare piercing through the dim illumination, jolting Mason to the present. His heartbeat thumped like a bass drum, and he blinked to steady himself. There was more than Shunnar's final grade weighing on his shoulders; the dad he wanted to get to know all over again had signed away his soul.

Thirteen years of a grief-stricken relationship was enough. It was time to prove himself as the leader he was meant to be.

Chapter 4

White Flag

Back slapping the ashlar wall, Mason peered up at the late demon's castle, small and scaled to perfection. Stones crawled up each layer, ascending in size to pointy turrets. The rear of the five-story dwelling grew right out of the powdery cliff, leaving the same slim walk-through his mom and he had used during their earlier breaking and entering.

He looked at her now, short blonde curls slicked behind her ears. Mia stood wide-eyed and alert next to a straight-faced Shunnar. With camouflage gear and gem-handled weapons stocked on her utility belt, she looked like the seam keeper she'd assured him she once was.

For Mason, she'd only been Mom. Would she ever be just Mom again? When they got Max back—*if* they got Max back—what would happen next? He was human. She was a seam keeper. Could they continue where they left off after years of lies and monsters and hiding? Could they be a family again?

His stomach backflipped into reality, apprehension scattered.

Get a grip!

His mom blinked his way, oblivious to his mental state. Ashton's hand hovered over her belt, set for battle. Shunnar scanned the tall windows lined up on the back of the house. There was no sign of movement behind the glass, and as always, the light inside and out resembled dusk or early dawn.

Mason swallowed his bile-tasting doubt…time to get his family back. One nod at Ashton, and she ducked along the windows until she reached the back entrance. Eyes pinched tight, as if that alone might turn the knob, she beamed when the door opened, still spurred by her gifts.

Inside, Mason led them past the dark kitchen to the stairwell. He remembered from his last trip the stairs rounded up five floors with wide landings between each level. It was early morning in Toria, their home in the Spiritual Realm, but he had no idea of the time here. Jumping realms always scrambled things. With no sun or moon, sconces on the walls flickered candlelight as if it were late, and no activity in the castle proved otherwise.

"Shunnar, Mom, start here and work your way up. Check every room. Ash and I will go from top down." He slipped up the stairs, Ashton behind, thankful the ominous space absorbed any creaks in the floorboards or shuffling of steps. Silence hung as they ascended to the top floor, with no explanation for the strange atmosphere. It seemed the realm didn't know it existed, didn't realize it should creak or moan with a disturbance in weight.

Mason peered into the library, the room that had recently housed his dad's unpublished books on demons. Back home, Max had hidden the manuscripts behind his published mysteries and ancient histories. Somehow, he'd dragged them out to seal his deal.

Mason pointed left, and Ashton slunk between the

right-side wall and a bookcase. A noise swelled from the center of the room, the sound muffled before the cause could register. As Mason crept around a shelf, he saw the source: messed blond hair, unshaven and disheveled, Max Deed. His stepdad's glasses tipped off the end of his nose like an old man. His elbows slumped over a table covered in books and scrolls, his shirt sleeves rolled up high on his arms. Before Mason made another move, he saw Ashton across the room. She circled her finger in the air and gave him a thumbs-up. Perimeter secure.

"Dad," Mason called, not wanting to startle him.

Max jumped, his chair scraping the floor before the sound cut short, lost in the strange thick air. His gaze swept the room, fear pressing the poised man Mason once knew as Dad into the shell standing before him.

"Dad, it's me." He stepped into view. Ashton stayed hidden.

"Mason?" Max turned, his glossy brown eyes doubling in size. "But I haven't finished my work. How—how are you here?" He scanned the room again. "Where's your mother?"

"She's downstairs. Come on, we're taking you home." He motioned for Ashton, and she approached slowly from Max's other side.

"Hi, Mr. Deed." She set her hand gently on his arm.

Max gaped between them. "Where's Ian?" He stumbled back. "Dominic?"

"Ian's dead. We need to go." Mason stepped closer.

"Dead?" Max turned the word over in his head. "Then, my work is done? You said your mother is…downstairs? Mia's downstairs?" Hyperventilating, he bent over, gripped his knees. Mason stared at Ashton. She shrugged. His dad was anything but this. Max Deed was clever and bold. He was pulled together, clean-cut, shaven, and only spoke with necessary words. This broken man before him was a mess.

"It's okay, Dad. Let's find Mom and get you home." Mason glanced wide-eyed at Ashton, similar confusion wafting across her face. *What happened to him?* They each took an arm, leading Max out the door.

The hallway was clear until sounds of a scuffle echoed from the floor below, before clipping to silence. Ashton's weapons belt lit up golden yellow, and she unsheathed her amber-handled sword. Nodding to Mason, she slipped out from under Max's arm and moved ahead. Mason pulled his dad's weight onto his shoulder and followed.

In the stairwell, Shunnar held an elegantly dressed old man against the wall. Mia fought hand to hand with a servant. The thumps resounded like faded distortions in the odd environment. The servant had impressive skills, so maybe they weren't all human. Though Shunnar and his mom were holding their own, Ashton raised her sword in warning.

"Stop!" she demanded, and the fighting froze. Mia turned, saw Max leaning against Mason, and all color drained from her face.

"Max!" Simultaneously she grabbed a dagger from her belt. Blue light flickered from the hilt as she sank the blade into the servant's chest. He dropped to the floor in a pile of ash as she ran to the husband she'd been dead to for the last thirteen years.

"Mia?" Her name barely crossed his lips before he

collapsed, dead weight like a kickstand snapping, and Mason stumbled onto the landing with Max in tow.

Shunnar raised his knife to take care of the elderly man, when a sudden blast deafened them from above. Lights sparked, smoke billowed, and a face from the not-so-distant past emerged: Ian, but not Ian.

Demon.

He had the same coloring and sharp features that resembled Ian, but with thick facial hair, a long black mane, and piercing green eyes. He was taller than Ian had been, yet had the same build, strong and fit. This larger demon arched his shoulders and cracked his neck as if his exploding entry had merely been uncomfortable. "What do we have here?"

The man Shunnar held braved to speak first. "Sir Kelvin, these maniac keepers have killed your brother and half the servants in his house. Please have mercy and spare me." He straightened his suit jacket.

Kelvin ignored the cast, closing the distance between the old man and himself in a stride. He touched the man's frail cheek. "My sweet Dominic. How long has it been since you once cared for my brothers and me?"

Dominic shook in response. He seemed more afraid when Shunnar loosened his grip and backed away, as if pleading to the wrong captor.

Think! Mason bellowed inside his own head.

He pushed up to his knees, Max still in tow, and heaved to his feet. Kelvin hadn't noticed or didn't care, his attention gathered on the old man.

Mason blinked a wordless message to Ashton, her sword still drawn. He glanced at his mom, now supporting his dad's other side, bloody dagger clutched in her free hand. Telepathically, he delivered a message to their cast outside. An ambush had been unexpected, but they would fight.

"What is this place, Dominic?" The demon peered around, his black leather vest exposing bare, muscular arms. "I only discovered it through my dead brother's spirit. I'm uninterested in waiting for his rebirth to expose the details." His glare snapped to the trembling old man. "Tell me!"

"It-it's a s-secret r-realm between realms, m-my master, Kelvin. Your brother C-Cillian created it. He wanted to sh-show your father—all of you when it was d-done. He wanted to sh-share it as a gift." The eerie quiet absorbed most of his stuttering.

Kelvin's green eyes shone like fog lights, small and fixed on something conjured behind his stare. He looked around again. It wasn't long before a smirk grew from under his scruffy black beard.

"Please, sir, I cared for you when you were young. I—"

Kelvin shot out a hand, squeezing the man's neck.

Dominic clutched the fingers over his throat, then slumped to the ground.

Dead.

Ian's brother exhaled and turned to Shunnar. He seemed indifferent to Mason and Mia hauling a passed-out Max or Ashton armed in a fighting stance. "You. Tell me why seam keepers have breached these walls? You have no business outside your Realms."

"Your brother took one of our own." Shunnar spoke with authority. Mason soaked it up, mentally prepping for the battle raging in his mind. If only he could think through the blur of emotion burning his veins.

"This human?" He pointed to the unconscious Max. "And this one." He sniffed at Mason. "You have demon blood."

His words blared in the stairwell, stinging before falling away. Mason panicked, dropping Max, and shoved the larger demon like he could simply push him down, as if in a school yard fight. Kelvin didn't budge, but Mason's careless act had shifted Max's weight onto Mia, who toppled down the stairs, her unconscious husband tumbling behind.

Shock thrust into chaos. One of his cast, Bronwyn, crashed through a small window in the stairwell from the southern front of the house. Her white hair flowed like an angelic banner as she flipped down acrobatically to her feet. Her hawk, Nigel, had to have flung her through.

The disturbance gave Shunnar enough time to pull knives from his vest, aiming for Kelvin's back. As if he were made of marble, each throwing blade ricocheted to the floor. Adam and Hannah, second line from his cast, ascended from the stairs in one fluid movement. Mason hoped they would help his parents escape as he thrust his foot into Kelvin's chest, barely teetering the beast.

Ashton and Bronwyn stood together, armed with blades and daggers in both hands, and aimed for the monster's heart, his back, his sides all at once.

Nothing.

His skin was too thick to draw blood. Or was it a charm? He smacked them away, knocking them each into the wall.

"Kiiiaaarrr!" Cries from Nigel, in hawk form,

blared as he soared through the broken window Bronwyn had created. He attacked the back of Kelvin's head with sharp talons.

Kelvin clawed at Nigel's hawk, feathers scattering like snow. Mason threw another punch, pain pulsing from the edges of adrenaline. Ashton, already on her feet again, brought down her sword. It chiseled off his shoulder, throwing her back. Was he made of stone? Bronwyn caught Ashton. The demon swatted his arms as if Mason's crew were irritants.

Hawk cries arose from outside, along with eerie screeches before snuffing out flat. Demons! Another battle raged outside.

"Did you think I would come alone to an unknown realm?" Kelvin grunted.

Nigel's hawk cried again, unable to penetrate Kelvin's thick skull from behind, but offered the needed distraction. The demon turned to fight off his winged oppressor.

"Go! Now!" Mason thundered as he dropped to shift. He glimpsed Bronwyn pulling Ashton down the stairs, the direction he'd seen his parents fall. He should have known Shunnar wouldn't flee; his hawk wings spread wide, transitioning faster than him.

Mason's bones split through tightened skin. His breath lodged as his razor-hooked beak tore through gums and teeth. His eyesight zoomed while his body twisted into its new shape.

All three hawks continued their dance of attack— striking, sliding to the floor, launching into flight, assaulting again. Movements were difficult in the tight landing, Kelvin spinning and ducking as he batted away each bird of prey. Hushed blasts from outside somehow carried through the broken window.

In his hawk form, Mason received Ashton's mental message. He deciphered her meaning as he flew in sync with his team. The servants were dead. Mia and Max had survived the fall. Hannah and Adam were leading them out.

He had to believe his cast outside was dealing with Kelvin's legion. The only keepers left inside were Nigel and Shunnar. Mason swallowed as Shunnar's voice broke through telepathically. *What's your call?*

My call? This seemed like a perfect time for Shunnar to make the freaking call. The mission had already ventured way past wrong.

The hawks continued in their drive, but nothing slowed Kelvin down. An expression of interest plastered his face.

Ashton's voice erupted through Mason's head. *We're all out, west side.*

It was the message he needed. Decision made.

Retreat! West end of the trees. We have Max, Mason delivered to the minds of his cast.

The three hawks made a final round, attacking Kelvin's shoulders and blocking arms before he crouched down. Oddly the monster stopped fighting, exposing his concrete back to take the brunt of the battle. Still nothing penetrated. Time to go.

They all swerved out the broken window and flew away from the estate. With the colorless surroundings below, Mason easily found the rest of their cast trekking away.

Max was still unconscious, held up by Hannah and Adam. After the guys shifted back to human forms, Ashton sent Mason a panicked look of relief. Mia grabbed Mason's arm, release spilling from her own eyes. The rest of their cast arrived. Hawks shifted, riders grew, adjusting to their regular size. Everyone looked at Mason for orders.

"The demons outside are wounded, not dead. They won't be far behind," Clara, rider from their third line, called. Black blood smeared her dark cheek.

Mason scanned the paper-thin woods as Mia called over the dread, "The tree portal, it's the only way out. Kelvin may not know. Exiting is different from entering."

"She's right, follow her," Mason ordered.

They all ran, picking through the soundless woods, drab gray trunks with pale ashen branches. If the air was a color, it would be a mix of yellow, gray, and brown.

Suffocation.

Pressure weighed on Mason's chest with each trot across the dustless soil. But he kept going. He had to get Max—everyone—out of there.

Mia held up a hand, halting before a random tree. It was no bigger or smaller than any of the others, nothing magical around to identify it as a portal. It was purely her prior knowledge that gave her certainty. She'd initially found it after being stuck in Ian's realm for three human days. That had been back when she was pregnant with Mason. It was when she'd learned the truth…she'd been tricked by a devil.

Mason strained to focus as Mia pushed Bronwyn through the portal. The others followed, one at a time. Adam and Hannah were left holding a slumped over Max, along with Ashton and Mason, and Shunnar and Mia.

Adam took on Max's weight and pushed Hannah through. She turned to pull Max on her way, but the tug was greater than she most likely expected, and she flew backward with a squeal before fading out of sight. Adam jumped in response to his mate, clutching Max to his chest. Like a brake thrown in a speeding car, his movement was interrupted. Adam swept through the portal, while Max's body jerked to a stop on the ground before the portal.

"What happened?" Mason spat.

Shunnar helped him pick up Max's crumpled body.

"I don't know, but we have to go." Mia's head shook back and forth, blonde curls loose in her panic. She must have appointed herself as lookout. "Get him through!"

Mason glanced at Ashton and tilted his head toward the portal. "Go. Mom, you're next. Shunnar and I have Max."

Mia continued checking behind. "Ashton, go."

When his mate hesitated, Mason eyed her. "Please. We'll be right behind you."

Ashton nodded, climbed through, but Mia refused. "I'm going last. Go!"

No time to argue. Kelvin might not be able to fly, but if they didn't hurry, he'd easily find them on foot. Shunnar and Mason hitched Max up by the shoulders and plunged themselves through the hidden portal of the otherwise thin tree. If they were lucky, maybe they could escape this plague of a realm and lock Kelvin in forever.

The thought took purchase in Mason's mind when he fell to the forest floor in the Human Realm. He rolled to a stop and leapt to search his surroundings.

Shunnar did the same. The rest of their cast stood ready, but no Max.

"Where is he?" Mason bellowed. It was only a one-way portal.

Shunnar whipped around. "I had him." He peered at Mason. "We had him."

"Dammit!" Mason growled. Wiping sweat from his forehead, he looked to Shunnar for help. He'd have flown a white flag if he'd had one.

"Search the area," Shunnar directed, hazel eyes locked on Mason.

I don't know what to do. His message sent only to Shunnar, as he locked down the recipients with his newly acquired telepathy. He didn't need other shifters picking up his fear.

The group dispersed, searching through the woods for any signs of Max. The setting sun sent that lingering glow before day faded to dusk. Color was back in their world now that they were in the Human Realm.

Mason's strength set with the sun. But still, he scanned the ground, tromping back and forth around the place he'd fallen, stirring up earthy scents of wet cedar. His dad was nowhere to be found, and neither was his mom.

"We should go back." Ashton dug in her pocket for her mirrored compact. "The portal inside is too far away, but I can take someone through a reflection."

Shunnar put up a hand. "If we go back, we need a new plan."

The tree shadows were dark, pooling into each other like spilled ink. They were losing light. Mason could think of only one thing: how could he lose his parents…again?

Adam stepped forward. His partner Hannah moved with him, always connected. With their matching auburn hair and flushed pink skin, they were a unified one. "I don't think Max can come through. I held him tight when I pulled across. It felt like he was the one who broke the energy flow."

"His blood oath?" Nigel offered, his long lean shadow blended with the tree shapes on the ground. "The contract binding even in Ian's banishment?" His height from the back of the group was a safeguard. Mason, grateful for his team's vigor, couldn't gather a single thought.

Shunnar set a hand on Mason's shoulder. "It makes sense. You and I both had him as well. His body was *forced* back. Keepers, return to the Seam. I'll assemble the Blessing Council. We'll need their guidance." He shook his head. "We may need more than that."

"My parents could be dead by then!"

"Kelvin isn't stupid. With our team attempting to extricate a human from his brother's secret lair, he'll want to know more. To do that he'll need leverage." Shunnar spoke coolly.

Mason couldn't move, frantically contemplating a backup plan. Darkness clouded his ability to think. He scarcely caught Shunnar motioning to Ashton. A moment later, she approached Mason, pulling him to walk with her. Together they led the cast through the woods past Mia's cabin. They didn't go inside though Mason paused for a breath at the base of the front steps. Ashton rubbed his shoulder, soothing the soreness already registering in his body.

"We'll get them out." Ashton tilted her head, catching his gaze. "I promise."

But her words only melted with the last lights of the day.

Secluded on Mia's property and the darkening sky, the males shifted into their full-sized hawk forms, something they wouldn't typically do in the Human Realm. The female riders stretched as their bodies resized slightly smaller and climbed on to take flight in the cool night air. Mason inhaled the deep breath he'd craved inside Ian's hidden realm, though it didn't refresh.

He could have traveled home through Ashton's reflection, through her Centennial gift as they'd entered the hidden realm at the start of the mission. But Mason needed to fly. With only a glance, she understood. He rolled his shoulders and curved his back, neck twisting, before his human body dropped into its hawk form. Soaring up and over his mom's cabin, he gave Ashton time for her form to meld in size before he swooped down for her to mount. Together they lifted off the ground, dirt and leaves rustling in their wake. It wasn't long before he fell in line behind Shunnar, his wings barely stroking the wind.

Shunnar knew the quickest route to the Northwest Portal, then back to the Spiritual Realm. Mason had tapped out. First mission in charge: fail.

Chapter 5

Internal Keepers

Zander tore off his death-soiled gloves and tossed them into a bin. His team stripped down in silence, peeling gear from their dream-soaked bodies. The Dream Realm had never sounded dreamy to Zander, especially since it was his consolation assignment, but the reality of protecting human souls was a wet and messy job.

Ansel, always done first, whistled on his way to the showers.

Daiya grumbled, "It's getting worse out there." She wrestled to free a leg from her wetsuit.

Zander didn't look up. He cared she was upset yet respected her privacy. Internal Keepers lost all modesty early on, but that didn't mean they were insensitive. Something he learned on day one when the three of them mismatched together. It wasn't anything he'd prepared for. He'd trained his whole life to be a seam keeper at the *borders* of the Dream Realm, to shapeshift into a hawk and fight the demons threatening to cross its boundaries, but a year ago, the Blessing Council had sent him to fight internally.

No explanation.

A change of destiny.

Done.

He hadn't flown since, the hawk inside dormant.

When he didn't respond, Daiya stormed off to the showers. Zander lingered longer in the semi-quiet space, Ansel's whistling seeping from the showers. The changing room was free of keepers, his crew finished for the day, night crews already departed. Steam from behind the adjacent wall beckoned, and he took the needed steps through the door, to an empty stall on the end. He craved the release of a shower, his body sluggish from the weight of their mission. Daiya had been right. Demon activity was at an all-time high. But today he had other concerns on top of that reality, burdens from his past, unfinished.

When the water spray hit his shoulders, he closed his eyes and fell into the heat, letting the streams pulse against sore muscles. His rattled mind also longed for healing, though expectations were low that his shower might provide mental renewal.

Ansel's whistling faded, signaling Zander to finish. His physical soreness had eased, as keeper bodies healed themselves, but his mental inflammation still burned. Memories unloaded in the safety of the shower walls. He pictured himself ten years old, back in his green-treed childhood village, Valley. The memory was from his first training days at camp where he'd learned to become a keeper at the Seam.

No.

He scrubbed away the image and focused on the leftover demon blood that had soaked through a claw cut in his uniform, blacker than his own dark skin. But the distraction didn't last as visions of the Seam, where the Dream and Human Realms met, crept back in.

Zander shook his face under the shower spray, but

images of his past forced themselves through. The first time he'd morphed into a hawk, he'd flown the brilliant blue skies at the border with his new castmates, friends for life…at least he'd believed so. He blinked to another vision of his younger self sparring in human form with Nigel and Adam, two of his closest friends. Zander's black hair was shorter than Nigel's, but both of theirs a contrast against Adam's fiery red, and their black skin the bookends to Adam's freckled ivory. The three of them had been inseparable until the destiny he'd grown to honor—out of nowhere—shifted.

Shutting off the water, he shut down his thoughts.

Done.

Zander was the last one to the cafeteria to meet his team for dinner, not because he was perpetually late, but intentionally. He not only took the needed time for his demon-caused wounds to heal but also drained his memories. They always found him after his duties, alone in the shower.

Tables overflowed in the tiny eatery, but every space was small in the Dream Realm, a world floating on docks and energy. Teams clustered together, usually in their own groups of three, but at times of celebrations they would pull their tables together. Zander glanced behind as the cafeteria door closed. The typically pink sky, hidden by night, still shone misty glimmers of magenta through the cracked door and windows. Their town, Reverie, stayed a perfect sunset at night, a perfect sunrise each day.

A roaring fire blanketed the multitude of table conversations yet also helped with the constant chill. Zander sat down and picked up his fork, the silence at their table awkwardly thick. Ansel had already inhaled half his plate of meats and fruit, while Daiya slid her food around without taking a bite.

"What's wrong?" Zander asked as he placed a napkin in his lap. There was a problem if his teammate wasn't eating.

Daiya looked up, her dark eyes like the forest he'd once night-trained in back home. He clenched his teeth, not because of her. The shower drain should have swallowed up his memories of Valley.

But he knew why.

The Blessing Council summons had arrived that morning. The notice had all three of them tangled in dread. But not only the meeting, or going back to the Spiritual Realm, his original home, threatened Zander's peace, it was seeing his old teammates again. The team he'd once trained to lead.

"Now you notice me?" She jutted her pointed chin, her jet-black hair falling away from her face. The blunt chin-length cut swooshed like liquid night. "What's wrong with *you*?"

Ansel stopped eating and glanced between the two of them.

Zander eyed Ansel, then Daiya. "What are *you* talking about?" He sipped his wine.

Daiya pushed her plate away. "You get a message from the BC and shrink back into that cold shell you arrived here with."

Ansel lifted both blond brows. He rubbed a hand over his shaved head and nodded. "You have been weird since it came."

"What do they want?" Daiya pushed.

"Probably nothing."

"Nothing?" She slugged the last of her wine.

Ansel stared at Zander, his green eyes glowing expectantly.

"I have no idea what they want." He folded his napkin over his still full plate. "But I'll let you know when I do." Pushing his chair in, he made for the door. No way would he show his true feelings about this meeting. It had been a similar gathering a year ago that had revoked his pairing with the Centennial seam keeper. They had needed him elsewhere. Or more, they had no need for him *there* anymore. Within days, he was swimming for demons in the core of the Dream Realm, his hawk form grounded for life.

****

Zander didn't jump at the knock on his door, already expecting the late night visit. He glanced in the mirror hanging in the small entrance way. It had been the only thing mounted among all the naked walls when he first moved in. Slowly let out his breath, controlled and even, until it fogged the reflection staring back. His dark brown eyes practically pierced the other side, so he took another breath until they softened, until his jaw relaxed. He rubbed a hand over short black hair, almost hidden in the dark room. Flipping the hall light on, he opened the door.

Daiya stood on his porch holding a handful of plums. "Sorry?"

Not a word she offered to just anyone. "It's fine." He waved her in.

Standing over his small kitchen counter, he accepted her offered gift. They bit into the purple fruit, eyeing one another in the process. Nothing had ever transpired between them, other than having each other's backs in combat and their strange way of understanding each other with only one look. She knew he had a secret chip on his shoulder but would never ask because she had her own. They were the same that way.

Ansel was their buffer, always watching their silent banter with gleaming green eyes and a cocked grin. He never took sides or claimed to understand their unspoken relationship. Somehow the two of them entertained him. His amusement often drove Daiya crazy, and she'd haul off and belt him at times, reacting first and thinking later.

But Zander knew Daiya. She was always starving after a mission. She liked lying in the sun on her days off, even if the constant cool temperatures brought tiny goosebumps to her smooth olive skin. And he never attempted to stand up for her in a demon fight. She did her own slaying.

"You're worried." Plum juice dribbled down her chin.

He snatched a hand towel from his kitchenette and threw it at her. "No."

Her dark eyes glowered with a matching smirk, as she wiped her lips. "Yes, you are. And it's okay." She chewed off another bite. "You're the one who wasn't supposed to be here. You can't tell me you aren't curious they'll pull you back to the Seam?"

Zander threw his pit in the garbage, shrouding the surge of anger that flushed his face. He washed his hands and leaned against the sink. "It's just a meeting."

"And you're not worried one bit they might pull you back to your original destiny? Your hawk inside isn't itching to fly right now at the thought of finally being free?" She stretched around him to toss away her own plum pit. "Your Centennial *girlfriend* isn't scratching your thoughts at all?"

"Seriously, D?" He scowled. He'd never spoken about his past with anyone, though rumors had flown. He hadn't taken her as one to buy into gossip...even if this time it was true. "We've never met. I'm sure it's only a meeting between realms because of some new threat. I'm a liaison between worlds. I grew up there. That's all." Besides, Ashton, the Centennial keeper Zander had once been destined to pair with until the council ripped him away, had been newly mated with some mystery shifter from the Human Realm. That also had him confused. Only female Centennials grew up in the Human Realm until their eighteenth birthday. It happened every hundred years, but never with shifters.

What if they *did* want him back? He bit the inside of his cheek to alleviate his forced sense of duty. Destiny had been a farce. So he'd anchored himself to his new position, locked everything inside, and focused on the now.

Daiya slugged him in the shoulder, bringing him back to the moment. "You better be staying." Her eyes glimmered for a split second. Then she made a face, lips curving, and pretended to wipe her plum-wet hands across the countertop, awaiting his reaction. When his eyebrows lifted, meeting hers with an unspoken sense of *don't you dare*, she used the towel on her hands and wiped any drops from the counter.

He faked a laugh. He couldn't handle the thought of sticky hands messing up his clean countertops any more than the fear of whatever the Blessing Council had in store for him. He had grown used to his new duty as an internal keeper. He'd tethered to that truth each morning, went to bed locked in that truth every night, and never thought about the future.

There was no point. Internal keeping was surely messier than border patrol outside the realm, but at least he still slayed demons.

Chapter 6

Teams Torn

Zander stopped outside the council room entrance, gripped the doorknob, and measured his breath. A final attempt to cool his emotions before he faced his old team—the friends he'd trained to battle with since he was ten years old.

Enough!

He popped each familiar face bursting in his memory. It had been a year since he'd been removed from his post. He'd moved on.

Hadn't he?

"Zander?" Shunnar's voice cut in from behind, catching him off guard. "Good, you're here. Let's go in."

So much for pleasantries. But he wouldn't have expected more from Shunnar. It had been a long time since he'd trained under him, and even then, the man was all business. No wonder he was a favorite of Mr. *Head-of-the-Northwest-Casts-so-don't-mess-with-me* Gavan. Zander smoothed his expression, unsure if it was Gavan's constant intensity that irritated him or the fact he was Ashton's father, so he must have had something to do with his assignment change.

"Sure." Zander tightened his jaw, grinding resentment with his teeth. Seeing Ashton for the first time was the only thing that might unhinge him. But he'd practiced his stone-like responses in the mirror that morning, keeping his emotions unreadable. She would never know this meeting had his insides twisted with memories of what could have been. None of them would.

Chin up, shoulders pressed flat, he followed Shunnar through the door.

The council room was enormous, since the entire Spiritual Realm was larger than his current home. The only village in the Dream Realm floated atop boardwalks, all the structures small in comparison. He imagined at least two or three meeting rooms from Reverie would fit into this one. His gaze flitted to the high ceilings and grand walls with no windows, omitted for privacy. Gossamer lights glimmered silver-blue from the intricate lanterns hung in each corner.

All the attention rushed toward him upon entry.

Shunnar had barely opened his mouth when the room's occupants, Zander's old team, jumped to their feet in greeting. Tiny Bronwyn slid around the wooden table and leaped into a hug. Her giant-tall mate, Nigel, reached a long arm across to fist-bump, though Zander had to reach around a gripping Bronwyn. After a squeal, she backed up for the rest of the crew.

Zander breathed out an unexpected laugh in time to greet Adam and his mate, Hannah, still twin-like, with matching auburn hair, as they leaned over their chairs to grip his shoulders. Hannah rested her cheek on his arm. The rest of the cast all smiled as if seeing him again was good news.

Emotions pooled in his heart. He'd worked so long practicing his reaction at seeing them again, assured he would come out strong and unhurt by the *great divide*, he hadn't thought about their reaction upon seeing him.

Shunnar faced Gavan, speaking privately, though Gavan did toss a stern blue gaze at Zander before turning to hear his second in command. His stare was somehow softer than Zander remembered the cranky commander. Then the warmth in the room radiated with the lantern's silvery light, as he found her.

Ashton.

He coughed to collect himself.

She looked at him but didn't appear to know him. Or at least she might not realize she had, or…did. It took time for the Centennial's memories to return. He didn't know where she was in the process. It was obvious he was staring, and he glanced quickly at Bronwyn, who had glided back around the table next to Ashton. Bronwyn's white hair illuminated under the lights, and she beamed her unforgettable smile.

"Zander, this is Ashton." She glanced at Ashton before moving on to the keeper next to her. It was quick, but Zander had caught it. Was Bronwyn also looking for a sense of recognition?

Ashton's lips caught in a word she might have been trying to say.

"And this is…Mason." Bronwyn paused. "Our new castmate."

"Hey." Mason threw his hand out to shake. His face was red, anger rolling off his aura. Zander wasn't sure what had him out of sorts. Maybe it was the reason for the meeting. But Zander nodded, shook his hand with a stronger grip than needed, and glanced back at Ashton.

"Hi." She scrunched her face, rich blue eyes

searching. "You look familiar. Have we met?"

"No," he said flatly and turned to find his seat. He didn't trust himself to say more, especially with her new paired teammate already heated.

Gavan called the group to order, and Zander took a seat across the table, as far as he could from Ashton.

Not a wise choice.

From his vantage point, looking at Gavan, Ashton was directly within his peripheral vision. He couldn't *not* look at her and pay attention to Gavan at the same time. Her hair was as golden brown as he'd imagined, oak tree branches in the gleam of the morning sun. He'd seen it in his mind's eye back home in Valley. But Ashton was the Centennial. She'd grown up in the Human Realm, spent her first eighteen years unknowing she was a seam keeper. And Mason? The rumors were vast, but the one where he'd grown up in the Human Realm was the most common. The fact that he had demon blood was another racing story.

Ashton glanced over at him, and his stomach tightened. She'd thought he was familiar but didn't seem to remember why. He hoped she never would.

By Divine intervention, Shunnar cleared his throat to get to the purpose of the meeting. A new mission was at hand, and it wasn't every day they brought an internal keeper to help with the borders.

Something critical had to be happening.

****

Mason had never felt his inner hawk itching to release more than it was now, confined in this meeting room, while both his parents sat trapped in a hidden realm with a deranged demon—a demon who had murdered his own childhood caretaker without a blink of sympathy. What could that mean for the safety of his parents?

Ashton placed a hand in Mason's lap. He gripped the charms on her bracelet and let his shoulders drop. Freaking out would not get the council to execute a plan any faster. The charms were smooth under his thumb, and he worked to hold his emotions in check.

Finally, Gavan got to the parts that mattered. "Bethesda has done the readings, and it appears the contract is binding. Max *must* publish his book on the reality of demons in the human world. It is the only way to free his soul from the hidden realm."

The room's occupants lost composure at once—gasps and wide-eyed desperate expressions. Mason let go of Ashton's bracelet for fear of snapping off charms.

"Hold on." Gavan put up a hand. "This doesn't mean it will all happen at once. We can buy time if we can find Max and slow his progress."

"A demon like Kelvin doesn't strike me as being patient." Mason threw in. "We can't put my da—Max in any more harm."

Gavan's regard landed bluntly on Mason's shoulders. "He already sealed that fate dealing with the Devil."

Mason flew to his feet.

Shunnar shot up, his voice raised over the silent challenge. "Our healers are trying to reach your mom through that mess of a realm, Mason. If we can get word to Mia, she can help with Max, help him stall and aid in planning. But attempts have failed."

Was Shunnar consoling him or shutting him down?

Gavan cleared his throat. "We've brought in Zander Mara. He's trained with the team—" His attention snapped to Ashton. "—well, with most of you. As an internal liaison, he knows the Dream Realm *and* the Seam. With his knowledge, alongside Ashton's new gifts, we will take a strategic *offensive* approach to enforce the safety of human souls."

"We're going to let the book happen, then *strategically* clean up the aftermath?" Mason looked at Ashton, then Zander. Zander was staring at her, but she glared at Gavan, the birth father she hadn't spoken to since the last time they sat in this room. Not so long ago, the council had contemplated how to free his own mom, Mia, and Ashton's birth mother, Althaia, when Ian had held them hostage. It was also the battle where everything changed. Ashton had soared into the seam keeper she was destined to be while Mason died and came back to life. Now they were sitting in this same room trying to save his stepdad from the worst mistake of his life.

Was this all payback for Mason's second chance at life? It didn't seem fair to come back only to have everything go wrong.

Gavan glared until Mason reluctantly found his seat and attention resumed. "Zander and Ashton will work on a plan to counter the internal spill-over. The amount of negative energy sleeping human souls are predicted to leak will upset the balance to the Dark. There is no telling what higher level demons could do with that much power. And now, Kelvin's calling the shots in his brother's absence..." Gavan shook his head.

"Why not take Kelvin out first, so my parents are safe? *Then* deal with the contract." Mason tightened his fists but stayed anchored to his chair.

"I understand the concern for your family." Gavan set his glare.

Mason clenched his jaw. It was more of Gavan's retribution for their last battle, when the council had cleared Ashton to join the mission conquering Ian. He'd wanted her to sit out because she was too new, or too young…or his only daughter. The only difference? Mason had no intention of sitting out any battles. He raised his chin in defiance.

"Kelvin has surely discovered the barter with Max." Gavan continued to glare. "He will push it through."

"All the more reason to stop him now." Ashton jumped to challenge her birth father. "Mason's right. Defeating him could buy us time to find another way. We might not have to leak anything about the truth of demons." Ashton shot a dagger of a glare at Gavan.

The room silenced like the deafening aftermath of an explosion. Gavan softened his gaze toward her. "That is the plan, but we must be ready for every outcome. We still need casts at the borders. Before his banishment, Ian's army had grown larger. Even now, demons swarm the Seam in higher numbers. But we will spare some members from Ashton and Mason's team with added hawks from my personal cast." He squared his shoulders. "I will not be challenged again on the subject. Shunnar?"

Ashton's fingers flexed at her sides. Mason stood to support her when Shunnar's attention flashed his way.

Enough. Shunnar's voice blared mentally through Mason's mind followed by sparks of pain down his spine. Shunnar's disciplinary warning. Mason thought a few choice words in his leader's direction before pulling Ashton down to her seat. Zander's eyes still locked on Ashton.

Shunnar exhaled, then called out the mission. Their cast would split, one part sent into battle with Kelvin. Another part, including Mason, would go to the Human Realm to prepare for the book release, while the rest continued their shifts guarding the Seam. Evidently, Mason's team, Seattle-bound, would prepare for combat through fake social media posts and devised computer viruses. Whatever it took to stop the forward motion of book sales.

The room filled with silence, dropped jaws, and wide expressions. Mason thought he might implode. Seam keepers in the Human Realm? From what he'd learned in training, and aside from the Centennial, this hadn't ever been protocol.

Mason gripped the table's edge. Not only was his team splitting up, but he'd also be separated from Ashton. Because of her gifts, she would travel with Zander to the Dream Realm. Their task, to work out a back-up plan for the potential incoming human souls, soon to be overloaded with fear from the reality of demons. He'd be dealing with social media. They were purposely keeping him away from the action, more proof they couldn't trust him to lead a team.

Rory glanced at her mate, Shunnar, and rose. "It is a new generation, as you know. Humans are far more frazzled than in previous centuries. They need saving from their own thoughts and self-inflicted fears. Though we've never resided in the Human Realm for duty..." She shook her head, long red curls spiraling. "The information age torments; misleading and misconstrued information overwhelms to a lack of faith in *anything*." Her eyes found Ashton, empathy in her gaze. "This knowledge comes from our Centennial connection. If we add demons to the mix, would their sleeping souls even survive?"

More silence.

Rory lowered herself to her chair. Mason rubbed the back of his head, the unease in the room thick.

Suddenly familiar notes trilled in Mason's head with the arrival of their final council member, Angel Sandalphon. Bright lights blinded as the room bowed their heads. The musical message flooded through Mason's body. Fingers tingling and chest swelling, the wordless song filled him with strength and renewed energy, just as it filled everyone there. When the soft blue glow lulled, he searched above, always trying to catch a view of the angel. Nothing but residual radiance clung to the ceiling. A slow sway of lantern light created movement along the walls. Teammates sat taller.

Isleen, representative from the Dream Realm, stood in her flowing violet frock, with Nurzhen, representative from the Spiritual Realm, in ivory white. They rose to give their blessings. And though the earlier angst dimmed in exchange for refreshed courage among the group, there was still a stir about the room. This would be a unique mission—something never encountered in any realm.

Shunnar called for teams to deploy at once. His orders were food, armory, departure. No time for sleep. But Mason didn't care about that. His head spun at the thought of not fighting Kelvin himself, at not being the one to rescue his own parents...not that it was even possible with Max's blasted contract. But the fact that he wasn't going at all had him seething. Was Shunnar holding him back? Or Gavan?

Everyone was risking their lives and the lives of each human soul because his stepdad had done something stupid. And Ashton? For the first time in keeper history, she was heading off to the Dream Realm with some internal keeper who couldn't seem to keep his eyes off her.

Chaos!

Mason stormed from the room, despite his angelic blessing.

Outside, the sun cut through the needles of each evergreen surrounding the assembly building. It wouldn't be long before twilight encased them, and though it typically held a gentle seclusion in the Spiritual Realm, Mason was suffocating.

****

Ashton found Mason pacing in the gardens outside. She approached carefully, having been accidently knocked in his quick turnarounds one too many times.

"Ash," he said, glimpsing her too late, grabbed her shoulders to steady her. "Are you okay with this?"

"Are you?" She circled her arms around his waist to stop him from further movement.

"My dad is stuck in that hell. And now my mom, with Ian's sociopathic brother!"

Ashton held him tighter, her cheek on his chest. His heart pounded in a scary-fast way, one that usually directed him down a road of impulsive decisions. She didn't want to see him, or anyone else, get hurt.

"I think all we can do now is trust the process." She gripped him tighter, feeling him relax, slightly.

He rested his head on her shoulder, scooped handfuls of her hair behind her neck. "We're going to be separated. I thought the whole point about being paired meant we wouldn't be—shouldn't be—apart."

Ashton shared the same thought. It was what they'd been told when Mason recently contemplated leaving the Spiritual Realm because of his demon blood. She cringed at the thought of it almost happening. She liked to think her close company with Mason was an elixir keeping that part of his heritage buried deep.

"These are extenuating circumstances."

Mason growled, "Because of my dad…stepdad…" He dropped his head.

"Come on, let's grab food." She pulled him toward the market. "We'll need strength for the mission. Then we do whatever it takes to clean up Ian's mess." Even saying the words, her heart rippled. They'd never faced such a complicated assignment, more than simply slaying demons. Too much was riding on her abilities to create a backup plan for the coming negative energy. She'd barely discovered her Centennial gifts, let alone been able to control them on demand.

They passed Zander on their way to the café. He was talking with Nigel and Adam, but he glimpsed Ashton's eye. Something about him tugged at her. How was he trained as a seam keeper but now worked internally? What if she couldn't help him? Her need for *more* still pinched from the inside, but this wasn't quite how she'd imagined it. Mason must have noticed her contemplation because he slowed his pace on their approach to the café.

"Okay, Ash. We do whatever it takes to clean up

Ian's mess." He paused at the door, street lanterns creating shadows around them. Ashton saw the rest of their cast inside until Mason tilted her chin and held her face in his hands. "I *always* love you, Ash." His familiar words coated her insides as he pressed a kiss to her mouth, lasting longer than her next needed breath. But he wasn't letting go, so neither would she.

Chapter 7

Goodbyes

Their hasty meal provided more time in the armory. Still, Ashton didn't know what weapons she'd need in the Dream Realm. Would she be demon hunting internally with Zander or stuck in an office brainstorming new ways to protect human souls?

"Standard gear is fine." Rory blazed in behind her. Ashton spun to face her commanding officer. "Zander will supply any other required weapons. Think strategy. We must find a way to protect the souls from the overspill damage when that book releases."

We must find a way? Ashton gulped. Her use of *we* didn't sound convincing…more like *you* must find a way. "Rory, you know I lack control over my gift to resolve problems."

Rory patted her back, curved her lips. Though she might be small in stature, she made up for it in authority. "You wanted more. This is more. Your mind will click into place at the proper times when you begin trusting it will. You are the one in your way." She held up a hand.

Ashton swallowed her complaint and thought about her various Centennial gifts. Opening locks wasn't a big deal, unless they ended up captured and chained. Her gift of solving puzzles, with that strange clicking behind her eyes, was probably what Zander hoped to use in their current mission, just as Rory said, strategy. Aside from her discovery of flower-power invisibility and her ability to portal through reflections, she had nothing clever to offer. She pushed down any mental acknowledgement of her new gift, which they had no idea how to practice or control. Anything that wild would be the exact opposite of strategy.

Rory's gray eyes peered brightly, a promise of sunshine through overcast skies. "Remember your gift of unlocking should work in every aspect of the word. You can reveal, uncover, and release anything hidden. Focus on connecting each meaning as you learn about the Dream Realm. This is a rare opportunity for you, Ashton. Seam keepers haven't joined with other realms before."

Flop. Her stomach dropped. As much as Rory encouraged her, pressure pressed along Ashton's spine. Any words of feigned agreement lodged in her throat, so she simply nodded.

"Good. Now Zander awaits outside. Say your goodbyes and be off."

****

Ashton found Mason in the doorway. He smiled with little joy behind it. She understood why. Coming so close to getting both his parents back had him revved up, not to mention the failure of his first mission, forcing him to the sidelines, in *his* eyes.

"Are you good to go?" He held the door as they walked through.

"I suppose. I'm meeting Zander out here somewhere."

"Over there." Mason lifted his chin to the left of

the assembly building.

Ashton glanced over the courtyard to the gardens. Ivy trickled from the roof of the assembly building, down the trunk of a tall hemlock, to a wooden fence surrounding the garden. Benches sat at the entrance, as well as throughout. It was a beautiful place she imagined painting one day, always in bloom with colorful flowers. A place where her adopted mom would have loved to create art.

No. As grief began to stir, she shook off the gloom. This wasn't helping. She blinked to focus on the group by the gate.

Positive thoughts!

Mason had too much at stake if this mission didn't pan out. With Ian's demon-bully brother, so did humans. Across the courtyard, night had folded over the small keeper village, Toria. Nothing but shadows of colorful flora played in the lantern light, silhouetting Zander with her cast.

Mason dropped his duffel to the bottom step. "I don't like him."

"Zander?" She tossed her bag next to his.

"He's always staring at you."

Ashton laughed. "You mean in the hour we've known him?"

"He hardly took his eyes off you at the council meeting." He scowled where their cast cheerfully mingled with their old teammate.

"He's familiar to me, or at least my keeper side. But the memory is stuck." She stared at Zander. He was slightly taller than Mason, not as tall as Nigel. Though reserved and overly stiff in his movements, he seemed relaxed to be with his old team.

She caught Mason's eye roll and shook her head. "Are you jealous of the history he has with our cast?"

Mason pulled her closer. "I'm not jealous." He smoothed her shoulders. "I'm wondering how this place—this realm with so much order—has somehow become a disaster we must clean up or innocents suffer. All because of my dad."

He was mostly right. Nothing had gone smoothly, starting with her transition into the Spiritual Realm, jeopardized by Ian's early detection of her. Never had a centennial been exposed in the Realms. Then Mason, her surprise paired mate, had grown up in the Human Realm...that too had never occurred before. Now a human meddling in otherworldly matters, Max Deed. It was a colossal mess, though she couldn't blame Max for trying to save the only son he believed was his.

Like dominos, every event tipped into the next. Ashton put a hand to her forehead, trying to mentally close her mind's file drawer of worries. She wasn't going to be that girl anymore. She'd beaten those inner demons when she battled Ian.

Hadn't she?

"Ash?" Mason squeezed her shoulders.

She bowed over, and Mason rubbed her back. It'd been a while since her last asthma attack. She had no clue where she might find an inhaler, so she took slow breaths of the overly fresh air surrounding Toria.

"You okay?" Mason guided her to sit on the assembly steps.

"I'm fine, just a lot of *unorder* as you called it." She took in another cleansing breath.

Mason drew her into his shoulder, loosely so she could breathe. "Never a dull moment, right?" He laughed, half-heartedly.

Of course, he made it a joke. That was the old Mason. She snuggled in, soaking up more of him. It had barely been a month in their new roles, only days since enhancing their relationship status, and she already admired his growth into the keeper he was choosing to be. Just sometimes, she missed her silly human friend.

"Thank you." She smiled. "I needed that."

Mason kissed her long again. Always a long kiss because he never simply loved her. He *always* loved her. Of course, he could never simply kiss her goodbye. He always *kissed* her, weighted with every part of him.

"I hate being away from you."

She pulled him closer. "I thought being paired meant we never had to be."

"Never say never." Rory's voice trilled from behind. "Time to go."

Mason only held her tighter, his lips soft against her ear. "I *always* love you."

"I always love *you*." Ashton clung for another breath, then stood to find her full cast gathered with Shunnar and two of his private shifters, Desmond and Connor. Everyone looked uneasy with the change in protocol.

Shifters wore dark camouflage pants with black T-shirts, boots, and jackets. Riders, like Ashton, wore the same, only khaki and white. Each shifter had their thin silver throwing knives concealed inside their vests. All clothes and weapons morphed into their hawks and back again without a hitch. Ashton rested her thumbs on her weapons belt, same as each rider. Their jewel-hilted daggers and swords were sharpened and blessed for the assortment of demons they may encounter.

Zander wore his own uniform, dark blue pants with a matching tight, long-sleeved T-shirt, and a navy jacket laced through the crook of his arm. With his darker skin, he blended into the night. She had no idea what an internal keeper's weapon of choice was. He looked her way when she glanced at him, then veered his attention to Shunnar, barking assignments.

"Rory remains in Toria, researching the contract. All teams report to her."

They split their cast of twelve into four groups. Six would remain at the Seam for patrol duty. Two would travel to the hidden realm with Shunnar, another attempt at battling Kelvin. Three, including Mason, would head to the Human Realm with Des and Connor as co-leads. After their last mission, she was sure Mason was grateful not to be in a leadership role, though it had to sting a bit. Ashton would join Zander in the Dream Realm to strategize for the anticipated negative energy blast. They didn't know the timeline for Max Deed's book, but it was bound to come soon.

The group stared at each other in cold silence—the weight of the mission stormy in the otherwise calm Toria night. There was no protocol for what they were about to do.

Mason squeezed Ashton's hand one last time, then grabbed their duffels. He handed hers over, shouldering his own before Shunnar hustled him toward the Northwest portal. Ashton lost his amber eyes in the darkened night as Zander approached, his gaze glistening under the hanging lanterns.

"Ready?" Zander said flatly, as if she wasn't traveling to yet another unimaginable realm.

"Sure." She grabbed her bag, trying to look as calm

as possible. Deep inside, familiar butterflies bristled, mocking the confidence she'd rallied after winning her battle with Ian. Her seam keeper memories had finally melded with her human ones, so she wasn't as confused as she had been a week ago. But whatever memory of Zander her keeper side might know seemed bolted tight.

Who was he?

"You'll need a coat." He slipped his jacket on as Ashton kneeled to the grass, pulling a brown leather one from her duffel. Toria was never cold. She only wore her jacket in flight. Interest piqued about Reverie, the village of internal keepers. She'd wondered before what it might be like past the colorful borders she and her cast guarded. She was actually going to find out.

"The portal's this way." His lean form headed away from the assembly building, past the gardens. She followed, the lanterns illuminating the trail just enough to see. A short time later, he stopped to let her catch up. His strides were long, but even with her curiosity about visiting the Dream Realm, uncertainty contributed to her snail's pace.

"Nervous?" He moved in step with her now.

"No." She'd never admit she was. Mason would've already anticipated her anxiety and coached her along.

"The Dream Realm is…indescribable. I think you'll like it."

He stopped at a passage on the left. She'd never been this far before, the gardens lovely enough never to need a step farther.

She passed through the gate into a cluster of weeping willows. Curly leafed branches draped with what looked like strings of twinkling lights. But as she moved closer the lights sparked in little spotted patterns.

"Fireflies." Zander half smiled. It was the first time she'd seen him do so, even if it was quick and under the glow of insects.

"They're beautiful."

"You might want to save that word for later."

He kept moving through the glittering willows without looking back. She followed as the trees gave way to tall grass and cattails. Her boots sank as the ground changed to sand, reminding her of Mason's beach house on the Oregon coast. The wind was cooler than Toria, more like the Pacific Northwest shores, and she felt a mist on her cheeks.

"Are you ready for this?" He looked back.

Her mouth stuck in a shape somewhere between yes and no. Zander held out a hand and after a quick wish for luck, she gripped his fingers.

They stepped onto a boardwalk appearing atop the sand. Within five steps, the spritzes of something cool and fresh misted her skin with a strange sense of warmth. A chilly air ruffled her hair. Her fingers, sticky and wet, clung to Zander's clammy hand. The pressure under his grasp tightened as a layer of moisture coated her face.

A watery wind tugged her along, increasing in force with every step, like plunging through a waterfall. Her eyelids squeezed as she relented to trust each step behind the internal keeper leading.

Finally, the spraying stopped. The temperature chilled, and Zander wasn't moving anymore. She opened her eyes, pulling her hand free to wipe her face.

"We're through the portal," he said, giving her

time to compose herself.

She blinked, but the aftereffects of the gateway left a pinkish tinge to her vision.

And the landscape!

Tall grasses and cattails replaced the shade trees of Toria. Swirls of airy fog speckled the edges of what looked like an enormous meadow, but the hues were more lilac and indigo.

The wooden slats swayed beneath her feet, and she could almost hear the sloshing of water. She leaned over, unable to see any solid ground. *Whoa*! She put a hand on her stomach, an arm out for balance. The dock was surely moving even if she couldn't see the water.

"What kind of lake is this?" She stepped back when the dock lurched, and she lunged for Zander, afraid to fall.

He caught her with a steady grip. "Take it slow." He waited for her to gather her bearings again.

The boardwalk trailed farther ahead where it connected to smaller paths along each side. They must be on a main dock because the boards beneath them appeared wider. Where was the land?

"Reverie's a floating village," he said as if reading her mind.

At least he was patient with her baby steps and white-knuckled grip on his arm. This place was unlike anything she'd seen before, even in the Spiritual Realm. The air smelled of coconut and sugar and sparkled like a fairytale setting.

Beneath the sweet aromas came a briny scent, like the sea. Beyond the docks, on all sides, were high rocky cliffs with mountainous waterfalls. Rolling fog tumbled up to the pinkened skies. It looked as if the sun was rising...or setting...or somewhere in between, a contrast to the blue skies of Toria. Sounds of crashing water rushed in the background.

"It's...beautiful." She stopped, still clinging to Zander's arm, still trying to blink away her rosy-tinted vision.

"You said that already, about insects."

She smirked. "Show me more."

He peeled her fingers from his arm and took her hand, allowing them to walk more freely. Swallowing her nerves she forced herself to take bigger steps in pace with him. The dock was wide enough for two people. She could do this.

The farther they went, the more she adjusted to the gentle swaying of the boards. But the more she peered over the edges on either side, the more she realized it wasn't water at all. It was...mist. Air. Nothing.

"What is it?" She stopped to investigate, still gripping his hand for fear of falling in.

"We call it aether; it's energy." His eyes lit up as he peered into hers. "It's where souls travel. Dreams emit positive and negative energy. You're already aware humans process their emotions as they sleep. Joy, sorrow, fear; everything releases through dreams right here."

"So, the energy released creates this pink *stuff*?"

"The positive energy creates freedom and movement. You can actually see the light swell around each soul. They look like little orbs of light."

"Orbs?"

"You'll have to see for yourself. The positive light keeps Reverie afloat."

She knew about positive and negative energy

released from dreaming souls, but to *see* it was something remarkable.

Zander kneeled, and she mirrored him. He studied the soft waves of aether as he spoke. "Negative energy sinks to the bottom, anchoring the tormented souls. As you know, demons feed off that energy. They soak it up, then return to their higher-level demon masters to expel it. This increases all demon power. But—" He stood up, folded his arms. "The more negative energy a soul releases, the stronger they're tied to their anchor, and the lower their souls dwell. The Dream Realm is fluid. Rigid energy like that, heavy and unyielding—" He eyed her. "It's unknown what might happen if the tethered souls snapped or fell."

A cool rush lifted from the mist, and she hugged an arm around her middle.

Ashton remembered her birth mother, Althaia, telling her that misery begets misery. Damaged souls were damaged, and it wasn't up to keepers to fix them. They could only help protect the borders from demons.

But what if that wasn't enough anymore?

Silence settled before Zander pulled her up. His full lips sealed, as if that was enough of the story. As if he were reciting legend, but it was time for bed. Her eyes begged him for more.

"We can start on all that tomorrow. Let's grab dinner, then I'll show you where you're staying." He pulled her along the slatted walkway, puffs of lavender film swirling from under the dock with every step.

She blinked again, but her vision hadn't changed. Glittering lights sparked from the waterfalls, like the fireflies at the portal's entrance. They rolled with the violet mist so Ashton couldn't see clearly. But the constant rhythm of movement was proof something unbelievable transpired around them.

A tear slipped, and Zander turned as her words spilled. "It's beautiful."

He raised a finger to catch her tear, and something about it jostled her insides. "You keep saying that. We may need to add a vocabulary lesson onto our list of saving the world."

Lingering only seconds before withdrawing his hand, his eyes lit up. She wished again for her keeper memories to fill in the gaps about him, but enough for one day.

She shook off her thoughts and let him lead her down the dock.

Chapter 8

Seattle Surprise

Mason followed Nigel and Bronwyn, the only cast members from his own team, across the grassy hill away from Toria. Their crew was small as keepers didn't typically venture into the Human Realm.

Des and Connor, two of Shunnar's private cast, were with them as they approached the oak portal. The two were polar opposites. Des was tall and dark-skinned like Nigel yet wore his hair in long black braids. Though Connor was shorter, he was built with muscle upon muscle, freckles covering his skin like constellations. They were usually together, paired maybe, and even though they were in charge, Mason knew he'd have to step up his game, especially entering his home realm. Still he trailed behind the group, each of them shouldering a small duffle.

Mason marched through the tree-portal as if he'd done it a hundred times. It had only been days since he'd followed Shunnar through for the first time. He let the strange, webbed sensation coat every limb, enough to irritate his skin before the white lights blinded any view of passage.

Once through, the industrialized scent of a city cloaked him.

Seattle. *Home*.

Not home. Not anymore. He shook his arms and stomped off the invisible remains of portal travel. His new team of five did the same, all squinting west at the tops of freight ship cranes raised like dragon heads from behind the warehouses. When he turned to the east, sleek buildings stood tall as if soldiers strutting their material power. If only they knew what real evil awaited.

"Why are we here?" Mason cemented his boots onto the concrete. "If we take Kelvin out first, the book may not *need* to be released. Our focus should be there."

Connor, his typical grin nonexistent, clapped a hand on Mason's shoulder. "A team's in play to do that. But we must be ready for anything."

Mason swallowed his grumblings and glanced at Connor's hazy-blue gaze, serious and comforting at the same time. He nodded as they crossed the street to a parking lot. Des pulled out a pair of keys and clicked to unlock the white van Shunnar had arranged. He climbed in behind the wheel, while the others crawled in back, leaving the passenger side open for Mason.

"We're thinking it's best to hide in plain sight, and since we don't have a place established here, your house it is." Des started the engine.

Of course, his house would be vacant. Mason closed his eyes and pictured it on the street where he'd grown up, Ashton's house right next door. Or at least its burnt remains. His neighbors wouldn't notice anything out of the ordinary. They would think Max Deed was on a book tour or teaching summer courses at the university. His dad had always kept to himself, hiring out lawn care and prearranging housekeeping. He was out of town so often, he auto paid his bills online and in advance.

The thought of such an organized man disheveled in that monster's library…Mason unclenched his jaw and grunted directions.

As they drove away from the city, toward the suburb where he and Ashton had grown up, he glimpsed the Space Needle in the side mirror. It used to represent home, but now it was an empty landmark. The July sun leaned low as the van's AC hummed. Traffic creeped, still eternally slow.

Mason closed his eyes.

If none of this otherworldly business had ever happened, he'd have been packing for college by now. He'd have saluted his goodbyes to Seattle and started a whole new life adventure, calling his own shots. Regret jolted up his spine. Reality wasn't giving him any more time in his world of *what-ifs*. If he hadn't learned about other realms, he'd never have learned his mom was alive or his dad actually cared.

And Ashton?

He opened his eyes, anxious to handle their current mission. Wasn't living in another realm, protecting human souls from demons, the definition of adventure? But he hadn't counted on so many others *depending* on him or that his dads (both step and biological) would be the ones unveiling these new realms around him.

"You okay?" Des asked, eyes glued on traffic.

"Fine," Mason shot back. "Where'd you learn to drive?"

He laughed. "Shunnar taught me yesterday."

"Whoa!" Mason straightened and double-checked his seatbelt. He examined the mirrors and the distance of cars around the van. "*I* can drive."

Des flicked a glance at Mason. "No way, man. This is awesome."

Of course, Des, advanced hawk in Shunnar's private cast, would think driving a van through Seattle traffic would be awesome.

Mason glanced to see Bronwyn leaning against Nigel in the seats behind. Only Connor's propped boots were visible from the third row of seats. He was probably asleep. Their teams hadn't had any downtime in the last weeks.

"Next exit." Mason's stomach rumbled, though he wasn't sure if it was due to Des's driving, hunger, or the thought of seeing his house again. He hardly blinked for the rest of the drive.

It was the house…or more, what remained next door.

The remains of Ashton's home sucker punched without warning. Ian had recently burned her home to the ground, killing her adopted parents. Someone had cleaned up the destroyed yard around the massive, charred heaps of foundation jutting from the ground, but it was ugly, with tape blocking off the area.

The scent of burned wood, plaster, and everything that made up his best friend—girlfriend's—house assaulted as he stepped out of the van.

All he could do was stare.

The others crawled out, standing behind him. When the silence grew too long, he realized they were waiting for him. He peered at Des, but Des only looked down, his long black hair falling in ropes across his eyes. Mason lifted heavy lids at Connor, Nigel, and Bronwyn; their lips frowned in sorrow.

Bronwyn gripped his arm. "Take as long as you need."

He glanced back at his burnt past, then stepped away, heading for his house. After he entered the code to the alarm, the garage door moaned its release. His dad's car was gone. Still at the beach house? But Mason's black jeep was there, right where he'd left it before his world changed forever.

Mason pushed through the kitchen door. The group followed, standing around the island with gear in hand. He hadn't had that many people in his house at once, since—since his fifth birthday party. After his mom died—faked her death—his dad never entertained again.

Mason shook off the memory. "The bedrooms are upstairs." His four teammates followed him up to the second level hallway. "Clean sheets should be there." He thumbed at a cupboard. Then he pointed. "My dad's room is here, guest room there. This is my room, but I can share."

Bronwyn and Nigel were closest to the guest room, so they headed that direction. Des and Connor marched straight into his dad's room without a word.

Mason huffed a breath at the empty hallway. "Okay, make yourselves at home."

He pushed open the door to his childhood bedroom, another place too full of memories, and slumped onto the bed. How was Ashton holding up in the Dream Realm? It had to be a beautiful place. He hoped she might find a moment to sketch a picture. The thought of her creating art again made him smile and a spark of warmth flickered in his chest.

There was a thump on his door. He stood in a flash,

hands reaching for knives.

"Should we figure out dinner?" Bronwyn laughed at his scrambling.

Mason pocketed his weapons…and his thoughts. "Yeah, dinner."

****

Pizza boxes littered the length of the table, along with two-liter bottles of soda. But the conversation wasn't as casual as their choice of dinner.

"We'll follow your dad on all social media platforms." Bronwyn went on as Mason choked down his pizza. "We've been briefed on the human information age." She tossed her crust into an empty box. "We'll need to be sly about it." She winked.

"We're hacking his accounts?" Mason coughed.

Des stretched. "We're going to have to immobilize his credibility."

Mason pushed up from the table, tipping his chair. The thick carpet absorbed the dramatics, but he didn't care. They were there to slow book sales somehow. But to discredit his dad on every front? What kind of life would he return to?

The crew cringed, already realizing that was the plan.

"When were you going to tell me?"

Nigel stood next to Des, two giants, both well over six five. "Mason, how else are we going to pull attention away from the book if it releases?"

"*If!*" Mason's mouth gaped. "This is all *if* it even happens."

Bronwyn and Connor found their feet, expressions sympathetic.

"You'll ruin his whole career! Why can't we stop

the spread of this *one* book?" Mason ran both hands through his hair, fingers catching on winding curls.

"Mason, we'll try. But we must be ready for anything." Connor leaned over the table, the pale blue of his eyes matching his serious tone. "If humans believe this level of evil is real…" He blew out his breath. "And now a higher demon like Kelvin is involved? We must shut it down."

Bronwyn reached for Mason's arm. Her mouth moved, but all he could hear was his heartbeat pulsing in his ears. He could barely feel her hand; he was shaking from the inside out. Trying to calm the rage, he cracked his neck. Ashton would have recognized he was losing it, but this team had no idea.

Mason exhaled as slowly as he could. It was what Ashton would have instructed. She would have run her hand along his shoulder and gripped until he released his pent-up energy. When that wouldn't have worked, she would've pushed him down and practically sat on him, applying pressure to every muscle in his back until he breathed steadily again.

But Ashton wasn't here. She was in some other realm he'd never been to with some other keeper he'd only just met, and Mason was about to incinerate.

His team must have believed deep breathing was enough; that the matter was settled because Connor collected pizza boxes, and Bronwyn grabbed a rag from the kitchen and wiped the table.

Mason stormed into the kitchen.

He'd had no idea the plan was to ruin his dad's human life. How was he supposed to destroy his dad's reputation and then expect him to return to his old life once the contract was paid? But then again, if the book did come out, would Kelvin even honor the contract and release him?

Mason couldn't see straight. He grabbed his keys off the kitchen hook. "I'm going for a drive."

If anyone protested, he didn't hear it. The kitchen door slammed with a thud, and he was in his jeep, the garage door rising as he revved the engine. Four faces peered out the front window when he backed out and sped down the street. He had no idea where he was going, but it didn't matter. He needed to drive.

****

The night dimmed as the radio blared. Mason drove straight through the sunset, straight through the city he used to call home. The outside air rushed through the open windows as the jeep twisted along back roads, south of his neighborhood.

Fresh air mixed with the blasting AC supplied a needed chill against his skin, calming his mind, or was it only a distraction? His gas tank was full, so he drove. He couldn't remember the exact time he left, but when the radio announced it was ten thirty, he pulled to a stop on a narrow shoulder, turned off the engine, and cradled his head in his hands.

The sudden silence competed with the aftereffects of the thumping bass in his head. Any calm or distraction from the ride faded. Mason pictured his dad again, but not the one stuck in a hidden realm—the one who stood in the hallway of their beach house and claimed to love him after thirteen years of disregard. He'd wanted a second chance, and Mason had given him hope that he could have it.

But he would have said anything that night to settle his dad before transitioning into the Spiritual Realm.

All this trouble! Who knew Max Deed would go to such extremes to make their reunion happen? It would've been easier had he gone on ignoring Mason. Now if Max did return, how often would Mason be able to see him anyway? Reason enough Max would need his work to fall back on.

His team planned to destroy that.

Mason rubbed his eyes and looked up, finally noticing his surroundings. His jaw dropped. "You've got to be kidding."

He hopped out onto the gravelly dirt road. To the left was an old dilapidated green barn. And straight ahead, the woods he'd entered as a human after two weeks of hauntingly strange dreams.

The hawks had called him, and finally, the day before graduation, he'd figured out the message. He'd brought Ashton with him and made her stay in the jeep because the dream had said to come alone. But when had he ever followed instructions?

Mason glanced around, almost expecting his spine to burn at the thought. As soon as the hawks had forced his first shift, he was thrust into the world of seam keeping…and the task of getting Ashton safely to her eighteenth birthday so she could transition into a keeper herself. It had been his last day as a human.

He had no desire to step foot into those woods again.

Hey Mas, Connor's voice in his head. *We've got a situation here.*

Mason rolled his eyes. He'd already turned the engine over, whipping the jeep around, when Des joined in.

You have a visitor.

Mason had asked who, but the connection severed. It must be taking all their concentration to deal with the problem. He sped back along the old highway until he hit the city limits, then forced himself to slow down. Cops pulling him over wouldn't be a good idea. His ID was probably still at the beach house.

****

As Mason pulled into the driveway, his heart sank. Parked along the curb was a familiar blue truck. Mason stood in the garage and took two deep breaths before opening the kitchen door to find the whole gang standing around the island. Leaning against the stove was one of Mason's closest childhood friends, aside from Ashton.

"Hicks." Mason forced a smile. What was he supposed to say? Bethesda had explained his and Ashton's family and friends would still remember them, just not wonder about them. It would be as if they were on a trip.

"Mas, dude!" He reached out a hand, and Mason gripped it. "It's been awhile. How was the road trip?" Hicks's light brown hair was clipped short as always. His muscular shoulders bulged through his T-shirt.

"Road trip...yeah...adventurous." Mason changed the subject. "You still working out?"

"Of course." Hicks laughed, then scanned the room. The cast all raised their eyebrows. "And you, too." He returned his gaze to Mason, but not before taking in his shifter uniform.

"Oh, um, these are my new..."

"Co-workers." Bronwyn stepped up and looped an arm through Mason's crooked elbow. "We sponsor Iron Man competitions, and we were in the area."

"Was there an Iron Man this weekend?" Hicks tilted his head.

"It was in Oregon. We stopped to visit." Bronwyn tucked a magazine into her other arm, pinching Mason. When he looked down, he glimpsed the Iron Man article.

"Yeah, I wanted to stop and say hi to the fam." Mason faked a half laugh.

Hicks turned his attention to Bronwyn, still linked through Mason's arm. "Bron—sorry, what's your name again?"

"Bronwyn." She glanced at Mason.

"Yeah," Mason said again, still tongue-tied. "We've been working pretty tight together all summer." He slapped his forehead. "Guys, this is Michael Hickson, um, Hicks. We grew up together."

"We sort-of met while you were out. But, man, I'm sorry I haven't called." Hicks scratched his head. "I don't know why I haven't." Confusion weighed his brow.

Des leaned over the island, clomping Mason in the shoulder. "Well, it wouldn't matter. This one always forgets his phone."

They all laughed, and Mason joined in. Of all things, he never once thought about running into old friends. But of course, he would. Technically, he was home.

"We'll give you a chance to catch up." Connor ushered the team into the living room, his red hair like a beacon, *remember the plan*.

Once alone, Hicks said, "How's Ashton? I can't believe what happened to her parents. To her house." He shook his head, true sorrow glinting across brown eyes. He'd been Ashton's friend too. "Where is she? She okay?"

Mason loosened the breath sticking in his chest. "It's been rough, but she's getting better." His mind raced to figure out a lie. "She's staying with some family friends in Oregon."

"It's wild I ran into you." He rubbed a hand down the back of his neck. "I never come this way home, but I'm sort of dating this new girl who lives close. I saw the lights on." He looked around. "Is your dad working?"

"Turns out he's out of town." The mention of his dad hit like a punch, but he shrugged, hoping he came across more casual. "So, new girl. Anyone I know?"

Hicks laughed. "Her name's Kali, and no, you wouldn't know her. She didn't go to Mountain High. I met her at work."

"Are you still at the diner?"

"For another few days, then I'm taking some time off before heading to college." He peered into the other room. "How long are you home?"

Mason would have loved to catch up with everything normal and human with Hicks, but there was a demon prince holding his parents hostage in another realm, and his team planned to destroy his dad's reputation. His own demon blood sizzled under his skin.

He rubbed his arms. "Dude, it's been a long day of traveling. I need to get to bed. Can I text you later?" Why did he even say that?

"Yeah, sure." Hicks headed for the front door but stopped to lean into the living room. "Nice meeting you."

"Same!" Bronwyn cheerfully answered from Nigel's side, squished into an overstuffed chair together. Des and Connor were side by side on the sofa, a shared laptop between them. They each glanced up to say goodbye.

Mason's heart pounded in his chest as he bolted the lock behind Hicks. Nothing about this mission would be simple, a perfect description of his life now.

Chapter 9

Sink or Swim

Everyone glanced their way when Ashton and Zander strolled into the busier part of the village. They'd crossed several docks before everything opened, resembling a coastal pier, minus the boats, clustered with small busy shops and structures. Too enamored by the scenery to ask, Ashton assumed the trading of goods and services in Reverie was like Toria. Elementals, or Els, she'd learned, crafted their work as art to provide, while other Els supplied the resources to create. Keepers were elementals too, their art, protecting the souls in the Dream Realm.

Had something so evil dared to upset that balance?

A chill wafted across her face, and she pulled her jacket tighter. The pink evening skies had dimmed, teasing night to settle. The pressure to abate the coming levels of harmful fear kept her from drifting away into the pink mist. She followed Zander deeper into the heart of the village, eyes widening as Reverie spread in size.

The tiny town floated atop rows and rows of wider boards. Little wooden huts with grass roofs lined the larger planked paths. A central structure sat in the middle surrounded by a moat-like sandy courtyard. Designs in the sand looked intentional, a Zen garden, with raked marks trailing the premises. A stone path led across the sand, appearing to be the main entrance to their Assembly Hub. Trails of white flowers and green vines draped from the straw rooftops like icing on a cake. There was more to see along the edges of the winding path, but Zander pulled her onward.

Smaller huts encompassed the larger one, like a pinwheel, with other elementals and keepers buzzing around. Finally they stopped in front of a café. And since traveling between realms always messed with time, she was already hungry and grateful they went inside.

****

Ashton sipped her wine, relieved a fire roared behind her in the small eatery. Even her bones shivered. Zander sat on her left. His teammates, Ansel and Daiya, across from them, dressed in the same blue that Zander wore. Ashton stood out with her blinding white tee and khaki pants but painted a team-supportive smile on her face.

Their small group of four had finished dinner with a variety of appetizer-like food choices, similar to the meals in Toria. Each plate was a masterpiece of craft and flavor, delivered by proud elementals. Despite the tasty food, everyone seemed on edge. Was it because of her joining their team, the growing demon problem, or were internal keepers just less chatty?

"I take it she's coming with us tomorrow?" Daiya hunched over the table. Her blunt cut swayed against her chin, hair so black it might be blue. Ashton had just met this internal keeper, but already sensed animosity.

"That's why she's here, right?" Ansel eyed Zander with a half grin, as if he was the butter between two crispy pieces of toast, but Zander peered at Daiya.

Ashton opened her mouth to agree with Ansel, then thought better of it. Daiya held Zander's gaze. Or glare? Her eyes, brown as Zander's, glinted with silver. Steady and smooth, they delivered more than words could say. It reminded Ashton of the staring contests she'd fallen into with Mason over the years. They could solve a spat in under two minutes because one of them would cave and laugh.

None of that was happening here.

Ansel rubbed a hand along his shaved head, then scratched at the light scruff along his chin. His bone structure was all angles as he drained his glass and set it abruptly on the table more to get their attention. It worked. They both snapped their heads in his direction. "It's a mock mission tomorrow. There'll be other crews on duty, so let up."

"She knows that." Zander turned to Ashton. "Ready to go?"

"She's supposed to bunk with me." Daiya pushed her chair in with a thud. Her sinewy build was different from the keepers in Toria. She was still muscular, but far leaner.

Ansel, similarly built, stood with her. His green eyes reflected the light of the fire, emitting a truce, or kindness, or maybe compromise. All the internal keepers she'd seen so far were smaller in height and weight, except Zander. He was a giant compared to the others, maybe because he wasn't originally from here.

"Not a good idea." Zander's wooden chair scraped across the floor as he pushed from the table. Ashton stood to join them, dinner obviously over. "I have an empty room. Ashton, are you comfortable with that?"

Around Zander's shoulder, she caught Daiya's tilt of head. Her short, silky hair fanned across her angry face. No way Daiya was comfortable. Even Ansel's brow arched.

"I don't want to be any trouble."

"It's no trouble." Zander didn't wait for a response before heading for the door. Ashton followed, not looking back to say goodbye. She didn't like the direction of conversation, hating to be the focus of their team's animosity. But she was familiar with being the guy's friend who happened to be a girl *all* through high school. She'd dealt with enough of Mason's ex-girlfriends to know when space was warranted.

She'd start over with Daiya in the morning.

Ashton awoke to a soft knock. It took a minute to remember she was in Zander's extra bedroom. In the Dream Realm. The place where the Spiritual Realm was depending on her and her gifts to save them from a new soon-to-be-released evil.

But how?

"Coming." She pulled the blanket up to her chin. Pink lights glittered from the crack in the curtain. She sat up, pushed open the fabric, then fell back into her warm spot under the comforter. How was it so cold?

Maybe she could summon her mind trick right from this room and solve the realm's current crisis without ever getting out of bed. Closing her eyes, she listened for the clicking sound that accompanied her problem-solving gift from the back of her mind. It was similar to her ability to open locks but on a figurative level. It had worked before but only when she was desperate. Right now, as her stomach growled, the chill and hunger were her only enemies.

She sent a sweet thought to Mason, knowing he couldn't hear her mental message. He'd need to be in hawk form and in the same realm. But it made her feel closer to him. She threw off the covers and dragged her bag to the bathroom.

After dressing into fresh seam-keeper gear, she found Zander in the kitchenette. "Is that café-awake?" He was swirling a pot of something deliciously coffee-herbal smelling over a little burner oven. Café-awake was her favorite way to start the day in Toria. It was like coffee and tea with something floral and earthy all mixed together.

"It is. Would you like a cup?"

She smiled and leaned against the counter. There weren't any chairs or bar stools. A glance around the room revealed a sofa and coffee table claiming a center spot in the bare space. He passed her a mug and then offered her a wrapped breakfast bar from a cupboard. It must be standard realm food, as her castmates in Toria ate them too.

"So, what's the plan?" She crossed her fingers she wasn't the only one ridding the realms of evil. She uncrossed them just as fast because the sooner they figured out a plan, the sooner she could get back to her team.

"Did you cross your fingers?"

"What? No." She gripped her mug with both hands and took a sip. Sweet, but with a bite, and warm all the way down.

"It's a human thing, isn't it? Making a wish or something?" He stared across the counter. She couldn't tell if he was curious or mocking her.

"I guess, but it was nothing. How would you know about human things anyway?"

He washed and dried his mug before placing it in the cupboard. When she looked around the kitchenette, it was as stark as the rest of the flat.

"I studied the Human Realm when I was younger. It was kind of a…hobby." He stopped short. "So, what were you wishing for? Or I guess un-wishing for?"

She laughed to blanket her discomfort. There was no way she'd admit weakness to him. But was he hiding something too? She swallowed a gulp of café-awake. "Nothing to wish or un-wish. So…the plan?"

He wiped the already clean counter with a cloth. "Today we swim for demons."

****

Ashton waited for the group to leave the locker room before dressing in the skintight gear Daiya had left for her, and not without a smirk. Ashton rolled her eyes—what was Daiya so worried about?

Space was limited, as Ashton was learning on the tiny floating island of Reverie. Males and females changed in the same room, not something she was used to in the Spiritual Realm. But with the group waiting for her, she didn't want to give Daiya another reason to be rude. She tugged on the silvery-blue second skin that covered her from ankle to neck. It was like an underwater diving suit, minus the tanks and mask. Zander had assured her she wouldn't need them because they wouldn't really be diving into water.

What had Ansel said?—think of it like sticky air. Then he'd shrugged, smiled, and offered her a rubbery black strap to wrap around her thigh.

Ashton held up the strap. On the underside were

smaller slats that held up to five daggers. She'd eyed them earlier on her new teammates. Internal keeper weapons were larger than Mason's throwing knives, but smaller than the daggers and half sword she usually wore on her hip at the Seam. How close would she be getting to these demons under the *supposedly* non-watery realm?

Exhaling the thought away, she bent to put the strap on her leg. Daiya had attached hers without effort, so she followed suit, looping the end around and through the opening, tugging it taut. There were no daggers loaded. Maybe they would provide them later. She'd only trained as a keeper at the Seam. Was internal keeping so different? The end result was the same—slay demons.

Ashton pulled on her booties, made in the same stretchy fabric as her suit, swept her hair into a messy bun, and headed out the side door to meet up with her new team.

The morning air was as pink as it had been the night before. Squinting above was like wearing rose-tinted glasses. She saw the crimson outline of the sun, bright and shiny, through the atmosphere and blinked at its brilliance.

Zander, Ansel, and Daiya waited by a bench, outside the center courtyard she'd glimpsed the night before. In the daylight, she noticed more décor surrounding the structure. Giant globes of colorful glass spheres lay scattered atop the sand, some in clusters, some solo. How had she missed these lovelies last night?

Filtered light glinted brightly off their hues—greens, yellows, purples, blues. They were larger versions of the three tiny soul-spherules she kept in a leather pouch on her weapons belt. One tiny rose-tinted explosive, no bigger than a giant marble, had been powerful enough to expel the demon prince, Ian. Well, for her anyway. Her personal connection had sealed the deal that fateful day. Though she had no intentions of getting personally involved with any more demons. Ever.

She clutched her chest; the vision of Mason physically dead at her feet still haunted. Shaking off the sudden chill from her memory, she forced her thoughts back to the present. *Deep breaths.* She breathed. *Focus on today.*

The glass spheres on the sand were the size of desktop world globes, the ones on human classroom shelves. Gleaming in every hue, they were *beautiful*. That word again. Zander was right, she needed more adjectives.

Ansel's movement drew her attention. He motioned at an array of knives placed on the bench, five of them. Zander picked one up and handed it to her by the hilt. She felt the weight of it in her palm, lighter than her daggers, but heavier than Mason's throwing knives, before placing the blade into a slit on the rubber strap around her thigh. She attached the other four.

"Now what?"

Daiya hitched her thumb toward a smaller dock leading away from the center. "It seems you need a taste of the demons below."

"Not just demons," Ansel said, pulling her down the dock, past Zander, whose lifted brows arched at Daiya. "The souls we protect."

Ashton huffed at Daiya's smugness. It didn't

matter. As much thrill as Ashton had recently gained in demon hunting or her curiosity about the souls, going under the water—or the non-watery whatever it was— caused her heartbeat to slip in waves. "Aren't we just strategizing?"

Ashton startled when Zander's voice responded behind her. She glanced to see he'd caught up.

"It's important you see the whole picture, the reason this all matters. You've already learned about the increased demon activity, but it won't make sense to plan a strategy when you've never been below." Zander nodded to where Daiya had indicated earlier. Ansel grinned sidelong at her, his green eyes glowing in the morning light, before sliding over to make room for the four of them to walk side by side.

"You've killed demons before, right?" Daiya patted her strap of knives, then adjusted a stretchy headband holding her hair back from her forehead. Disdain coated her voice.

Daiya hated her for sure.

Ashton rolled her eyes to the unapologetic cherry sky and trudged along.

The open courtyard forked into smaller wooden paths all heading in various directions, each so long she couldn't make out where they ended. Mounds of tall grasses poked up through the mist along the docks. If she could have pushed back her long tight sleeves, goosebumps would've popped from the chill.

They zigzagged down dock after dock, their line of four shrinking to two and two, until they were closer to the wall of outer waterfalls. Ashton felt the spray of whatever it was, *not* water, wafting against her cheeks.

Finally, the dock widened at the end like a giant T-shape. On one side there was a bench, as if keepers might sit to enjoy the magenta-peachy view...and it *was* breathtaking. But being this close to the falls also included the constant pounding of water-like haze about thirty yards away. It swirled and gusted, blowing the stray hairs falling from her bun. The sound thundered in her ears like band drums.

Ashton swiped the very real wetness from her face, not that it mattered because the spray continued its blast. Strands of her hair stuck to her skin, though her skin suit glistened, impervious to constant battering from the falls. Underneath she felt dry as a bone.

"You'll get used to it," Ansel whispered over the roar, though he looked to strain in his delivery.

Zander touched her elbow, tilting his head to the opposite side of the T-shaped boardwalk. A small, enclosed structure sat ready with open doors while other internal keepers strode in and out. Some paused, half smiling at her as they passed. But mostly, their faces were intense, appearing to be on a mission. Before she entered, she watched a few cross their hearts with their hands and jump from the dock into the...what *was* it again?

"Zander," she called over the noise. "You said it's not water, but—" She wiped the dewy film off her face and held up her hands.

He leaned in close to her ear, and the sense of familiarity flowed through her before rushing away with the blowing mist. "The water is an illusion. It's energy, remember. But it does feel a little like water. Just stickier. Trust me. You'll be okay." He walked through the open doors of the small hut.

She stepped inside, out of the dewy energy, and it

was instantly quieter. Zander checked in with a woman behind the counter. She was lithely built, similar to Ansel and Daiya, but older. It wasn't that she had wrinkles like Ashton's human grandma had, but more like her cheeks were weathered. Her long gray hair laced into two dangling braids down the breast of the same blue uniform they all wore, though hers hung loose, like a jumpsuit.

Her voice crackled as she spoke, as if permanently damaged from years of talking over the perpetual noise. "Here ya go, sweet." She handed over a black earpiece to Zander, and another one to Ashton. "I'm Nanna. And you must be our second little seamer come to see what you've let loose past the borders?"

Ashton bit her lip, unsure whether to laugh or apologize. Nanna's expression appeared benevolent, but her message was loud and clear. They wouldn't need internal keepers if seam keepers did their jobs. Her shoulders drooped at the weight of everything connecting.

Nanna noticed her discomfort. "It's okay, little heart. We're all a team in the larger scheme of things. Another cog in the wheel of creation." She patted Ashton's hand in the transference of equipment. Ashton accepted the tiny rubbery device in her palm and looked to Zander, who was twisting his into his ear.

"Nan always finds some kind of silver lining." Zander shook his head at Nanna, and she shrugged.

"The earpieces are only for *our* team. Ansel and D can communicate under the surface without them because they were born here, but we weren't."

"Because you two aren't inners." Nanna let out another jab but with a full grin. "Is your destiny askew like his?"

Ashton still couldn't tell if she was joking or not.

"Destinies change, Nan." Zander laid his hand atop hers. "And aren't *you* glad they do." Nanna reached her other hand atop Zander's, and they locked eyes a moment.

Then, without another word, Zander headed back outside where Ansel and Daiya stood waiting. They had the same little black devices in their ears too. It must be to communicate with Zander, which now made sense. They were from the Dream Realm; Zander wasn't.

"Ready?" Ansel asked, swiping wet film from atop his hair-spiked head. His voice emitted clearly through the device in her ear, even with the hammering waterfall of energy. Refusing seemed out of the question, so she nodded, squelching her creeping nerves.

She stepped closer to the edge of the dock. *Here comes the* more *she'd told Rory she wanted!*

Without any details or training or tips about what to expect, her new borrowed team lifted their fists. Daiya held up one finger. Ansel held up two. And Zander, three. Then Daiya crossed her heart and jumped, disappearing under the surface without a splash.

Ansel was next. Midair he swiveled his body around, flipped, and grinned as if a circus act, before fully submerging.

Zander reached out to take Ashton's hand, and she gripped it tightly, letting him pull her off the edge with a trust she would've once only sworn to Mason. If he saw her now, taking a huge leap of faith—without question or complaint—he wouldn't believe it.

Chapter 10

Rainbow Souls

Zander clasped Ashton's hand to anchor her from the swirling aether, their joined effort a friction in the plunge. He hadn't told her much about the rosy energy-filled atmosphere.

How could he explain? Experiencing it firsthand was the only way to comprehend what the Dream Realm truly was—sticky, airy, weightlessness—like swimming without water. His first time under had been a disaster. Of course, Ansel wasn't kind in his initiation. Zander wouldn't leave Ashton alone to discern which way was up.

He watched as she held her breath, blue eyes bulging in a state of panic, legs kicking to keep afloat. The deeper they sank, the more indigo swirls of color formed, flickered, and dissolved as she floundered. He wanted to give her time to adjust, but...was she breathing?

Ansel and Daiya kept watch, giving her space to acclimate. He could see their outlines through the heavier, mostly translucent air. Their team wasn't officially on duty. This mission was about showing Ashton how things worked on this end of the spectrum. He would keep guard though. Lately, it wasn't *if* they ran into demons, but *when*.

Zander steadied her. "Slow down. You're all right." He pointed to Ansel and Daiya. They hovered in a relaxed stance, legs bent, arms out to the side, slowly moving back and forth in the soft indigo currents.

He pointed to his mouth. "It's okay, you can breathe. Relax. Let yourself float."

After a moment, her swinging legs slowed. Her gaze followed the luminescent sparkles bubbling in reaction to her movements.

She let go of his hand, air bursting out through her nose, then in again. She splayed her legs, as if to balance, and spread both arms out, swaying them forward and backward less frantically.

Her eyes drifted from Ansel and Daiya to Zander, then to the thick substance all around. But her lips…they were a thin line. She was probably afraid to open her mouth.

He pointed to his face. "You can talk."

"Let's go." Daiya's voice came through his earpiece, so it must have rung through Ashton's too. She startled at the sound, glancing toward Daiya.

Zander gently gripped her forearm. "Remember, we have earpieces to communicate as a team. Our voices only carry a few inches without them. But you can talk."

He watched various expressions cross her face. She was pretty, and though she may have meant something to him long ago…would have meant something to him now had his destiny not altered, there was nothing between them. She didn't remember him. And he'd moved on.

Hadn't he?

Until yesterday, when the Blessing Council had

summoned him, cracking open a locked part of his past.

Zander glanced at Daiya, long swirls of color dancing in sync with her impatience. The aether deepened in hue, thickening and thinning around her movements. Even if she could hide her expression behind distance and the thicker airlike substance, he knew what she was thinking. Daiya was the stubborn teammate in their trio, suspicious the council would order him back to the Spiritual Realm. She didn't want him to leave their team, but really, she didn't want him to leave her.

Nothing official had transpired between them, nothing lasting longer than their usual silent gazes, or his lingering thoughts when he closed his eyes at night. But she'd always carried a chip on her shoulder, and since he understood that kind of weight, he never asked about it. They had a way of understanding each other without talking at all, exactly what he needed.

Whatever *it* was or wasn't, the Blessing Council had caused a ripple…again. He exhaled a breath, wafting the aether in front of him. Would he always be the one ordered away?

Ansel pulled Zander's attention as he closed in next to Ashton, the atmosphere swooshing against his chest. He knew Ashton would also feel the currents push against her.

"It's like extra-thick oxygen." Ansel halted before her. "Just don't take deep breaths."

Ashton stared at him, her chestnut brows crinkled together, until finally she opened her mouth. The movement pulled against the flow of currents as she coughed into the thick air and regained composure.

Zander reached out, but Ansel already had both

hands steadying her shoulders, breathing with her until she was steady.

"I said no deep breaths." His head tilted in jest.

"Oh my God." Her voice came through Zander's earpiece. He watched the muscles in her neck relax, her face brighten.

"You've got it." Ansel backed away, throwing his body into a backflip, then popped up in front of her again. "Now you try."

Ashton shook her head. "Oh no." She gasped, air swishing as she looked between Zander and Ansel. She accepted both their offered arms, holding her breath as they lifted her, effortlessly, up and over. She almost made it around before curling into a ball and kicking her way back down.

"I'm not ready for tricks," she said before Daiya's voice cut through.

"Are we done playing?" Daiya kept her distance.

Before swimming away, Ansel gave Ashton a thumbs-up. "Let's go!"

"Ready?" Zander asked, slowly stirring the aether back and forth with his arms and legs.

Ashton watched him with big blue eyes, mirroring him. So he backed away, stretching out horizontally, backstroking toward the team. She leaned forward, swooshing her arms up, over, then back to her sides, gaining speed through the thick substance of dream energy.

A quick learner, just as he'd always believed she would be…when he used to think of her as part of him.

****

Ashton breathed in the airy substance that lived beneath the docks. It was the freshest air she'd ever inhaled and full of aromatics like coconut and spinning sugar, vanilla, and…what else? She couldn't name the scent. Her lungs felt full, her body buoyant.

She was swimming through sky!

Daiya led through swirling indigo and lavender currents. Ashton soared next to Zander with Ansel trailing behind.

At first, everything appeared clear. It seemed she could see for miles. But as the forms ahead blurred in and out of view, she figured her vision was maybe sixty yards in each direction, the short side across one of Mason's soccer fields. Her chest tightened at the thought before she let the sting of human memories fall away. And they did, swooshing with the tingling bubbles fizzing around her exposed ankles and neck.

Every direction looked the same, and different. Tall grasses swayed from somewhere far below, like ocean seaweed. When she peered down, the dark silhouettes of vines twisted and swayed into a muddled bottomless nothing alongside the seagrass…or reeds…or mystery vegetation. Soft colors, with subtle hints of magenta and darker blue, swirled.

It was all surreal.

Ashton had never gone deep sea diving, but she'd watched the quiet beauty of underwater worlds on television. This couldn't possibly compare. Moving felt both efforted and effortless through the energy. Surely there was less gravity than at the Seam. Falling from Mason's hawk form that fretful night Ian's goons came after her was still fresh in her memory. There'd been no floating in that dreamy air-like substance, but *inside* the Dream Realm…

Daiya led them farther from where they had dove

in, and the deeper they swam, the darker the hues became. She glanced over to Zander, and he pulled on his left cuff with his right hand. Light streamed from the stitching around his wrist like a flashlight. She did the same, and a glow beamed from her sleeve, the rays bending around invisible tides wherever she directed her arm.

Now she swam through the night sky.

"Lights out. We're approaching the nest." Daiya's voice, abrupt in her earpiece.

"Nest?" She peered at Zander, and he tugged his sleeve again. The lights cut out at once. As they approached what resembled an underwater waterfall, she copied what Zander had done and pulled on her sleeve, snuffing the glow.

The view took her already oxygenated breath away. Standing before her was a gray-blue wall of energy. It dropped before them like a curtain of thunderstorms and appeared as large as the rocky cliffs encircling Reverie above.

Looking down, she couldn't tell where the curtains of color and movement ended. It was the same when she ogled up. The colors were lighter toward the surface and darker down. The edges blurred out of vision, as if they kept going.

How far? How wide?

Ansel swam next to her, his voice low through her earpiece. "The energy runs vertical, the entire length of the realm. The walls flow from the circle of cliffs above Reverie." He shrugged. "We don't know how far down. Sleeping human souls collect inside, nestled to the center like little orbs of light. Pretty remarkable, don't you think?"

"Remarkable doesn't begin to describe this. And orbs?" Ashton squinted to see through the swirling curtain, but the concentrated color was thick. She couldn't imagine anything getting through. Even demons.

Daiya approached, rolling her eyes. She took a deep breath, then dove headfirst, into the mantle of energy until she was gone.

Ashton's hands flew to her mouth. She strained to see through the barrier, but it literally appeared like a torrential rainstorm. Ansel's chuckle carried through her earpiece as he followed suit, taking a big breath before diving into the deluging wall. The force swallowed him in a matter of seconds.

"Ready?" Zander held out a hand.

She shook her head and floated back from the massive flow of contained energy that had just sucked up two keepers.

"It's okay." He offered a hand.

His brown eyes, darker than Mason's, grounded her, making her want to trust over arguing for another option. So before chickening out, she grasped his hand and nodded. This couldn't be worse than her first flight on the back of a hawk. As terrified as she had been then, by the end she hadn't vomited, and she'd almost sat up...almost.

Zander laid a hand to his chest. "Hold your breath. It takes almost a full minute to get to the center. Aether's too thick to breathe inside the borders of the nest. And close your eyes. The pressure's pretty strong."

"Wait—what if I get stuck?"

"The energy flow will pull you through. Don't

fight it." He raised his brows as if to ask again if she was ready.

"Okay—hold my breath, close my eyes, don't fight the pull." Was it too late to opt out of this part of the Dream Realm tour?

Zander's grip tightened. Ashton sucked in a breath and squeezed her eyes shut as he tugged her into the curtain of energy. She kicked her feet to keep up, or at least help move herself through, but he was right. The powerful force already lugged her, so she focused on gripping his hand.

Hold breath, close eyes, don't fight the pull.

If it was only a minute, it was the longest minute of her life.

Pure force thrust her body through the wall—curtain—border. Whatever it was, it was warmer than the less condensed parts of the strange atmosphere, and loud, like the raging waterless waterfalls above Reverie.

Shades of dark and light glinted behind her eyelids, as if someone swung a flashlight. But she didn't dare open her eyes as Mason may have tried. A flicker of ache passed through her heart, wishing he was there to experience this incredible ride. He was the one who craved terrifying carnival rides, spinning hotdog-filled-passengers upside down.

Not her.

After a jolt, the force lifted and the air cooled. She swallowed a lungful of air and blinked to see Zander, Ansel, and Daiya studying her with great interest. They floated in the same magical *stuff* she'd swam through earlier, but now the colors sparkled and glittered as if rainbows scattered from all angles across her team's faces.

When she looked back, the energy wall stood with its deep indigo hues flowing up and down, dropping vigorously like the wildest of waterfalls. The air was richer on this side, the fragrance of peppermint so strong it stung her nose.

"Wow!" A rainbow broke across her palm. She spun around and light blazed from behind her team.

Her mouth dropped at the round globes of light floating as far as her eyes could see.

"Each orb is a human soul." Zander's voice, soft through the earpiece.

"I thought—" She fumbled for the right words. "I thought they would look like...bodies, I guess." She peered in every direction. There had to be thousands of them...millions!

"Their bodies are in their beds—or wherever they're sleeping. These are their essences. Their thoughts, their souls. When they awaken again in the Human Realm, their light in this realm blinks out."

"But it returns when they fall asleep?" Ashton couldn't stop scanning the sea of color.

Zander explained, and Ashton tried to listen as she took in spheres of light glowing in shades of every color imaginable. They were the size of melons, hovering like giant stars in the night.

She wondered if she could cradle one in her arms, they were so enchanting. Each soul's glow refracted off the others until their bent and married lights scattered the airy aether in new silvery-edged hues...like a disco ball.

Ashton spun in a circle, despite the stickiness. She wanted to dance under the spectacle. And she'd *never* wanted to dance before. The energy sparking from each orb intoxicated. Invigorated.

"How are you not *giddy* with all this light?" Her words came out more breathless than she'd meant, and she labored to push her torso around in another circle.

Above and behind the team floated a sea of candy-colored splendor. Her legs flailed and her arms swirled in the soupy, rainbow air; she almost braved one of Ansel's flips. But it was so syrupy-thick. Her team had backed up to give her space, their features like shadows behind frosted glass.

Finally Zander reached through the gooey air and clasped her arm, pulling her closer. "Welcome to the nest."

Ansel wore a broad smile. "What do you think?"

She opened her mouth to speak, but the miracle of the souls swept away any words. It was then she noticed the blinks of lights snuffing out, then popping in again somewhere else, and it made sense. "I see orbs blinking asleep and awake. Like a string of twinkling lights. They're—it's—"

"Beautiful?" Zander curved his lips.

She lifted her fist to thump him on the shoulder, but her arms moved in slow motion. By the time she reached him, it was a tap. "How do you fight demons like this? I can hardly move."

"Easy. You cut it." Daiya appeared, knife in hand. As she shot an arm out, the air fell away under her blade.

Ashton scanned her leg of weapons and withdrew a knife. She aimed away from the group, stabbing into the viscous air. It worked. The point cut straight through the sludge she'd felt when swinging an empty fist at Zander. She could feel the pressure, but it was swifter with the sharp blade edge leading.

"Thanks." She eyed Daiya, who nodded back.

A nod? Progress.

"Other teams are here. We'll get as close as we can without intervening. We're not on duty, but demons don't care about that. Be ready for anything. And speak in a whisper. The earpiece will pick it up," Zander coached as they eased closer to the glowing spheres.

Ashton followed, a blade in each hand, taking everything in as they swam toward the souls. Daiya had been right, she was grateful for her knives.

Heading into the masses, her gaze locked onto a blue orb, larger the closer she swam. Its light, fragmented like an Independence Day sparkler, spewed bits of color into the atmosphere. Sapphire and royal blue sparks sprayed until blending with the colorful effects from other surrounding souls.

Although, darker bits of tarnished light descended from the same orb. Tumbling down, they disappeared into the depths like inky black beads on a chain.

Unmoving, Ashton watched as the team meandered through the glowing globes, without touching any of them. *How?* There were so many.

Zander looked over his shoulder. "You okay?" he whispered through her earpiece.

"I'm afraid I'll damage them with my knives."

"Watch." He waved an arm toward a sphere of yellow light. As his arm neared, the soul inched away. With every pass, the golden light swayed out of reach. With his other hand, he pointed a blade toward a violet sphere hovering on his other side. The ball of light eased away as if caught by a breeze. "They have a protective shell, impenetrable."

Ashton leaned forward, gently swooshing an arm toward the blue one she'd studied. It swerved out of reach. "Unbelievable…as if trying to connect the like sides of magnets." She chanced another swipe, and it swayed, light expelling from some source of endless supply. The brightest of colors flickering to mix with the others while darker bits fell.

She squinted to see below. "What's at the bottom?"

"We can't go down there. It's where the negative energy falls forever—if the demons don't get it first."

"Are the dark parts negative energy?"

"Yes." He looked somber as he eyed the same blue orb's shadowy leash.

"Can we break the chain?"

He shook his head. "We've tried, but as you can see—" He swiped his knife to cut away the darker energy spewing from the soul. It glided out of reach. "Impossible."

"So that's where the demons are, right?" She pointed into the gloomy darkness where a labyrinth of tarnished light trails vanished out of sight. "Then isn't that where we should go to stop them?"

When he didn't answer right away, she looked up. His brown face, brown eyes, darker in the airy atmosphere, contemplated.

"The oxygen farther down is too thick for us to survive." He looked toward the center of drifting lights. "Come on. We need to stay together."

She glanced below once more before kicking her feet through the field of rainbow souls and easing herself into the soupy mix of aether behind Zander. Souls slid out of their way without the need to maneuver around them.

They caught up to Daiya and Ansel, who waited beyond a cluster of feathery green and blue grasses. She wanted to ask about the vegetation here, but she could barely make out her team with their silvery blue suits. They camouflaged with the deeper indigo aether, and the glowing spheres played tricks on her vision.

She mimicked Ansel, grabbing hold of a long vine to anchor herself. But Ansel's next move had her on alert. His wide eyes scrutinized through the depths of the nest...to see what? The rest of their team did the same. Demons? Glancing down, all she could see was a smear of charcoal-gray darkness.

Ashton glanced at Zander, but he was pointing down.

"D, six o'clock." His voice was barely audible. Daiya was already gone, cutting through the smoggy soup in a flash.

"Ans, back her up."

He already dove her way.

"Nan, we need a crew!" Zander swore under his breath, scanning the area. He looked back at Ashton. "Stay behind me."

Ashton squinted her eyes in the direction of Daiya and Ansel. She clutched her knives tighter as the image of a demon bobbed up under an emerald orb. It didn't seem to hurt the soul. The ball of green light buoyed away with every approach from the blob-shaped monster, appearing more like a walrus with horns. Most of the demons she'd encountered at the Seam looked like an odd combination of earthly and mythical animals.

Daiya surprised the creature, dropping from above.

But the creature wasn't after the soul. Through the

blurry distance, Ashton could see that. The tarnished bits of light she'd seen before sputtered like Fourth of July duds. The chain of light descended down, down, down.

The demon—*demons*, as more congregated from below—gulped the descending deeper shades like water from a hose.

Clear lines were hard to make out, but Ashton saw the silhouette of Daiya's knife tear through a monster's back.

Ansel arrived in time to counter another blob ascending. His knife plowed into the demon's head as it turned its ugly face to where Ashton scarcely made out slots for eyes.

Another!

Her seam keeper side ignited. She itched to move, but Zander stood as a sturdy barrier. Didn't he realize she could fight these demons under the surface as easily as she could outside the borders?

Whoa! A walrusy demon creeped up from below, its movements choppy. Ashton could make out its red eyes creating a trail from the dark below.

"Daiya!" Ashton shouted, swimming forward. But Zander, already moving, turned and pushed Ashton back.

Daiya turned, just as a demon reared up, catching her calf with a horn. Her scream crackled through the earpiece, as pink-tinged swirls from Daiya's leg seeped into the blue aether.

Wounded, she threw her knife into the demon's neck when it came in for a second attack. The swarming colors deepened with the monster's inky bubbles, leaking from its lethal gash. It turned belly up before falling farther than Ashton's vision could follow, the aftermath of ichor and blood saturating her view.

The other demons all turned at the same time, following their fallen into the dark below.

Soon Daiya's form appeared through the clearing aether. She held her wounded leg with one hand; a knife in her other, cut through the airy atmosphere, still searching for danger. But even with the demons gone, Ashton saw a purple spot clouding the water behind her.

Daiya's blood.

"Let me help!" Ashton cried out. She hadn't been trained as the Centennial keeper to hide on the sidelines. That'd sadly been her choice as a human, but she wasn't that girl anymore.

"No, we've got this. Stay there!" Zander called, his attention on Daiya.

"Left calf," Daiya gasped through the earpiece.

Zander joined Ansel, their bodies back to back, creating a sandwich, with Daiya in between. When the air currents stopped pushing, and the quick movements of shadowy blobs fell away, Zander swam back to the spot Ashton hid, pulling long grasses up to cover her.

"You okay?" He peered in every direction, surely hunting for more danger.

"There could be more. I can fight," Ashton stressed.

"Just stay here." He didn't wait for her answer and was through the liquid air, swimming laps around his team once more. But the demons were gone. Zander grabbed Daiya's shoulders and stared into her eyes. If he said something through the earpiece, Ashton couldn't hear it.

Ansel pulled something from a front pocket and clasped it over Daiya's wound. The blood, discoloring the air, stopped instantly.

A second later, another team whooshed past Ashton, their currents rippling the vegetation around her legs. The group of three halted before Zander, Daiya, and Ansel.

"Three down. Same breed. Clear," Zander reported, his voice louder in Ashton's ear.

She couldn't hear the other team. When Zander spoke again, he was the only voice. They must be on a different communication system…or didn't need one.

She had to get closer.

With only two strokes out, Zander maneuvered toward her. "We're done here. You okay?"

She was fine, but *not* okay. He didn't trust she could handle herself in a fight. She opened her mouth to tell him what she thought when a movement swept in from the right.

Ashton rotated, both knives ready. Another blubbery creature sprang from the darkness, horns cutting through the aether. Ashton was closer and hurled herself onto the beast with a twist, her knife tearing into its head. Dark ichor spilled into the mix of air, like a shadow melting. Zander finished it off with a blow from his foot. It hovered for only a blink, releasing a warbled cry, before falling into the gray-blue mist below.

"Yeah," she said in response to his question. "I'm fine."

Chapter 11

Coffee, Milkshakes, and Complications

Mason rolled out of bed with one mission in mind: *coffee*. Nostalgia lingered as he pulled on a pair of sweatpants and a faded T-shirt from his childhood dresser.

Standing barefoot in his kitchen and staring at the coffee machine, waiting for water to press through the caffeine pod, his mind slipped to Ashton. What was she doing this very minute? Time was different in every realm, so in Reverie she could be asleep, working over a stack of playbooks, eating dinner, or whatever strategizing looked like with *what's-his-name*.

"Morning." Bronwyn ambled in, dressed in leggings like Ashton used to wear and Nigel's T-shirt. "This stale human air...I was up with the sun, but I *still* feel sleepy."

Mason stared as she slouched her small frame against the counter and frowned. The slump of her shoulders matched the turn of her lips as she exhaled and ran her hands through long white hair. He'd never once seen her frown. Serious expressions during battles? Yes. Smiling or laughing? Always. But frowns? Bronwyn was an optimist.

The machine stopped dripping, and he pulled out his mug, holding it up as a peace offering. "Coffee?"

"Will it help this sluggish sensation disappear?" She pushed off the counter, palms open, welcoming the gift.

Mason laughed and threw in another pod for himself.

"Mmmmmmm." She sipped the steaming liquid. "This is awful and delicious at the same time."

"I'll have an order of awful and delicious." Nigel stepped through the doorway and bent to kiss Bronwyn's head. He hadn't bothered with a shirt, his dark skin a contrast to Bronwyn's silvery-white hair.

Mason laughed under his breath and readied a third coffee pod. They all stared as the machine performed its magic when Des and Connor sauntered in.

Conner leaned over Bronwyn's shoulder, inhaling the contents of her cup. "Will this concoction ward off Human Realm hangovers?"

"Worth a try." Mason pulled the box of pods down from the cupboard. "Sorry Earth's atmosphere doesn't pump in pure oxygen like the Spiritual Realm," he snarked, passing the next filled mug to Nigel.

Connor slugged Mason's shoulder…in gratitude, perhaps?

Mason popped in another pod.

Soon they all sprawled in the family room, mugs in hand, including Mason. He swallowed his first gulp with relief…*finally*.

Bronwyn sprang up to retrieve her backpack and passed out energy bars. They engulfed them in silence, leaving a pile of wrappers in the center of the coffee table.

"What's the plan?" Maybe it was the coffee, but Mason sensed they might be afraid to bring up sabotaging his dad's name after his freak-out the night before. At this point, he just wanted to get it done.

"We'll need to start with Max's social media accounts." Des sat up from leaning against Connor. "I believe you call it *trolling*."

Mason arched an eyebrow.

"First we're going to catch up on what the world thinks about him now, so we know how to approach the situation later," Bronwyn chimed in.

Mason shrugged. "He doesn't have a social media presence."

"He has enough of one." Connor grabbed the laptop, left on the side table from the night before. "He's got a link—no, wait, an account, right?" He looked up, rubbing his short ginger hair.

Mason nodded approval at his lingo. His team must have had some hell of a crash course.

"He has a small following." Connor pecked the keyboard. "Mostly academia. I found a list of all his college tour chats. But his mystery books have a few numbers too."

"If this book releases as nonfiction, like we assume it will, and it holds the proof Max is being provided with from the Dark Realm, then he'll surely focus on the college circuit and avoid the cult culture." Des set down his empty mug.

"Who's going to believe a book about demons anyway?" Mason asked. It'd bugged him during the night when he couldn't sleep. "Especially the educated?"

Bronwyn held up a hand. "Humans never had any proof before. Who knows what kind of information Max has now?"

Mason clenched his jaw. The reality of monsters was still sinking in. How might the rest of the world take it?

"They won't want the book picked up by fanatics at first, at least Kelvin won't," Connor added. "From what we've learned, those groups aren't taken seriously. My bet is it will be more fact-based, a…what's it called when it's a film?" He looked at Des.

"Documentary." Des tied back his long hair.

"It won't pause radical group ranting." Bronwyn smiled for the first time that morning. "That's where we come in."

"I get it. We *want* fanatics." Mason stiffened. He thought of the *Blaire Witch Project* from the nineties before he was even born. The low-budget horror film became a cult hit as a documentary about real and dangerous witchcraft to the masses. The movie was a hoax, but the fear created was real.

"Of course. We need to throw off the majority of believers," Bronwyn continued. "If we can help fuel them ahead of time, they'll do most the work."

Mason grunted his understanding—the mob mentality of fear.

Nigel set down his empty mug. "Mason, I believe there will be all kinds of religious masses panicking. Whatever facts Max puts into his book will confuse and torment the public at the same time, right?"

Mason looked down. "It has to."

Bronwyn wrapped her hands around her middle. "Unfortunately, all panic leads to negative energy, whether it's belief in the book or not. The confusion alone will slough off in their sleep…when they dream."

"Kelvin's picking up where Ian left off, stirring the

pot." Mason exhaled, his coffee acid in his stomach.

"If we can get the majority to believe it's a hoax…" Connor set the laptop down and grabbed his mug. "*Before* there's a chance of readers taking it seriously, then the fear count goes down."

"What do we do?" Mason set his unfinished cup on the coffee table, no longer craving caffeine.

Bronwyn pulled Nigel to stand. "Time for *Max* to do some trolling."

"And to find those interested in the supernatural." Nigel squinted at Mason. "I think we use something called *hashtags*?"

Connor scooped up the napkin-like wrappers from the table. "Okay, let's plant seeds of mistrust in the world—" He glanced at Mason. "I mean selectively add posts about the absurdness of demonic activity."

Mason leaned back against the sofa. Slaying demons at the Seam felt less complicated than this plan.

****

Mason's eyes blurred together by the time Connor leaned into Max's office. "You hungry?" He'd been staring at the computer screen for hours. They all had. Somehow each of his team had been provided a laptop, due to Shunnar's mysterious connections to the Human Realm. Would he ever figure out this hierarchy of keepers?

The time on the computer read 2:43, past any typical lunch break. But there wasn't anything typical about this mission. He rubbed his hands down his face. "Yep."

Mason slid out of his dad's desk chair and followed Connor into the kitchen. The gang joined one by one as they opened and shut the refrigerator and cupboards to no avail.

They all gawked in his direction.

"What?" He leaned against the island countertop. "No one's been home for weeks."

"Didn't your friend, Hicks, say he worked at a diner?" Nigel offered.

A chorus of *yeses* filled the room before they all piled into Mason's jeep. As soon as they pulled into the parking lot, memories from not so long ago swarmed Mason's chest.

Jay's Joint, affectionately called J's, was an old dive made new again by a retired computer tech and his partner. They'd staged the place like it was from the seventies but with a modern flair. Bold colors like goldenrod, turquoise, and orange filled Mason's mind, along with long oval tabletops instead of rectangular. Graffiti plastered the walls in forms of art prints from…Jean-Michel Basquiat. Mason smiled for remembering the artist's name. Ashton had once explained he'd created more work in the eighties but echoed a seventies vibe.

Vehicle doors cranked open and slammed shut, forcing Mason back to the task at hand.

Food.

He climbed out with his crew, unblinking at the bright light shining from the overhead blue sky. As a human, he'd always kept sunglasses in the glove box…sunny summer days were Seattle's best kept secret. But this weather was the norm in Toria.

Filing through the diner door, bell jingling, Mason pointed his group to a booth in the back. It sat to the left of an empty stage where acoustic guitar bands and poetry readings happened at night. Thankfully J's wasn't as busy as he'd expected, only a couple at a table by the window and a few teens at the sidewalk tables outside. Of course, it was between typical mealtimes. He could only hope he didn't run into anyone he knew. The thought of more lying or worse, dragging anyone else into his mess, added to his already sour stomach.

A server, wearing J's standard uniform of jeans and a black T-shirt reading *You Jivin' Yet?* in flowery white lettering, approached the table. "How's everyone doing?" The teen girl passed out menus. "I'll grab waters unless you all want milkshakes?"

"Milkshakes?" Bronwyn perked up. "Sounds totally huma—I mean refreshing. They're cold, right?" She looked at Mason.

The server clicked her pen. Mason laughed. "Um, yeah. Chocolate's the flavor." He glanced at the others, not wanting to make eye contact with the server, as she scribbled down Bronwyn's order. The fewer people he involved in this mission the better.

Des saved them all. "Chocolate milkshakes for everyone."

She walked back to the kitchen, and Mason let his shoulders slump.

"Sorry." Bronwyn blushed. "I almost messed up."

Nigel wrapped an arm around her. "Easy mistake."

They all laughed. It wasn't loud, but with the lack of other clientele, their release must have reached the kitchen because the server leaned out again. Mason waved her away.

After a unified approval of the delivered milkshakes, they ordered hamburgers and French fries, eating in silence. The food actually settled Mason's stomach.

They'd just finished their meal when the door jingled.

"Mason Deed. Two days in a row, man." Hicks approached the table, held out a fist to bump. He wore J's black T-shirt, ready for his shift. "I thought that was your jeep outside."

Mason stood up, greeting his friend, when the bells jingled again. Hicks turned and opened his arm up to the girl waltzing through. She was shoving sunglasses into her bag as she made her way to an employee door behind the counter. Her long black hair swept across her face, but it was her arms, bare below the short sleeves of her J's T-shirt, catching Mason's attention. His team must have noticed too because they all shuffled out of the booth, knocking Mason aside in their quick withdrawal from the table.

"Kali, over here," Hicks called to the girl.

Kali looked up, tucking long locks behind her ear—her ashen-gray ear matching the ashen gray skin on her arms.

She was a demon.

A *fade*.

Mason had recently fought two of them when searching Ian's warehouse for Ashton. They were the lesser demons harnessing enough energy to hold a shape in the Human Realm. What was it—she—doing here? And with Hicks?

Kali turned with a smile, slowly slipping away when her eyes scanned the group.

"Babe, this is my friend, Mason. We went to high school together." He stretched out an arm for her to join them.

She inched forward, Hicks's arm wrapping around her shoulder as she approached. "This is Kali," he said, grinning.

She eyed the group with a blank stare. Her pupils dilated so much, Mason couldn't tell the color of her eyes. They were just...dark.

"Hi," she whispered, casting her gaze down.

She had to know they were keepers. As if she could hide her identity from them. Mason exchanged knowing glances with the others, rolled his shoulders, hands flexing at his sides. But Hicks didn't seem to pick up anything out of the ordinary.

"We're closing tonight," Hicks said to Mason. "Come back at ten. We can hang out and catch up. You all should." He scanned the group. "We'll be out of here pretty fast since it's a Tuesday."

Kali's gaze drifted up at Mason.

Mason kept his eyes glued on Kali, but responded, "Yeah, tonight would be good."

"I have to punch in." Kali pulled Hicks toward the employee door. "So do you."

"She's right." He teetered backward and caught his balance. Laughing, he said, "See you tonight."

The team was already heading out the door, bells chiming as Mason paid the bill with a card from his dad's desk drawer. Then he hurried behind them. No one dared a word until the doors shut tight on the jeep.

Mason's lungs burst. "What the hell?"

"One of Ian's leftovers? How would Kelvin already know about Mason's former life?" Bronwyn voiced what everyone was thinking.

"He's a high-level demon." Nigel scanned the parking lot. "There could be more fades."

Mason inched the jeep into the road, eyes peeled. Was Kali on a new mission with Kelvin or left behind after Ian's banishment? His core burned thinking of Hicks with a demon. Another person he cared about snagged by the supernatural.

Chapter 12

Doom and Overwhelm

Ashton awoke to another knock on the door; rosy light streamed through the curtains she'd forgotten to close. Events from yesterday replayed in her mind like a movie trailer. The misty-aired Dream Realm, the floating spheres of rainbow souls, the blubbery-horned demon attacking…and the tension of her knife tearing through its skin.

Hissing a breath, she rolled out of bed. Too much too fast! She sent *miss-you* thoughts to Mason, craving his revved energy as a welcome distraction.

"Morning." In the kitchen, Zander slid a mug of café-awake across the countertop.

Ashton sipped twice from the warm herbal goodness. "Hey." She kept her voice neutral, snatched an energy bar from the counter, and headed to the sole sofa in the center of the room. She would have asked approval to eat there, but after yesterday, she still had sea legs. Or air legs. Or realm legs. Whatever explained the wobbliness in her limbs.

Zander had stayed with Daiya at the healer's sanctuary late into the night. Ansel, tightlipped about any deeper relationship between the two, had instead given Ashton a tour of the assembly hut and shared the most recent demon reports. The only change noted was an increase in quantity and the oddity of red eyes.

Ashton had pored over the report the night before, but this morning, the sudden change in demon eye color from the typical black, gray, or no eyes at all screamed *clue*. Too bad she'd never been a mystery buff back in her not so long-ago human days.

The silence grew awkward. "What's the plan today?"

Zander offered her a napkin and sat down. "We aren't diving, if you're worried."

"Why would I be worried?" She took the napkin and glared at him side-eyed. "I'm a trained keeper."

Zander pushed a coaster closer to her, so she set her mug down and opened the bar.

Did she look worried? Had she appeared nervous the day before? It was a unique environment, one she hadn't been prepared for, but that could have happened to any keeper who'd never traveled internally before.

She rubbed her eyes with a free palm. She *was* tired and maybe a little overwhelmed by the stress of fixing such a complex situation. It *had* kept her up most of the night. But she could battle a few monsters. Hadn't she proved herself with ol' red-eyes yesterday?

"I mean we'll be strategizing above the surface today. No demons."

"I'm not afraid of demons." She bit the chewy oat and fruit bar as if she'd clamped onto a demon's arm. The thought made her wince.

Zander scratched his head, exhaled a breath as if hanging on to something he'd rather say. "Okay."

"Sorry." She lifted her mug. What was wrong with her? "I think I'm stressed about finding a solution. But the demons from yesterday…I could have helped."

He lingered in her gaze before responding. "I didn't want you hurt on your first day. Big mission ahead."

That couldn't be all of it, but he leaned back and closed his eyes. What time had he gotten home last night? Dang! Ashton hadn't asked about Daiya. Guilt rippled through her chest.

"Daiya, how's she doing?"

"Our healer called out of realm for support. This wound's *different* than we've seen before, but she felt a little better by the time I left."

"Different how?"

"It's not healing as we typically do."

"I'm sorry I fell asleep. Are *you* okay?"

He huffed, maybe surprised she was concerned. "Fine. We should get going."

"Where to, if not below?" Her arms prickled with goosebumps, some from the chilly air in the room, some from the cooler air that seemed to follow Zander. What was his deal? And what would cause a demon scratch not to heal?

"The office. Amit, our head, will have an updated report."

She didn't move, not with the rest of her warm café-awake and bar to finish. "How long have you lived here…in Reverie?"

Zander's gaze flicked to hers in a flash, creases carving across his dark forehead. "Why does it matter?"

"It doesn't." She swallowed her last bite. "Just curious. At the meeting, they said you trained as a seam keeper. How does a shifting hawk end up here?" Maybe she'd crossed a line, but if she'd be collaborating with Mr. Serious Pants over the next who knows how long, it would be nice to know a little more about him. About his team.

Zander opened his hand for her empty wrapper. She placed it in his palm, and he stepped the three strides into his kitchenette. "If you're ready, we should go."

Okay…conversation over.

****

As they approached the larger central hut that housed Reverie's command offices, Ashton surveyed the outside sand garden, surrounding the structure like a moat encircling a castle. There weren't any birds, though tiny butterflies and other winged insects fluttered about the glass sphere sculptures, reminding her of the fireflies from the portal entrance.

Inside, busyness swarmed. The main entry, filled with small sofas and chairs, extended into a hallway exposing three doors down each side. Other internal keepers buzzed throughout the central space dressed in their indigo blues, though Ashton wore her regular seam-keeper gear.

Zander led her to the back room on the right to find Ansel—and Daiya—already working.

"You're here?" Ashton blurted at Daiya.

Ansel looked up from his stack of journals. Their wounded teammate leaned against the arm of a small sofa, her leg elevated, calf wrapped in bandages.

"Still not healing?" Zander strode to her side.

"It's fine." Daiya adjusted her position. "The healers said the wound should improve by tomorrow. You know internals don't heal as quickly as hawks." She sneered, but an air of jest laced through her words.

Ashton watched Zander's jaw clench. "It's been at

least twelve hours." He leaned to inspect her bandages.

She shooed him away. "Nanna fussed over me this morning. And of all people, *you* wouldn't want to mess up her wrappings." She offered him a small smile.

Ashton stepped back. It would take a while to figure out Daiya. Stabbed by a demon horn or not, something about her teammates caused her to soften. What was her story?

"Well, yesterday, while you two were slacking..." Ansel cut the moment of sentiment with humor. "Ashton and I compared the journals from the past month." His smile slipped away. "The demon count, already high, continues to increase." Ansel pushed back from the desk. "But that's not the worst part."

The room fell silent, awaiting his reveal...yet Ashton's guilt was already snared. It was *her* cast, and other keeper teams at the Seam, responsible for stopping demons from crossing the borders. If more monsters found their way into the center of the Dream Realm, it was because seam keepers weren't doing their job. Her fingers folded into her palms, the pressure of each fingernail a reminder of the cost.

"What is it?" Zander glared at Ansel, his eyes like a storm.

"In just two days, negative energy has *doubled*. Something is happening. And it's happening fast." Ansel lifted his chin, ever so slightly, toward Daiya, though his gaze never left Zander's. A quiet message passed between the two.

The seriousness of the situation pressed on Ashton's shoulders, but she didn't dare move. Holding her breath, she prayed he'd say more. Something like *I have a plan!* She cut to Daiya. *She* must know what to do. Nothing terrified that keeper, not even the state of her slow-healing calf.

"The demon was different, this wound is different, so the souls are reacting to the change." Daiya lifted herself to sit straighter. "Is that what you're saying?"

Ashton guessed she hadn't missed Ansel's subtle chin movement to Zander. She doubted much escaped Daiya's scrutiny.

"I'm saying it can't be coincidental." Ansel rubbed his head. "And yes, it's causing more souls to anchor!"

"Those demons were like every other monster we've battled before, except for the one with red eyes." Daiya's black hair shimmered in the pink light splattering through the window. "Clarify."

Ansel shoved the journals across the desk. He didn't seem angry at his team, just frustrated. Ashton had only known him for a couple of days, but already his carefree air had disappeared, his green eyes steady between his teammates.

"The red signifies *something*. Nan's already working with Amit on this one. But we need a permanent fix." Ansel locked eyes with Ashton. "Maybe you have an idea, Centennial?"

"Me?" Ashton scanned the room, the group suddenly quiet. Frustration already brewed to return home and fix what she could at the Seam. Her gifts had to be stronger in the Spiritual Realm where Rory could help. But here in Reverie? The pulsing in her chest knocked against her ribcage like it used to when she was human. Her gift? No.

Anxiety.

Her keeper inside—the cleverer part of her—used the buzzing beat as a battle chant.

Ashton's human side inhaled, wanting to say something useful, but no words formed.

"Isn't that why you're here?"

"D—" Zander cut in. "This intel is new for all of us." He restacked the journals.

Daiya huffed.

Ashton forced herself to move, to pull a chair next to Zander. "I'll help any way I can." Her heartbeat thumped, suppressing the unease assaulting her insides.

The door flew open, and they all jumped. Nanna waltzed in, gray braids swaying with every step. Behind her was a man, medium in build, with a giant head of black hair, brown skin, and a scrunched face. A sense of urgency bloomed around them both.

"Updates." He dropped a handful of reports onto the desk. "Gavan just sent word. Mia is safe with the human, Max Deed, but his team barely made it out alive. Kelvin has some powerful monsters guarding the estate." He shook his head. "Healers connected with Mia, but not for long. The strange atmosphere in that pocket of a realm is thick, but they're working on it." He scanned the group, noticing Ashton. "Oh—hello."

"I'm Ashton." She softened her tightened jaw but didn't stand or smile. It didn't seem the time for pleasantries.

"Amit." He nodded. "It's good you're here. We're in need of your Centennial gifts more than expected." He studied his reports, as if waiting…for her to summon her gifts upon command.

Ashton's stomach flip-flopped. She wasn't a superhero, here to save the day.

Scanning her abilities, she made a mental checklist. She could harness the ability to transport herself and one other keeper through reflections. Using Toria's purple flower power for invisibility had come to her naturally, the petals handy when she'd once hidden from two demon goons outside her birth mother's tree portal. But her ability to hide wouldn't help the entire Dream Realm. Unlocking chains, like the ones she'd once freed herself from in Ian's warehouse, didn't seem helpful. And her new gift? Demons with strange red eyes and vicious bites weren't anything like a storm to stop.

Her gift for solutions remained the most viable bet, but this ability revealed itself in its own time, and time wasn't something they had. Rory knew all this! Ashton's fragile confidence shriveled to the size of a raisin. She opened her mouth to explain when Nanna took the floor.

"Mia and Mason Deed's stepfather remain trapped. I'm sure you've read the latest numbers for Reverie; God help those souls. Now a fade has mixed with your human friend—what's the place called again?"

"Seattle." Amit ran a hand through tousled hair, distractingly, off his forehead in thick, dark tufts.

"That's it." Nanna continued. "We need—"

"Wait, what did you say?" Ashton leaped to her feet, cutting her off as the context of what Amit had said registered with another flop of his hair. Was Mason okay? What human friend with a fade? "Who?"

"I don't know the name, sweets. I'm sorry."

Zander rose. "I'm sure they're managing like we are."

"How are we managing? Daiya's injured, and the souls are leaking—wait—what does a double amount of negative energy mean for the realms?" Ashton's heart rate joined in chorus with the anxious chant in her abdomen.

Nanna's hands dropped from her hips.

Amit spoke instead. "Souls leak energy, as you know. But negative energy is heavier and weighs the souls down."

"And with this new demon..." Ansel held up a report.

Amit cringed, but continued, "Yes, the new demon." He exhaled. "We fear they're connected. If weighted souls fall too low, they anchor too deep in the depths. It's rare, but it happens. Then the demons, new *and* old, can easily extract the fuel that pools along the edges."

"Then why not send teams down to battle them where they are?"

"Pressure." Zander slipped in quietly. "Our teams can't swim that low. We've tried."

The room grew soundless, gazes easing toward Daiya. Her eyes were downcast. She wasn't saying a word. Nothing snarky or smart.

Ashton thought Daiya might need saving and chanced pulling the attention back her way. It's what Ashton would have wanted, had awkward stares ogled at her. "Okay. So, we can't go low. But I thought you said *no* creatures can swim to the depths?"

"No creature can...*usually*. But this recent species may be able." Nanna covered her lips.

The back of Ashton's mind tingled, as if her gift picked up the first pieces of the puzzle. "The souls are pouring negative energy...more than usual...into the monsters' laps, figuratively speaking. Mason's team is dealing with a fade, right? And stronger, higher demons are creating the fades." Her heart skipped a beat, as the group nodded, but she kept going. "Now there are demons with red eyes and evil bites." It didn't make sense. "Would Kelvin be behind these new demons? Could one monster prince handle all this chaos on his own? And what would cause demon injuries to change?"

Nanna raised her hands into the air. "That's what I don't understand. A demon's bite's a demon's bite. They slow keepers down, but they recover." She knelt beside Daiya. "It's a mystery that she isn't healing." She glanced at Amit.

"Ian's brother must have infested his army with something newfound. Something lethal to keepers. And yes, I'd say he's powerful enough to do it. But why now?" Amit clasped a handful of his hair again. "Thankfully, Rory hasn't reported any of these new injuries from the Seam. Daiya's the first case."

"I'm healing." She whipped her foot down from its elevated position and pushed off the sofa. "Ahhhhh—" She was down as fast as she'd tried to stand. "Dammit!"

Zander scaled Ashton to get to Daiya. "Slow down." He readjusted her leg, and she let him, eyes sealed tight.

As bad-tempered as Daiya had behaved, Ashton still worried for her. Something had happened, involving Daiya, with keepers going too low in the negative energy pool. Ashton would find out *what*, though now wasn't the time.

"What can we do?" The buzzing behind Ashton's ears lessoned, making her wonder if she'd even felt the workings of her gift. She peered at Nanna hoping for a miraculous remedy. But that wasn't Nanna's responsibility. The elder keeper oversaw operations and documented the dives. There had to be someone! "Is there another healer?"

"She came last night." Nanna pushed Daiya's hair off her forehead and again the girl who'd earlier snapped and scowled at Ashton allowed the gentle act. "I wonder if she might reexamine the wound. What do you think, Amit?"

Daiya's dark eyes flew open. "I'm staying here to help!"

"You can't help anyone in your condition." Ansel winked at her dirty look. "Rest up, fighter-girl, then you can tackle the new demon scare." He glanced at Zander, another look passing between them, before he inched closer to Daiya and offered his hand.

The room held until she accepted. "Okay."

Ansel gently pulled her to her feet. She bit her lip and limped with him across the office floor. The sunrise-tinted morning penetrated the window, saturating her black hair in shiny purple hues.

She peeped over her shoulder at Zander. "I want updates."

"Of course." His lips curved, but Ashton sensed the worry on his brow. Daiya probably picked up on it too. Weren't locked puzzles Ashton's expertise? As soon as she figured out this latest infiltration, she'd work on unlocking Daiya.

Amit didn't lose any ground. Once the door clicked behind Ansel and Daiya, he barked orders. "You two, pay attention. First, we continue protecting those souls. Rory's working on the venom problem. Since Max and Mia are stuck in that blasted hidden realm, she's also researching Kelvin. We need to establish his endgame. At the same time, the demon count must come down. I mean *down!*" He peered at Ashton. "I'm afraid that's even more pressure on you. Whatever gifts you have to offer, Centennial, we need them now. Time to counter those blasted levels of fear!" He stormed to the door, tufts of hair spiking like he'd never owned a brush.

"Amit, we need more help." Zander's voice held an edge.

Desperation?

He hadn't trusted Ashton's ability to hold her own below the surface, and now he didn't think she could handle the job she'd been sent to do. She swallowed the sour part inside that agreed. Her old human side, who'd never actually been human, rolled her eyes.

"Ashton's only just realized her keeper status." He peeked over, seemingly apologetic for making such a judgement, more than her birth father Gavan had offered on her last mission.

Maybe she should feel grateful…more help would be warranted. But his words weighed like an insult. Her anxiety, having receded in the last week, was back in full force.

How was she supposed to solve a multi-realm catastrophe…alone?

Amit stroked his hair in the opposite direction he'd just wrenched. "We have no extra soldiers. They're all battling the excess of demons, avoiding injuries as best they can. Extra crews are cleansing the currents beneath the souls. You must do the job dealt to you by the Blessing Council. A job you were destined for. All our realms depend on it."

All our realms depend on it—depend on us—

depend on me! The knots in Ashton's side tightened as Amit disappeared through the door.

Zander brushed invisible dust off his pants and coughed, as if he hadn't just insinuated they needed more help than her alone. "Should we get started?"

Ashton's stomach churned.

Chapter 13

Predator or Prey

"Fades." The word spat alongside various curses under Mason's breath as they climbed out of the jeep. Des stormed through the garage door into Mason's house. Everyone followed, gathering in the kitchen. Connor flopped against the island, looking as stunned as Mason felt.

"How many do you think there are?" Mason gripped the edge of the counter.

Bronwyn pulled her white hair into a knot on top of her head. "It's hard to say. Fades are rare. It takes enormous amounts of energy for a lower demon to take on human form. They need a higher-level demon to activate. They also buzz with a frequency easily picked up by other realms." She leaned in next to Nigel, silvery brow lifted. "Ian wouldn't have wanted attention from the Dark Realm, right?"

"No." Nigel arched his long spine in a stretch. "Rory and Shunnar reported Ian had been working solo from what the healers confirmed. He'd contended with his brothers for centuries while trying to prove his worth to his father, the king of Hell himself."

Mason sneered. "What might happen if *Daddy* found out?"

The silence of the group bounced like an echo from

each wall. Connor opened his mouth to say something before clamping it shut. Bronwyn ogled wide-eyed. Nigel stared at his feet.

Finally, Des splayed his fingers on the countertop, as if to ground himself. "If Lucifer discovered any of his sons meddling in the Human Realm, they would answer to an indescribable wrath and consequently, human destruction. Evil lives everywhere, never doubt that. But Lucifer dictates every extracted ounce. He has no paternal instincts."

Connor rested a hand on Des's back.

Mason fumed. "Then both demon princes wouldn't have wanted to be noticed. If Kelvin's flying under the radar, there *can't* be more fades. So where did that thing back there with her claws into my friend come from?" Mason's hands twitched, his body aching to fly. He wasn't fully comfortable shifting but soaring on the wind soothed. "Was she even involved with Ian?"

"We have to assume she was." Connor grabbed a laptop. "Let's check out Hicks's social media. Maybe he has some new followers."

"Good idea. Kelvin wouldn't have had time to set Kali up in Seattle anyway," Bronwyn added. "She and Hicks seemed as if they'd been together for a while...long enough for him to call her *babe*." She peered over Connor's shoulder at the computer screen.

The July sun poured in through the kitchen window glinting off Bronwyn's silvery knot. Mason's shoulders fell with his mood. "But we haven't been gone long. A month maybe."

Des pulled his hair to the side. "Kelvin *is* one of the eldest brothers, a powerful demon prince, ranked higher than Ian in their hierarchy of darkness."

Connor glanced up. "Are you suggesting Hicks's mind has been altered?"

A hush pinged off the beige painted walls, across the quartz countertops, and reverberated in Mason's ears.

"Think about it." Des threw up his hands. "Fades belong to the Dark Realm, but they are nothing without their masters. Kelvin must have traced her energy."

"So why didn't our healers pick up Kali's presence beforehand?" Mason pressed against his forehead…This demon was now his friend's girlfriend.

"They must have believed the threat diminished with Ian's banishment."

"It's because Max made that deal." Mason pushed off the counter, pacing around the island. Each teammate took steps back to avoid collisions. "How can they do their jobs when my human stepdad goes rogue with the devil?"

"Mason, this isn't your fault." Bronwyn reached out, slowing his steady stream of ranting. "Healers aren't meant to monitor the Human Realm. Their focus is on the souls in the Dream Realm. Our job is to keep the demons out. Getting mad won't help. We *need* you."

"For what? I'm the one to blame for this mess. Now my friend is dating some demon spawn with absolutely no idea of the danger involved. What can we do, without risking his safety?" Mason's frustration clanged in his head, the noise a contrast to the quiet outside. "What are *we* going to do?"

"Talk to Shunnar?" Nigel suggested.

"Already done." Connor leaned into Des. "Made contact the moment we met the fade."

Mason stared at him in disbelief. "How?"

He shrugged back at Mason. "Perks of being Shunnar's special cast. Des and I don't need to be in the same realm to communicate telepathically with our team. And we don't just have mental connections with only a mate or Shunnar, but with any shifter. We're always on."

Mason pressed the crinkles on his forehead. He'd been curious about Shunnar's private team of shifters, but this wasn't the time. The thought of hauling Hicks into this otherworldly chaos had Mason dangling over a slippery slope of control. Only a month ago he was protecting Ashton from demons in the Human Realm, forbidden to explain. Here he was again saving another friend from monsters he couldn't talk about. *Is this my penance?*

Not your penance. Nigel's voice seeped through Mason's mind.

Mason's head jerked in Nigel's direction. His giant-tall castmate stared back with knowing mahogany eyes. Stress had Mason locked down tight, he'd forgotten he could communicate with his own hawk team. For now, that consisted of Nigel.

Only in the same realm. Nigel's voice pierced through him.

Okay, okay, I get it. Out of my head.

Nigel smirked from across the kitchen. *You're the one letting your guard down. I taught you better. Remember the tricks? Lock it up—I mean, unless you want to talk about your self-loathing guilt instead of the mission at hand.*

Mason shook off Nigel's invasion. He was being the castmate and friend Mason trusted him to be, but he didn't want a therapy session, especially with Hicks in trouble.

I'm good, thanks. He sent the quick response to Nigel, then forced his guard back up the way Nigel had taught him in Toria. Now Shunnar or Gavan could contact him, as well as his own hawk team, if they needed to, but they wouldn't necessarily hear what he was thinking.

"Why mess with Hicks down here?" Bronwyn questioned the room. "Why not simply carry out his brother's plans?"

"I wondered that myself." Des added, "How would he even know about Mason's old friends? It goes against free will to mess with Hicks this way—if it's how he bound him to the fade so fast. If that's the case—" His dark eyes matched his darker skin, matching the darker mood of the room. "—Kelvin must already know we're here."

The lights flashed in all their eyes, awareness unraveling.

"He's here." Mason's blood ran like ice.

****

The jeep's digital clock blinked to 9:30 p.m. in the parking lot outside J's. A faint twilight gleamed, though the sun had sunken low behind the buildings and trees. Nigel, Bronwyn, and Mason waited in Mason's jeep, while Des and Conner sat next to them in the white van.

"What's the plan again?" Mason kept cracking his neck. He'd never felt more confined, even with their group spaced out in two vehicles.

Connor reported from the van's passenger seat, his voice quiet as he spoke out his side window to Mason on his right. "We need to figure out if she's alone or not. According to Shunnar, Bethesda's working on readings now, but something seems to be blocking this whole Pacific Northwest area."

Mason wrenched around in his seat to fully face the van out his window. "When were you going to mention that last part?" There was a block in their area? He glanced over his shoulder at his passengers; Nigel and Bronwyn seemed just as surprised, twisting to stare at Connor.

Connor's expression looked like a deer in headlights before he leaned back against the seat, groaning in frustration.

Des leaned over Connor's lap. "We received the intel minutes ago. The block complicates things, but let them worry about it for now. Our plan's the same. We need to figure out if Kali is working alone or not."

"And you still think it's better for you two to be seen here and not join us?" Mason leaned out his window. "Is it wise to show them our hand?"

"Of course. An essential part of the plan. Our presence here shows Kali, and whoever else, we aren't afraid."

"Okay, but play it cool," Mason warned. "I don't want *anything* happening to Hicks. I mean it." He gripped the steering wheel for control. What he really wanted to do was punch the dashboard, then throw the jeep into gear and rip out of there. Tension rolled over his shoulders like the waves outside his Oregon beach house. It seemed a lifetime ago he was there with Ashton, fighting off Ian at the shore, when in reality, it had only been a week.

Reality? Reality didn't exist anymore.

"Of course, Mason." Bronwyn brushed his arm.

"We're a team. I know you feel less connected to us because of your time in the Human Realm, but we're a destined cast. Together. And we're all for one in every battle."

He glanced at her frosty-blue eyes at the word *destined*. She exuded positive energy—opposite to the cranky, tired teammate feeling sluggish in the Earth's atmosphere that morning. She was the Bronwyn he'd been getting to know from Toria, clever and tough, always encouraging. But was she correct in her belief of destiny? It didn't seem as if any of this would have been Hicks's foretold fate. Mason half smiled in gratitude. It was all he had, and he hoped she understood.

"We're just going to chill tonight. Act casual." Connor leaned forward from the passenger seat in the van. All gazes fell to him. Even Des turned to stare.

"Yeah." Mason laughed at his choice of lingo. "We'll just *chill*."

****

"Hey, guys." Hicks strolled up next to Mason's side of the jeep.

Mason nodded his chin to his friend and checked the rearview mirror to find Kali locking up the main doors.

Hicks put out his fist to bump. "Not much happening tonight, but we can hang at my house. Folks are in Europe."

"Right before you leave for college?" Mason fist-bumped him back.

Hicks tilted his head as if he wanted to say more.

"Are they coming home before you leave?"

"Umm, yeah. Of course." He didn't sound

convinced.

Kali approached, stalling in Hicks's shadow. Her long, dark hair fell over her face, making eye contact difficult. The summer night had already stitched itself up, covering the parking lot with a dark sense of doom. Or maybe it was Mason's dread. He needed Hicks to stay safe.

The start of their evening felt awkward. But Mason wasn't leaving Hicks alone with a demon, especially now that she must know who they were. And that meant contact with Kelvin. Could demons speak telepathically like shifters?

"Hanging out sounds perfect," Bronwyn mustered, probably to break the strangeness.

"Great!" Hicks seemed upbeat and back to normal again. "Meet us there."

Mason watched them walk across the parking lot, arms entwined. Kali tossed a glance over her shoulder, but any expression became lost under her hair. Hicks gave him a thumbs-up through his truck window before speeding off.

Mason saluted the white van, complete with Shunnar's special team of two. They would provide surveillance on the outside while Mason, Nigel, and Bronwyn were inside with Hicks and the fade.

J's was only a few miles from Hicks's house, so they arrived in no time. Mason sat still after he turned off the engine. The last time he'd been there was graduation night. With Ashton. The night she'd met Ian.

"Wait!" Mason twisted toward his castmates. "Whatever happens in there, keeping my friend alive is mandatory."

Nigel patted Mason's back. "Priority number one. We don't need panic to spread to the neighbors."

Mason blew out a quick breath and threw his head back, his gaze catching Bronwyn's in the rearview mirror.

"Fades aren't easy to take down, from what I've heard. We don't see them at the Seam." Bronwyn's icy gaze flickered like rays of hope. "But we can do this."

The blue in her eyes reminded Mason of Ashton…he wished she was there. They'd finally proven they were stronger together, so when would that happen? Factors beyond their control always took precedence.

"True." Nigel responded. "Battling a fade is new for us all."

Mason scanned the group. "Well, here we go."

They all hopped from the jeep.

Hicks's house was just as Mason remembered. His parents were wealthy and liberal in allowing him and others the use of their space, even when they weren't home. Mason had dragged Ashton to many parties here. She'd hated all of them—homebody that she was—but somehow, he'd always convinced her to go.

The group stood at the front door, waiting for Hicks to come through the garage. Kali wasn't with him when he let them in.

"Where's your girlfriend?" Mason tried to sound casual. Hicks tipped his head in the direction of the family room, and they followed him into a spacious area next to an equally enormous kitchen. An oversized, cream-colored sectional sat across from two overstuffed chairs Mason knew reclined, though they looked more formal. How many times had he been in this house?

Too many to count.

But tonight, it felt like the first time.

"She's changing." Hicks glanced down at his work T-shirt, then shrugged. "Can I get you something? I have energy drinks, water…beer?" He looked over at Nigel and Bronwyn.

"Water would be good." Nigel spoke for the group, authoritatively. Hicks glanced at Mason, as if wondering why this guy was speaking for him when any other time, he would've grabbed a beer.

Mason's eyes widened as Bronwyn responded, "We're still in training."

Hicks's expression dropped. "Oh yeah, the Iron Man. Hang on." He left through a pantry door, returning with a handful of water bottles. "Do you have another competition already?"

"Not for a while, but we train full time." Mason cringed at the thought of more questions and changed the subject. "When do your folks come back?"

Hicks cocked his chin to the side. "Ummm, I'm pretty sure next week." He scratched his head, not that it moved his short, clipped hair. It was dark in the lamplit room, his glossy brown eyes reflecting the dim light. But Hicks shook off his quick daze and passed out waters. "Have a seat."

Bronwyn and Nigel sat on one side of the sectional, Mason on the other. After another trip to the pantry, Hicks tossed a couple bags of chips onto the coffee table and planted himself into one of the recliners.

"How'd you meet sweet little Kali?" Bronwyn grinned, elbows on her knees. Nigel exhaled a breathy laugh. Mason tapped his fingers, eager to know too. With his friend's life in danger, he cared less about formalities.

Hicks swallowed a gulp of water. "At work."

"She must be new," Mason added.

"When did she start?" Bronwyn chimed in, tucking stray hairs behind an ear.

"What's this?" Hicks surveyed the room with a half-smile. "An interrogation?"

Busted. Mason forced a laugh and after a few seconds, Hicks joined in.

"Just catching up." Mason clapped him on the shoulder before settling back on the sectional. "I've missed you, friend."

"Well, he's been in good hands," a syrupy voice sang from the hallway.

Kali appeared from around the corner, her jet-black hair pulled up in a pony, long bangs catching her eyelashes when she blinked. They were a perfect distraction from the strange ebony hue of her eyes. She sat on the arm of Hicks's chair, and he lifted a hand to her back.

"Has he now?" Bronwyn met Kali's singsong voice with her own. Her smile matched Kali's, though something passed between their piercing stares. Mason wasn't sure if he'd need the knife tucked under his shirt.

He eyed Kali. Was she armed too? Her flimsy tank and shorts did nothing to hide her ashen skin tone, not that Hicks or any other human would notice the gray coloring. She already knew who they were. She had to.

What was her game?

"Of course. And it's a good thing I stepped in since two of his best friends moved away." She squeezed his shoulder, staring directly at Mason. "No offense to you and…Ashton, is it?"

Mason's blood boiled.

"She's just kidding." Hicks pulled her onto his lap. "I wasn't a lonely puppy waiting by the door."

"I know, I know." She kissed him on the mouth. "But aren't you glad I brought you home?"

"Yes, I am." His gaze lingered on her face before reaching for a bag of chips. "Funny, I didn't think I mentioned Ashton. Or Mason." His eyes glossed over again before ripping open the bag.

"You did, babe." She placed a hand on each side of his face, peering into his eyes, then kissed him again.

"I remember now." He plunged his hand into the chip bag.

Kali smiled at the group from her position in front of Hicks's.

A warning.

Message received.

Mason glanced at Nigel and Bronwyn. Their plan was to find out more about *this* fade and if there were others without Hicks catching on. Maybe the shiny-eyed look he wore was some kind of spell.

"Where are you from?" Bronwyn asked Kali. "Hicks mentioned you didn't go to school with them."

"I just moved here from…down south." She snatched a chip from Hicks's hand, and he winked at her.

"South?" Mason pressed. She had to have used some powerful magic—force—whatever it was on his friend, enough to send away his parents and keep him latched like a pet. Mason was ready to take Kali outside and pummel her.

He glanced at Nigel, jaw twitching. Couldn't they

take her out now and deal with the aftermath later? Bethesda could work her magic on Hicks's memory. Maybe then he'd snap out of his glossy-eyed trance and realize they'd saved his life.

Nigel eyed Mason and sat up straighter. *Slow down. We can't blow this without getting the information we came for.*

Mason cracked his neck to shake off Nigel's mental warning. He needed a minute to contain himself and hopped to his feet.

"Oh no—I'm hitting the bathroom first." Nigel rose and swept past Mason, knocking him down on the sectional. "Is it this way?"

"Yep, down on the right."

Mason clenched his jaw, glaring at Bronwyn in question of Nigel's behavior. She barely shook her head, enough to convey *stand down*.

What are you doing? He sent to Nigel, but his castmate's mind was locked.

Hicks continued the conversation none the wiser. "Kali is from Cali." He laughed at his play on words and squeezed her leg. "After high school, she moved up with her older brother."

"Brothers," she corrected in a louder voice, glancing in the direction Nigel went.

Hicks tossed down the bag of chips, dusting off his fingers. "Yeah, brothers." He smiled sideways at her. "But Vin's the only one I've met yet so far."

"Vin?" Bronwyn's eyes widened, meeting Mason's.

Could Vin be short for Kel*vin*? Infuriation sparred in Mason's mind at the confirmation of more fades, one of them being another demon prince. There was no way this monster had known Hicks for weeks. Kelvin hadn't even been in the picture then.

He had to be under compulsion. What had Des said about messing with free will? Kelvin was breaking the rules right under his father's nose.

Kali smiled and sank against Hicks, pushing him deeper into the overstuffed chair. The whole scene reminded Mason of an animal forcing its prey down, slow and steady.

"What about you and tall, dark, and handsome?" Kali addressed Bronwyn, changing the subject and keeping control of the conversation. "Where are you two from?"

Bronwyn didn't miss a beat. "Oregon."

"Go Ducks." Kali smiled craftily.

"Hey now!" Hicks teased and leaned into her more.

"You know I'm kidding. I swear I've converted." She held up her hands in feigned surrender.

"That's my girl." Hicks grinned and glugged a drink of water. "Sorry, Bronwyn, we're *dawg* fans in Seattle. I hope we haven't offended you."

"Did I miss an offense?" Nigel strode into the room, eyebrow raised. "Something about ducks and dogs?"

Hicks and Kali belly laughed as if one of them had told the most hysterical joke.

But Mason stood up, giving Nigel room to step by. "Just college sports talk, but Kali was telling us about her brothers. How many did you say you had?"

Kali stopped laughing. Her hand brushed the side of Hicks's hairline, arms tightened around his shoulders.

A snake image drifted into Mason's head as Hicks

peered into her eyes and clung around her middle. Mason scowled. The thought of his friend turned on by a monster, as if she was really a girl, was disgusting.

She leaned over and kissed his cheek.

"I have far too many brothers to count." She giggled, snuggling into Hicks before resting her glare on Mason. "Big family."

Chapter 14

Lunchtime Confessions

Ashton slumped over the desk, her third time poring over the reports from Nanna. All she'd gleaned was amplified activity, the oddity of red-eyes, and the sudden heaviness of dream energy. "Souls are even *more* weighted now. Has this ever happened before?" She stretched.

Zander sunk into the sofa. "Not like this." His response hung in the air. They'd been silently working for hours. The information was the same, with puzzles of solutions only mocking.

Ashton's mind teetered between her immediate task at hand—stopping the level of negative energy soon to surge with the release of Max's book—and this new problem involving more dangerous, red-eyed demons—not to mention the slowly sinking souls. At the same time, she desperately wanted to contact Mason.

A fade in Seattle?

Mason had shared his previous encounter with fades when his team had recently searched for her in Ian's warehouses. But they'd put them down. With Ian gone, where had this new lower demon come from?

"Umph—" Ashton's guttural noise escaped her lips.

"You okay?" Zander looked up.

"My brain hurts." She left out the part about wanting to contact Mason. "We're staring at this data like it's supposed to speak some magic tongue." She threw her hands in the air, struggling to hide defeat. "I don't know what I'm doing. I'm too new at this, just like you told Amit. *You* don't even trust me."

"Listen." Zander straightened, his face softening. "This situation is new for us all. I didn't mean—"

"Situation?" Ashton fell back in her chair with more momentum than expected, knocking it sideways. Their eyes locked as he jumped to help, though she caught her balance.

He bent and scooped up the papers he'd dropped. "This is unfamiliar territory. It's not that I don't trust you. *None* of us have encountered anything like this before." He closed his eyes, releasing a slow breath. "I just thought we needed more help, that's all."

"Someone higher up?" Her stomach growled internally, and the pangs of a headache formed.

"There's nobody *to* help. Teams are split left and right. The last I heard, Gavan's working the Seam himself. Look at us. I've only been internal for a year, but from what I've gathered, the realms have never joined to fight a cause."

"Okay. I get it." She held her stomach. "Then we need a *different* strategy. I know demons never die. But how are they *made*? There must be a reason we're finding them with new red eyes and the power to inflict slow-healing wounds. How are they getting through the border?"

She had to believe the teams at the Seam were doing their jobs. But if Gavan, head of the northwest casts, was out there himself, they were obviously shorthanded. She imagined her birth father out patrolling. Aside from him asking her to stand down during the final battle with Ian, she'd only ever seen him at council meetings.

He'd asked to speak with her after Ian's banishment, to explain his side. But knowing he'd left her birth mother, Althaia, just because she'd been chosen as Centennial still vexed. She had no desire to hear anything he had to say.

Not then. Not now.

"That's just it. Nobody knows." He stared at the ceiling. "Amit said the Seam is doing all they can."

Ashton couldn't let the idea go; Rory had thrown her into this new position too fast. Regret about asking for *more* soured her insides, and she pressed her hand on her belly. She'd been too cocky. Something she'd never been before…before her keeper memories plowed over her human ones. Before she'd somehow battled Ian and believed she could take on *anything*.

Zander squeezed the back of his neck. He couldn't have slept much the night before, staying with Daiya so late.

"I know I have this Centennial gift of solving puzzles, but I-I have nothing."

He considered her with a heavy gaze. "You've had to learn everything about your gifts and our worlds rather quickly."

"I never finished the keeper crash course before the whole Ian debacle. Then Mason's dad wound up trapped, and now Kelvin's carrying his brother's torch." She rolled her eyes. She may be the Centennial, but her title hadn't provided any deeper knowledge of her own heritage…too many years absent. Was that why Althaia had referred to her loss of childhood in the Spiritual Realm as a sacrifice? Her earned gifts, payment for all she'd missed.

"But your keeper side has fully wakened, right?" He moved across the room, his voice as soft as his steps.

"Supposedly." She thought back to the dizziness upon her first transition. Her awaited eighteenth birthday had become more than she'd bargained for. Rory had explained it would take time for the memories of who she would have been, and who she was, to settle with her human experiences. Mostly they had. But even with less anxiety here, worry still reared its ugly head to the disappointment of her keeper side.

"And your memories have reminded you that you *are* a warrior?"

"Of course." She could hear Mason's voice reminding her of the fact.

"And you know you are…the Centennial?" He was closer now, sitting on the edge of the desk. "I'm sorry my faith in you faltered. I was worried about Daiya. I'm also worried about the souls." His eyes glossed over, a rich brown. "Does your keeper side remember me at all?"

She sat forward, chair creaking in her swift movement. "Should I?"

He gazed a moment longer, then moved on as if he wasn't trying to relay something more. "No. Probably not. Anyway, lower demons form through collected negative energy emitted from the souls."

Was he changing the subject?

"That's why they look like blobby, half animals.

It's hard for them to hold any real shape." He squeezed the back of his neck again. "For a higher demon to create a fade, it takes enormous power. Once a lower demon claims life through that power, they gain more of themselves with every moon cycle."

"What does *that* mean?" Hadn't he just peered into her with something more, something he was maybe going to say but changed his mind.

Was she supposed to know who he was?

"It means fades can become strong enough to continue *without* their makers—the higher-level demons who create them—but it wouldn't be wise."

"Because they want their own glory but don't know how?"

"Exactly. Too many of them can mess things up without a higher demon controlling them. Not even the Dark Realm wants that."

"If we know there's a fade in Seattle, shouldn't we handle that first?"

Zander's lips lifted in a half smile. "Ambitious, but we have enough to do executing the job the BC gave us." He straightened the messy report papers into a neat pile.

"BC?"

"Blessing Council."

She rolled her eyes. "Fine, BC. But what if our job here is connected to that fade in the Human Realm? You said yourself, they're dangerous if left unrestrained." Mason would have already planned to sneak out and find the fade himself. How was Zander so reserved?

"Our job isn't to stop the fades. There are other teams in place for that."

"*Mason's* team, which consists of only a *third* of our cast." Ashton slapped her hand onto the pile of reports Zander had just straightened. "Those are the numbers we should be paying attention to. The souls here are safe. You said so yourself, not even *we* can touch them."

"Did you hear Amit? They're releasing too much negative energy. We can't go that far down, it's…dangerous." He pushed the papers out of her reach. "Not only does the energy empower the demons—and their higher-ranking masters—but who knows what would happen to those souls. From what we've learned, they don't recover."

"What happens to them?"

"They're anchored in agony. Even when they wake in the human world again, if they seek to find joy, well, it would be difficult. They'd probably find themselves saddened, or worried, or…what do you call it there?" He looked down to think. "What is it when one clings to something until it controls and swallows them whole? *Addiction*, I think."

Her lips parted to ask how he knew such a term, when she remembered he'd mentioned studying the Human Realm.

She turned to the window, head spinning.

Would the world be better off knowing the energy humans created with their own emotions caused them so much damage? When she'd asked her birth mother, Althaia reminded her that knowing the reality of demons would cause even more unstable emotions.

She released a long breath.

The sky looked more apricot as her stomach rumbled again, and she blurted, "I need food to deal with these new complications."

Zander pulled open the office door. "After you."

****

The café, near the central hut, was less crowded that afternoon, though Ashton still ran smack into Ansel.

"Oh, sorry!"

"It's fine." His quick arms steadied her fall. "Lunch break?"

"A late one, but yes." She followed Ansel's gaze to her newest teammate.

Zander greeted him with hooded eyes. "How's D?"

"You know—cranky." He leaned against the front counter. "I'm bringing her lunch to the infirmary."

Zander blinked. "She's actually staying put?"

"You don't want to know what it's taken to keep her there." Ansel laughed, his green eyes shining like a cat.

A look of concern crossed Zander's face before he smoothed it away with his palm. "What's Amit have you doing?"

"Just keeping D down and checking in with Nanna. She's measuring the energy depths every hour, then we analyze the data."

"She's not diving herself, is she?" Ashton cut in.

Zander and Ansel both shook their heads, but Zander added, "Soundwaves."

"Wow, okay. When are *we* going down again?" Ashton's keeper side was ready to leap, and she lifted her chin even if her human side hesitated.

"I'm jumping with another team tomorrow. D's furious being grounded. But *you*." He peered directly at Ashton. "You and Z are stuck in that office until you figure out how to soften the blow of negative energy Max's book will cause. The BC fears it's going public soon." He rubbed his head. "With the demon count this high, a fade loose in Seattle, and terror soon to rise in the Human Realm, your gifted solutions can't come fast enough."

Ashton's efforts to hold her back straight caved.

"Adequate pressure applied." Zander glared at his teammate. "We've got it."

Ansel shrugged. "Sorry, but we'll all be in trouble if you can't fix the problem—"

"Here you go, Ansel," voiced a café-elemental. He handed off a wrapped package of food, tied neatly with twine, before Ashton could sarcastically thank Ansel for the added stress. "Tell Daiya to heal quickly."

"Thanks, Daniel." Ansel took the bag, but before heading out, turned and winked at Ashton and Zander. "See you later, heroes. Can't wait to see how you save the day."

"Thanks, mate," Zander scoffed as his teammate disappeared.

Ashton stared at the closing door as the pressure of their—her—impossible task tightened its ugly grip.

"Let's sit." Zander headed to a table.

Ashton followed, thankful he'd chosen one by the fireplace. She'd worn her jacket all morning. This place may glow like a summer sunset, but the temperatures bit like a winter storm.

Before long, they had plates of tapas-style food on the table, each delicacy arranged like tiny sculptures and warm mugs of café-awake in hand.

"I want to get a message to Mason. Is there a way to do that?"

"Of course." He said it like it was the simplest thing.

So why hadn't she been told? And if there was a way, why hadn't Mason already contacted her? Or maybe the *newbies* were still stuck in a faraway land of catch-up.

Zander leaned in, seemingly rethinking her question. The fireplace glow reflected across his dark eyes, and a wrinkle scrunched above his nose.

"Well, can you show me?"

"Sure." He narrowed his gaze, evidently surprised. "I'm guessing you've never needed to contact him because you've always been together." He took a swig of his drink.

"Well, mostly." She thought back to the time Ian kidnapped her from the Seam. "Why couldn't anyone get hold of me when I was taken before?"

He tilted his head. "Taken?"

She shrugged as if it was nothing now. "Ian swiped me on a night mission and held me in the Human Realm until we transported to his little homemade realm between realms." She sipped from her mug. "I couldn't communicate with my team from either location."

He swallowed his bite. "Ian must have shrouded you. I'm sure the healers tried to make contact. They may have gotten some readings the closer they got, but auras can be covered by all kinds of magic."

"Magic? Like witches and wizards?"

"You're living in a world of demons and floating dreamer-souls, and magic sounds impossible to you?"

"I mean—"

"It's not the same magic the Human Realm is

obsessed with. What's the place that makes all the fantastical movies? Holly—*something*?"

"Hollywood." She set her fork down. His studies of the Human Realm had to have been vaster than she'd imagined.

"When one realm needs to contact another, they send a whisper-note." He put his hand up for her to let him finish. "That means they use a special parchment paper created from a unique tree in the Angelic Realm. The ink is from the runoff here in the Dream Realm. It's from a cave under the falls. I could show you—if we ever have time."

"Wait…I have so many questions." She tucked lose strands of hair behind her ears. "First of all, yes. How do I get this paper and ink? Secondly, how does it actually work? And third, I thought you said the falls weren't really made from water?"

He wiped his lips with a napkin. "The ink is a residue from the aether. Once you write the note, the sender whispers the name of the receiver and blows it into the wind. The note disappears instantly and appears at the correct location soon after."

"Seriously?"

"Yes."

"Why have I never seen a magic letter appear in front of anyone?"

"It's not needed most of the time. The BC handles all realms' communications. Teams have their unique methods of telepathy during battles. And the elementals within a realm are already together."

"Wow, back home we use our phones for everything. I guess maybe we have an overflowing amount of communication."

"I noted that in my research."

"Exactly when and how did you study the Human Realm?"

He laughed. "Like I said, it was a hobby. I studied when I could, but training was intense. We all worked together, wanting to be exceptional for our Centennial and expecting you to return—and I-I wanted to be ready." His smile slipped with what appeared to be nervousness.

"Everyone prepped for *my* return?"

"It's been abuzz in the realm for as long as I can remember." He glanced at the fire.

She studied him, not sure what direction to go. She tried not thinking of how the keepers in the Spiritual Realm…especially her team…had been expecting her for far longer than she knew they existed. "How does it work in Reverie? I noticed you only have teams of three. Is that the norm? Are there pairings like at the Seam?"

He inhaled a deep breath, and for a moment she wasn't sure he would answer. "Teams are small here because, well, the Dream Realm's an island. Reverie floats as you've seen." He stacked his finished plate and silverware together tidily, dusting microscopic crumbs from the table onto his hand before swiping them onto the plate. "The Seam needs pairings because they protect from the air. They need a *bonded* rider and shifter so they can safely communicate telepathically. But we don't need that here."

"Because each fighter works independently on a team? Is that why Ansel can hop into someone else's crew?"

"Yes."

"But you and I were the only ones with communication devices yesterday. Can all the keepers born here communicate somehow?"

"Only under the surface. It's similar to the way you and Mason communicate with each other when he's in hawk form."

Ashton thought about the need to think messages to each other under all that soupy air. Then the question she'd wondered before struck again. Maybe this time he'd answer. "I still don't understand what brought *you* to this realm. If you're a shifter, a hawk, then why are you here?"

Zander looked around like it was time to go.

"You really don't know who I am?"

It wasn't the answer she'd expected. "We just met. Remember?"

"I thought your keeper memories were supposed to bind with your human ones."

"They did. I mean, it took a while, and I still struggle with my human side agreeing with my keeper side. But am I supposed to know you, Zander?"

He stared at her, considering, then picked up his mug. After a long, slow sip, he placed the cup down, adjusting it several times to some kind of precise position before responding. "When keepers reach their tenth year, they're sent to battle training. It's like a boarding school, I believe you would call it in the Human Realm, but more intense. It's located in Valley, where many keeper families raise their children." He glanced at the fireplace again, deep in thought.

Ashton followed his gaze into the bright orange flames, slowly dancing along the stone hearth. When she had turned ten, Mason took her to the movies without parental supervision for the first time. They'd eaten sour candy until their mouths swelled and consumed enough soda it sloshed in their bellies as they walked home.

"When I arrived, I was immediately selected for a cast." He glowered into his mug, and she blinked away her ten-year-old memories to focus on him. "There were eleven of us, and we all became fast friends. We learned to fly, to fight, to use weapons…to have each other's backs." The straight line of his lips curved at the edges, ever so slightly, his jaw almost relaxed.

These were obviously fond memories. They had to be, seeing his facial expressions soften. So why all the secrecy?

Then it hit her.

"Wait!" Her mind raced…seam keeper casts consisted of twelve members. "Eleven?"

His eyes locked, and the lines of his almost smile stiffened. Ashton thought back to when she'd first met him with the Blessing Council in Toria. They'd introduced Zander as a past teammate. Her whole cast was happy to see him. Bronwyn had leaped to welcome him. Ashton's wheels spun as she pieced together the puzzle that was her past.

The chilly room, in constant disagreement with the crackling fire, flooded her with heat. Zander watched her, the brown in his eyes rich like tree sap.

"We were—" She started again. "You—were on *our* team, not just any keeper training, so—why—how?" Her words jumbled.

Finally, he saved her—or pushed her over the edge. "Yes, to all you're trying to piece together. For seven years, I trained to be paired…with you."

The fire sizzled louder. Laughter carried from a table across the room. Ashton's heartbeat wedged itself between two ribs, pounding in her eardrums, as everything she'd learned about pairings came tumbling back. She gripped the sides of the table with both hands. "I didn't know. I'm sorry."

Zander shook his head, his gaze lingering. "It's okay. It's been a year. I'm…over it." He adjusted the dishes along the edge of the table again when Daniel swooped by, gathering everything. He must have sensed the seriousness of their conversation because he didn't linger.

Ashton waited until he was out of earshot. "I can't imagine how you felt then, or how you might feel now, especially with us working together." She sat back from the table and let her shoulders fall. "Did you…"

"Have feelings for you?"

Ashton frowned. Uncomfortable didn't begin to describe how she felt. Was it pity for what he must have gone through? Yes. Emotional carnage? Probably. Guilt? Of course. She didn't know if she was the one to blame. Was it because she fell in love with Mason before knowing her actual destiny? Would that even be *her* fault? Though if she was destined, then wasn't it always supposed to be Mason? Her mind zigzagged to connect the timing.

"I did. But obviously it was because I was supposed to. I guess. I think. But how could I have felt anything real when I'd never met you?" He shook his head. "I've tried to make sense of it myself. From what I know, diverting a destiny has never happened before."

"Well, what did they tell you? Why would they alter your life in your final year?" She'd never regret her pairing with Mason. She loved the best friend she'd grown up with, loved him even more now that they were *more*. But it had taken Mason a longer time to settle with their relationship being a *realm* decision, as if they had no choice in the matter. What could it mean now that maybe it wasn't?

"They've never explained. The BC summoned and told me they were making a change in my calling—straight to the Dream Realm. They said one day it would make sense." He pushed back from the table. "I'm still waiting."

"So where does that leave you?"

He opened his mouth to respond—Ashton wouldn't have blamed him if he would've said lonely, or even livid. She knew how hard Mason had worked to accept his role in the Spiritual Realm. How might Zander have dealt with losing it. But he stood up instead.

"In a new realm. And right now, in a bigger mess than when I arrived. Let's head back."

Ashton followed him out of the café and into the chillier outside. Lavender tints smudged the skies, the color of Bethesda's eyes. She longed to see the Spiritual Realm's healer again. Mason trusted her, and she appreciated that Bethesda had taken him under her wing. Who had Zander had to help him work through all his changes? Daiya? Maybe Nanna? He hadn't only left his planned duty at the Seam but his castmates. His friends. The keeper—*her*—who he'd expected to share his life with. Ashton couldn't imagine leaving her team behind, and she'd only worked with them for a month.

Had she somehow messed everything up?

The beauty of Reverie's constant sunset skies sank to the pit of her stomach.

Chapter 15

Organized Chaos

The cat and mouse game Kali played sent shivers down Mason's spine. He needed Hicks alone. "Hey, do you still have my Mustang hat?"

"Yeah, I was surprised you left without it."

Mason hopped up. "I kind of left in a hurry. It's my only souvenir from our years at Mountain High." He shook his head, picturing how stupid he sounded. Over a hat? "I mean, Ash asked for it. You know how she is." He forced a laugh.

"It's in my room." Hicks stood, lifting Kali with him, and plopped her gently in the chair in one fell swoop.

Bronwyn must have realized Mason's scattered, possibly weak, plan because she jumped up too. "Come on, Kali, let's go scrounge something more than chips in the kitchen." She winked at Mason.

Kali noticed. Her expression narrowed to match the sharp angles of her bone structure.

Mason booked it to the stairs hoping to make it before any minds changed. Hicks's footsteps tromped behind.

"I don't think so." Kali's voice deepened like gravel.

Mason and Hicks whirled around. Kali lifted from

the chair like a prowling cat. Nigel found his feet cautiously as all eyes rested on the fade.

But Hicks, unknowing of her origin or anything otherworldly, reached out. "Babe, you okay?"

Her long black ponytail swooshed to the side. The black in her eyes gleamed as a force of energy released against Mason. He felt it like a blow but didn't topple over. It was more like a warm poof of air whooshed between him and Hicks.

"I'm not feeling well, Michael. I think it's time for your friends to leave." Her voice was smooth, even sweet, as it carried through the strange energy force filling the room.

Mason took a small step back, thankful he could. He watched the rest of his team lift their arms or push their hands forward. They must have felt it too.

Hicks paused a little too long, staring in Kali's direction, before finally responding. "Of course, babe." He closed the distance between them in long strides, wrapped an arm around her and faced Mason. "We can do this another time, right?"

Mason glanced at his team. They obviously needed to regroup. But leaving Hicks with this monster? Sweat collected in his palms. "Sure, I'll grab my hat and we'll take off." He turned to bound up the stairs.

"Maybe later?" Kali offered, leaning her head into Hicks's neck. "I don't know what's come over me, but it would be better for Michael and me if you came back another time." She emphasized Hicks's first name, like another warning.

Nigel grabbed Bronwyn's hand and passed the couple on the way to the door. They turned once they stood beside Mason. Hicks laughed strangely, obviously under some sort of fade-spell. Could he feel what was happening to him yet be helpless? Was he in pain?

"Thank you for understanding." Kali chimed, looping an arm around Hicks's back. "See you all later."

Mason nodded. "Hicks, I'll call you tomorrow. Are you working?"

"We're both off tomorrow." She snuggled in closer to him, and he squeezed her tightly, almost protectively. "We have the same schedule."

Nigel pulled Mason's shoulder. "Let's go." He started toward the door and Bronwyn followed, glancing back with glaring blue eyes. Mason could tell Kali had pricked her battle side.

Mason was the last to move, his eyes cut to a stone-faced Hicks before latching onto Kali's glare. Reluctantly, he turned and stepped out onto the front porch. Bronwyn pulled the door closed and they all stood there for a moment, waiting to hear something from inside the house. Nothing happened, save the warm night air enveloping them from the *strangeness* they'd just witnessed.

Slowly, they moved toward the jeep, but Mason paused on the sidewalk and looked back. The curtains had already been drawn, the house still. As the moon stared down from the clear black sky, surrounded by a saturated spray of city-buffered starlight, he couldn't shake the feeling that his luck might not withstand another trial.

He'd made it through Ashton's transition into the Spiritual Realm. He'd made it through the discovery of his heritage—his demon birth father and tainted bloodline. Hell, he'd been dead and miraculously revived not long ago!

Was everything happening his fault?

He had to be the bad omen. A disease to everyone around him. Hicks didn't deserve to suffer for his mistakes. Mason needed to fix this. He had to save Hicks, free his stepdad, and pray his team didn't regret accepting him back into their realm.

****

Alarms buzzed as Ashton and Zander strode into the central hut. Gear-clad keepers raced briskly in various directions, mostly out the west doors toward Nanna's.

"What's happening?" Zander demanded, catching the arm of a keeper.

"SOS from every team. The souls are sinking— seriously going *down*." He broke free, fleeing through the open door.

Zander glimpsed Ashton, dark eyes delivering the intensity of the message without a word. Instead of Amit's office, he stormed straight to the gear room. Ashton swallowed her knotting ball of worry and followed.

Amit found them in the hallway. "Zander, Ashton. We need everyone under. Souls are falling like Earthly rain. Get down there, and I'll be in contact."

"Demon count?" Zander called over his shoulder as Amit stormed the opposite direction.

"Zero!"

"What?" Zander's mouth dropped.

Amit faced them with a look of dread, his brown face pale as ice. "There are no demons from what Nan can tell. Zero."

"What's pulling the souls down?" Ashton chanced.

"Your job just grew in size, Centennial." He wiped the sweat blanketing his brow. "Go below, both of you. This situation usurps our original crisis. For now."

****

Mason slammed a fist against the steering wheel as the jeep whirled away. "Why did we leave him alone with that fade?"

"You still don't know everything." Nigel had one hand on his seat belt, the other gripped the door handle. "If we wake your friend now, while he's under the influence of that fade, he could die. The pressure of that kind of—"

"Dark magic," Bronwyn stated flatly.

"Magic?" Mason thought of his mom using what she called *help* from the dark side, back when she was hiding in Seattle from all the realms.

"It's rare for demons to use magic. They don't need to. Their suggestions are enough to break the will of humans. That means something else is going on." Nigel looked back from the way they'd come. "What would make them go after Hicks like this? *He* doesn't matter."

Mason shot him a look, but he was still peering out his window.

"I mean in the larger scheme of things."

Bronwyn curled her body around the seatback. "Kelvin's already here. We can all feel it. He must be using Hicks to get to *us*, so we don't foul up the release of that demon-secret-leaking book." She held her palms together as if she was praying. "How do we find him?"

"Would it matter if we could? He has too many layers of rebirthed skin. How do we even fight him?"

Mason jerked the jeep into the garage.

The white van was gone. Mason didn't have to wonder about Des and Connor knowing they'd already left Hicks's house. They'd be patrolling the area.

Bronwyn pushed open the jeep door. "We'll wait for the others and get a message to Bethesda to do a reading. If we can track Kelvin—Vin." She whistled through her teeth. "I don't know. We're going to need more backup. The Blessing Council needs to make the call."

****

Zander nodded at Nanna, who gnawed her lip from the door of the diving hut. He cut to Ashton and Ansel, crossed both arms over his chest, and jumped. Ansel tilted his head in the direction of open aether and dove after him, leaving Ashton alone on the dock.

Her human side quaked, but her warrior side tightened the strap of knives on her right thigh and followed suit, leaping after her new teammates into the pinkish airy mist.

Once below the surface of the curious unwatery substance, she took a minute to regulate. The panic from before swelled in her chest, but she overcame it quicker, allowing her lungs to fill with aether. Spreading her limbs, she found balance in the buoyant space and opened her eyes.

The indigo sparkles of energy glistened in their strange mysterious way. Through the swirls, she caught the focus of both teammates and leaned their direction, her pace faster this time as she thrust with her feet.

Ansel's voice came through her earpiece. "Orders are to fill the space below the orbs. We must create a current to counter the strange magnetic energy pulling the souls down."

Zander surged ahead, a knife in each hand cutting the wispy aether.

Everything darkened on the way down, the airy watercolor hues deepening to rich velvety swells below.

Ansel's voice rang again. "Remember you can breathe down here." He glanced back, and she released another breath into the whirling mist.

"Let's go," she willed herself to say, relieved she *was* okay. She'd only been under the surface once, but she had to trust her instincts to help the souls.

She could do this.

Up and over, she pulled herself close behind Ansel, who swam directly behind Zander. The aether swooshed as she caught up to them. Soon, they'd arrived at the ginormous curtain of light; long swirls of blue-green sea grass swayed below her fabric-booted feet.

As far as she peered, the force of light rushed downward. The nest of souls was through this magnificent wall of indigo light. But there wasn't time to gawk.

Zander glanced back, his sense of urgency radiating. "Remember what to do?"

She nodded, inhaling a deep breath. Zander held out his hand, fingers wrapping around hers as he pulled her into the pounding steams of energy. Her stomach tilted, unafraid to admit her unease. The sucking sensation plucked at her torso, and the fretful warnings she'd heard the day before about keeping her eyes closed haunted.

As before, the minute-long slog through the curtain was surely longer. Though once complete, her caution collapsed. If it wasn't the scariest scene since her adopted family's house fire or Althaia's possessed tree killing the love of her life, this current sight was a close second. The scattered orbs of light she'd viewed just yesterday, like rainbow stars dotting the Milky Way, hung *below* her.

A day ago, she'd swum *up* to the blurry spheres of light, each moving away the closer she swam, like two north-sided magnets with no opposite to attract…until now. Hundreds upon hundreds floated down, bobbing momentarily, then inching farther below.

Internal keepers swam laps beneath the orbs, thrusting the currents *up*, to force the souls closer to where they should be. The haze of the deeper nest and distortion of swimming keepers clouded her vision.

Organized chaos.

Zander and Ansel led her deeper until the aether was an eerie shade of midnight blue. Even the sparkles barely glinted. And the thickness? This heavier syrupy *stuff* felt impossible to swim through. She hadn't gone this far down the day before. Now, peering out, the glow of souls looked like hints of holiday lights through layers of fog.

But there wasn't anything cheery about this situation. The sense of the mission, grim.

Ashton pulled out her knives to help cut through the cloudy aether. She stayed as close to Ansel and Zander as possible and followed them into the dark. She couldn't count the number of teams swimming underneath the orbs, continually bobbing as keepers streamed back and forth. It looked like an endless count of Olympic-sized swimming pools set up as far as the eye could see, which wasn't far in this atmosphere, but she sensed the teams of swimmers continued.

Keepers bearing knives took turns racing laps below the lights, their energy compelling the orbs upward. They were shepherding the souls like sheep, but the sheep didn't retreat for long, ebbing right back down.

"How long has this been going on?" Ansel called through his earpiece. He was talking to someone else and reported back to Zander and Ashton in a lower voice. "Began an hour ago, a few souls at first, then clusters. Now they're all falling."

Already the three of them had joined in with another collective group, taking on laps. Ashton wasn't sure what direction she was swimming, but she pulled thick airy aether through the longest strokes she could muster, following behind the pounding feet before her.

She worried her knives might cut a crewmember, but with the porridge-like sludge of currents streaming back, she let the thoughts go. Better a surface wound than to lose the souls. A quick glance up was evidence enough it was working. The swirling balls of light bounced against whatever energy-like force field their combined motions created, keeping them at bay.

But for how long? Her arms already ached.

"Demon count?" Zander demanded through her earpiece, as if he was right beside her, but she'd lost him in the swarm of swimmers.

"No traces." Nan's voice, breathless.

Ashton's legs burned by the end of their allotted pool length, but after only a couple beats of rest, she backtracked the way she'd swam, behind another unknown keeper.

Amit's voice cut through authoritatively. "Blessing

Council is meeting. Will report back. Current orders stand. Save those souls."

"How many have we lost?" Ashton peered down, unable to see any light. Hadn't she learned it was dangerous to swim this low? She swam through the doom spreading over each extended muscle.

"I'm sure Nan's calculating," Zander whispered over the roar of wind, or currents, or whatever hullabaloo their continued movements created.

Despite the heat her body generated with each stroke, she started to shiver. She clamped her teeth and kicked her feet, throwing herself into a third lap. The work it took to trudge through this stuff had to produce enough warmth to keep her appendages intact. *Right*?

Keep going, Ashton chanted to herself as she pushed through the atmosphere. If Mason could see her now, he wouldn't believe she hadn't quit already, or at least complained about wanting to quit. *Keep going*, she chanted again, her keeper side towing her along.

She wasn't sure how many laps she'd completed, the words, *keep going*, sounding on repeat when her mind began to click. She'd almost missed it, only a beat off from her two-worded mantra. Numb and achy was all she knew, *keep going*, then somewhere in the craze of pressing on, *keep going*, a picture formed in her mind. It was like an opening scene to a film where a camera fanned across the setting.

Lavender fields, rolling across rounded hills, swayed freely under a vast blue sky.

She slowed, reached out as if she could touch the scene in her mind.

Pop.

"No!" Ashton cried when the vision burst from her

mind, dropping like a falling orb.

A keeper swimming behind her almost slammed into her, swooshing around her just in time. She tried to focus, but another keeper pushed her aside, as if leverage to keep moving. Striving to see the lavender hills in her vision, she hovered in her spot to gather her bearings when another keeper knocked into her.

She needed out of the way, needed to think!

Ashton plunged below the rhythm of swimmers. She closed her eyes, searching for the clicking sounds to tap the solution to her mind. Letting herself sink a bit, she felt a strange sense of pause.

"You okay?" Zander's voice came through. She opened her eyes expecting to see him, but he was lost above in the factory line of swimmers.

"Fine." But she wasn't sure she was. The heaviness of icy aether tightened around her calves and shoulders. The currents from swimmers overhead looked like a patchwork of silver winds. She was deeper than she'd thought. "Ummm, maybe not."

"I'm tracking Ashton—fifty yards below you." Nanna's voice burst through.

Ansel's voice sounded. "Heading down."

"Take caution," Nanna said. Her tone, gruff.

Ashton formed words, but her head was swimming somewhere in the depths with her body. The darkness was like a blanket. Or was she passing out?

Gelatinous air stuck in her lungs, and any sought visions of lavender fields warped into a mental image of her old asthma inhaler. Right there on her nightstand. If only she could reach it.

Instinctively, as if some part of her knew what to do, she directed any remaining energy into her right hand, willing it through the dark muck to her left cuff. She pulled with all her might. The seams of her gear shirt lit up like hope.

Lost hope because it didn't last long.

Yellow beams of light flickered to black with every weighted blink, competing against her will to stay awake. She reached a hand for her inhaler, though she knew it wasn't there.

A mind trick?

Sleep tugged. Before its final pull, fingers gripped her torso, lifting her upward faster and faster to the top. Her breath caught in the less viscous atmosphere, but whatever coated her mind still lingered.

"Ashton, wake up!" Zander's voice echoed in her ear, hands rubbing her arms. More hands rubbed her legs.

"I'm here," she muttered with effort, her focus regaining shape. The blue-black aether from below transformed to a lighter twilight.

"What happened?" Ansel must be the one rubbing life into her legs. Zander, in front of her, waited expectantly for an answer.

She treaded the airy space. They had to be above the souls and swimmers now. The rushing noise coming from below.

"My mind did that clicking thing." She wiggled herself free of their hands, inhaling the smoother oxygen. "Sorry—I know that doesn't make sense to you." She put a hand to her head, tucking loose strands of hair behind her ears, but they only floated free again.

"You can't go that far down," Zander scolded. "I told you that."

"A vision came. I needed to slow down to see it

better."

"Do you remember what you saw?" Ansel came up beside her, nudging an angry-faced Zander out of the way.

A lavender field flashed in her mind. What could that possibly mean in their current situation? "No."

"Let's get you out." Zander squeezed her shoulder, his eyes kind again.

Maybe his earlier harshness had been out of concern. She hadn't meant to take them away from the souls, and she wasn't giving up. Her mind *had* clicked in the midst of swimming laps, always tending to reveal solutions in the middle of chaos.

"No, I need to stay and help." She inched away from their fretful faces. "My Centennial gift tends to come in desperate times. I must go back."

"Can you? Physically? Sinking that far down takes time to recover from." Ansel's emerald eyes gleamed apprehension.

"I'm sure." She forced through exhaustion. Even if she only had the strength to swim one more lap, she would try. The souls depended on her Centennial gift. Mason's dad depended on her gift.

"Let's go." She dove toward the river of lights below.

Chapter 16

Sinking Souls

Mason paced the living room as Connor and Des pored over a laptop. Nigel and Bronwyn had disappeared upstairs shortly after their return to rest. They were all sleeping in shifts, and Mason insisted on first watch.

Des leaped to his feet. "Kitchen, now, everyone!"

Nigel and Bronwyn bounded down the stairs wearing alarmed expressions. Mason's jaw clenched as he focused on Shunnar's two keepers, each of their heads tilted in a way that meant they were still receiving news telepathically from the Seam.

The room held, and Mason stared, taking in the contrast of their skin tones under the bright kitchen lights, fair and brown, a drastic opposition in their hair color, red and black. In every way Des and Connor appeared opposite of each other, yet radiant with the same strength and emotion. He ground his teeth in wait. *Please let this be good news!* The thought of this whole nightmare ending so he could get his family back…reunite with Ashton…

Hope rustled across his shoulders.

Des nodded at Connor, the subtle movement cutting Mason's thoughts short.

Connor relayed the news. "No new demon energy

has emitted around Hicks's house in the last two hours. But there's a new situation *inside* the Dream Realm."

Where Ashton was? Mason pushed off the island. "What?"

"Slow down." Nigel stood to his full height, then turned to Connor. "Explain."

"No demons." Connor shook his head, as if doubting what he was about to say. "The souls are simply slipping into the depths."

"The depths? What does that mean? Souls can literally fall *out* of the Dream Realm?" Mason's volume increased with each word, even in relief to hear there were *no* demons.

Bronwyn squeezed his shoulder. "Not exactly. There's a bottom, of course. But keepers can't go that far down."

"What happens to the souls?" Mason scanned the group huddled over his kitchen island, their complexions paled, mouths drawn tight. *Was it that bad?*

"If a soul dies, the body's left an empty shell. The person still lives on Earth until a natural death occurs, but it's never the same. And lost souls are harder to find, especially without a body in which to connect. The Heavenly Realm takes over then. That's their department, sending spirits to keep the bodies sound in hopes the souls can reunite—"

"*If* they can reunite," Connor added.

"*If* we do our jobs, we won't let that happen," Bronwyn said with gravity. She looked at Connor. "What else?"

Connor blew out a weighted breath. "We were right about Kelvin. He's in Seattle. He's four times as unpredictable as his banished brother. Ian was working off grid, so his casualties were minimal. His brother, on the other hand…"

Mason cringed at the word *casualties* thinking back to the loss of Drew and Maggie Nichols, Ashton's adopted parents. They'd treated him like a son. Now they were gone, because of Ian. Yet Kelvin was four times *more* trouble? "What are we doing about this?"

Connor rubbed the back of his head. "Bethesda reported a rallying number of fades at Ian's old warehouse."

"He must have some grand plan, unafraid of a few keepers, because he's using the one place we already know about…somewhere easily trackable." Des's voice waned at the end, as if he wanted to say more.

"Maybe that's what he wants." Bronwyn added. "He knows we're here. Kali didn't hide the information about her *brother*, Vin."

"It's a trap," Mason exploded.

Connor shrugged. "We know the layout of the place. Could Shunnar send more support?"

"We act now before he can conjure up a defense." Mason headed toward the stairs. He always carried a weapon, but he wanted every last one of his knives. "Connor, tell Shunnar to have support keepers meet us at the warehouse. Let's do this!"

"Wait—we need surveillance first. There will be eyes around that place." Des raised his voice. "We've already deduced it could be a trap."

"We don't have a choice." Mason gritted his teeth. "That demon monster—fade thing—has my friend, and now there's more of them—"

Nigel pulled him back by his shoulder. "I

understand your rivalry with this demon. He has your parents locked in his den. He's messing with your friend. But we have a duty not to bring evil to innocents in the Human Realm."

"That's it!" Bronwyn slapped her hands atop the counter, turning all heads. "That's what Vin wants." Her silvery hair glowed under the overhead kitchen lights. She wasn't looking at any one of them, instead her gaze danced along the intricate designs of the island granite, seemingly interpreting her mind's idea.

The room was quiet for too long. Agitation won. Mason couldn't wait. "What is it?"

She looked at each of them, taking more of Mason's thinning time to make eye contact. "He wants to create a scene. That's why he's not hiding. He *wants* us to come after him. Stirring alarm will play perfectly into his ploy to frighten the masses."

"You're right." Nigel threw up his hands. "And with souls falling in the Dream Realm, he's busied the Blessing Council, and any extra keepers sent to aid."

"True." Des put up a finger and cocked his ear away from the group, receiving more information. Connor must have received the same message because his open mouth clamped shut. They both dropped their stances.

"What is it?" Mason pressed.

Connor enunciated each word clearly. "Orders are to stand down."

"What? No!" Mason's inner hawk twitched. If he didn't calm down, he'd shift right here on the kitchen floor. He inhaled a ragged breath to slow everything down.

Des put a hand on Mason's back. "All focus is on

the souls."

"Are they sending outside keepers to Reverie?" Bronwyn asked.

"They must." Des shook his head, then locked eyes with Connor. "This has never happened before. We're in a new chapter now."

Connor put an arm around Des and pulled him into his shoulder. They turned and left the room.

Bronwyn placed her hands atop Mason's. "We have time. Vin has a master plan, but our team jumping into war with him only executes his schemes quicker. For now, we need to figure out those lost souls." She reached for Nigel.

He leaned down, whispered in her ear. She placed a hand on his chest before leaving the room alone.

"I know what might help." Nigel headed toward the back door, then turned. Waited.

Mason's arms and shoulders trembled. He couldn't utter a word if he tried. So, he pried his fingers from the counter and clambered across the floor to follow Nigel into the night's cooling air.

They hadn't made it to the backyard when Mason's bones snapped. He tried to stop the turn, but when he looked for Nigel, his castmate had already shifted. Mason let the change roll over him like a quilt folding him into the wind.

Kiiiiiiaaaaaaarrrrrrr!

****

Ashton pulled herself to the edge of the makeshift pool, her section of relay swimming still ongoing. Trying to stay out of the way, she cradled her abdomen while her feet slowed in oscillation.

"Ashton, Ansel." Zander's voice seeped through

the under-aether noise. "Reinforcements arrived. We've been ordered to rest."

Ashton didn't have to be told twice, moving past the numbness in her arms and legs, she forced her body to exit the busyness of kicking keepers. Making her way to the rushing wall was slow going. She hovered only a moment before risking entering on her own. She had no idea where her team was. If she stopped now, she may not be able to move again.

Swallowing a gulp of air, she slipped an arm through, allowing the force to pull. The pulsing of the air-chamber struck her like a blow. Had it hurt like this before? Maybe being in a stronger physical condition mattered.

After her lungs felt ready to burst, she opened her eyes on the other side. There were other blue-geared keepers swimming toward the surface, also released to rejuvenate. She followed them up, their pace slower than she imagined they should be.

How long could this go on?

As she climbed higher, indigo swirls turned pink. The lighter air kissed her cheeks. Ashton stretched one slow arm after another, lazily making her way to the top. The distance between her and the swimmers above fell away. All she could do was watch the current's bubbles grow smaller. When other keepers passed her, their looks of exhaustion were a horrible reminder of the grave situation.

How much longer?

She didn't remember the dock being this far away. No way would she call Zander and Ansel for help again. She'd already been the weak link, already wishing again for her earthly prescribed inhaler. Maybe if she rested for a bit.

She swayed to the left, out of the stream of keepers. It couldn't be *that* far to the top; the aether around was already brighter.

Ashton closed her eyes to slow her breathing. Maybe this was how Mason felt after flying in a battle? Back at the Seam, she only had to hang on to slay demons. She hadn't trained for this level of physical endurance. At least she wasn't feeling that sense of sinking anymore, her body buoyant and floating with only a few kicks from her feet.

As she opened her eyes, something nudged against her back.

Busted!

She didn't want Zander and Ansel thinking she couldn't make it on her own.

"Just a short break." She swooshed her arms to turn around, eyes growing two sizes. Staring back at her were the beady *red* eyes of a demon.

"Ashton, where are you?" Zander's voice. He must have heard her through the earpiece.

She couldn't speak. Not with the monster hovering before her. Its gray scales layered across thick mounds of blubber, with bulges forming where ears should be. Short arms and legs, and a long, thick tail seemed to help it balance. More concerning was the bumpy alligator-like snout protruding off its lumpy head, complete with a mouth full of razor-sharp teeth.

Ashton's scream buried beneath the breath she couldn't find. Those eyes—those red gleaming eyes like the monster that had attacked Daiya.

"Ashton, report." Zander's voice shattered through her earpiece. "Nan, track her."

"Demon near the surface, thirty feet down, southwest from the docks." Nan's voice was stern. "Ashton's there. Go!"

"Diving back in." Ansel's voice.

She couldn't respond. The only thing in her mind was summoning the last of her energy to kill this demon.

Closer to the surface, the air was more fluid, her movements more sinuous. She swung a knife across the snout of the beast. Even with its enormous size, the demon flinched back with oddly disjointed reflexes, rotating left and reappearing above her. As its jaws came down, to close around her head, she ducked, sitting into the lowest squat of her life. This freed her legs to thrust up under its belly. When her feet made contact, she propelled off...managing one of Ansel's backflips in the process...then righted herself, ready.

The beast didn't slow, lurching at her, teeth chomping for effect. And those crimson eyes lanced through the swishing air currents. Its grunts echoed like drumbeats.

Could she use the confusion of the swirling energy in her favor?

She flipped back as the monster drew closer, catching a current, and kicked her limbs with all her remaining strength. The action tossed her back, but the undercurrent she created whooshed toward the demon, providing her needed seconds. She twisted the opposite way, breaking from her backward motion, and scooped her aching arms wide, streamlining her body up and over like a swan dive. With her last breath she curled above the beast to plunge her knife down into the top of its head.

The demon shook and screeched as a team of internal keepers swarmed the scene.

She didn't recognize the faces of the keepers taking over the twitching demon, only Zander and Ansel supporting her arms on either side. Zander pointed up, and it was then she realized her earpiece was gone. Red-eyes must have knocked it loose in the battle.

Depleted, she never looked back, didn't wait to see the monster sink or even hear an explosion of soot and ichor. She let her team drag her to the top and haul her onto the rocking dock without an ounce of care.

****

Mason soared the open sky, hardly a wing beat needed with a southern air flow warming the night. The longer he flew, the calmer he became, though he never mistook calm for compliance. Not anymore.

Better now, thanks. Mason sent to Nigel. *Feel free to head back. I'll take another dip over the city and be right behind you.*

I'll stay. I don't mind. Nigel's voice came back equally relaxed. Mason could tell their little unplanned recreation also soothed his castmate. Shifters needed flight.

You sure? Bronwyn will have my head if I keep you out too long.

Nigel slowed, circling in one spot. It was a clear night, the moon a runway spotlight. His hawk vision would make it possible to see all kinds of scurrying rodents below, just as Mason could. *Des and Connor will appreciate it if we return together.*

And we live to make them happy. Mason huffed. He didn't have any beef with Shunnar's higher-level shifters. But right now, Mason wanted to check on

Hicks. He kept the lead and headed in the direction of his house. Just as he lowered over his backyard, he tipped right, toward Hicks's place.

What are you doing?

Relax. Just checking to see if my friend's still breathing.

Nigel swooshed up next to him. They were both the size of typical Earthly hawks, rather than the slightly larger form they took to carry riders at the Seam. Nature's way to protect their identity in the Human Realm.

Mason perched on a roof across from Hicks's. Nigel landed beside him, feathers ruffled.

Make this quick, Mason. Des will *freak out.*

But Mason wasn't listening. Like a creeper, he peered with his intensified hawk vision into Hicks's bedroom window. Whatever Kali was—it wasn't a girlfriend. Mason lifted off without word and landed on the sill outside Hicks's window. He could see the lump that was Hicks asleep on the bed, alone. He picked up voices from somewhere else in the house and hopped his way to the backyard, settling on a gate.

Nigel landed beside him.

The backyard had a patio, decorative lights zigzagging from one end of a pergola to the other. Mason knew they were on a timer and would blink out at midnight. In his high school days, Hicks and he had waited for that midnight blackout many times before sneaking out.

He eyed the French doors that led into the family room where the voices carried louder, his hawk vision picking up every nick and scuff in the paint. He also made out something through the glass.

Who's with Kali? Nigel sent.

Mason strained to see more, but the angles were all wrong, the bigger body facing the wrong way. He could see legs and shadows of multiple forms. A lamp shone inside the family room, but the kitchen and hallway lights were off. Mason was about to suggest it had to be Vin, when several forms passed quickly through the hallway and out the front door.

Stay here. I'll follow them. Mason had already flown to the top of the house. Nigel didn't argue, thankfully. Whatever mess they were in, they were *in*. A vision of a pissed-off Des flickered through his thoughts, but he locked it down.

Three people—*fades*—fled into the night and down the street. *They're on the move. I'm following from above.* Mason sent only to Nigel as he soared from rooftop to rooftop, trailing the trio.

Mason, you might want to come back. Kelvin just crept out of the shadows with Kali.

Mason's heart pounded. Could it be this easy? He changed flight from the group when he realized the trio's intentional turn. Two lefts and a right—if they made another left, they'd be on Mason's street. *Dude, they're heading to my house.*

Stay on them. Signal Connor. I'll focus on Des. Nigel's tone clipped.

Don't leave Hicks. And don't engage unless you have to.

The connection cut like a dead wire. But he knew Nigel was in battle mode now, communicating only if necessary.

Connor! Mason flew at lightning speed, soaring home. *Danger coming! Three fades heading your way, less than two blocks away.*

Mason hurled through his upstairs bedroom window, shattering the glass. He rolled in a flutter of snapping bones and dispersing feathers, as talons shrank into booted toes, and his beak shaped into his mouth. Red blood trickled down his human neck as he leaped, fully dressed, to his feet and whirled around the doorframe—*bam!*—straight into Connor.

"Whoa." Connor cursed, hands bracing himself. "Slow down and explain exactly what's happening."

"No time. Three fades walking over from Hicks's house." He bent over his knees to suck in a breath. Already beat from his previous long flight, racing over and crashing through his window, his adrenaline pumped sporadically. "Nigel's—"

"We know where Nigel is." Des stormed into the hallway. "I sent Bronwyn to help. We'll hold the fort here." He turned to Connor. "Shift and take the roof. Mason, front upstairs window. I'm heading to the garage and will take the side window that faces the yard."

Mason didn't argue. He fell into soldier-mode and followed orders.

The night was getting uglier.

****

Ashton sipped whatever warm concoction the healer had provided before leaving to help other exhausted keepers. Thankfully Amit hadn't grounded her to the infirmary. She wasn't hurt, just depleted.

Zander set her up on the sofa in Amit's office, while Amit left through a portal to meet the Blessing Council. Ansel had gone for food again, but at least he was bringing sustenance back for everyone.

After a few minutes, Zander dropped Nanna's latest reports into a perfect stack and thumped his fists on the desk. "Tell me again, what happened?"

Ashton rubbed her head, still woozy. "It's like I said, I got winded and swam aside to take a break. The demon literally bumped into me."

"The beast never registered on any of these reports." He pinched the bridge of his nose the way her human mom would have with a headache. "It's like it was never there."

"Listen, why don't you take a break. You don't look well." His naturally dark skin had a clamminess to it. Was he getting sick or worried sick? Whatever was going on under the surface of Reverie was beyond critical.

"I'm fine. Just a headache." He pulled his chair up next to her. "The red eyes. There's something about them. You're sure you've never seen them at the Seam?"

Ashton sipped her tea because he already knew her answer. "What do you think it means?"

Up again, he strode slowly and steadily to the window and back. Maybe this was his way of showing frustration, completely opposite of Mason's crazy-fast pacing.

Zander froze in his calculated steps. "What if Kelvin's creating his own unique type of demons?"

"How's that possible? It's only been days since he discovered his brother's lair. Would he have had time to create something so massive?"

He rubbed the back of his head, turning to face her. "Time shifts in every realm. I think since Kelvin's under the safety of that invisible pocket Ian made; he doesn't have to follow the same rules. Who knows? Maybe he was already scheming long before finding his brother's hidden location. Maybe that discovery only fast-tracked his plans."

"I second that." Daiya hobbled through the door. "Vin must have already had plans of his own until he found a quicker means to an end."

"Why are you up?" Zander helped her sit. With a bag over one shoulder and a crutch under the other, she somehow waved him off. He pushed a small side chair up to the other end of the one she planted herself in and helped her elevate her leg.

Ashton clutched her tea. "How are you feeling?"

"Better. The healers are still working on me but agree I'll recover." Her tone was softer than before. She smiled in Zander's direction. "I have interesting news to share."

"Wait for me." Ansel flew through the door with bags of food in both hands. He divvied up the goods from the café across the desk.

Daiya pulled a bound book from her bag. "I've been researching demon princes."

"Rather than resting," Zander snuck in as he passed out napkins.

Daiya shot him a glare. "Cillian is—was—will still be the youngest demon prince, even after his rebirth." She tilted her head, and her bluntly bobbed hair framed her cheeks, like iridescent black butterfly wings.

At first, demon hierarchy was confusing for Ashton. When she'd killed Cillian, or Ian, or whatever other names he might have gone by, she'd only banished him back to Hell for a hundred years. How she understood it now, he'd be reborn, though his place in the family line would never change.

"I remember Ian talking about his father never supporting any of his sons' interests." Ashton thought back to their first coffee date in Seattle. Her shoulders shivered at the memory. That had been before she knew who he was—*what* he was. And far before she'd known anything about herself.

Daiya nodded as if Ashton said something right. "There are seven brothers. All of them reckless. But from what I can find, Kelvin is the eldest, and the worst." She glanced at her book.

"You have books on demons here?" Ashton took the tiny plate of blackberries and cheese Zander offered.

"We have books about *everything*." A momentary look of annoyance returned to Daiya's expression as she glimpsed Ashton, but it faded fast. Maybe she remembered she wasn't in any position to be rude. Ashton had killed the demon that attacked her…with Zander's help. But she'd also taken the attention off Daiya during Amit's earlier tirade. "We have historians in every realm. They track the happenings of each day in a log. After a year, Binder Els copy and make the collections into books."

Ashton remembered Rory's office filled with bookcases. Maybe she could learn more about her own past reading some of the histories.

Daiya raised her voice to bring attention back. "Anyway, Kelvin's been banished multiple times, and every time he returns, he's stronger."

"Stronger how?" Zander set down his plate.

"It says here that after rebirth, his body actually callouses, creating extra thick layers." She looked up from the page. "Like the skin of a scar maybe? And he's larger too."

"When my cast fought to retrieve Max, our blades couldn't penetrate his skin." The memory soured Ashton's stomach. "Every weapon slid off—like he was made of stone."

The group fell silent.

"How do we battle that?" Ansel pushed his plate aside, his usual grin sagging.

"Well…" Daiya looked directly at Ashton. "How'd you wipe out his brother? Those tiny pink soul spherules, right? Don't all seam keepers carry them?"

Ashton pictured the three marble-sized explosives hanging on her weapons belt in a tiny pouch. She shook her head as shame seized her confidence. If she'd only figured out how to use them sooner, there might have been less damage. Maybe Max Deed wouldn't have been caught in an evil hidden realm.

"It's complicated. They work best with a personal connection." Her human time with Ian flickered across her mind. That magical kiss. But that had been before the truth of other realms existed. "Seam keepers hardly use them—if at all—because keeper emotions shut down in battle. I-I was only able to make it work because of my human connection with him." Her lashes fluttered at the thought. That history book probably hadn't been bound yet.

"So how do we get personal with Prince Kelvin?" Ansel leaned back, defeated.

Ashton set her teacup down, the cup as empty as her solutions.

Chapter 17

Demon Chant

Mason peered through the corner of the front bedroom window. The fades weren't even trying to hide. The three of them waltzed right into Mason's yard. It was after midnight, the neighborhood resting far too quiet. They had to be on the porch by now or maybe they were circling to the back. From his position, he could see nothing.

Connor, report! Des's demand filtered through his head. Mason strained to listen and pressed his face against the screen. Where are they? All mental blocks were down. He needed to hear everything. If only his activated hawk vision could see through hedges and around walls.

Two on the front porch. One in the—the bushes. What's it doing?

Bam bam bam!

Mason jumped. What the hell? *They're knocking?*

Hold position. Des ordered.

Mason slowed his breathing, centering himself the way Bethesda had taught him. But his heart pounded like thunder. He'd only practiced meditation in a calm healing center. Right now, he felt anything but calm. He was hungry for blood—anything to put these fades down.

"Knock-knock," a deep voice sang from outside. "We just moved in and want to welcome ourselves into *your* world."

"That's right," another voice rang higher than the first. "We're here to stay and love to play. Come outside!"

Their cackling carried through the night and surely to the houses close by. If they kept the racket up, human busybodies would investigate in no time.

"We've already met your friend, Michael Hickson. Charming human," the deeper-voiced fade shouted.

Are they trying to wake the neighbors? Mason sent, blinking as the porch light clicked on across the street. The Williams family had lived there his whole life. Another house lit up next door to them. *Neighbors waking! Time to shut this down.*

Back me up. Des's message blared as Mason heard him storm through the house and open the front door.

"Well, you *are* home—Mason Deed, is it?" the higher-voice fade shrilled.

"What do you want?" Mason heard Des ask.

Crap. He needed to be closer. Mason sprinted to his bedroom, crawled out over the broken shards of glass, uncaring if he cut himself, and dropped to the lower eave. Peering through the darkened side yard, he checked to see that the grounds were fade-free, then eased himself onto his belly, dangling over the side of the house.

Conveniently angling himself away from his mom's prickly roses, he aimed for the softer bushes planted between. This wasn't his first time sneaking out of his house, and he knew exactly how to arch his back to miss the roses. He let go, twisting to a squat before finding his feet. With his back pressed between the house and shrubbery, he inched toward the front yard.

Connor screeched from above, but Mason's adrenaline pumped like iron, pulsating in both ears. If his hawk mate had called out a battle plan, Mason missed it. Disaster spread across his front lawn.

"Come join us outside," the monster belted with the volume of a sports announcer.

"I have a better idea. Why don't you *three* come in? You're waking the neighborhood," Des responded in a lower volume.

Mason heard him loud and clear, but wasn't sure it was because he'd moved closer, or Des's voice sounded through his mental connection. It didn't matter. Mason peered around the corner, finding the two demons poised at the bottom of the steps.

He scanned the yard for the missing third.

"Ah-ha." Deep-Voice chuckled. Long black hair topped its human-looking face, similar to Kali's. "Precisely the plan." It wasn't large, maybe five nine and on the lean side. Mason could take it.

The other one was the same size with shorter, brown hair. They both wore sweats and T-shirts with Seattle logos splattered across their chests, but as Mason took a step in their direction, the brown-headed fade stretched into a phantom shape of shadows and claws, twice its original size. Mason scuttled back, eyes bulging.

Des leaped off the porch, two knives hurling from his hands, and dove into the black illusion of smoke.

Hooting shrieks escaped the dark mass that entangled Des.

Since when do fades actually *fade*? The only two

fades he'd killed before had stayed neatly locked in human form until their ichor bled over Ian's warehouse grounds.

Connor squawked again.

Mason pulled a knife from its strap under his shirt. *Attack!*

Deep-Voice, the black-headed fade, screamed at a pitch so high Mason covered his ears. "The earth is fresh, the night is new, the demons now return to you." It repeated the words again and again as Des and the shadowy blobbed demon scrabbled on the grass.

Mason bolted from his spot, knocking the singing fade onto the ground. It jumped up as fast as Mason, hands ramming hard against his chest. Mason tumbled back, blade sailing, and landed on his backside.

As he scrambled up, Connor descended. His hawk form clawed onto the fade's face, tearing out long black locks, as he suspended it from the ground. The monster's T-shirt oozed dark blood, distorting the space needle graphic pictured across his chest. But the thing laughed, even with talons embedded in its face, still warbling bits of the song: *The earth is fresh, the nights are new, the demons now return to you.*

Lights flickered as neighbors appeared on their lawns, flashlights swinging. A man bellowed from somewhere down the street, "I've called the cops, you maniacs!"

A faint sound of sirens broadcast in the background but between that and the commotion of bystanders stalking closer, Mason searched for his knife, one eye open for the third fade. He didn't know how long Connor could hold up the other demon.

A trill carried from the side of the house. There it

was, snickering as if someone had shared a hysterical joke. A ginger-headed, gray-skinned demon stepped out from the shadows. Its outstretched hand gripped a cellphone, camera aimed and *recording* the whole bizarre scene.

Mason scanned the yard. Des still fought the fade that had transformed its body into black mist and claws. Connor's talons continued dragging the other fade like a ragdoll, though it now screamed less with song lyrics and more gurgling cries.

In long strides, Mason stalked to demon number three and lunged for the camera.

The fade leaped backward, red hair flailing, and disappeared toward the darker side of the driveway. *Damn!* Why draw so much attention? Mason glanced up, expecting Kelvin to drop in while his cast was occupied.

Nothing.

They had to shut these demons down. Now.

A new keening whirred above the noise as a police car skidded to a stop, lighting the dark in flashing crimson and blue. The video-recording fade, now illuminated by the eerie glow, smirked, its ashy skin lavender in the glare of police lights. It also wore a Seattle themed T-shirt, this one with the city skyline outlined in metallic paint.

"Stop! Police!" Two officers barreled out of the vehicle. "Put your hands in the air!"

Mason threw up his hands, his back to the police but couldn't take his eyes off the fade. The ginger demon inched back, its form fading into the night. Mason, now the only body visible on that side of the house, would look as if he was running from the scene.

Connor dropped the demon he'd been dangling and flew away. The fade fell into a clump.

"Turn around, nice and slow."

Great. Mason rolled his eyes and edged around to face a female officer. She had a gun drawn between him and the monster on the ground. To her, the fades would look human. But the bloody one was still in hysterics. The officer's expression was more than mortified.

"Be quiet!" she bellowed at the fade. The monster held its face, rolled onto its back, still halfway wailing to the tune of its earlier chant. The officer addressed the goggling neighbors, eyes still flickering between Mason and the fade. "The show's over, people. Step across the street until we can take proper statements."

The officer aimed her gun between the same laughing hyena and Des, who'd been commanded down to his knees. The shadowy clump he'd wrestled was suddenly nowhere in sight.

The cop shared a glance with her partner, a tall, balding male, then ordered Mason down to the ground next to Des. "This one here needs to shut up." He leaned a foot into the chanting demon's hip. "And someone else needs to start talking. What's going on?"

"Sorry, officers—" Des began when something huge and shadowy slammed down onto the top of the police car, crushing the hood, yet sticking the landing. This demon, dressed in black, muscles bulging, stood taller than all of them and wore a smirk as if carved into his thick skin.

Kelvin.

Once more giggles came from the side of the house where the third fade had disappeared. Mason wrenched his neck to see better, and there it was with a tiny white camera light piercing the night.

Both officers jumped back, guns ready, as if they were any help against this level of evil.

"Don't even think about it," the bald officer hollered.

Kelvin leaped from the top of the car to the ground…right within camera range. He grinned and opened both of his hands, as if to show he meant no harm. But the menacing expression on his face told a different story.

Mason squinted to get a better view.

He looked so much like Ian, with dark eyes and sharp bone structure. But where Ian had appeared youthful, like any typical human their age, Vin's sculped muscles flared like a body builder, his long mane billowing off his forehead. He appeared older than Ian, maybe in his thirties, but nowhere near his true multi-century-old age. The demon prince was enormous.

"Make this my declaration to the human world," he proclaimed to the camera. The red-headed fade continued filming as the police officers looked on, guns leveled, jaws dropped. "Evil is real. Hell is alive. And thriving."

The fade who'd earlier disappeared into mist rematerialized and flanked Kelvin. Mason flinched away from the strange energy pushing out like fire.

In a blink, the police officers froze, completely still, as did the neighbors who'd only moved to the middle of the street. There were no sounds. Even the wounded, once laughing fade on the ground was quiet. It crawled up and took its place next to a towering

Kelvin.

Every human stood in a trance.

"We meet again, Mason Deed." Even though the other fade had assumed Des as Mason at the door, Kelvin knew exactly who he was, shadowy eyes piercing.

Mason and Des shot to their feet.

"What do you want? You already have my family," Mason spit through his teeth. Adrenaline flared, or was it fear? He remembered his blades spinning right off those chiseled shoulders not so long ago.

"This." He opened his arms to the scene on the lawn. "I want this." He turned toward the camera. "Here is your proof; demons are real. Your fear is all we require. So, *feel* all those scary, nightmares-come-to-life *emotions*. We'll handle the rest."

Connor's voice whispered through Mason's mind. *On three.*

One. Des counted mentally.

Two. Mason let his impulse lead. He had no idea what was coming but ran with it.

Three. Connor dropped atop Kelvin's head, going straight for his eyes.

With the distraction, Des and Mason leaped into attack mode. Mason tackled Kelvin from the right, tensing his body for contact, and slammed into his hard-as-stone torso. His knuckles burned with each connection, but he pounded his fists with every bit of strength.

Des reclaimed his knives, or maybe he had more on him, stabbed and swiped alongside Vin's face. Each effort chiseled off the demon prince's cheek landing Des on the ground and up again. Just like they'd fought demons in hawk form, it was a relentless rotation of drilling.

Mason and Des took turns striking at him from every angle while the other fades stood back filming and chanting…*the earth is fresh, the nights are new, the demons now return to you.*

Connor's shrieks haunted in unison with more sirens. With each distraction, Mason moved fast, snatching one of Des's blades from the ground. He sprang, and as if rock climbing, mounted his foot onto Kelvin's thigh. Using his lap as leverage, he pushed up, then rammed the knife down hard above his shoulder. The sharp edge barely pierced his skin, but the bombardment seemed to disorient enough. The demon prince didn't know which way to look, shielding himself from the hawk's sharp stabs and Mason winding up for another blow. Then Des.

Chaos filled the air like burned rubber.

Keep it up, Connor! Mason sent. This time he stabbed his blade into the demon prince's ear. He wasn't aiming for it. But with whatever luck they had, he found purchase.

Kelvin roared like a wounded animal, finally stumbling back, though he shook off both keepers in the process. Mason landed in a thud on his shoulder before rolling through the pain to his feet. Des vaulted to his feet. Connor's feathered form flung through the night air into the next yard. Mason couldn't hear the thump of his landing as more police sirens shrilled.

"Come, my children. The night is young," Kelvin called to his fades, one massive hand pressed against the side of his head. The place where Mason had struck his ear oozed black goo. The fades disappeared into smoke, as Kelvin recited foreign words like a spell of magic.

Before Mason blinked, Kelvin vanished into the July night air, somehow releasing the trance-like hold on the scene around them.

Chapter 18

New Division

The team was quiet when Zander stood, collecting napkins and food trash from their meal. His mind churned at how they might defeat a monster made of stone. There had to be a reason the BC wanted him to work with Ashton. Could this have been what they meant a year ago, after stripping him of his destiny, that everything would make sense one day?

Could this be that *one* day?

Maybe the council asked for his help because of his expertise in both realms. Right now, he knew only one truth. He didn't fit into either world.

Not really.

Zander ground his molars. His teeth already hurt from earlier worry, and equally sore, his body burned from hours of swimming. He tossed the food bag into the bin under the desk, then peered at his team. They all looked defeated, including the one keeper he never thought he'd meet.

Ashton was kind, just as he'd imagined she would be. After seeing her in battle, she obviously had skills. She was the trained and gifted Centennial, though managing her gifts evidently wasn't solid yet.

Everyone slouched in a strange universal silence,

eyes downcast, halting the already stressed mood in the room to a low crawl. Daiya shoved the history book on demons back in her bag.

"How long between shifts?" Ansel stretched, breaking the calm.

"Teams are resting in four-hour increments." Amit blew through the door as if on cue. "You each have new assignments." He dropped a new stack of files atop the desk.

Zander swallowed a cringe as his own reports, once arranged neatly in the corner, shifted, their edges now askew. He blinked toward the window to the naturally pinkened skies and took a breath. Then another. He'd already worked himself up with this new mission, and he didn't want a pile of papers besting him. He locked his shoulders and focused on what was constant…the eternally disheveled Amit.

"That was fast." Daiya dropped her book bag to the floor.

"Time is of essence." Amit rubbed a hand down his face. "Ah, Daiya. I heard correctly then that you've been researching." He scratched his head as if another thought crept in, but he kept going. "Until your leg fully heals, you're reassigned to support Rory in Toria. There's a high healer there, and between her care and your knack for unrest, the Blessing Council believes you will be an asset." He rocked his thumb at Zander and Ashton. "You two are headed to the Human Realm."

"What?" Zander voiced over Ashton. Both sprang to their feet.

Daiya pulled herself onto her crutch. Ansel, already rising, helped her find balance. Amit shook his head, as if he knew what they all might say. What could be happening in the Human Realm that would cause them to take away keepers needed to keep the souls afloat?

Maybe this *was* the *one day* the BC had spoken about? He swallowed mouthfuls of stress to pull back his emotions.

Ansel huffed, rubbing his shaved blond head. "What about me?"

Was he nervous? They'd never broken up the team…especially after Zander had been the one to glue theirs back together after the—tragedy—they never spoke about.

"Ansel, you're escorting Daiya to the Spiritual Realm, see that she's settled, but it's not to stay. You'll be working with the team infiltrating Kelvin's hidden realm. We need fresh blood in the mix to figure out how to free Max and Mia. When that book releases, finalizing the contract, there's no assertion Max, being mortal, will survive the event. You'll work with keepers Adam and Hannah, from Ashton's cast."

"Aren't we needed here? There're hardly enough bodies to keep the souls afloat." Ansel sent Zander and Daiya a brow-crossed stare.

"You're breaking up our team?" Daiya's voice rose.

"I don't understand this decision," Zander stated as firmly as he could. His thoughts, once folded neatly atop the other, slid sideways, confusion fraying the ends. He ran his fingers along the window, steadying himself, but also to feel the coolness that penetrated through Reverie's constant low temperatures.

Amit put up his hands. "Before you start objecting. Here's what I know—straight from the council." He looked directly at Ashton. "Now don't go panicking, but Mason and Desmond have been arrested."

"Arrested!" Ashton raked both hands through her hair, ripping free her hair tie.

"They're fine. Gavan's team is working on it. The healers are easing every human memory involved at the police station as well as the neighborhood."

"What happened?" Ashton's hands trembled, and Zander moved to stand by her.

"It's complicated. There's recorded footage of a demon fight on Mason's front lawn—released over the human World Wide Web. The video's gone...viral?" He glanced at Ashton. "Is that the term?"

Ashton didn't respond as she dropped onto the sofa.

"Who would record something like that?" Zander squeezed his fingers into fists.

Ansel backed up against the closed door. "Can the healers erase that many memories?"

"I don't have all the details. But the team reported the public spectacle appeared to be Kelvin's intention." He held up a finger when Daiya started to interrupt. "From what we know there are at least four fades working for Kelvin—evidently known as *Vin* down there—and they're wreaking havoc by involving humans."

"Are they hurting them?" Ashton looked pale.

"They aren't hurting humans—although they did a number on our keeper team—they seem to be illuminating themselves instead."

"They're frightening the masses before the book comes out." Daiya scowled down at her leg. "I need to get down there. I can help."

"Rory is overloaded keeping tabs on Max and Mia in that hidden realm, the team in Seattle, and our situation here. Every last keeper is out on mission. Rory needs help, and since you're still healing, it's where you'll be most useful." He slumped down into the desk chair, eyeing her book bag. "And bring those histories. Maybe there's something from the past to help our future."

Daiya shook her head, seething to say more. Zander knew her all too well. She despised standing down. But maybe this was a blessing in disguise. Daiya was smart. If she let herself, she might help Rory out. And part of him felt better knowing she'd be out of danger.

He exhaled deeply to clear his mind.

"What are Ashton and I supposed to do in Seattle?" His jaw tightened under his skin, lips a thin line.

"We can't send high numbers into the Human Realm; our hands are full everywhere else, regardless. Ashton has the knowledge of living as a human, and you…researched it for several years in preparation for…anyway. It's you two, so meet back here in one hour." He leaned over his desk toward Daiya, more files and papers sliding in various directions. "Rory's waiting. You're going to see their healer, research that demon wound, and figure out those red-eyed monsters. These are the Blessing Council's wishes."

A ripple flooded Zander's spine. The Blessing Council's wishes.

He huffed a breath.

Amit rubbed a hand through thick tufts of dark hair. "Now go and pack, all of you."

"Wait, what about the souls?" Ashton uncurled

from her shrunken stature on the couch. "Isn't the Blessing Council able to step in with the souls at least? I mean, aren't they protected?"

All three of them stared at her. Amit walked around the desk and put a hand on her shoulder. "The world was put into motion long ago. The souls are as strong as the humans in which they harbor. It fully depends on them," he said. "And *us*."

The room hushed as she seemed to make sense of the whole free will thing. Then Daiya turned and hobbled toward the door.

Zander stepped around everyone to follow her. Their lives would never be their own.

****

Ashton's mind ached with visions of overwhelm. Maybe it was the state of lost souls. Maybe it was Mason being arrested. Maybe it was absolutely *everything* falling apart around her. She'd been sent here to strategize, to help solve one major problem. But how could she do that when more setbacks continued knocking everyone down?

Ansel approached. "Hey, I'll take you by Z's to grab your stuff."

Zander and Daiya were already gone. There was definitely something between them. But she looked up into Ansel's kind eyes, the corners of his mouth lifting like everything would be okay. Once they made their way onto the stone path that crossed the raked sand and onto the faintly rocking dock, Ashton asked the question she'd been wondering about. Her brain needed a break from the general peril demanding attention.

"What's the story with Zander and Daiya?"

Ansel laughed. "They're both stubborn and carry

their pain across their backs like wings."

"Pain?" She stepped carefully on the swaying dock.

"Not literal pain. Emotional. Z lost his destiny to some surprise shifter who arrived out of nowhere—" He glanced over with wide eyes, the evening's purple glow making them a deep shade of emerald. "Sorry."

She suppressed her shock and shrugged for him to continue. Of course, Zander had been slighted. He was supposed to have paired with the Centennial. With her. She wrapped her arms around her middle, not only because the later hour was cooler, but because the situation sliced her heart. She didn't know Zander well, yet he'd already felt *something* deeply for her...for *seven* years!

"Anyway, it took him a long time to adjust, not only to losing his place there—in the Spiritual Realm— but being ordered *here*. I mean, it's not a demotion by any means. Our internal work is critical. But he hasn't flown as a hawk since." Ansel stared at the ground.

Ashton could see he cared about his friend. Knowing that helped a little with the guilt she'd messed up his future. A small *little*, but it was something. "I feel terrible about everything. I didn't know." Her arms dropped as the path widened.

"He knows that."

"What about Daiya? She hates me."

Ansel pulled up his collar and huffed a laugh. "Daiya hates everyone. But she's earned some life-long patience." He looked at the rising mist along the horizon as they turned onto the larger boardwalk that held rows of sleeping huts. He let himself into Zander's place, holding the door for her.

"I don't understand. What happened to her—if you don't mind me asking?"

He closed the door, then turned to face her. His expression was serious and sad, which didn't fit his typical persona. "The love of her life was Maria. She was one of the keepers who dove too far down, about a year ago. It was an exploratory mission. Maria, Daiya, and another keeper, Jonah, were seeking a way to clean up the negative energy collecting at the bottom. As you've learned, it attracts more demons but also anchors the leaking souls. Daiya's team was running tests, trying to break the ties." He fell quiet, and Ashton held her breath.

"Maria and Jonah died. Daiya barely escaped. She was really lucky."

Ashton wiped a tear from the corner of her eye. "I doubt she'd describe it that way."

"I guess Zander and I are the lucky ones. She's one of the best keepers I know. She's tougher than Z and me put together." His voice sparked, but mostly it seemed an effort to change the mood.

"But what about *their* relationship? Do they have one?"

His lips curved. "They have one. They just won't admit it."

Ashton lifted her brows. They still had a big night ahead of them. "Thanks for sharing. It helps to understand where they're coming from."

"Of course." He grinned one of his telltale smiles.

Ashton headed toward the spare room when it struck her. "What about you?" She peered over her shoulder. There wasn't a lot of time, but they were all working so closely together. *And* she was curious.

He put his hands in his pockets and shrugged. "You know, I'm pretty happy on my own right now."

She wasn't sure if he didn't want to share, or if he really wasn't interested in anyone. But one thing she sensed, his endless ability to comfort. No wonder he was a good balance to Zander and Daiya.

Heading to her room, she grabbed her duffel. It only took a minute to stuff what little she had inside. It wasn't like she'd unpacked or planned to stay long. She glanced around the empty room, then walked out to find Ansel waiting by the door. One last look around the stark apartment concluded her assumption: this might be the place Zander slept, but it surely wasn't his home.

****

Zander folded and rolled each piece of clothing Daiya tossed onto her bed, then he tucked them neatly into her bag. She'd rambled nonstop about the messy condition of the realms and her abhorrence at having their team split up, cursing her leg with every other breath. She was overly dramatic, as usual, but still he listened.

Finally, leaning the crutch against the wall, she hopped to the bed. "This thing slows me down. I *detest* weakness." She heaved her bag closer as she sank to sit. "Of course, you have everything organized and efficiently placed…with extra space?" She peered up.

Her eyes were the deepest of browns, so rich Zander could see plum. Her shiny black hair draped to the sides of her cheeks, exposing her full face, a gift for him alone. She never hid her eyes behind her hair because she was shy or scared. It was about trust for Daiya, and there weren't many she included in that category. The two of them had come a long way.

Now they'd be moving farther apart.

He tightened his jaw, sharing in her frustration, and maybe a little added guilt packed in with her gear. Earlier in the week, when the BC first summoned him, Daiya had been scared his old world was reassigning him for a third time. Secretly, he'd worried about the same thing. But now his displacement wasn't the only concern. Their entire team was severing.

He fisted his fingers on his lap, his stomach sour, until the rainbow of sinking souls crossed his thoughts and forced his hand. He swallowed the rising bitterness. There were things bigger than him. Or his team.

She nudged him back to consciousness, loosening his sharp-edged thoughts.

"You know me. Efficient to a fault." He faked a laugh to which she raised an eyebrow.

"Will *you* be okay?" Daiya leaned in closer.

He sat up straighter on the bed's edge, body still tingling after lapping the aether. "I don't like our team separating."

"Well, you and Ashton will be together."

He frowned at her sarcasm. "Not what I meant."

"You two seem to be getting along, like old, destined lovers-to-be."

"Knock it off." He leaned closer. He wasn't sure why. Did he expect her to kiss him goodbye and wish him well? That wasn't their style. "She doesn't even remember."

"But you do."

He glowered into those dark stubborn eyes. Though she seemed jealous he was leaving to work with Ashton, he'd never been able to get past her walls.

"She's already paired, Daiya. What's your deal?"

She huffed a breath. "I don't have one. It's obvious you two get along. That's all." She pushed herself off the bed, looped her bag over her shoulder, and hopped across the floor to grab the crutch.

Zander didn't know what to say, and he didn't jump to help her. That would have made things worse. She was right, though. He and Ashton did get along. It was difficult not to wonder what might have happened if things hadn't changed.

But he *got along* with Daiya too—usually, when she didn't cut him off at every turn. He watched her hobble out the door and rolled his eyes. She was a sharp one, and though her astuteness was high, it was her jagged edges that marked him.

Chapter 19

Together Again

Mason staggered into the kitchen exhausted and hungry after spending the night in a holding cell. He'd refused to talk to the police, upon Des's request, but how would he have explained demons on his front lawn anyway?

It had taken all night for Bethesda to work her magic on the police department and the neighbors, manipulating their memories. The problem now: the internet. Kelvin's fades had posted the video of their demon fight on multiple sites for humans to like, comment, and share.

His first concern had been Hicks, though Bronwyn and Nigel had kept watch all night. Their last report confirmed Hicks was sleeping. Nine thirty in the morning was early in the summer, especially for a brand-new high school graduate. That gave Mason a chance to breathe. He hadn't slept a wink in jail; sleeplessness stretched over his shoulders like an itchy sweater. Rest sounded like a better fit.

Des grabbed a coffee pod from the cupboard and chucked it at Mason. "Make this work." He looked as tired as Mason, dark eyes drooping.

The night had been rough. And the Human Realm air was stale, the earthly oxygen making it more difficult to heal and revive after a battle.

Battle?

Mason moaned, bending to pick up the coffee pod that had bounced off his chest. How could they call it a battle when the demon threw them to the ground more times than he could count? He *had* slowed the monster down by stabbing him in the ear.

A soft spot?

Achilles' heel thoughts filtered through when footsteps bounded down the stairs. He wrenched the lever down on the machine and turned—attacked again for the second time in less than twelve hours.

This time, his attacker was soft and smelled of lavender and honey.

Ashton.

"What—I mean, hi!" He pulled back to see her face, her lake blue eyes, her long brown hair. She was a cool breeze on a sweltering day.

"I missed you."

"How are you here?" He leaned them both against the counter.

"New orders. But I feel better now that we're together." She nestled into that spot under his shoulder, the one only she could fit, making him feel lighter.

Their two bodies melded like an inner link stitching itself back together. He wrapped his arms around her tighter, and just as he lifted her chin for a kiss, Connor coughed.

"We should probably all sit down so I can brief you on the latest intel. Shunnar had to lock both of your abilities down, Mason and Des. That's why you couldn't communicate mentally while Bethesda completed the memory blocks. But there's more."

"Since we've just arrived, we need a full update anyway."

That voice.

Mason found his balance and set Ashton on her feet. There Zander stood, dressed in his blue gear shirt and navy pants. Mason glanced at Ashton. She wore the same thing, irritating him more than it should have.

"Living room. Everyone." Connor clasped a hand on Zander's shoulder, then moved down the hallway with the others.

Mason craved a caffeine boost, but he wouldn't miss a single word. Having Ashton back already revived his energy. He plopped next to Ashton on one end of the sofa. Des sat opposite, long legs angled around the edges of the coffee table, while Connor leaned on his knees over the table and pulled up a site on the laptop.

Zander sat in a chair across from everyone else.

Good. Mason cut him a glare as Connor began.

"Let me share what Gavan reported, then you can ask questions. I'll do my best to answer them."

Connor scratched the back of his head, his red hair orange against the deep burgundy sofa. "As we all know, Kelvin is here in the Human Realm, going by the name Vin, and he's creating demons faster than our healers can track. That brings us to the fade." He exhaled. "Kali has Hicks under a dark magic spell."

"Who?" Ashton sat forward.

"The fade acting as your human friend's girlfriend. He's fine for now." Connor gave her a sorrowful look, but his short nod seemed to say that was all they knew for now.

Mason pulled her back, trying to keep his fingers

soft even if his own insides stabbed like daggers. "We'll figure this out. I promise," he whispered, though it already felt like a lie.

"Here's the kicker." Connor touched the screen, whipped the computer around, and let it play.

Zander and Ashton watched the demons' video with dropped jaws. It was obvious Connor had already viewed it in dealing with Shunnar and Gavan. When Mason glanced at Des, he recognized the same expression he wore himself.

Shame. Embarrassment. Anger.

How could they let this happen? It broke every rule about keeping the human world unknowing of other realms. But Kelvin had also violated them. Without care.

Mason cracked his neck. "I'm still learning the laws between realms, but how is that bastard getting away with this? Doesn't he answer to a higher power?"

Des gulped a swig of his coffee. "That's just it. There should be repercussions."

"He's breaking all kinds of protocol—black magic, free will, and now this. Alerting the world of their existence." Connor leaned back.

"The human world has always known about demons." Ashton's voice, slow, as if she was thinking about her old life. "I mean, there've been stories, movies, exorcisms, and all kinds of paranormal activity throughout history. But this." She pulled her knees up to her chest. "This is *in your face*—here's a video to prove it—*real*. What are we going to do?"

"This amount of fear will tip the scales." Zander glanced at Des.

Mason rolled his eyes. "Of course it tips the

scales."

"Wasn't it your mission to begin with? To shut down the fear factor here, so when Max's book released, people would believe it to be fiction?" Zander leaned forward in his chair.

"Wasn't it *your* job to protect the souls in your realm instead of letting them fall?" Mason threw back. Connor had relayed the news about the souls on the way home from jail. But saying it out loud soured his stomach.

"Mason—" Ashton turned to him in a flash. "Protecting souls is all our jobs."

Des put up a hand. "She's right. Calm down."

Ready to pounce, Mason stared at Zander. Zander straightened in his chair, but his expression, ridiculously unreadable. A poker face to match Max Deed's.

The room stilled.

Mason inhaled, then exhaled, ebbing the energy threatening to peak. He closed his eyes, thinking of Bethesda's lavender ones shining back at him. "I only mean we've all messed up. It's probably not the best idea to rub it in." Mason corrected himself, not only for Ashton, but for the group. He needed to stay in control.

****

Zander glanced at Ashton, and she mouthed the words, *I'm sorry*.

He hadn't picked up positive vibes from Mason before—when they'd met at the BC. Mason had been red-faced and angry at the meeting, rightfully so with both his parents trapped in that evil-created realm. But afterward he'd only glowered from the assembly building steps as Zander reconnected with his old cast.

Being assigned to work with Ashton probably hadn't helped matters.

Zander released the pressure between his molars, relaxing his jaw. Maybe Mason had discovered she'd been *his* castmate first.

Ashton's crinkled forehead brought him back. He nodded, accepting her apology, though it wasn't her fault Mason was on fire. Wouldn't he feel the same way? The BC had stripped him of that option last year. He'd moved on with Daiya in Reverie. Hadn't he?

He froze. Thinking of her that way seemed to break their unstated rules.

Connor closed the laptop and stood. "Immediate orders are to rest until tonight. They can't send extra keepers. The balance of energy is already askew. Every spare keeper has been sent to Reverie."

"The video's out there." Des stood with Connor. "All over the internet. Keeping balance is a moot subject."

"Rory insists the focus of energy is *only* here. Although the video released worldwide, the views, likes, and shares trace back to the Seattle area *only*." Connor shrugged.

Zander's thoughts stirred. "That means Vin *is* working to stay hidden from his own laws—and his father. But containing his video reach to one location would take a lot of power." His gaze fell to the wooden floor, seeking the organic flow in each plank. He found a long oak stripe where the grain changed color and followed it, his mind reaching for meaning under the surface. He stopped at the edge of an ornate rug, colors of amber, red, and green contrasting against the wood when it hit him. "Kelvin's using the souls to fuel his strength." He looked across the room at Ashton. "But how?"

"The red-eyed demons." Ashton spoke slowly, sat up straight.

Connor jumped in, beaming at Des and Mason. "Yes, that was another detail. There've been demons found in Reverie with red eyes."

"In all my years at the Seam, I've never seen a red-eyed demon." Des looked down, as if thinking back to every encounter.

"One wounded a teammate. She's not healing well," Ashton added, and Mason cracked his neck at her use of the word *teammate.*

Zander asked Connor, "Is Rory researching these odd demons from our history?"

"She is now. That's part of the new team assignments." Connor slid down to the floor. "I think some of your cast—I mean *team*—is there."

Zander didn't miss the slip. Connor shrugged, obviously apologetic. An honest mistake, but Zander swallowed to hide his sucker-punch reaction.

"I ran into one, and it literally came out of nowhere." Ashton pulled the attention, and Zander was grateful.

Mason jerked his head in her direction. "What?"

"Are you sure?" Des's face scrunched in disbelief as he eased back down next to Conner. "Maybe a reflection?"

"The eyes were red when I stabbed it," Ashton challenged.

Des held up his hands in mock surrender. "I believe you. It's just strange."

"Demon eyes only appear red in *this* world. At

least that's what I've learned in my earlier research." Zander's mind raced to put the puzzle together. Kelvin must be behind these new creatures. Or had Ian already created this new demon? Was Kelvin's plan sped up by discovering his brother's hiding place?

"I hadn't realized it before, but you must be right." Ashton stood up. "Every demon we've seen at the Seam has had *no* eyes or *dark* eyes. Never red."

"This sounds bigger than it needs to be." Mason scanned the room. "Can't the healers do their voodoo on the entire human race? Let the book come out, alter human memories like they did to get us out of jail? Voilà. Problem solved." He picked both hands through his knotted hair. "*Then* we deal with these new demons?"

Zander's fingers twitched in his lap, and he fisted them again. This guy was a loose cannon seeking an effortless way out.

Connor interjected. "It's too many minds for the healers to manage, plus it breaks our laws about intervention."

"They intervened in my life and Ashton's family, when they placed her here as Centennial—" Mason flashed her a sorry expression. "They mind-warped the entire police department and my neighborhood just hours ago. That's pretty big interference."

"You're right," Connor said. "It *all* upsets the balance of good and evil. Typically, we stay out of human lives, no matter the dangerous choices they make. Our Centennial interference only occurs once every hundred years."

"Except this time." Des yawned. "The healers can't suppress the memories of an entire world. And we can't do anything to stop what's happening until we all get some rest. Let Rory and her new team do their research." He met everyone's gaze. "For us, everybody down. Hold all decisions until ten o'clock tonight." He pulled Connor from the room but called over his shoulder. "We'll keep first watch."

Mason peered at Zander. "You can stay in the room Bronwyn and Nigel were using. Or there's a sectional in the family room." He pointed down the hall.

Zander didn't care where he slept. He just needed to close his eyes. Picking up the coffee mug Des left on the side table, he headed from the room. With a squirt of blue liquid found by the kitchen sink, Zander rinsed the mug, dried it, and after opening a few cupboards, put it away. Then he dropped onto the sectional in the adjoining family room. A blanket draped over the back of the cushions, but he wasn't cold. He merely covered his head to block the light.

Soon, flashes of colorful sinking souls filled his mind...then Daiya's half-filled bag on her bed, her whole face staring up at him, her unhealing leg...the demon with the red eyes...being transferred to a yet another realm in only a year's time...

Chapter 20

Stress and Choices

Mason pulled Ashton closer, as if she might slip away while he slept. His bed was comfortable and having her nearby, even more comforting. He could barely keep his eyes open; at the same time his thoughts ran drills up and down the soccer field from his high school days.

He had to trust Hicks would be safe with Bronwyn and Nigel on duty. They would relieve his castmates later that evening. This talk of red-eyed demons coming out of nowhere, wounds that wouldn't heal, and the heaviest of all weights—his mom and stepdad still trapped in that private hell.

Standing down sucks!

Bethesda's advice prickled in his head...*The energy you suppress is the drive you need for guidance.* He could lead this mission and get his family back. Needing a deep breath, but not wanting to wake Ashton tucked against his chest, he staggered his inhale.

"Mas—you asleep yet?" Her voice resonated against his chest.

"Yes."

She huffed a knowing laugh. "What if we can't figure this out? What if it's like doomsday for the Dream Realm, which means it's doomsday for the all the souls, which means the world as we know it is...*doomed*."

"Shhhhh." He rubbed her shoulder. "This is the old *human* you. You're a warrior now."

"You heard the others. This is new for all the realms."

"That doesn't mean we won't find a way." Though he wondered the same thing. The typical business of the realms had begun unraveling the moment he and Ashton had arrived. Then again, maybe it was just *him*.

"Rory said the Centennial transitions to bless the realms, connecting us to the human world. In her training, I sound almost *heroic*. But that's not reality. I'm stumbling." She rotated to face him. "And Mas, I know I was a scaredy-cat as a human. But I-I want this. Maybe it's my keeper memories returned, but I want to defend the Seam. I want to be part of something magnificent."

"*You* are magnificent." He brushed her hair back. No matter how dark his thoughts were, he'd shine light all over her.

"It's all falling apart. Just like before, I can't control the one gift they need the most. My mind isn't clicking with any possible solutions."

"You're under a lot of pressure."

"I have no idea how to save those souls from the excess negative energy. What happens after the book gets out?"

"There's still time." Though his words didn't ring true.

"No. I have zero ideas about keeping the souls from falling to the depths of Reverie." Her whispers grew. "And now these crazy-eyed demons inflicting wounds that won't heal and—"

He kissed her. Soft and slow, as if to say everything would be okay because they had to be. Even with his own list of growing worries, he cut off the racing fuel of thoughts and held onto her kiss, willing her shadowy thoughts away even if his lingered.

Ashton took over, kissing him back. Her arms tightened around his middle, her encouragement rocketing to his heart.

Message received.

They were both in over their heads, that much was true. But Mason had to believe his second chance at life was for a reason bigger than himself. He held Ashton's cheek with his palm, her soft skin easing him to remember that truth, to relax and let go.

For now.

"I love you," she sighed sleepily. He could feel her finally relax.

"I *always* love you," he murmured into her hair.

****

Ashton woke in Mason's old bedroom more rested than she'd felt in a long time. But when the night filled with voices from downstairs, her doubts tumbled back. She didn't need to organize them in her mental filing system, although traces of her human side desperately tried. There was no cleaning up the other messes until she solved the big disaster before them.

Another demon prince catastrophe.

She rubbed sleep from her eyes, then wiggled from under Mason's arm to perch on the edge of the bed. Like a bird she stretched her wings. But also like a bird, she should still be asleep. It was the end of the day for Seattleites, the start of a violet night sparkled around the edges of Mason's boarded-up window.

She'd have to ask about that later.

New relief flooded because right next door would be the charred mound of what remained from her earthly house. She'd averted her eyes upon arrival…not ready. And tonight?

Not ready.

Mason mumbled, needing five more minutes and rolled over as she lifted off the bed. She padded across the floor to suit up.

"You okay?" Grogginess slurred his words.

"Yeah," she whispered. He needed to be up anyway, with disaster at bay. Then, again, the gifted Centennial should be able to solve realm problems to begin with. She bit the inside of her cheek, pulled her hair into a ponytail, and tiptoed from the room.

Downstairs she found Zander and Des in the kitchen, the walls aglow with overhead light, a contrast against the dark windows. They were both dressed in seam keeper gear though she noticed Zander wearing a black T-shirt. Maybe he'd borrowed one from Des.

"Good morning." Zander greeted her with wide eyes. "I know more than the typical keeper about the human world, but *this*?" He held up a coffee pod. "Des has destroyed several attempts, and we still can't make it work."

Des huffed. Zander actually grinned, teeth and all. Ashton had never seen him smile that big, especially with his whole face, dark eyes squinting above pinched brown cheeks.

"Of course." She laughed, turning to the blinking appliance. "These machines get testy sometimes. Oh— you need more water." She grabbed a pitcher from the cupboard.

"Water. I told you," Zander mocked teasingly.

"Okay—okay, you were right this time."

Ashton glanced to see Des sulk. "Did you two know each other from Toria?"

Zander had shared in training with Nigel and Adam, and her other castmates, but he hadn't mentioned Shunnar's private guard.

"We go all the way back to Valley." Des was next to her now, peeking over her shoulder as she poured the water and set the coffee brewing.

"I thought you trained with *my* castmates?" She looked at Zander, already wiping old coffee grounds from the counter and into the sink to rinse.

"Cousins. My mother and his father are siblings." Zander dried his hands. "Twins, actually."

Ashton's face must have looked surprised because Zander added, "We all had lives before we began our service."

"Of course. That makes sense." She hadn't had time to learn much about her castmates or the world outside their *service*, as Zander put it.

"Everyone has a past. We visit relatives and friends when we can, or if we decide to have a family of our own. Keepers can take a sabbatical and then return when they're ready." Des yawned.

She handed Zander a mug. "Did you ever go back between your assignments? Or—I mean could you have if you'd wanted?"

"What would it matter?"

The room grew as quiet as the night outside. "I mean, could you have gone home after things changed for your…um…"

"Destiny?" Zander inhaled, as if to control something deeper inside.

Ashton didn't mean to upset him, but he looked at her with steady, kind eyes.

"Our homes in Valley are for raising young children and caring for elderly keepers. My destiny away from this cast—away from you—*changed*; it didn't dissolve entirely. I'm still a keeper-in-service, whether at the Seam, internally, or here."

"*You* were supposed to be in Ashton's cast?" Mason appeared from the hall, his long curls in their typical mess, brows crinkled together, though at least he was dressed. "Originally?"

"You're up." Ashton pulled him toward her, though his eyes pierced Zander.

"Yes," Zander replied.

"I knew you all trained together, I just didn't realize…" He looked as if he was putting the details together while Ashton's stomach balled into knots.

The room filled with uncomfortable silence until Connor strode through.

"Café-awake—I mean coffee, please." He held out a hand to Des, who placed his half-drunk cup in Connor's palm.

Connor downed the brew in one long gulp. "Have you shared the plan?"

Des shook his head. "I was waiting for everyone to come down." He moved to the coffee machine, checked for water, and tossed in a fresh pod.

"Like a pro," Ashton whispered to him over her shoulder, still squeezing Mason's hand.

Mason was disturbingly quiet.

Connor observed the room, ignoring the tension,

and cleared his throat. "Our first priority—banish Kelvin. The council believes it's our best bet to free the anchoring souls. Then, it's fade-fiasco clean-up. After that, we're back to prepping the world for the book release to free Max and Mia." Connor rubbed his stubbled chin. "Not too much, right?"

Ashton was impressed with his sarcasm though she winced with every uttered step. "How do we banish this invincible demon prince with all the fades around, not to mention keeping innocents safe and out of the know?"

"He's probably thinking the same thing, and that's our angle. We act tonight." Connor glimpsed Des. They'd obviously already communicated about the mission. "He won't believe we'd put humans in harm's way."

"Because we won't." Mason found his voice.

"I know you're worried about your friend, but if we don't do this now, we lose our window."

"Agreed. But not until we get Hicks out of there."

Zander stepped forward. "Mason, I understand the thought of losing a friend. But this is bigger than one person. The outcome affects billions."

"I don't care." Mason paced a lap across the short distance of the kitchen. "We're at least warning Hicks."

Des's expression dropped, mournful. "He's bound to that fade."

"Free will." Mason strained with desperation. Ashton reached for him as he stormed across the floor, but his arms were rigid. "I thought everyone had free will."

Des straightened to his full height. "Kelvin's not following rules."

"Do Shunnar and Rory know about this?"

"They ordered it," Connor barely whispered.

"Sometimes we have to do things for the good of the masses," Zander said loudly, catching Mason's attention. "Sometimes we don't have a choice."

Mason glared. "Maybe for you." He turned to Connor and Des. "I'm choosing to save my friend."

"You need to stand down." Des moved closer. "We have our orders."

"We can get Hicks out *first*, then follow orders." Mason pulled away from Ashton, his fists clenched, though he *was* keeping it together, to her surprise.

Ashton forced her way between them, facing Mason. "We'll try, obviously. Right?" She flicked her gaze at Connor. Hicks was her friend too.

Connor clapped his shoulder. "Keepers protect souls. That's what we do."

Mason cracked his neck and leaned back. "Okay." He rubbed his face. "Okay."

"Maybe we could all use more of those coffee pod things," Zander suggested.

Ashton smiled at his attempt to help, but her insides knotted into tight little balls. Saving the world would take more than a little caffeine.

Chapter 21

Another New Plan

Within an hour, Mason and his crew strode to the white van, a block down from Hicks's house. Connor tapped the van door with his knuckle. No answer. A hawk flew overhead, disappearing into a greenbelt. Nigel.

"Finally." Bronwyn's voice carried from across the street. Her white hair rippled under the streetlamps as she approached. "Tell me you brought food?"

Mason thumbed to Ashton. "In the bag."

Nigel ambled from the greenbelt. "We're starving." A sudden recognition crossed their faces as they each noticed Zander.

"Hey—good to see you again." Bronwyn's starved expression slunk into a half smile. "I mean, not under these circumstances." She hugged him, and Mason squirmed under the sudden itch her kindness caused. He hadn't had time to talk to Ashton about Reverie. Was it Mason's fault Zander had been bumped from their cast with his unannounced arrival?

"*Three* realms now." Nigel's jaw clenched when Zander's brow rose. "I didn't mean anything by that." Nigel's already dark cheeks paled a hue, even in the night.

Zander clapped his shoulder. "It's okay."

"The food? I need food." Bronwyn glanced at Ashton with more irritation than Mason had seen before. She and Nigel were both far grumpier than usual. But twenty-four hours surveillance in this less-oxygenated air would probably do that.

Ashton offered her the bag. "Sorry, we didn't want to be recognized, so sufficed with the corner convenience store." She pulled Mason's black beanie off her head.

Mason reached a hand inside the bag first, grabbing a blue lighter from the bottom. Ashton crinkled her face in question. The others seemed just as interested. "Just in case..." He flicked the switch to snap a flame. "If knives don't work, I want something."

"And that tiny plastic thing is going to help?" Bronwyn asked, seemingly genuinely interested.

He shrugged, pocketed the tiny contraption, and handed over the sack.

Bronwyn pulled each item from the bag onto the curb, a box of donuts, several small bags of chips, two giant bags of sour candy, and water bottles. "What. Is. This?"

"Let's do this in the van," Des said crisply, and they all packed in with one extra seat to hold the food-goods. "What's the recount?"

"Same." Nigel motioned for Bronwyn to divvy the grub first. "Hicks hasn't come out once since last night. He sleeps. He eats. He watches TV with the fade. He sleeps again."

Mason shook his head. "She's keeping him a prisoner in his own home. I don't get what he has to do with our realms?"

Ashton's eyes lit up when he mentioned *our*

realms. He caught it too. But it was true. Even if his human stepdad had ruined the natural order of how those realms worked...and even if Mason had been unexpected in the cast...they were still his. He took a breath, as Bethesda had taught him, and blew out all the angst and confusion he couldn't control. If it could help Hicks stay safe, he would keep it together.

"It's like he's on a timer." Bronwyn handed Nigel a bag of chips while investigating the white powdery fluff of a donut hole. "Kali wakes him almost every three hours, feeds him, hangs out awhile, then puts him back to bed."

Mason watched Ashton's expression grimace.

"They must be using dark magic." Des patted his pockets as if ensuring he was ready to go. "It's limiting."

"Because they *are* hiding, and it *is* traceable." Mason nodded.

Connor picked up where Des left off. "Bethesda cannot locate them. There's a layer of energy over Seattle. She thinks it's the ley lines."

"Ley lines in Seattle?" Ashton looked as puzzled as Mason. He'd read about the energy fields between famous landmarks, like the pyramids or Stonehenge. But here?

"They're everywhere." Connor grabbed a bag of sour candy. "Kelvin must be using the energy to create a cover."

"Where *is* Kelvin?" Mason toyed with the dangling seatbelt. With this talk of dark magic and ley lines, all he could think of was getting Hicks out even sooner.

"We haven't seen him since last night." Bronwyn held her hand with powder-covered fingertips awkwardly over her lap. "But he didn't leave by way of the door."

"Magical portal? I bet he's at Ian's old warehouse." Nigel leaned back after devouring two mini-bags of chips and a water bottle. "You know where that is, right?"

"Yep," Mason said at the same time Des and Connor nodded. He sat up, ready to go, the memory of that place tattooed in his mind.

"The plan?" Zander raised a hand.

"Simple. Go to the warehouse and kill Kelvin." Mason threw back but then thought about Hicks. "Wait, someone should stay here."

Des's voice deepened in delegation. "Ashton and Zander will stay with Hicks. Keep watch while still deliberating on your initial task for the souls in Reverie. Bronwyn and Nigel, rest, but be ready. The three of us will head to the warehouse. We've been there before. We know the layout." He scanned each pair of eyes in acknowledgment.

Mason started to make an audible noise in disagreement but stuffed it down his throat. As much as he wanted to work with Ashton and his own cast, it made sense. When he looked at Zander, he hoped his disappointment wasn't noticeable in his countenance.

"I'll drop Bronwyn and Nigel at the house, then double back to leave the van for these two." He pointed at Ashton and Zander. "The three of us will shift from here." He froze. "Wait, Zander, you'll need to shift to reach Hicks's bedroom window. Have you—"

Mason glanced at Zander, as did everyone else.

Zander's expression was somewhere between *no, it's been too long* and *say the word and I'll morph right now*. His gaze narrowed, and his cheeks pulled as if he was trying to remember how. Mason had only shifted a short time, still a lengthy and sometimes painful process, but the freedom of soaring across the open sky spoke volumes. Raised to fly, then never flying…he couldn't imagine.

"I can help you." The words were out before Mason realized he'd been the one to say them.

Ashton smiled with approval, more likely relief, that he'd offered. He tucked away the truth he'd heard and deciphered that morning, that Zander was originally *paired* with Ashton. He didn't know what to do with that. So, he ran a hand through his hair as if it might erase all the what-if's. Somehow, *he'd* been a surprise to the Spiritual Realm, as Zander might have been a surprise to the Dream Realm. Being displaced was something he could relate to. Plus, Hicks needed saving. Max and his mom needed freeing.

He would do this to achieve a higher purpose.

"While I appreciate your offer, I remember how to fly."

Mason whistled a breath but surrendered both hands.

"Then, let's move." Des ordered before they poured out of the van, all except Des, Nigel, and Bronwyn. After a few waves of goodbye and Ashton hugging Bronwyn, Des turned over the engine and pulled away.

Ashton's expression hooked Mason's heart, and he led her into the greenbelt away from Connor and Zander. The neighborhood was quiet, houses dark for the night. No traffic, only streetlamps like stars in parallel lines down the road.

"Here I thought we'd get to do what we do best—"

Ashton finished his sentence. "Working together as a team. I know." She leaned into his chest. "I hate being away from you."

"It makes sense for now, but—" Mason wasn't sure how much to say, his heart wrenching in too many directions. Ashton's blue eyes became the calming pool his soul needed. "Once we clean up this mess, I have to believe we'll get back to some kind of new—"

"Don't say it...normal?" she chastised, ponytail swinging side to side. "Mas, it's okay. Our lives aren't our own anymore. There are bigger stakes at risk." She ticked off her fingers. "We have another demon to kill. We have souls to save. Max needs to release his book, and I need to figure out how to soften the blow when that happens. Hicks needs to be freed from that fade. Plus, we'll have to clean up whatever collateral damage the dark magic leaves in the Human Realm...did I miss anything?"

"What about regretting my mom's surprise mistake eighteen years ago, creating a giant rift in your destiny?"

She stepped back. "What do you mean?"

He tipped his chin in Zander's direction.

"Seriously, Mas, I am not in the mood for you to feel less than the destined partner I'm proud to call my own." She fake-slugged him, a reflex from their childhood. "I love *you*."

He leaned down to kiss her perfectly soft lips, letting the loud silence of the sleeping street fall away to the chirping frogs and crickets he only ever heard through her influence. The sounds of nature grounded Ashton more than it did him, but they were always a connection. Holding her kiss as always, he escaped his inner demons telling him he wasn't good enough. And when the notions crept in with his next breath, he kissed her again, breathing her in like oxygen.

"It's time." Des was back, flashing the van lights, and blinking out the moment. "Connor and Zander went on a test flight. They're headed back now."

Mason walked Ashton across the street. "Keep watch over Hicks." He didn't have to say more. She knew the importance of the mission. "If you want to talk, I'll be in hawk form for the flight over. Wait!" He ran to the passenger side of the van, ruffled through the glove box, and pulled out the small notebook he'd found earlier. "If you need to draw."

She accepted the journal with a knowing smile.

"There's a pen in there and an extra hoodie for when you get cold." He pointed back to the van, but she caught his hand, clasped it to her heart.

"Thank you."

"No, Ash, thank *you* for standing by me." He didn't want the strain of reality—Zander as her originally planned partner—to cloud his emotions. But they were doing just that.

She lifted onto her tiptoes, pinning him with her gaze. "Always."

It was the only word he needed to hear.

Chapter 22

Teams in Motion

Zander followed Connor into the shadows of the greenbelt. He hadn't shifted into his hawk form in fourteen months. It was the longest he'd gone since first morphing as a ten-year-old boy. The last time was when the BC reassigned his future.

That horrid day sputtered through his mind…the news ringing in his ears, his feet stumbling into the gardens, his body dropping into hawk form and taking the longest final flight his bones could endure.

They want me to serve internally, like a fish! Natural hawks eat fish!

His raw emotions had almost spilled to his castmates—ex-castmates. But his team had recently learned how to lock down their thoughts, protecting their deepest and most private emotions, and Zander wasn't about to let anyone know how much this *shift* in his destiny actually hurt.

"You ready?" Connor's voice stunned him back to the present.

Zander shrugged false nonchalance as the blood in his veins bubbled in anticipation.

"If you want privacy." Connor started to turn around when Zander inhaled a deep breath, closed his eyes, and in one fell swoop, transformed into a hawk.

His speckled-brown wings caught a slight updraft, whooshing him into the air and ruffling his feathered body.

Alive again…at long last.

Connor must have shifted just as quickly because he'd already caught up, hovering below and letting Zander lead.

All was quiet at this higher altitude, although knowing Shunnar's special unit could override to hear all hawks, he locked down his thoughts before emptying his mind of *everything*—his duties to Reverie, his lost destiny to the Seam, to the Centennial, even his own team, Ansel and Daiya.

With the summer winds rolling beneath each wing, he needed to imprint this sensation into his soul. Hooked beaks didn't grin. But he was *happy*, if only for the moment as he surged above the neighborhood's darkened rooftops.

Holding back a *kiiiiiiiaaaaaaaarrrrrrr* rippling for release in his chest, he finally opened his senses to Connor.

Thank you for letting me have a minute.

Connor's voice filtered through. *Of course. I can't imagine being grounded for so long. Do you miss it?*

No—yes. He slowed to let Connor take the lead, following his lighter, creamier plumes. Each feathered wing stroke caught the silver moonlight.

Can you fly on rest days in Reverie?

*I—*Zander paused, soaring on a flux of southern warm air. It was like the universe wrapping its arms around him, welcoming back the elemental he was meant to be. That thought alone was enough to crack the hollow bones holding his mental frame.

I just don't.

He couldn't say the truth…that he didn't see the point in flying when it wasn't his destiny anymore. The BC assigned him *under* Reverie. The only seam keeper advantage was his hawk vision, masterful at seeing through the aether.

Somehow, though, he'd been the glue restoring Daiya's fragmented team. His feathers quivered as he looped lower.

Connor followed him down. *I'm sorry.*

There was nothing left to say, and no sky left to fly. The same tall trees in the greenbelt they'd launched from were upon them.

As the wooded landing strip appeared, Zander rolled his neck into his chest, willing his bones to morph back into his human form. He landed with a thud on his back.

Connor landed on his feet and offered a hand.

"Thanks." Zander accepted his help, feeling a little rusty.

Des, Ashton, and Mason all leaned against the van as he and Connor approached.

"All good?" Des tossed the keys to Ashton, but his eyes were on Connor.

"All good." Connor got down to business. "Okay, team—if we need to relay messages, Mason will shift to communicate with Ashton, or Des and I can communicate with Zander."

"Got it," Zander said, realizing he wouldn't be able to mentally communicate with Ashton's cast. They weren't his anymore.

****

Mason and Connor soared, flanking Des from

Mason's little suburbia to Seattle. City lights glowed like the home Mason remembered. The space needle pricked the dark with its illuminated outline. But Des's voice pierced behind his ears, shattering any nostalgia.

We're playing this like we hunted Ian. Take down every fade you come across.

Mason didn't wait for more. *It's not the fades I'm worried about. Remember our last brawl? Vin's literally made of stone.*

We know. Connor cut in.

Shunnar had already shared the history Zander's teammate, Daiya, had dug up about the demon prince's rebirthing.

Mason scooped his wings lower over Lake Washington. The waft of spritzing water refreshed, though still, he was tired. But didn't he do his best work when exhaustion led the way?

Connor's voice blew through. *So if Kelvin's skin has become his armor—well, except for—*

His left ear? Mason caught a gentle zephyr, catching up, and reveled in the memory of slicing through Vin's skin when his dagger found the monster's profile.

Ear, yes. Maybe even his temple. Rory and Daiya believe it's Lucifer's safeguard. Every one of his sons has a soft spot to be put down, if needed.

Ewww—creepy. I thought Max was cold. Or at least he used to be. Mason swallowed the guilt thinking about his estranged relationship with his stepdad. Tonight, he wanted nothing more than to save him from Hell.

Cutting through tall buildings now, the three headed northwest until Des circled down onto a dimly lit building several blocks from Ian's warehouse. In hawk form, they all perched on the rooftop, watching.

Mason studied the huge ship cranes as the moon's reflection rippled off Puget Sound.

He's only thicker on the outside, Des mentioned as if an idea brewed.

Then his wounded ear could still be damaged, Connor added. *That alone could slow down his hearing, his reflexes, or at least his psyche, thinking he's unbeatable.*

Mason screeched, his bird of prey reeling to take out the demon. It would be easier to deal with his dad's survival and reentry into the human world without a demon prince hellbent on...*what*? Did he want to follow in his brother's footsteps? Continue building a new realm? Mason's insides pinched and groaned.

We find his soft spots—ears, temple, eyes, mouth. Mason raised his wings.

It might be all we have. That and taking his fades down. There can't be many more. Des gripped and regripped his position on the roof's ledge with tipped talons. *It's surely too much energy to hide from the Dark Realm.*

Mason ruffled his feathers. Rory had said a forcefield covered Seattle. It must be how Vin was hiding his plans from his own world.

Again, what if we involved the Dark Realm—tell Daddy what Junior's been up to? Mason paced on the gravelly rooftop in awkward bird hops.

Des and Connor both shrieked their disapproval in unison.

Connor landed next to him. *If you want any of us to come out of this alive or any innocents down there, including your family, you* won't *involve the king of Hell.*

Des sent his message bluntly. *Devil princes? Take 'em down. The Devil himself—*

Hide, Connor squawked.

Okay, okay. Mason sent quickly. *But we handle this here. Tonight!*

Quiet. Des arched in the direction of Ian's old warehouse. He must be getting a message telepathically. *Rory and Daiya are working to buy time. If they tear a hole in whatever invisible net Kelvin's using to hide this area, he'll have to patch it.*

Time to hunt fades. Connor's wings opened wide.

Kelvin's the greater target. Mason's wings arched as wide as Connor's, ready for flight.

Des's voice, a battle cry behind Mason's eyes. *There're no reinforcements. We take down whatever we find in the window Rory provides.*

Kiiiiiaaaaaarrrrr!

Meet back here, Des ordered. *Go!*

But Mason was already in the air, soaring down streets as if dodging the cave rodents and thick trees where Connor had trained him not so long ago.

His teammates followed silently as he glided to the old, deserted gas station across from Ian's warehouse.

Mason, shift. Connor, sky. Tap in when needed.

Des and Mason rolled into their human forms, squatting low to the ground. They hid behind a giant garbage bin in the alleyway, behind the station, and amid a few unhoused souls hunkering down for the night. They paid them no mind.

Des waited, maybe to allow the dust to settle or maybe for a report from Rory. They didn't have an accurate number on fades yet.

Finally, Des crossed the street, and Mason followed, crawling under the same hole in the cyclone fence they'd cut when they were last there. The same three jet-sized buildings sat in a row, metal roofs slicing the moonlight.

Des held up a hand.

Mason halted, holding his breath to scan the surrounding darkness.

Dammit! Des sent frustration with his received message. *Rory says they can't find a thread to pull on whatever magical web is covering the city.*

Mason stepped around the shifter in the lead. *Well, there's no time to wait.*

****

Ashton rested her head against the back of the seat. Hicks's dark house was still in view although she'd moved the vehicle closer. This way she could see if any lights came on or if anyone left the driveway. Zander had shifted again, taking to the trees in Hicks's yard.

It was well past midnight. Mason, Des, and Connor had been gone for about an hour. Mason hadn't checked in, and she didn't have mental communication with Zander, another reason for moving the van closer.

Finally, after checking for moving shadows, she searched for a pen. Drawing was her first choice in making it through long nights. Thankfully her hand sketched her oak tree without too much concentration, allowing her mind to focus.

Lavender. She breathed out the dreamy word as if it might settle somewhere in the chilling van, and her previous vision from Reverie might make more sense. She pulled on Mason's hoodie, inhaling his scent.

The last time the clicking magic of her gift had surfaced, she'd been overwhelmed with stress, which meant she may need to be under duress for actual ideas to seed. How was this gift supposed to help the realms if she had to endanger herself to make it work?

Shaking her thoughts, she again envisioned the lavender field stretched across a blue sky. The vision she'd had in Reverie hadn't looked like any of her mom's old paintings, or like her old drawings. She'd visited a lavender farm on San Juan Island before, but how was that supposed to save the souls in the Dream Realm? *Sinking* souls—her mind echoed as the purple flowers in her vision faded into blurry-edged nothingness.

With every shaded line she added to her oak tree leaves, she imagined more and more lavender until out of the corner of her eye, something moved down the street. Sitting up, she tossed the journal and pen into the console and peered through the dark.

There it was again.

Someone—or *something*—moved in Hicks's driveway.

Zander must have noticed because his hawk form appeared on the rooftop next door. She couldn't see him clearly but assumed with the shadowy swoop of the larger bird's silhouette, it was him.

If it were Mason, he'd have communicated telepathically. But Zander wasn't able, leaving her semi-solo. She'd only trained to deal with lower-level demons at the borders, but she was all in, her gaze narrowing on the driveway as she approached on foot.

Earlier, Bronwyn and Nigel had reported nothing occurring during their twenty-four hours of surveillance. Of course, something would happen now.

She patted her vest pocket for a couple of jewel-hilted daggers. Getting caught wearing her weapons belt wasn't a smart idea in the Human Realm, but she wasn't battling demons empty-handed.

Ashton inhaled a slow breath, jogging closer to the side of the adjacent house, out of streetlamp glow.

Blink! A porch light flashed on.

"Ugh," she whispered, clamping a hand over her mouth. *Sensor lights!*

If she hadn't already announced herself, she might have a chance. Nothing shadowy or fade-like came her way. No humans either. The night quieted itself once more, not even a breeze during this bewitching hour. The light blinked off.

Hicks's house was right next door. She looked up to see Zander's hawk form peer over the roof eave. He was above her now, the houses so close together. Was he nodding? Nodding as if it was a good idea for her to sneak up this way or nodding like watch out, danger!

No time to consider! Hicks's garage door flew open, the grinding noise like a chainsaw through Ashton's heart. She plastered both palms behind her, cementing them against the house, as if to ground her.

Hicks's truck backed out of the garage, then stopped in the driveway. The sensor lights flashed again, and Ashton could just make out Kali's silhouette in the driver's seat.

"What are you doing?" Ashton murmured to the night.

Letting the truck idle, Kali hopped out. She left the door ajar and ran back through the garage, her black hair flowing like a cape.

Zander flew down to a fence between the garage and the house, while Ashton remained frozen against the neighbor's siding. She peered at Zander's hawk eyes, glossy pools reflecting the truck cab light.

"Let's go, babe," Kali's voice trilled, Hicks in tow, their arms around each other.

Where are they going? she asked mentally as if Zander could hear her.

As the two looked down, and before she could think, Ashton hopped into the back of the running vehicle, curling into a tight ball in the corner of the truck bed.

Please don't look in the back.

Zander launched overhead, wings flapping like a bump in the night. She couldn't see if Hicks or Kali noticed either of their sounds, but she guessed Zander might be glaring down with evil hawk eyes at her impulsive decision. This was Hicks, and she had no idea where Kali was taking him or if he'd come back.

Zander would follow by air. That much she trusted.

The rest of the plan?

"Here you go, Michael, just a few more steps," Kali fussed over the groan of the engine.

Ashton couldn't see a thing. She kept her face plastered against her knees, staying as low as possible. Shuffles came from the passenger side, as if Kali helped Hicks into the truck. It took everything in Ashton's power not to sneak a peek.

The click of a seatbelt and a few low-toned moans filled the air.

Was Hicks hurt?

"There you go," Kali said. "Now we're both on the run. We might as well go down fighting." She heaved a breath and shut the passenger door.

Seconds later, the driver's side door closed. The engine revved as Kali backed out of the driveway, a little joltier than Ashton thought was good for the truck or her body. The condition of her fingernails, already shot from fighting demons, flashed behind her eyes as she clutched the metal of the truck. But she left her trivial thoughts behind as the vehicle zoomed down the street.

Summer night air whipped Ashton's hair from her ponytail. It blew up the back of Mason's hoodie, chilling her skin. The sound rushed against her ears like crashing waves. What she couldn't hear, and only trusted was there, was the inaudible sound of hawk wings high above.

Chapter 23

Blowing Up Demons

Mason stalked forward, each stomp igniting frustration until he stopped. Pivoting, he shrugged his best *whatever* at Des, thumbing for him to lead.

No time for newbie mistakes.

He crept behind Des, his teammate's black hair, black skin, and black T-shirt disappearing into the shadows. Mason was hidden, dressed in their typical dark gear, yet his sense of urgency aglow. If they could stop Kelvin here and now, they could figure everything else out for his dad. And Hicks. It was the curveball of the sinking souls throwing everything off.

Des stopped outside the first warehouse building and glared at Mason. *Calm down. Your mangled thoughts are distracting.*

Then get out of my head! Mason sent back.

Des spoke in a grindingly low whisper, "You don't get it. We are *it* right now. All the realms are en route to save the sinking souls. Reverie is vulnerable. Internal is on high alert. Gavan, himself, is pulling duty at the Seam. Shunnar is working with Rory and Daiya." He threw both hands in the air. "Clear your mind!"

But Mason was just as enraged. "Where's the Blessing Council? The angels?" He threw back, unsure of his plural use of angels. He'd only ever encountered one, the Angel Sandalphon. But if they worked for a higher power, then wouldn't this be a good time for him—her—*them*—to step in?

Des gripped his hands behind his head. *We can't begin to comprehend the Angelic Realm's viewpoint in any situation. Their timeline is vast, not linear like ours. And we don't know the ultimate purpose for everything. We do our best in our duty and have faith in the rest.* His words pelted Mason's mind like tiny stones. *Now focus!*

Des turned, leading them onward, and Mason took one of Bethesda's cleansing breaths to clear his mind. No time for meditation. They had a demon prince, far stronger and more dangerous than Ian had been, to kill—banish—put down—stop—anything to get him back to his initial task: freeing Max from that blasted secret realm.

The two slid along the side of the building to the corner between the first and second garages. The July sky, rosy with muted starlight and city buildings, helped his eyes adjust to see more. Even better with his hawk vision, although he couldn't use it for long in human form because of the strain.

Des put up a fist stopping Mason in his tracks. He pointed to the second building, about fifteen yards away, then motioned for Mason to cross while he covered.

Mason didn't hesitate. He locked down his thoughts and glanced over each shoulder before sprinting across the concrete to the shadowed mock safety of the other side while a hawk-bodied Connor watched from the roof.

Instantly, Des was right behind him. As Mason

started to slide down toward the second building door, Des grabbed his shoulder and pointed above.

Up? Mason scrunched his face. They hadn't gone up last time. The buildings were like giant hangers without planes. The only clerestory windows were too high to see inside. With all that littered equipment on the outskirts of the building, going around the outside was a death trap, especially at night.

Shift! Des's command drilled his ears from the inside out. *Rory just sent word the healers tracked a high level of demon energy. Here!*

Connor's lighter voice seeped through Mason's stress. *Probably fifty fades in the second building. Third one's dark.*

Mason had only shifted in midair once or twice, out of desperation for his and Ashton's life. Morphing amongst the dead bones of machinery, with hardly any space to move, and working to stay undetected he tumbled into action. Des was already waiting with Connor on the roof when he finally landed, his body buzzing from the quick change.

Mason bounded about with talons until he found the edge, then stretched his hooked beak forward and over. It was a strange upside-down view, but with hawk vision, he was able to see more than he would have dangling as a human.

Connor flew back to the first building. Mason peered through the windows, straight across into second building's high windows. Des disappeared to the back.

Oh my God.

It was all Mason could think, and he'd inadvertently sent panic to both Connor and Des. Shock seemed to settle across the rooftop air. Mason's wings lifted to help him balance.

Fifty?

To hear the number was one thing, but to *see* them. Mason stared from his strange, inverted angle. The warehouse filled with too many human-looking demons, wearing the gray-tinted skinsuits that people didn't seem to notice.

Fades stood all around, some in groups, some alone, some sparring. Others gathered around a table with food. All of them preparing for what? A takeover? War?

Wait. If Kelvin was back with Hicks and Kali, then the three of them could deal with these monsters without interference.

He pushed past the thought of that evil beast with Ashton and Hicks.

Ash, can you hear me?

He knew his communication might be traceable, but he chanced it to check in. Besides, Kelvin was nowhere in sight.

Mason! Her voice came through, jittery and loud.

Where are you? He swooped upright.

Don't get mad—

You okay?

I'm okay. Kali loaded up Hicks in his truck and took off. I couldn't let them leave and not know where they were going.

Mason swore over the rumbling coming through on her side. *Tell me you're not hiding in that truck?*

I'm not hiding in the truck.

Mason barely loosed a breath when she elaborated.

I stowed away on the back truck bed. So,

technically, not in *the truck.*

Mason, let's go! Des's order cut through. Connor took flight in Des's direction, toward the back of the second building.

Colorful language spewed from his thoughts, but she was quiet…letting him calm down, he was sure. He sucked in a breath Bethesda would be proud of. *Is Zander with you?*

He's flying above.

Do you know where Kali's headed? Any idea on direction?

No response, and for a minute Mason thought he'd lost her. His own wings flailed in his hawk-version of pacing, but he dragged his taloned feet to stay put. He didn't even know where to fly to get to her. *Ash!*

I can't tell. She coughed. *Wait, I think maybe north on I-5.*

He imagined her poking up from the back, peering around, the wind pelting her face. It was the middle of the night.

Mason! Des shouted through his head again.

Be careful, please. We don't have our eyes on Kelvin yet.

*I don't think he's here either, but—*Her voice cut out as Des's broke through like shattered glass.

I've got Kelvin in view. He's in the back of the building, a private office.

Kelvin's here. I have to go. He hopped into the air. *Be careful!*

Mason cut the connection as he glided, wings low across the roof, to the back side of the building and another long high-level window at the top. Ignoring Des's rebuke in his ear, he joined his teammates.

Mason stretched his neck from the rooftop edge to see Vin standing over a blobby demon monster. It was the kind Mason hunted at the Seam—mindless and animalistic—yet somehow a formless mix of shadows, claws, and teeth.

The ugly thing squawked and stretched, as if being tortured, scraping its claws on the concrete floor. Mason regripped his talons, almost falling at the noise crackling through the glass. Appalled, yet unable to turn away, he ogled through the horror with raptor vision.

Kelvin had both hands raised over the moaning *thing*, head down. He appeared deep in concentration, and if his lips moved, his words couldn't be heard. Mason's hawk hearing picked up nothing.

What the- Connor sent, energy level high. *I can't believe we're going to see this.*

What's happening? Mason thought aloud. But the answer delivered before Connor or Des could respond, right before his eyes.

The low-level demon curled in on itself, let out a blood-curdling screech, and unfurled from the floor. Now a bigger mound of gray skin dripped black ichor. The new shape grew, then folded, then grew again, like clay forming under invisible hands. Finally, a red shadowy mist encircled it like magic until the once ground-hovering creature lifted a human-looking head, as it stretched itself into its new skin.

This one appeared to be a female with anatomically correct body parts. Kelvin tossed it a towel. It—she—soaked up the black bloodlike ichor with the cloth, though her drippings still covered the floor. Then the newly made fade bowed at the demon prince's feet.

I've never seen this done before. Des's voice was

hushed, but the tone came through Mason's mind as if he screamed. With the agonizing noise sounding from the new fade suddenly silenced, Mason thought their cover might be blown.

But Kelvin never looked up. He called for someone, his deep voice bellowing through the office door, and another fade entered to lead the new female-looking one out.

Mason remembered his encounter with two of Ian's human-looking monsters when he had been here only days ago. He'd killed one on his own, the other with Connor's help. They didn't go down without a fight, but when they fell, it was in a puff of smoke and soot.

He's creating them from some sort of energy source. Do you think it's coming from Ian's secret realm? Connor asked. *It would have to be strong to make this many.*

There's no way. Mason's mind raced back to when he'd searched for Ashton in that place before his stepdad even made the deal for his life. *That pocket of a realm barely had light. Trees can't grow* or *die. I think if he had some sort of power source there, he'd have already used it. He wouldn't have needed Ashton's gifts in the first place.*

Des sprang up to the flatter part of the roof. *Then it's coming from somewhere else.*

Mason watched as two other fades entered the office with a mop and began cleaning the floor. Kelvin leaned back into an office chair, head down, almost in a posture of prayer. All of a sudden, a small, eel-like creature slithered out from under the desk.

He summoned another one. Connor sent and hopped up to the top with Des. Mason followed. He had no intention of watching another shadowy, ichor-slicked, demon birth.

They're all in there together. Mason's mind was moving fast. *It would exhaust us taking them all down one at a time—*

Connor finished his thought. *But we could take out the whole lot at once.*

Sending word to Shunnar now. Get down there. Shift. Go through the old equipment. Look in the other buildings. There's got to be something we can use. Des ordered and took flight back the way they'd come. *And be careful. This seems almost too easy.*

That thought had crossed Mason's mind too. Kelvin knew they were in the Human Realm. Where were the lookout guards? But they didn't have time to question Kelvin's strategies. They had to shut his fade-making business down. Now.

Mason and Connor landed in the same machine-covered alcove they'd shifted in before. Mason bit his tongue to keep from swearing upon landing, but he found his feet and rose to a squat amongst the equipment, Connor right behind him.

Des still hadn't morphed back, probably still in conversation with Shunnar.

Mason wasn't waiting. Not with Kelvin creating more monsters for his army. Maybe the energy level it took to create the fades was too all-encompassing for him to notice he was being spied on. Maybe that was why their small team of three had gotten this far undetected.

"Ouch!" Mason whacked his knee on an old, rusted piece of machinery.

"Shhhhh!" Des reappeared from the shadows.

Mason's heart thrummed out of his chest. "Shunnar's order: take him down at any cost. Take them *all* down."

"Look," Mason said, glancing down at what he'd knocked against. It was an old trailer, tipped low on one side. Flat tire? No tire? Mason bent over to investigate. "There're chains attached to the hitch. Could we lock them in? Start a fire?" His whisper came out low and raspy, adrenaline racing.

"Let's do it." Des nodded, needing no convincing.

The clock was ticking. Who knew how long Kelvin needed to make these human-like demons? They could end this whole thing tonight.

Mason pulled at the chains, peering up at Connor. He wasn't sure how they were going to do this, but an equipment yard had to have tools and fuel. If they could find a cart or truck or something heavy to pull in front of the doors, they could block the house of evil inside.

Connor grinned a wicked smile, the dimness of Seattle's glow illuminating his freckled face. *We're blowing up demons!*

They had the makings of a quick plan with an explosive solution. Mason could only guess what kind of child Connor might have been.

Des shook his head. *Let's get busy.*

Chapter 24

Stowaway

Ashton pressed her back against the truck bed, her feet pushing along the perpendicular side, wedging herself into the corner. It had taken every tightened muscle to deal with all the stops and starts until they merged onto the freeway heading north on I-5. At least that was the direction she thought they were heading.

The trip was filled with a constant rumble and biting wind. She was grateful for Mason's sweatshirt, yanking the hood up early on. She couldn't see where Zander was, and every time she searched the sky, she'd whack her head, so concluded to trust he was there.

After what had to be almost two hours, the truck slowed, taking an exit. Stiff and frozen from the cool night air, she couldn't rise up fast enough to see which one. But they had to be somewhere outside Bellingham, maybe. In one of her glimpses, she'd seen a sign for Lake Samish.

The truck turned, continued at a slower pace, then turned again. At the gentler speed, she rolled over for a better view of the open sky...no streetlights...no Zander. She rubbed her face with her hoodie-covered hands. The cotton was soft against her windblown nose, though a wish for a hairbrush combed her thoughts.

Kali pulled onto a back road, driving for close to

another hour. The bumps and bruises she'd surely acquired would not be pretty. Ashton had just wished for a bathroom break when Kali turned onto a dirt road, which twisted down another bumpy road, until Ashton felt almost carsick. There were no streetlights wherever they were, but the stars were bright, casting a feathery glow.

The truck slowed again, as if the fade might be looking for a specific location. Ashton busied her mind by making star wishes. Her number one wish at the moment was for her world to stop moving. When Kali finally braked, Ashton's head clunked into the side of the truck.

Kiiiiiaaaaarrrrrr, Ashton heard from the sky, though it sounded farther away. *Zander.*

Afraid of discovery, she arched herself into a tight ball. But Kali and Hicks hadn't loaded anything into the bed of the truck before leaving. Would they look there now? As she uncurled to make a break for the woods, the doors on both sides opened. She squished back down, listening as they each hopped out, feet crunching along the forest floor.

"See, Michael. This is the perfect spot." Her voice was gentle, a contrast to the demon she was.

"Oh, babe—you're right! The constellations are practically in our laps." Hicks sounded happy, as if this monster could really be his girlfriend and they were on some starry-night date. "We should set up camp right here."

Ashton peeked over the edge of the truck, praying they were looking in the opposite direction.

"Wait, let me check the energy levels," she said, jolting back to the truck. Ashton ducked, her heart jumbling in her chest.

Hicks chuckled. "You and your crystals."

"I want everything to be perfect." She must have found what she needed because she slammed the door and crunched away. "I'm going to set these up."

Ashton took her chance, inching to the bottom of the truck bed, and with every step Kali made on the ground, perhaps placing her crystals, or whatever she was doing, Ashton timed her movements to creep out of the truck and into the shadows.

Hiding behind the first tree trunk she found, she held her breath. Had they noticed?

When all was quiet, except the patterned stamping of Kali's feet harmonized by Hicks's humming, Ashton let her shoulders drop. It was cold. And she was a mess, covered in dust from the ride. She adjusted her ponytail, tucking the stray tangles behind her ears.

Were they hiding from Kelvin? Or meeting up with Mr. Demon-Pants after all? Was she tricking Hicks…maybe sacrificing him in a crazy dark ritual? That might explain the crystals.

Questions brawled with flailing heartbeats.

Crap!

Ashton peered up through the dark trees, thankful again for the stars. How far away might Zander be? Hadn't she heard him call?

"Ready." Kali's voice, still sweet. "Walk with me. Do you mind?"

Hicks reached out a hand. "Lead the way."

Had Hicks always been this agreeable? Ashton had been to many parties at his house. She'd gone to every sports game he and Mason played together. He was the guy who always had a girl, but never a girlfriend. Or maybe Ashton had hidden too long in her bubble of high school life. Maybe she knew less than she thought about the boy who'd grown up as her friend.

Ashton surveyed, cheek pressed against bark, as Kali took his hand and pulled him in a wide circle, carefully stepping around every crystal she'd placed on the ground. How did she remember where she'd put them? Somehow, she found her way. From what Ashton could tell each one seemed evenly placed, maybe six feet apart.

Ashton didn't know enough about fades. Maybe these low-level demons were made stronger or smarter the longer they were human-like. Did they have supernatural powers? But hadn't her own gifts muted in the Earth's atmosphere? She still had her strengths, only dulled. And magic? Only an itch she couldn't scratch. Or maybe it was a new drawer of mental files needing order in her head. She had many questions to ask when she got back…if she made it back.

Stop thinking like that!

Hicks needed her, and she wouldn't let him down.

"It's smokey quartz and aragonite, along with clear quartz too. We walk three times around the grid I've made in each direction." Kali stopped and inhaled a deep breath. "Now you. Take a cleansing breath."

Hicks huffed in and out. "Like that?" he asked.

"Perfect," she said. "Now keep breathing and focus on the ground. Think about every step, letting your energy flow and take root. This spot is right on the edge of his veil. We can hide along the busyness of the energy currents, but not without camouflage."

"Who are we hiding from again?" Hicks's tone dipped in comfort level. Ashton couldn't see his facial expressions in the dark, but she heard the hitch in his voice. She saw his silhouette stop in his march around Kali's crystals.

"Michael, you remember." She embraced him in a hug. "I love you. You love me. We are going to forge our own way in the universe." She kissed him, and Ashton could hear by the smacking sounds he was kissing her back.

What was going on?

Ashton crept closer, taking the slowest steps she could, to stand behind two tall evergreen trees. The old trunks embraced in a hug themselves, with a tiny opening between them, like a slit for a window. The opening reached from about shoulder level on Ashton to maybe three feet higher, less wide. But it was enough to get a view and hopefully *not* get noticed.

Squinting her eyes, she saw Kali's hand fall strategically from his shoulder, down his back, to her pocket, then to his. Something glinted in the moonlight. A stone? A crystal?

Ashton couldn't help but think of Mason's mom. Mia used to hide similar rocks and minerals all over his house and in his pockets. It made sense when Ashton was a child because she only knew his mom to be a geologist. But Mia was a seam keeper, hiding in the Human Realm from every other realm. And she used resources to hide, like stones and crystals.

"I remember now." Hicks must have taken a breath from his lip lock.

"Good. Let's finish this last rotation, walk three more counterclockwise, then we should be safe in our cocoon for a little while."

"Sounds good. Then I'll pitch the tent." Hicks's

voice was sugary-sweet.

Ashton leaned her head against the double-treed trunk when a hand came up from behind and covered her mouth.

Her first instinct was to elbow whoever or *whatever* was behind her. But hadn't Kali fortified this place?

For scaring her, she elbowed the culprit anyway. The sounds of a grunt blew forward from behind. She turned, dagger drawn, to find Zander, bent over and covering his own mouth to keep quiet.

Chapter 25

Curiously Sour

Zander righted himself, glanced between tree trunks, and nodded as if an all-safe sign.

"Hey." He stepped back and shrugged.

"Don't spook me like that."

"I wasn't sure how to approach." He pointed to the couple walking circles in the dark.

Ashton shook her head. "How much have you heard?"

"Enough to know she's using crystals to hide their energy. Did she say *cocoon*?"

Ashton checked over her shoulder as the couple made another round, this time in the opposite direction. "Yes."

Zander raised an eyebrow, then moved closer to peek between the trunks.

Peering over Ashton's head, he watched the shadowed pair walk in small laps. After the last rotation, the fade knelt down and pressed both hands to the ground. It was too dark for him to see what she— it—was doing, but it appeared the thing was digging in the dirt. After a few minutes, it stood up and dusted off its hands.

Hicks used the cab lights from the truck to set up camp in the center of the area marked by crystals.

Zander couldn't see those either, but assumed they were there.

Ashton stretched herself higher on her tiptoes as they spied the strange scene. But neither of them talked or stopped ogling until Hicks grabbed two bags from the truck, and Kali joined him at the entrance of the tent. Once they both crawled in, zipping the flap shut, Zander stepped back.

"I contacted Connor from the air. His orders are to stand guard here," he whispered louder than expected, then froze, assuring he hadn't blown their cover. Energy still zinged through his veins after the long flight, a sensation he'd almost forgotten existed. "I'll keep first watch."

Ashton looked around. "I wish I knew where *here* was."

Here was quite a contrast to his birds-eye view on the journey over. The woods were silent, as if any nocturnal animal business was on pause. No wind. No bats. No scurries from nocturnal animals. He'd read about various habitats in the Human Realm. And lots about the weather…intriguing. So many different conditions. Growing up in Valley, his Spiritual Realm home outside of Toria, every day was a perfect spring day. Constant warm breezes, blue skies, white fluffy clouds, and if it rained, it was gentle and quick. Refreshing. Reverie was as lovely, but more distinct. The weather the same every day, pink and chilly, a winter sky lost in perpetual sunsets.

Though never this quiet.

"Do you think the animals are under a spell? It's awfully silent for a forest."

Ashton tilted her head, as if listening. "Maybe."

Zander gazed over his shoulder. Hopefully whatever crystal magic Kali used would benefit them all. No time to worry about bears and coyotes along with demons. But, with everything awry in the realms, he'd stay alert.

"Did it sound to you like Kali might be hiding from Vin herself?" Zander had trained his whole life to slay demons, but they typically appeared as shadowy blobs with animal-looking features, like fangs and claws. He'd learned fades looked human, though he'd never seen one before.

"She did," Ashton responded. "It's been bugging me because Mason said she'd spoken of him as her brother."

Laugher from the tent caught their attention. As he turned, his stomach growled.

Ashton stifled a giggle.

"Sorry. I forgot how much flying takes out of me."

She held up a finger, then cleared a spot to sit with her foot. He helped, as quietly as he could, before joining her on the cold ground.

They'd settled, twin trunks behind their backs, when more giggling spewed from the tent. Zander and Ashton froze, eyes locked as they inclined their chins to listen. Hicks was saying something Zander couldn't quite catch, and Kali laughed.

Ashton eyed him with a smile, slipping her hand inside the front pocket of her sweatshirt.

He curled a corner of his lips. *Curious.* Her starlight features held a soft glow. Back at the BC meeting in Toria, when he'd first met her, he couldn't help stealing glimpses. And in Reverie, watching her experience the beauty of the Dream Realm, something unraveled inside him, something previously tied down.

What might it have been like—he blinked. Her indigo eyes stared at him.

Whoa—had he checked out? *Get it under control.* He stiffened his back, pushing into the rough edges of bark. No time for *what ifs.*

"I'm sorry, did you say something?"

She smiled, full lips curving. "Of course not. I'm contemplating. I don't share these with just anyone. Consider yourself lucky." Her raspy whisper matched her sly expression as she pulled out a bag of something—then stopped.

The noise from the bag crinkled through the woods, sounding nothing like an animal. She gaped and glanced over her shoulder.

All quiet.

Slowly, she tugged again. Stopped. Another centimeter. Stopped. This could take all night. Was it even worth it?

His stomach decided it was. But as the contents of the package became visible, he cringed. Strange cartoon children decorated the bag. "Candy?" He remembered their stop at the gas station before meeting Bronwyn and Nigel.

She smothered a giggle, then opened the bag labeled family size. The chorus of crumpling remained an issue. He pulled a throwing knife from his vest to help when she managed a tiny split down the seam. Slower still, she separated the two pieces until enough of an opening allowed some to fall into her palm.

He put his blade away.

"Here." She sighed. "Not dinner, but they are one of my favorite desserts." She nodded for him to open a hand, then tipped the edge. Candy figures, resembling human cutout shapes, tumbled from the plastic bag, one yellow, one blue, and two green.

"Lucky—the green ones are my favorite." She smiled, snagging a green character from his palm, and bit off its head.

He popped the other green candy into his mouth—regretful at once.

His eyes had to have grown two sizes. They teared up as if he'd eaten the sourest lemon. Arching his back from the trunk, he turned to spit the devilish concoction out when the flavor smoothed and finished with a sudden sense of sweetness. The candy stuck in his teeth, but he worked out the bits with his tongue…watching her do the same.

"What do you think?" she asked, throwing an orange one onto her tongue.

He grinned back. "Okay, once I get past the initial shock."

She covered her mouth with one hand, possibly locking down a reaction, and tossed him the bag. He wasn't sure why but accepted her offer. It was the only food they had.

The moment was nice for a while, the moon bright. The night air chilled, but it wasn't freezing. In any other circumstance, this might have been a perfect evening…if they weren't after an evil demon prince, in another realm, so her unexpected castmate—boyfriend—could save his earthly father.

Now the moment was properly strained, as it should be. He rolled his eyes at the night. *Touché, destiny.*

After their candy feast, the temperature dipped. He

and Ashton sat side by side, nestled behind the trees to stay warm. They hadn't spoken in the last hour.

He peeked at her closed eyes, nightfall covering her like a blanket, and hoped she would find rest. Stretching his back a little taller against the tree, he focused on the sugar streaming through his veins to stay awake.

A while later, with his tongue still tingling from the sour candy, a rustling sound seeped from the tent. He glanced at Ashton, though it was darker and harder to see, her eyes opened wide. She pressed a finger against her lips, and he nodded in agreement, straining to listen. Neither of them moved.

"It's time again." Kali's voice carried to their shelter between trees. She must have believed they were alone and undetected because she wasn't whispering. "We need to make our circles."

"Can't we wait until morning?" Hicks complained. "It's late, babe."

Zander heard the tent flap unzip, followed by movement clambering across the ground.

Ashton hoisted up without a sound, peering between the trees as he crawled to stand behind her. As Zander made it upright, Kali froze and stared their direction. They'd been caught! Whatever light was left from the moon reflected off her eyes, glinting like a predator.

He ducked.

Ashton must have realized too because she almost lost her balance jerking back. This time her feet crunched the ground as she balanced on a protruding root. Zander caught her arm, helping her settle.

"What was that?" Hicks asked, voice steady, but

scratching on the last word.

"Stay here," she warned.

"No way," Hicks argued.

Ashton froze in Zander's grip, her feet barely planted. She'd taken her hair down before resting and now it draped across her face, hiding any reaction or silent expression she may have wanted to send. If he let go, he wasn't sure she'd stand on her own without wobbling.

He glanced back at the fade and Hicks. They were coming straight toward them.

What was the plan?

Chapter 26

Burn it Down

Mason rounded the corner of the warehouse with a long chain across his back and another shorter one looped over an elbow. It was better he wore them than announce his arrival clanking. The closer he strode, a low rumble of racket carried through the door of the second building. They obviously weren't expecting company, distracted by whatever was happening inside. If Vin was creating fades, using dark magic atop his already profound powers, wouldn't he have some kind of wards in place?

Connor's thoughts broke through. *I wondered the same thing. Maybe it's taking all he's got to create his army.*

Mason imagined Connor heading to the doors on the opposite side of the building, equally loaded with chains they'd confiscated from the fences along the outer gates. Des, in hawk form, kept watch from the roof. Mason wasn't sure which side was the bigger threat, Ian's brother or the fifty-plus fades.

It's probably the energy net over the area. Des sent.

Mason adjusted the chains. *He must think it's all the protection he needs.*

Or he thinks there's no chance we'll get past his

newly made demon spawn? Connor huffed. *I'm at the south entrance.*

The chains were heavy, but Mason had arrived at his destination. *Ready at the north.* He stretched his neck to hear better.

Voices carried, as if these human-looking demons had no concerns about anything beyond the warehouse. The walls muffled any comprehensible words, only the din of grunts and laughter filtered through.

They don't seem worried about an attack. Time to prove 'em wrong, Mason sent before feeding his chain through the door handles. He hoped it slowed any monsters attempting escape. After twisting the links of metal around to the ends, he wedged a throwing knife between various links. It wouldn't hold the door for long, but hopefully, long enough.

Done. Mason retraced his steps to the east side of the building and waited.

Thoughts of Ashton filtered through, but he had to believe Zander, originally chosen for Mason's post, would keep her safe. He huffed a breath, releasing the thought as a new image surfaced—her mocking voice loud and clear: I don't need protecting.

Connor approached from the south, moonlight illuminating his pale skin. It startled Mason for a half breath, but he didn't spook easily anymore—not when dealing with evil on a daily basis.

They eyed each other before dropping to shift, Mason changing faster this time. He barely felt the prods of pain before dissolving into his new shape and joining Des and Connor atop the roof.

By the time Mason fully landed, Connor was mid-shift. His back bulged under autumn-hued feathers and bone-protruding skin before rippling into human form. Mason blinked under the crimson glow of Connor's aura, then lifted his own wings to activate the transformation again.

"Ouch," he coughed, lying flat on his human back. He was faster, though not used to morphing so many times so close together.

"Let's go." Des's human boot nudged Mason's hip. Mason stifled a moan and crawled to his feet. The old Mason would have backflipped from the graveled roof to his feet, but how much trampling could the fades underneath detect?

He followed his team to the side of the roof with Vin's office below. Mason dropped to his stomach, as Connor had, and scooted as far over the edge as possible. Looking down at the possible hundred feet of distance to the ground, he swallowed hard. He'd never been afraid of heights, but he still didn't want to slip. He wiggled out to his hips, tightened his core, and craned his neck over the edge to better see through the long horizontal windows.

Kelvin had another blob of shadows on the floor. Mason held his plank-like stature but already felt the burn of back and forth shifting in his core. Comparing the amount of energy to turn mindless creatures into human substitutes and his ability to shift into a hawk, Mason could only imagine the effort to create was more. And Vin had made so many.

How's he doing it? Mason grunted in his mind.

Can't all be on the same night, Des offered, a hopeful hitch in his voice.

Mason shuddered. He needed open communication with his team but slacked on keeping up the boundaries in his own mind. Distractions. His energy was zapped, but his mind also coiled with worry about his family, Hicks, and Ashton.

Now! Des's tone ripped him back. *While he's busy.*

Connor popped up like a surfer, not that he'd know that. Mason clambered up behind him, meeting Des at the center of the roof. They all stared down at a trapdoor, used for maintenance, Mason guessed. Using his boot, Connor kicked. Dusty muck flew up as it opened easily. They all lifted their brows. Had it even been locked?

Mason followed his teammates, dropping into the closet-sized space, to find another door. Des looked back before pulling the handle. Locked.

Connor used his boot again to kick the door. When it didn't open, they all froze.

Des shook his head as Connor lifted his leg again. "Noise."

In a jumble of black flesh and brown feathers, Des appeared in hawk form. With a flutter of wings, he swooped onto Connor's elbow, using his beak to work the flat circular lock. Finishing it off with a sharp talon, the latch released.

Mason swallowed. This had to be a perk from being in Shunnar's special force.

Connor peeped around the doorway, then nodded all clear. Des had already shifted, his human presence breathing down Mason's back as they moved along a dark hallway. Mason peered with hawk eyes, burning a mental map in his mind. With the front and back building doors chained, their exit would be the same as they had entered.

They crept down the hallway opening to a loft-like

half wall. Mason cautiously leaned over the edge, then jerked back in a flash, pointing down. Fades.

They were on the top level of three floors, if he remembered correctly. When he had last stood on the first floor weeks ago, he recalled the second and third levels looking out over the larger jet-sized main floor. Glancing up, the same clusters of chandeliers over the balcony-like edge dangled, an odd lighting choice for such a dingy warehouse.

Connor tapped his arm. They had work to do.

Des motioned for them to check the rooms as he headed the other way. *Work fast. I'll check for wires in the maintenance room.*

Mason followed Connor, opening one of the two doors off the small hallway. It was a storage room with boxes stacked from floor to ceiling. One of the boxes was open, holding multiple pairs of sweatpants and Space Needle printed T-shirts in every color.

Connor thumbed the boxes. "For the newbies."

He was right. The noisy demons from his lawn had all been wearing Seattle-themed clothing.

"These will burn," Mason whispered, but he had to check the other rooms first. Ashton had once been held here. He wouldn't be responsible for any innocents getting hurt.

They crossed the concrete floor to the other door, finding an empty bunkroom. There were three rows of bunkbeds, two against the side walls, and a third set perpendicular to them against the back wall. The beds each had a pillow and sleeping bag.

"For fades?" Mason cocked a brow. Did these monsters even sleep? He'd only trained for the blubbery, nursing demons that filled with negative dreamer energy and then waited for their masters to milk them. Disgusting.

These human-like creatures were different, and he didn't know enough about them.

Visions of his birth father flooded his mind. The late Ian's voice haunting as he'd once tried convincing Mason to kill his castmate, Adam. Didn't Mason have this same demon blood running through his own veins? Mason winced. Ian had never been a blubbery monster first. He'd been a prince, part demon, part angel, part— whatever it took to create him. That was how the Blessing Council had explained it.

Mason wasn't a monster unless he chose to be.

And he wasn't choosing it!

Connor pushed out the door, his movement pulling Mason from the room to the stairwell. His sketchy heritage would have to wait.

Hurry. The shadow's taking shape, Des's voice seeped through Mason's mind. Connor nodded. A dual message.

One more floor check, Mason sent, then followed Conner down the stairs.

Bam!

The impact connected with the back of Mason's head the moment his foot touched the second floor. His body knocked into Connor, and they both hurled into the narrow hallway, smacking the walls as they went down.

The clanging in Mason's ears only sent him to his feet faster. Blood wetted the back of his head. Connor climbed up from under him when the fade who'd jumped him was in his face again and far too eager. The demon hadn't even called for help, undercutting Mason in the gut and thrusting him into Connor.

Curses flew as Mason caught his breath and launched his body into the demon, forcing it onto its back. *You like that?* he cried internally, for fear of alerting other fades. Mason held it down as Connor kicked the monster's head until all movement stilled. Connor helped Mason up as they scanned for more fades.

"Gotta start this fire," Connor hissed. "Out of time."

Mason leaned into a room on his left, another bedroom like the one upstairs. He swiped a pillow off the nearest bed and pressed it to his head. It wasn't ice, but it could soak up blood while his body healed itself—slower in the earth's atmosphere.

"Finish this floor." Connor wiped sweat from his brow.

Mason tossed the bloody pillow, hoping there were no humans anywhere near this place.

Three of the four doors led to bunkrooms. One was a bathroom with a shower and a washer and dryer in the corner. Even a shelf with hygiene products, shampoo, and—Mason picked up a can—hairspray?

If he was infiltrating these fades into society, this was bigger than they'd expected.

Light it up! Des barked though Mason's aching head.

Mason fumbled with the lighter he'd pocketed from the convenience store. A brief memory of buying sour candies before his and Ashton's movie nights flickered behind his eyes. But the colorful memory went up in smoke, as they hoped this warehouse and everything inside might too, if their plan worked.

Connor grabbed a T-shirt, keeping watch as Mason lit the corners of each bunk. A souvenir maybe? But Mason rushed to hit the next room as Connor closed the door. They needed the fire to burn slow enough to get out first, but long enough to inflame the building. If the sleeping bags were fire retardant, they would hopefully burn slow enough to buy them some time.

Sweat dripped from Mason's hairline as thoughts of fire alarms rushed his heartrate. They didn't need human firefighters saving the day—or night. Hopefully Des was able to disarm them.

Climbing over the downed fade, they headed back upstairs. But Mason froze, motioning for Connor to wait, and turned back down the hall.

Smoke streamed from under each door as he yanked the neck of his shirt over his nose. No alarms yet. He pushed open the bathroom door and scanned the room. Letting his makeshift mask drop, he grabbed a towel thrown over the shower and tossed it into the dryer—along with cans of hairspray—then pushed button after button until it turned on.

He bolted without even shutting the door, smacking into Connor as he did. Connor's face scrunched in confusion, but they righted themselves and ran.

"Go!" Mason voiced gruffly. They needed to time this perfectly with Vin's energy levels. The smell of smoke already filled the air. He could only hope Vin was preoccupied below and the new fades were mindless without their master.

Connor slammed the door to the small space housing the roof's trapdoor when Des's voice vibrated through Mason's mind.

Get out now!

Connor wiped blood from his forehead, smearing it into his ginger hair, and crawled up the ladder first. He reached a hand down for Mason, pulling him up singlehandedly. Mason would ask about his upper strength workouts later.

"Light this up?" He held out the T-shirt he'd swiped from the storage room, and Mason set it on fire. Connor tossed the T-shirt down into the hole and slammed the door.

Des was already airborne as Connor dove off the ledge shifting midair. Mason plunged into his impulsivity and leaped, wings breaking free under snapping bones. His lips tore on teeth as his hooked beak broke through, feathers choking down any reluctance.

The brethren soared across several streets to the ledge of a taller building.

They perched. They waited.

Nothing happened.

Mason's wings refused to settle. He was ready to leap. To fly.

Still, nothing happened.

Nothing—*boom!*

The explosion was small, not enough to take down the whole building. It was only a dryer unit. But then another blast, larger than the first. The long windows running along the north and south sides of the building shattered. Blue-gray light flickered like a blinding strobe light.

Screams, smoke, fire.

Boom! Another eruption.

Mason couldn't see if any fades escaped. They

were too far away to hear chain-bound doors rattling in the roar of commotion. Whatever energy Vin was drawing to create those human-shaped monsters had to have helped Mason's attempt at blowing up the building.

Smoke bloomed after the blue light settled. Fire alarms wailed from surrounding buildings, the explosions triggering them. Sirens soon blared from emergency vehicles moving in their direction.

We need confirmation. Connor's tone rasped in Mason's mind.

The three of them watched gold flames scratch the night sky. But was there a portal inside? If so, Vin would have fled, taking as many minions as he could. It wouldn't be easy killing a major demon. Not that this haphazard plan had been easy. But the smoke was too thick to see anything.

Mason fumed as firefighters began their work on the blaze. He hadn't thought about the aftermath, hadn't wanted humans getting hurt. The only goal was to stop Kelvin and save his dad. Save Hicks.

Had it worked?

Chapter 27

Discovered

Ashton found her feet as Zander steadied her atop the forest ground. She hid her squeal with a hand across her mouth, though Kali had to have heard.

"Who's there?" The fade walked to the truck and opened the door.

Ashton hoped she might get in, but instead she snagged a baseball bat from the floorboard. What if Ashton was a bear? Wouldn't hiding *in* the truck be safer than the unknown in a dark forest?

But Kali was the monster.

"Hang on," Hicks forced through gritted teeth, a flashlight swinging in one hand. "I'll do that." He swiped the bat and stepped in front of her. "Get in the truck."

Ashton pushed her hair back, panic swooshing. "It's me." She ignored Zander's glare and leaned out from behind the tree. "Ashton."

"Ashton Nichols?" Hicks shined the light, glow blinding, and stalked closer.

"What are you doing here?" Kali's voice hitched as if…in relief?

Ashton glanced to see Zander standing in the shadows. Both hands lifted in question, but she shook her head, pretending to shake off dust. "You wouldn't happen to have any wipes? That truck ride was brutal from the back."

"You stowed away in our truck?" the fade asked.

"Hicks's truck, and yes. He's *my* friend. You're—"

"—as concerned as you are," Kali interrupted. "That's why we're here. *Hiding.*"

"Ashton, Kali's brother is abusive, and now that he's found her, we're taking off for a while." He tossed the bat back into the truck, the flashlight's yellow stream drawing zigzags in the dark as he moved. "Until he gets bored and wanders off like she said he will." He pulled out a plastic tub of wet wipes. "Here." He tossed her the bin.

"And the crystals?" Ashton asked Kali directly. Even though the fade stood back, her demon eyes glinted in the dark.

Hicks pulled Kali under his arm. "That's a Kali thing." He smiled at her. She grinned back, and if Ashton hadn't known who—or *what* she really was— she would have believed the kindness.

"So, you're camping in the middle of *nowhere* for how long?" Ashton pulled out a wipe and set the bin at her feet.

"It's not the middle of nowhere." Kali sneered. "It's in a specifically chosen spot. I told you; we're hiding."

Ashton cleaned her face and hands. Was it the truth? Could a demon be afraid of another demon? Ashton's chest jittered, hoping Zander would fly for backup if things went south.

"Is Mason with you?" Hicks called into the woods. "We have food!"

"Just me. I stopped by your house when you were

pulling out. I-I don't know what came over me." She wrung her hands with another wipe. "I was worried about you."

"Me?" His eyes glazed again, posture shifting. "I'm fine. Kali and I are fine."

Fine? Hadn't he said they were on the run from her violent brother?

Ashton clumped the wipes into her fist and faked a laugh. "Well, now I feel silly."

Kali rolled her eyes.

Hicks motioned her to the tent. "Hungry?"

"No—I mean, maybe a little." The sugar from the half bag of sour candy still zipped through her blood stream *and* sat in the bottom of her stomach. "I don't want to impose."

Hicks chuckled. "No way. Kali brought enough for an army."

"That's because of *your* big appetite." Pulling her hair back with a hair tie from her wrist, she walked back to the tent. Ashton stared, but it was too dark to see how gray her skin was.

"I'll stay out here." Was she blushing now? "I don't want to be a third wheel."

Kali reappeared with a grocery bag full of food. "You can sleep in the back of the truck if you like? I brought extra blankets. I won't need them since this guy here is my personal built-in heater." She looped an arm through Hicks's elbow as if claiming him.

Probably a warning not to try anything.

Ashton heaved out a breath. "That would be great. I can figure out a way home in the morning, unless you're going back tomorrow?"

Hicks eyed Kali.

Kali shook her head. "No." Then she grabbed blankets from the truck and tossed them over the edge into the back.

Ashton faked a yawn. "Okay. What time is it anyway?"

"It's already tomorrow." Hicks gaped at his watch. "Three in the morning."

Kali yawned this time, obviously also faking.

"You'll be okay by yourself?" Hicks asked.

"I'll be fine." She held up the bag of food as they padded back to their tent. "Thank you."

"Take this." He jogged back and handed her the flashlight. "We have another in the tent."

Kali's strange eyes glinted her way, reflecting eerily from the glow of the flashlight. "We have a few more rounds to make, but you have a good night."

"Really?" Hicks complained. "We're still doing this?"

"You don't have to walk with me."

Ashton risked prying. "Why all the walking?"

"It's something I do to feel safe from...my brother." Her glare pierced Ashton's.

"Let's go." Hicks pulled her back until she turned away. "Circle, circle, right. Circle, circle, left." His voice faded away as they crunched through the woods together.

****

Zander listened to the whole strange conversation and watched the even stranger ritualistic strides around their perimeter, until finally Hicks and the fade went to bed. He waited until no sound seeped from the tent before creeping slowly to the back of the truck.

"Ashton?" he whispered so softly he wondered if

283

she'd actually heard him.

"Climb in."

Her shadowed silhouette sat up, and he held his breath hoping the couple in the tent hadn't heard. When all was quiet, he climbed over the tailgate. Halting between steps, afraid to continue until the quiet of dark filled his uneven efforts of stealth, he lowered himself beside her.

"Hungry?" She handed him a granola bar. "Wait, I'm betting you'd like this first."

He accepted her gift of a wipe, letting out a little breath of surprise she knew. His emotions scattered as hunger leaned in and he washed his hands.

A granola bar, handful of grapes, and a water bottle hit the immediate spot. He rested against the cab of the truck and exhaled. Now he could think about a backup plan.

She tossed part of the blanket she was under across him. He wasn't that cold. The temperature reminded him of Reverie. And his blood still seemed to pump after the heated events of the evening—flying such a long distance, worry about Ashton, the strange sugar high from the sour candies…

"I wondered if you'd flown back to get help."

"I'm not leaving you here." Thankfully she wouldn't be able to see his expression in the dark, but his jaw dropped. "I'm pretty sure Mason would kill me for *that* alone."

She stifled a laugh, which meant his assumption was right. "Mason's running on empty, that's why he was cranky with you earlier. We'd finally put an end to Ian when the deal his dad made was discovered. When we couldn't get him out of that place…" Her voice lowered, all laughter gone. "His family hasn't been together in a long time. It's a last opportunity."

"He's desperate."

"*Hopeful.*"

"He lets emotions make his decisions." Zander plopped another grape into his mouth.

She rolled over and pulled the edge of the blanket up to her chin. "He feels things first, then reacts. That's not necessarily bad."

"I didn't mean to offend you." He reached out to touch her shoulder but pulled back. "I'm sorry."

She yawned, and not the fake kind he'd detected from her earlier when talking to Hicks. "It's fine. I'm fine. Goodnight."

"Wait. What's your plan? Des instructed us to stay with Hicks."

"You talked to Des?"

"They're dealing with the fades at the warehouse…something about a fire. But they don't have eyes on Vin or his cronies. His orders are to stay here. Keep watch over those two."

Her body went stiff next to him. Then she sprang up. "He's not answering."

She meant Mason and their mental connection. He put a hand on her shoulder. "They're in the thick of it right now. Des was short too. I'm sure he'll make contact soon."

Ashton stared into the dark trees for a while before lying back down. Once she relaxed, he plopped another grape in his mouth. His shoulders were heavy, like rocks against the metal truck, and he wondered what Daiya and Ansel were doing that earthly moment.

Was he feeling homesick? Not for Reverie.

His teammates.

"I think Kali might be running *from* Kelvin." Ashton's gentle voice lulled him from his thoughts. "I don't trust her. Yet maybe she *is* keeping Hicks safe."

"That's what Mason wants, right? To keep his friend safe."

"Of course." She adjusted the covers, probably as uncomfortable as he was. "Our job just got a little easier, I guess."

He lifted to his knees to crawl out. "So, that's the plan then." But what about the souls in the Dream Realm? What about their original task, minimizing human fear after Max's book launched?

Confliction pierced his chest.

"For now, Hey, stay here." She reached out a hand. "We both need to sleep, and I'm sure we'll hear the tent unzip if they get up before us."

He froze under her palm. He *was* exhausted. And with a fuller belly, his body begged for rest. "Okay." He scooted next to her.

"Zander?" Ashton whispered after he settled. "When the BC introduced you that first day, they called you Zander *Mara*."

"Yeah."

"You're the first keeper I've met with a last name."

He laughed as quietly as he could. "We don't really use them, as there are less of us, and we often don't repeat names like they do in the human world."

"But couldn't there be another Zander one day?"

"Our last names are our mother's names, in case of confusion."

"Your mother's name is Mara?" Ashton's voice curled curiously.

"Yes." He adjusted the blanket, sleep calling.

"It's beautiful."

"You called flying insects beautiful," he murmured.

"You know what I mean."

"I do." He sighed. "Thank you."

Silence covered them for a long time. He could have sworn he heard her heavy breathing of sleep when she whispered, "I haven't forgotten about the souls, Zander. We're going to find a way to save them." She reached a hand to his. "We will."

He appreciated her hopefulness.

Chapter 28

Circle Confessions

Ashton awoke to the zipper of the tent, as she'd hoped. Had she even slept? When she opened her eyes to the morning light of the woods, she immediately shut them, squinting to see that Zander was still asleep. But someone walked closer. Too late to warn him, so she threw her side of the blanket across his head and scuttled over the top of him.

"You're up early," Kali whispered, letting her know Hicks was still asleep. She was wearing Hicks's high school jacket, blue with a white mustang on the back, and her black hair pulled up in a knot on the top of her head. Her eyes were dark, even with the sunrise gleaming apricot hues.

"Yeah," she whispered, respecting Hicks's sleep, but also hoping her climb over Zander and the knee to his back had woken him.

Ashton walked toward Kali, coughing over the thud and grunt coming from the truck behind her. Then she smoothed her tangled hair as best she could.

"Here." Kali handed her a hair tie from her wrist. "I have to make my rounds."

Ashton's brows rose. Was she being genuinely nice?

"What exactly *are* you doing?" She accepted the

elastic band and wrapped her locks up in a messy bun, too many snarls for anything else. She warmed her hands inside Mason's hoodie pocket and watched Kali begin her walk.

The fade looked back, her cheeks less ashen in the morning light, her voice low. "You can join me if you want. I'm not what you think."

Ashton glanced over, hoping Zander was in the clear, and caught up to Kali. At first, she couldn't see a proper path through the branch and moss debris, or the crystals Kali had placed only hours ago in the dark, but as she followed along, her eyes adjusted. By the third cluster of gems piled on the ground, she started to feel the energy before stepping past. She found the fourth batch right away.

She knelt to study them. One was brown, another red, and the third was clear. "How does it work?"

"The smokey quartz lifts negative energy creating a field of calm. That's the brown one. The reddish one is aragonite. It removes pollutants and fosters truth. And the clear quartz amplifies them both creating a sort of refuge within the edge of Vin's spell," she said matter-of-factly. "Of course, they're demon cursed." She continued her path.

Ashton followed, still perplexed, yet unsure how far to push. Even though Hicks had teased her about walking circles, they actually made a rectangle, with perpendicular lines and straight edges.

"I know you think I'm bad."

"I don't know what to think." Ashton kept in step with her slow pace. "Hicks is a longtime friend. I don't want him getting hurt."

Kali stopped. "I don't know how much you know

about fades." She dropped her chin at the word, as if ashamed. "But we grow. We *become*. I have an opportunity for a new life. And I won't let you or anyone else stop me."

Ashton wasn't sure what she was getting at, but if it involved hurting her friend, she wasn't about to let that happen. "Not at the expense of Hicks."

Kali's mouth dropped. "I would never hurt him."

The fade's eyes glossed over, blackness bleeding from each pupil which softened to gray. Tears formed in the corners.

Was she for real? Nobody had explained fades becoming more than their human-like appearances.

"I don't understand. I thought—"

"You thought all demons were bad." She wiped her eyes with the back of a hand. Her human-looking, skin-covered hand, with only a tinge of gray. In fact, its tone appeared more *periwinkle* in the light…if Ashton was choosing a paint color.

"I'm sorry. This is new for me too." Ashton wanted to believe her, but she had to be sure. She'd been played by a demon before.

Ashton couldn't read her expression. Was she going to elaborate on some monstrous scheme? Or was she about to come clean? Ashton's stomach twisted.

"I was created by Prince Cillian when he first arrived to find *you*." She started walking again, then looked back, waiting for Ashton to join.

Ashton shook her head to shut down her brain. She would listen first.

"Hicks doesn't remember, but I went to your high school. I was the one who found you and Mason. I'm sorry, but Ian created me to become his eyes inside your world. You must understand, when a higher-level demon raises a lesser demon into a fade, that fade owes them their life."

Ashton followed a half step behind, working hard not to interrupt. If this *demon*—and that's what she was—was going to spill her story, then Ashton didn't want to miss one line. She shuddered at the thought of Kali spying on her and Mason. That act alone had brought Ian into her life. Into Mason's life. And ultimately caused the death of her adopted parents. She swallowed the bile rising in her throat.

No. She wouldn't react. *Yet.* She would hear Kali out because that's who *she* was.

They returned for their second loop around the perimeter. Ashton, enthralled in the story, had forgotten to check the back of the truck to see if Zander had gotten out or if he'd fallen back asleep as Mason would have.

"I felt it the night Ian was banished." She tucked her hands in Hicks's jacket pockets. "My chest burned. My limbs froze. I could barely breathe."

"Where were you?"

"I was in Ian's warehouse, in the city. He had big plans. He was going to make more of us and start a new realm. A safe world away from his brutal family." Her smile warmed, as if he'd promised her a real future.

Then her expression fell. "He'd been planning for a long time. But he needed more power for the realm to sustain any backlash from his father. Before we found you, I'd been helping him gather energy from the minerals in this realm. Then I knew."

"Knew what?"

"Mason's mother had been using positive and

negative energy with her earth materials. That's how I found her…I'm a tracker. When I discovered you through Mason's mother, it was unexpected. Centennials are hard to find. Ian knew whatever gifts you gained in your transition would be exactly what he needed. I followed you at your school and learned more about Mason and Mia Deed's crystals.

"After you graduated and transitioned, Ian took over. He had me wait for him in the warehouse. I remained until one night I fell to the ground, writhing in pain for hours. I thought I was dying." She tightened both arms around herself. "Then it faded away, and…I was still here. I was still me, without him."

"Oh my God. You've been alone this whole time?"

"I wish." She moved forward again, beginning their third loop. The crunching of the forest seemed softer in the daylight. "Kelvin found me soon after. He'd somehow learned everything Ian was up to, taking Ian's plans to a deeper, frightening level. But I—" She turned, grabbed Ashton's hands.

Ashton glimpsed down, somehow expecting her fingers to spark with the contact. When they didn't, she peered into Kali's charcoal eyes.

"I want to be the *me* that Ian made. He didn't want anything in return after I found you. Which, I'm sorry about that." She let go, rubbing fallen strands of hair from her eyes. "I wanted a chance to be free. That's what Ian wanted too in his own distorted way. And for a while, I thought I was. But then Vin showed up, holding my existence over me."

"What does he want?" Ashton looked through the trees, as if Vin and his cronies might be watching. There were no birds. No scurrying squirrels. It was strangely quiet.

"He discovered my tracking skills and forced me to cast a spell over the city."

"You're the one—covering the city with a force field?"

"Force field?" She shook her head. "It won't protect anyone. But it will hide what Vin's doing from his father and the other realms."

Ashton pieced together the mental puzzle, but the outside edges were fuzzy. "How are you doing it?"

Kali glanced down at the rugged terrain. "Energy lines surround the city, but this place here..." She stomped the ground. "This location is like a conduit for all of them. The force hums in my veins. That's how I found it."

Ashton's head spun with questions. "Mason's mom used crystals and stones, both blessed and cursed, to hide from the realms. Is that something *anyone* can learn to do?" She locked eyes with the face before her—somehow more human now.

Kali's teeth tugged her bottom lip. "There are all kinds of lower demons. I was—*am*—a tracker. So, yes. There are others that could probably manipulate crystals this way. But they'd have to be made into fades, and they'd have to have the knowledge I learned from watching Mason's mom."

Ashton's brows arched. She wanted to believe Kali was under duress. That she had stalked them out of force and survival. But if she was a tracking kind of demon, there had to be others. And maybe it wasn't so hard to learn what Mia had discovered with her crystals and stones.

"It wasn't personal." She continued her circle.

"And it's not all me. Ian found an energy booster to hold up what I created. I did my part. But now I'm choosing to be free."

Ashton's mind roiled. "If you're the link hiding the city from all the realms, he's not letting you go."

"That's why you keepers need to do *your* job and stop him." She gazed over her shoulder. "I'm counting on you. And if you're the Centennial, this shouldn't be impossible."

"Wait a minute. Did he know we'd come back? Or did he lure us with the situation at the Dream Realm?"

"Once he learned about Max Deed and Ian's book plans to increase the fear factor in humans, he took it to the next level. He knew you'd do anything to squelch the book's release. He needs it out there but doesn't want the Dark Realm to know. So, he used me to seal up as much of the area as possible."

"What do you mean, seal up? No one can leave?"

She shook her head, long black pony swaying. "People can come and go as they please, but if they think they know something from inside the boundary spell, they'll forget as soon as they leave."

"Mia never spoke of anything like this."

"I don't think she knew what she had, as Ian didn't know the vastness of what he had. A lot of what I figured out was using her blessed and cursed stones with the hum I feel in my veins. I guess it is a me-thing." She peered up at the sun.

Ashton rubbed her temples, information overload. "So, why mess with Michael Hickson? He's innocent in all of this."

Kali turned to walk the circles back the other direction. "Michael was the only person I knew to connect the two of you. Even if I hadn't told Vin, he would have found out because of his angel blood, however diluted in his family line. It works in extremely convincing ways."

Ashton remembered the strange dream-summoning she'd experienced with Ian.

"The higher-ups can read us. I'm nothing but a tracking *hound* to them. And Michael was nice to me." She looked down.

"Hicks is nice to *everyone!*" Ashton's voice blew past whisper. They both froze, glances darting toward the tent.

Nothing.

Ashton blew out a breath.

"I got his parents out before Vin could hurt them. I'm *protecting* him now." Her strides escalated.

"How? By hiding in the woods. You can't keep him here forever." Ashton pulled her to stop.

Kali brushed her hand away and increased her pace. "By creating this bubble on the frayed edge of the energy lines. I'm hiding him in a fold of Vin's own power, to give *you and your keepers* time to destroy him." Her voice rose, along with her sense of urgency.

Ashton leaned against an old cedar, her mind whirling with her gut. Kali kept moving along her path finishing her ritual. Where was Mason? Zander had mentioned a fire, with orders to stay put. But she needed to make contact soon. If Kali was telling the truth, how long could she keep Hicks safe?

Ashton squatted to her knees, chin in hands. If the northwestern part of Washington was essentially locked up, that would help Zander's and her plight in dulling the fear in humans. If there were a smaller number of dreamers to calm, that would be easier.

Kali strode up, blocking the sun and pulling Ashton's worries to the shade. "Please. Do what you came here to do. I will keep Hicks away from Vin, but I don't know how long we're safe here. Vin will discover soon that I'm gone."

Ashton needed a bathroom, a shower, a hairbrush, and time to think. There were souls falling in Reverie and a fire in Ian's warehouse. A ticking sensation amplified in her head, and not the familiar clicks of a solution, more the frantic pressure of time running out.

"Do you know what's happening in the other realms?" Ashton's thoughts ran laps, thinking about the swimmers in Reverie.

Kali shook her head, shifting enough to let the sun pierce through. "I don't."

Ashton blinked, an image of her standing in Rory's office asking for more responsibility washed over. She was so sure of her abilities then. After one battle, she'd thought she could take on anything.

But wait—Rory hadn't hesitated to send her to Reverie. She still believed in her. Was she overthinking what she needed to do, forcing a solution when instead, she needed to trust her abilities and let the answer fall into place.

"Well?" Kali leaned the other way, and the contrast in light flashed behind her. It felt symbolic, like Ashton's previously snuffed light had illuminated. Her ability was always there…even in the dark. She'd learned that as a human. Hadn't she told Mason, never give up?

Ashton let the warm sun seep through her pores. She smiled, absolutely positive her adopted parents were looking down on her this very moment. They had always been proud of her. Yet she *was* stronger now.

"Are you okay? What's happening in the other realms?" Kali's dark eyebrow hitched.

"I'm sorry. It's a lot of information." She put her hands on her chest and sucked in a breath. "The souls in the Dream Realm are falling. Do you know anything about that?"

Kali shook her head. "I don't."

"Never mind. I'll go back and—" She glanced toward the truck. *Zander*!

Kali folded her arms, peering into the tree above them. "I think he belongs to you."

Ashton hopped up, following her gaze to Zander's hawk perched in the branches.

"You knew?"

"Of course." She winked. "The spell to hide us here creates quite the buzz in the animal world. Haven't you noticed the forest is pretty quiet?"

Ashton looked around. "Well, yeah."

"It doesn't hurt them. Critters just don't like the feeling and wander from the edges."

"How are you so much brighter—no offense—than the other fades I've come across? I mean…" Ashton's words tangled. "I've only seen a few, but you're different."

Kali smiled again, and she wore it well, her ashen skin almost ivory in the sun. "I was created with hope. Even if Ian's ways were faulty, he was trying to do something good. And—" She grinned. "—I learned a lot at your high school."

Ashton's eyebrows arched…definitely a turn of events.

Chapter 29

Reference Books and Purple Visions

Mason dropped onto a chair in his family room, a newfound layer of stress the only buffer between urgent thoughts and exhaustion. He glimpsed the kitchen under heavy lids, almost hearing his mom calling his four-year-old self in for dinner. Back then, his dad would have rounded the corner from his office. Mason would've dropped his dinosaur figurines and bolted toward the kitchen. His dad would have widened his stance, so Mason's nimble body could slide under his legs, across the tile floor, meeting his mom's feigned annoyance and his dad's holler, "Safe!"

Whoa! Mason sat upright.

The room was aglow with light, July's morning weather already warming the room. He hadn't thought about those memories in…forever. Glancing at Connor draped across the sofa and Des equally spread atop the corner chair, he rubbed both eyes.

They'd watched the warehouse burn through the night without any evidence Vin or his fades were dead or alive. Emergency crews had swarmed until daybreak when the blaze was mostly under control. The fire would surely be cause for an investigation. There hadn't been time for Mason's team to do their own inquiries. The most pressing, had there been a hidden portal out of that warehouse?

Hours had smoldered since checking in with Ashton. When they last connected telepathically, he'd accidentally woken her and was only successful decoding her mumblings about Hicks being safe yet still under Kali's strange spell. At the time, the warehouse was ablaze before him, so he sufficed to trust her. But trusting her right next to him was a lot easier than trusting her far away. He gritted his jaw.

"Why don't you three get some sleep?" Bronwyn called from the kitchen. "Or shower so you can wake up. I have coffee." Her voice carried a cheerful tone. She must have slept last night. Or maybe she'd adjusted to the Human Realm's thicker atmosphere. Whatever it was, her positive energy soothed.

Mason stretched before heading her way.

Connor rolled over, pulling a throw blanket over his head, but Des shadowed Mason into the kitchen.

"Anything new from Rory or Shunnar?" Mason sloped against the counter. If he sat down, he wouldn't get up again.

Bronwyn placed hot mugs in front of them. "Yes. Rory and Zander's teammate, Daiya, traced Vin's energy field to the Seattle ley lines. You'll never believe this, but that beast found a way to pull dream energy from *under* Reverie. Well, they *think* that's how he's creating his army."

"How?" Des spoke softly, glancing over his shoulder at a sleeping Connor in the next room.

"Shunnar's working out the technicalities. But Reverie's aether is somehow being drawn here like a magnet." She blew swirls of steam off her coffee. "Daiya believes it's from the same stuff Ian must have used to wedge in his realm between realms."

Mason drummed a finger on the granite. A fortified energy source made sense. "Maybe Ian didn't know how to make the energy work. He thought he needed Ashton's gifts, remember? He must not have known what Kelvin knows."

"Or hadn't figured it out in time," Des added. "Maybe Ian wanted it that way, his *own* private space to hide away from everyone without draining excess energy." Des held his cup mid-drink, something more on the edge of his thoughts. "But that wouldn't have lasted long without the realms taking notice."

"No. Vin's obviously not afraid to think on a larger scale." Bronwyn set her cup down. "He's managed to magically cut Seattle off from the rest of the world, realms included."

"Without their own knowledge or that of the Dark Realm." Des scratched his head. His ropes of hair dangled over the counter, dark eyes weighted. Mason shagged his fingers through his own long tangles. "Kelvin's not only more violent, but intentionally sloppy. Posting videos on the *internet*?" He glanced at Mason as if to check his vocabulary.

Mason nodded.

"That fight on the lawn had to have alerted his father. Pulling in our healers to shadow memories still causes unbalance. They can't mend everything," Des whispered.

"That's just it." Nigel stepped into the room, freshly showered and geared up. "He's concealing *everything* under that blanket of energy. From everyone. We need to figure out how he's doing it."

"And annihilate him." Mason slapped his hand

onto the countertop. The kitchen silenced as the smack ricocheted into the quiet morning. Mason's eyes grew wider than the pain shooting through his palm. He glanced over at Connor, starting to stir.

Bronwyn offered her mug to Nigel with a small peck on the cheek, then tossed another pod into the machine.

"I just want this to be over." Mason swallowed down the burn of emotions when something tugged his thoughts. "Then again, if I wasn't trying to save my dad, our realms would be busy managing keeper business. Would we have even realized what was happening here?"

"Not right away. But more importantly—*how* is he gathering the aether?" Des leaned on an elbow.

If Des was stumped, then what the hell? Mason and Ashton were the newbies. When the ones who should know what was happening *didn't*—then what? Wasn't there some kind of reference book on all this?

Mason slammed down his mug, coffee sloshing, his mind flashing to Ian's estate. *Reference books.* How many demons kept a library in their lair? "Ian had a room full of books, modern-looking, old, and even my dad's manuscripts. He must have been researching how to pull everything off without notice." He swiped the spilled coffee with his hand.

"Makes sense." Des set his mug on the island. "He figured out when our Centennial was returning. That's never happened before. But Ian's sights were obviously smaller than his brother's. Vin's simply picked up where Ian left off."

"And maybe the plan—or how they activated the plan—is in a book."

"We'd be looking for a needle in a haystack." Mason threw his head back, eyes burning with exhaustion.

When nobody responded, Mason opened his eyes. His team stared.

"Why would we look for a needle in a haystack?" Nigel seemed to speak for the group.

Bronwyn leaned in next to her mate. "I think it's one of their sayings, meaning...?" She glanced at Mason.

"It means this book could be anywhere, and who knows how much time we have." Mason stood straighter. "We need to get into his hidden realm. What if *whatever* power he's rigged up under the greater Seattle area mars it for life?"

Des interrupted. "We can't storm in there without a—"

"I know, I know, without a *plan*. Then let's hurry up and make one!"

****

Ashton gripped the plumy neck of Zander's hawk as they soared low over the forest. Every bone in her body ached after adjusting small enough to fit. The fact that her bones constricted to another size to fit atop any hawk still messed with her mind on a good day. But here? It was already difficult to use her special gifts in the Human Realm, the atmosphere so dense. She didn't have to shrink so small in the Spiritual Realm.

The plan was to travel to the wood's edge, a risk to fly together where others might see them during the day, but they needed to get home. And fast. She didn't have a mental connection with Zander like they would have had they remained destined. Ashton pressed against his back and tried to relax. The level of trust she had with Mason was not holding true with Zander—not that he wasn't skilled at flying, but everything felt wrong.

She cringed against the July breeze whipping in their flight. That was precisely why she needed to sort everything out. The sooner she deciphered the souls, the sooner she and Mason could return to some kind of normal and the safer human dreamers would be. A win-win all around.

This was where she'd expected Mason to say something snarky in her mind about overthinking their situation. God, she missed him. She had so much to process, like what was going on with Hicks and Kali with her circles and crystals and talk of *becoming* someone.

Zander dipped between trees at a slow, steady pace. Once they got to the edge of the tree line, they'd be on foot until they connected with the team. She'd tried to contact Mason, but he must not have been in hawk form. She was sure Zander had already spoken telepathically to Des or Connor, so she wasn't worried they couldn't get home. If anything, she'd call for an uber from a gas station.

Zander's hawk swayed gently, almost lulling Ashton to sleep. Almost. She blinked several times as he flanked the river below. The swirls of water reflected the bright summer sky, and she closed her eyes, letting her thoughts drift. Dreamily, the blue river from below became the indigo aether in Reverie, then violet bubbles in her mind formed shapes along the soul spheres until they all looked lavender. The river, the air, the bubbles, the souls, and now the flowers blooming in rows behind her mind's eye.

The lavender fields resurfaced from her vision in Reverie. Then one of her mom's paintings came to mind, but it wasn't lavender that she'd helped paint that day, in remembrance of her grandmother; they were irises. Abstract, tree-sized irises that could never have grown so big in real life. Her heart sank. That picture had burned in the house fire caused by Ian.

She readjusted herself, switching sides, so her other cheek rested against his soft down. Her vision grew stronger now. The giant purple flowers in remembrance. *Remembrance.* How did this all relate to lavender fields? Her mind started clicking like the pulses of a clock.

And then *click!* The pictures in her mind became clearer. What was the opposite of remembering?

Forgetting!

Click! The flowers didn't have to be lavender.

Click! They didn't have to be giant irises.

Click! The field wasn't a field at all, rather, a blanket. And the flowers were *her* purple flowers of invisibility. The same star-shaped petals she carried in her silver tin and whoever she touched while the tin was open became undetectable by sight, sound, or any other sense. They were invisible.

Forgotten.

She sat up straight and could tell Zander noticed. Had it been Mason she would have shared her insight through their paired telepathy. It didn't matter, she knew what to do. It wasn't her gift of unlocking she needed. It was the flower-power energy of invisibility. She needed to cover the souls with her flowers.

How would she trigger the magic without

physically touching the souls?

Her miraculous vision seemed impossible.

No. The tingles jarring her spine told her she was onto something. Maybe with the help of her team, she could figure the details out later. She kicked her heels into Zander's hawk sides.

"Whoops!" she laughed at the wind. *Not* Mason. "I don't know if you can hear or understand me right now, but I'm sorry I kicked you. I'm ready to get home. I have a great idea!"

Chapter 30

Inspiration

Zander shook out his hands after shifting. Vibrations zinged down his arms, both exhilarating and annoying at the same time. They reminded him of a different life not so long ago. His transformed future.

Perplexed and rubbing his sides where Ashton kicked him during the journey, he followed her out from behind the small cluster of trees. The temperature in the later morning was warmer here compared to the woods. Ashton had commented that lovely summers were Seattle's secret, since it usually rained the rest of the year.

"Des is meeting us there." He pointed at a small strip mall about a mile up the road. Ashton nodded but rattled on about a vision she had on the ride over.

"It must be the answer. If we can use the invisibility of the flowers, we could camouflage the whole realm from demons. I mean, technically it should work, *if* we find a way to extend the energy across a larger space."

She'd taken off her giant hoodie and tied it around her waist. Her hair was pulled back and her cheeks flushed, probably from shifting through the sluggish Earthly air. He could relate. Reverie was never this hot. He was starving after the flight, yet also curious about

306

her gift.

"Can you show me how it works?" He pulled her to his other side as they marched along the freeway. They were well out of the trees, cars blasting past them, and he needed her away from the edge.

"Sure, I always carry my compact of petals." She pulled a small silver case out of her pocket. "We can try at the gas station, with people around, so you can experience it." She wriggled her fingers, as if trying to be mysterious. The act came across charmingly silly.

He held back a smile. There was something comforting about how much she cared for the people around her. Even though she had seemed nervous before, she was making jokes now.

Daiya was never silly—only serious, unless she was teasing him about his need for order. But those were the quiet times when they were alone, when she'd tip her face and grin. She never did that for anyone else. Her charcoal-brown eyes were opposite from Ashton's bright blue ones, but somehow, they reached deep beneath his thickened skin.

How was Daiya's demon scratch healing? He didn't want her to be okay because she would go mad, but he needed her to be okay because he wanted her to feel whole. Because he wanted...*her*.

Ashton grabbed his arm. "Are you ready?"

They'd made it to the gas station, and she pulled him behind a giant, stinky garbage bin. Opening the compact, she tipped the lid around to fasten on the back, exposing tiny holes.

"The dried flower petals are inside." As she said the words, she started to vanish.

He smelled nothing but the trash, and if he hadn't

seen it with his own eyes, he wouldn't have believed it.

"Wow." Zander lifted a hand to touch her. When his fingers came to where her shoulder should have been, it moved right through.

Pressure gripped his arm, and he watched her materialize back into view. No, it was the other way around. He dematerialized out of view. "I don't get it. I touched you, and you weren't there."

She laughed. "It's amazing, isn't it? You can't see, hear, or touch me. Only I can bring you under the veil with me by touching you." Her face fell, the laughter dissipated. "So how can I possibly share this with the entire Dream Realm. How can I touch all the souls?"

That was a dilemma. "We'll talk to the team. Maybe Rory and Dalya can help?"

She pulled him around the building and into the store part of the gas station. He could see everyone, yet no one acknowledged their presence. Once near the restrooms, she opened a door and peeked in.

"Coast is clear." She called over her shoulder and jerked him into a stall. Once inside, she released his hand. He couldn't see her anymore until…he could.

She smiled, shaking the closed compact in the air.

****

Mason woke up with tiny tickles on the back of his neck, and he ripped out of bed, throwing knife drawn in a flash.

"Ash!"

She'd already jumped back, hands up, expecting his reaction. But she smiled, freshly showered and dressed. Her wet hair hung long down her back, making the neck of her shirt damp.

"Don't do that." He turned and threw his blade,

planting it into the opposite wall before whipping around and wrestling her down to the bed. "I've missed you. Are you okay?"

"Yes." She kissed his neck. "I think I've figured out a way to protect the souls."

"For real?" Mason pulled her up.

"With a slight complication." She raked her fingers through clumps of wet hair.

"Which is?"

"I believe if I—or we—can spread my purple flower power of invisibility over the Dream Realm, then the demons shouldn't be able to detect the souls. What I don't know is how to literally spread myself that thin."

Mason scooted back, his shoulders against the wall. Ashton sat crisscrossed facing him.

"It came in a vision, along with the ticking that rattles my brain when a solution to a problem evolves. I still need to talk to Rory."

"That's good, because so do I." Mason pushed his floppy curls to the side. "Remember that room in Ian's estate with all the books?"

She nodded. He imagined she saw the same thing in her mind. The library where she and Mason had fallen through an unexpected portal to her birth mother's oak. It led to where she'd watched Mason die and come back to life. Where she'd banished Ian. Now it was where Max and Mia worked to publish that terrible book about the truth of demons. Enough to create unfathomable fear in humans in hopes their dreams might surge with negative energy.

He sighed, the stress of reality more than taxing.

"I remember."

"We think Ian might have researched the hidden realm a lot longer ago than we thought. Vin's on a fast track with Ian's findings, and he's using the information to accelerate his own plans. He doesn't simply want his own realm. He wants a chunk of the human world, too—say Washington State for starters."

Ashton wrung her hands. If he had to guess, she'd probably thought of a solution and now another problem had reared its ugly head.

"Don't worry." He smoothed her fingers under his. "Something will work."

"I need to talk to Rory. I know she can help, or Daiya maybe?"

"Daiya?"

"From Zander's team. She's been researching with Rory. Maybe they could help with both our problems."

"Maybe." Mason stretched. "I think I finally slept last night. What's our timeline?"

She tugged one of his curls. "You must have been tired. I checked on you when we got back. You were out cold. Zander's in the shower now, then we'll all portal back to Toria to meet with the Blessing Council."

"What about Hicks?" He sat up in full alert.

"He's safer where he is."

"Which is where?" Mason couldn't imagine a safe place anywhere near Seattle right now. They were still waiting on confirmation the fades and Vin had been banished.

"It's a lot to explain. You'll have to trust me." She eyed him, chin tilted in challenge.

"Tell me."

"Kali's hiding him deep in the woods, north of here, by Bellingham. She wants nothing to do with Vin.

It was all an act to stay alive. She actually wants a life."

Ashton's blue eyes were soft, and they soothed his racing thoughts like nothing else. He rubbed both hands down his face. "What kind of life?"

"Trust me, remember?" She pulled his hands down, gripping them tightly. "She's not what you think."

"I know. She looks like a human pretending to be Hicks's girlfriend, but she's really a low-life demon. No way we're leaving him there." Spikes of agitation grew.

"We are. I believe her. We don't have the time or keeper power to cover all these areas. You've seen Vin's video!"

He nodded.

"Connor's been blasting social media with hoax posts and spreading fraudulent attacks against the videos. But people are freaking, and the book hasn't even come out yet."

"So why leave Hicks?"

"Because Kali is hiding him and his parents *from* Vin."

Mason had no words. His mind fluttered to Ian's library where he'd found his dad in a state of confusion. Now Hicks was folded into the mix of his unraveling life. But he was out of ideas. And energy. "If you think he's safer, then yes, I trust you." He didn't trust Kali, but the idea of being outside Seattle did seem safer.

She narrowed her eyes. No way had she believed he'd cave that soon. But their life hadn't been anything near ordinary these last weeks, and maybe he did need more than his impulses to go on.

"I think the details of how Ian created his hidden realm might be somewhere in his library. Remember all the books?"

She nodded, still holding his hands in hers.

"Maybe Vin found out how to extend that place here."

"In Seattle? Why?"

"Because he wants more territory, and he found Ian's human hiding place. I don't think he wants to start somewhere new when Ian may have already had this place mapped out." Mason rolled his eyes. "Can't let Daddy Lucifer find out."

Ashton shuddered.

Mason squeezed her hands. It was a creepy thought, especially when humans had no idea the other realms even existed. He didn't know the extent of the father of all evil, but if his own children feared him, then they should all be afraid.

"I need into that library. If we can see the direction he's going, maybe we can put up a roadblock." He let his shoulders slump. "I need this to be over."

"Going through his books is a good start. We don't have other leads." She leaned in closer. "Well, except that Kali is a fade who wants to be good, and she has the ability to manipulate crystals and stones to create energy…*magic*." Her eyes grew wide.

Mason studied her before responding. With the wood boarding up his broken window, his room was darker, making her blue eyes look indigo. Then he knew. "Like my mom?"

"Exactly, but there's more." She climbed to her knees, excitement brewing. "Kali's keeping Hicks at the edge of Vin's reach, at the border where he forced her to make Seattle invisible to the outside world. She's using crystals in a rectangular pattern, pacing three times in each direction every few hours. Like a spell."

Mason's jaw dropped. That was more ritualistic than anything he saw his mom do. "Sounds *witchy*."

Ashton shrugged. "I don't understand how it works, but she's hiding Hicks in the same fold of energy that Vin's using to hide Seattle." Her tone deepened. "Kali needs us to hurry and defeat Vin because she doesn't know how long she can keep the veil up. But if I can do something similar with my flower petals, maybe I *can* make the souls invisible."

"Let's go." He jumped up, throwing what little he'd brought into his duffle bag. They might as well move while Vin and his spawn were MIA. If the demons showed up later, their keeper teams could deal with them.

Ashton pulled him to stop. "Listen, we have a job to do. And we're going to do it. But Des is still assessing the warehouse damage and confirming whether Vin and the fades are actually dead—gone—whatever. Gavan's orders are to wait for that box to be checked before we move." She squeezed his shoulders.

"You're listening to your father now?"

"Birth father, *not* father." She scowled at him sideways. "Shunnar is in the field because we're low on keepers. I'm only following orders, not him."

He squeezed her hip bone, pulling her closer. "I'm know. I'm sorry."

She swallowed. "Connor reported that Bethesda is doing energy readings as we speak. Hicks is safe for now. And though I'll need to test the fruition of my invisibility idea with Rory, we have a minute." She pushed his hair back from his face.

"No time for mistakes." He perched on the edge of his bed, pulling her with him.

"Listen, we at least have an hour." She smoothed her thumbs over his hands. "You hungry?"

He was starving, as always, but at the moment her comfort was like a Thanksgiving feast. "I'm fine." He brushed her cheek, the tiny scar under her right eye. "Thank you."

"For what?" She looped an arm over his shoulder, pressing away all the angry knots along his neckline.

"For this." He took her chin in his palm and kissed her long and soft. She was as sweet as any dessert. Her freshly showered scent of lavender and honey was the only energy drink he craved. And her compassion and genuine love? She would never know how much he truly needed her.

Maybe she would.

He stifled a laugh behind locked lips when she pulled him closer, kissing him back with far more emphasis than he had. Somehow, lost in his own lovely thoughts about her sweetness, she took command. Hands roamed, breathing intensified, and in seconds they were lying back in the very spot Mason had slept. He wasn't tired anymore.

"Ash." He flipped her around, gently pulling her still wet locks over his pillow, so her back wouldn't soak through. "I love you more than you know."

"*Always*, right?" She moved both hands up to his face, shining eyes holding his own.

"Always." He kissed her again.

Chapter 31

Possibilities

Ashton stopped on the grassy knoll above Toria, breathing deeply. The air, so fresh and oxygenated, filled her soul. When she glanced around, the various members of their patchwork teams were doing the same. How had she ever survived in the Human Realm for eighteen years?

No wonder she'd suffered from asthma.

Their group moved along the trail, Ashton with Mason, Connor and Des behind them, Bronwyn and Nigel following, and Zander trailing last. When Ashton glanced over her shoulder, Zander was pretty far back, taking in the scenery.

Realization hit her.

He used to live in the Spiritual Realm, far longer than she had. Maybe he'd never made it to Toria, but from what she'd learned, Valley was close by and most likely filled with the same crisp air. She'd have to ask him if the same blue horizon with fluffy white clouds pushed around by a constant refreshing breeze were there too.

Mason squeezed her hand. Toria was in clear view now, and as always reminded Ashton of a fairytale village. It wasn't a town of magic, witches, or elves, but more colorful houses with thatched roofs, quaint cafes, and lanterns swaying from tree limbs. The town was a storybook and now the place she viewed as *home* more and more every day. If they could finish this mission, she could get back here and start living her new life.

Unless chaos *was* her new life.

"Head straight to the assembly house." Des's deep voice called from behind.

Mason quickened his pace, and Ashton impelled her legs to match his stride. Urgency pinged off his shoulders. Hopefully, this meeting would confirm that Vin and his fades were banished. Then they could publish that blasted book, free Max from his binding, and manage the aftermath…which got her thinking about the flowers.

"Mas, I still need to figure out how to transfer the flower's invisibility to the souls. What if it isn't possible?"

"What if it is? Ash, trust your visions. You're the smartest person—keeper—I know," he stressed as they strode forward. "Talk to the council. Share your idea."

No time to respond because they were there. Ashton climbed the assembly building's steps, the age-old trees blowing overhead. She glanced at the gardens, still blooming as they had been when she'd last walked through with Zander. Knowing the portal to the Dream Realm was right down the path roused her heart for the sinking souls, and for Max and Mia, still stuck in Ian's hidden realm.

She stomped through the door Mason held open. They had work to do.

Within minutes, various team members sat around the large wooden table, sapphire lights from each corner casting a soft blue glow. According to Gavan, who Ashton refused to look at, the Blessing Council would arrive momentarily.

Ashton had hugged Adam and Hannah as soon as they walked in, two of her original cast she hadn't seen since they'd all split up. The remainder of their group was with Shunnar on patrol. The realms were short-handed with all extra keepers supporting internally.

"Daiya," Zander voiced aloud, then snapped his mouth shut at the attention drawn. He rose from the seat next to Ashton, slowly, as if she hadn't heard the eagerness in his voice and greeted his teammate or whatever she was to him.

Peeking to see Mason still talking to Adam and Nigel, Ashton noticed Bronwyn and Hannah catching up on her other side, parts of their conversation weaving in and out of earshot. But Ashton wasn't eavesdropping; her mind was stuck on how to spread invisibility flowers atop the souls. She needed to talk to Rory, who she'd expected to come in with Daiya, though she hadn't.

But Daiya. She walked in on her own, no crutches or help. Her sleek black bob swooshed along her chin like an exclamation point. Had she finally healed? Ashton stared as the snarkiest internal keeper marched up to Zander and pulled him in for a hug. It seemed like such an intimate moment for them, especially since neither showed affection nor emotion.

"Can we talk?" Gavan's voice intruded.

Ashton pulled her gaze from her new friend and his *maybe* more than teammate and glared up at the chief of casts. Gavan was the keeper in charge of their mission, and the man who'd left her birth mother when Ashton was a baby, all because she'd been chosen as the new

Centennial.

She raised her eyebrows in response.

"Des mentioned your idea to help the souls. Your invisibility gift with violettias."

Of course he did, but she wasn't upset. They were running out of time.

She sat up. As unnerving as it was to see she resembled him, she would never describe her own eyes as piercing. The icy blue, though, was a match.

"Can you tell me more about it?" He sat down next to her. "I'd like to process the concept before the council arrives, although I have passed the information Des shared to Rory."

She glanced at Mason, knowing he'd already caught a glimpse of what was happening, one of his eyebrows arched. She could handle Gavan. She'd proven him wrong before.

"So that you can plan a way for me *not* to be a part of the mission?"

He exhaled, more as if steadying himself than exasperated by her snippiness.

But she didn't know him well enough to read his tells. Maybe this was Mr. Calm and Cranky's way of dealing with opposition.

"We can't very well carry out your gift without you." He pushed his already short dark hair off his face and leaned in closer. "Ashton, when this is over, I would like to discuss what happened between your mother and me, after you were born. If I've learned anything from how you handled the situation with Cillian, you are worthy of your role. Your Centennial knowledge linked our realms with strong, positive energy. I apologize for not trusting your warrior inside.

Can you please elaborate on your plan?"

There it was. Compassion she hadn't expected to see.

Tearing her gaze from his, she scanned the room. No one seemed to notice their conversation, except for Mason, who was inching his way closer even as he spoke with Adam.

She took a breath. "Are you being honest?"

"I don't waste time with lies or formalities." His frosty eyes peered into hers. "You are my daughter, and I have more to say to you, but this isn't the time." He stopped abruptly, obviously done sharing, waiting for her to elaborate more about her plan.

Or possible plan. She smoothed a few stray hairs into her ponytail. They'd tickled her cheek, which prickled her nerves. Then she swallowed. "I'm not sure how much Des told you, but I had a vision about a lavender field, then a painting I'd made with Mom— my adopted mom." She squirmed in her seat. "The painting was abstract with tree-sized irises. As the images blurred together, I saw the soul orbs floating under Reverie. I didn't understand the connection until I remembered the purple flowers of invisibility. What if *they* were the giant irises? What if the lavender fields from my vision didn't literally mean lavender fields but my gift of inconspicuousness. Maybe it was an image of how a purple blanket of invisibility might look covering the souls in the Dream Realm?"

"Interesting." He scratched his chin, and she saw dark traces of stubble. He looked down at a slight angle, and she recognized the movement for speaking telepathically, maybe to Shunnar. She had no idea if he had a new mate, since he and Althaia weren't together.

"Have you worked with Rory on transmitting your gift to more than one keeper at a time?"

She sunk back in her chair. "There hasn't been time."

Gavan was quiet for a moment longer, his glare on the wood floor before looking up, lips sealed. He shook his head as if shocked at what he was about to say. "What if we brought Mia back?" He visibly gulped, Adam's apple bobbing. "Do you think her knowledge of minerals and crystal energy might be of use?"

Her eyes bobbed as much as his larynx, which got her thinking of apples and the color red—glowing red like the eyes of those new demons in Reverie—and her mind began clicking. "Yes!" she blurted pushing up from her chair. Mason was there in an instant, hand on her back.

"Ash?"

Everyone in the room who wasn't standing before found their feet. Those already standing stared her way.

"Sorry—" She clamped a hand over her mouth. The clicking pounded behind her temples, her shoulders, and vibrating knees. "I need to see Mia, right now."

Her teammates rushed closer, and Mason put up an arm as if to brace her from a riot.

"Everyone, sit," Gavan ordered, and the room halted in their inquiry and obeyed. He stood at the end of the table demanding attention. The room obliged, although Mason's eyes were on Ashton's. She was relieved to have his arm draped across her shoulders, grounding her. The clicking echoed through her body like it had never done before.

Just then members of the Blessing Council poured

in through the main doors. The air in the room lifted, and Ashton was sure if Mason let go, she'd take flight. Everyone stood to greet the three representatives from the Dream Realm and five from the Spiritual Realm.

Mason helped Ashton stand.

"Thank you for your patience in our delay. The crisis in Reverie is beyond grave." Nurzhen bowed his head to the group, white robes shimmering under the lanterns.

The council members, dressed in their typical silky garb, Dream members in indigo and Spiritual members in ivory, also wore looks of concern. They bowed their heads in greeting.

As the last council member's head lowered in acknowledgment, a familiar tune hummed in the back of Ashton's mind, sapphire light melting over the already blue lanterns in the assembly room corners, a glow so great Ashton squinted until her eyes shut completely. The melody from inside her mind flooded through each limb and finger and toe until she transcribed the blessing from the Angel Sandalphon.

This only empowered her more, and the trembling that had rattled her body stilled. A refreshing chill swept over, followed by warmth, before the music dispersed with the bright blue lights leaving a soft whirr in its place. She opened her eyes to see that every teammate appeared more relaxed. More confident.

Whatever they had to do, whatever battle they needed to endure, they would gladly accept the challenge.

They would fight.

She would fight.

Chapter 32

Ley Lines and Reverie

Ashton held her head in her hands trying to hold tight to the blessing they'd all received.

"From what Rory and I have researched"—Daiya flipped the pages of her notes—"we can't find a power strong enough to sustain away from its source. However Mia managed her stones and crystals, it was on a smaller scale. We don't understand how the evil-eyed demons are entering without detection. What we do know is that without Ashton physically touching the souls, which she cannot do, there's no known way to spread her gift."

"We must be missing something." Ashton spread her fingers atop the table, pressing her palms into the wood to ground her thoughts. The ticks and clicks had returned in her brain, swirling in hues of crimson and lavender, as if on the verge of springing with a solution. There had to be a way to connect the creepy red eyes of those strange demons and her ability to channel the invisibility nature of the flowers to the souls. *Violettias*. Gavan had called them by the name Rory had taught her. But collectively, they would always be purple flower power in her own mind. *Her* gift. There had to be a way to share them with an entire realm.

"We've only seen a couple of red-eyed demons.

The one that almost got to Ashton—" Zander glanced at Mason, his inhale drawing attention.

Ashton squeezed his arm, whispering, "That we killed." Then aloud to the group, "But now that I think of it, I was already outside the nest of souls."

Daiya put down her notes. "The one that scratched me was inside, but on the outskirts, along the edge. Remember?"

Zander stood, pushed in his chair. His jaw flinched as if he chewed on some kind of revelation, but Ashton didn't know him well enough to know how he processed information. It struck her then: there were two keepers in this room, her birth father and her first chosen mate, who might have been the most important beings in her life, had she not been chosen as Centennial.

But she had.

And there had to be a reason for that.

Her mind played its tune, like an orchestra cadenza building to climax, the volume in her head growing. She pushed back from her chair. "The red-eyed demons, they're *conduits*. They don't seem to be extracting energy *from* the souls. Maybe they're keeping a line of energy *open*." Her voice scratched a little in its delivery, but she was confident.

Zander added, "That makes sense. Vin would need a power that didn't have to be syphoned and refilled."

"It must be connected to the ley lines that Kali spoke about." Ashton worked the puzzle pieces together. "She used energy from outside Seattle."

"Kali?" Gavan stood. "The fade claiming Vin to be its brother?"

Ashton faced her birth father. His head tilted as if

valuing what she had to offer. "Ian created her. Originally, she worked against us. After his banishment, she tried to live her own life in the Human Realm, but Vin found her and forced her to finish what Ian started." Ashton rolled back her shoulders. "We already discovered a shield around Seattle. Turns out Kali created it, to hide Vin's actions from all the realms."

"How?" group members asked at the same time.

Ashton studied the room. Everyone looked tired. They'd never battled anything like this before. A recent glimpse of her cast cheering their first demon kill at Toria's local café crossed her mind. If only she could go back to that time again, when her cast only had one job, and they knew how to do it.

Nurzhen nodded for her to continue. She'd almost forgotten the realm representatives were there, they were so quiet. Mason touched her leg, drawing her attention, his offered encouragement to keep going.

She sent him a half smile of thanks, nodded to the council, and locked her gaze on Zander. He had to have overheard her conversation with Kali the morning she spilled her guts and begged Ashton to do what their team had originally planned…get the demon book out, tone down the human fear, set Max free, and banish Vin.

"Ashton, how did she create a shield so large?" Gavan brought her back to the reality she was trying figure out *as* she explained.

"It was Mia's stones and crystals. Kali had been spying on Mason's mom." She glanced at Mason. "Ian created her to find me, but she found Mia first."

Mason rubbed a hand down his face. This news

had to cut deep. She squeezed his hand, tried to relay that it would be okay. But he'd blame himself for *another* circumstance where *his* family caused a greater danger.

"That's it," Zander blurted. "The red eyes. *They* must be the crystals transferring a constant stream of energy from Reverie to the ley lines. It's the eyes, not the demons."

The color red filled Ashton's mind again. She rushed to Zander, her mind clicking with every step. She barely glanced at the assembly staring at her. "Ian could have already had those red-eyed beasts down there. Keepers just hadn't come across them yet."

"Maybe Ian only had *one* conduit-created-demon, enough for his personal needs. If it stayed on the outskirts, avoiding the souls, we could have easily missed it." Zander shook his head. "But his brother wants more than that. And with the information Ian left in his realm, plus the skills Kali learned from watching Mia—"

"My mom was only trying to hide herself." Mason flew to his feet.

"That's just it." Zander glared at Mason. "She used blessed and cursed stones to do so. I heard Kali say her old demon form was a tracker. They're like hounds in your terms." He returned his focus to the group. "But Kali paid attention at the high school. She learned more than collecting information about Ashton and Mason. She studied Mason's mom, and how Mia caused a small trickle of energy to hide behind. Kali created—"

"A rushing river." Ashton finished, cut her attention to Daiya. "Is the energy source from the aether in Reverie or the ley lines?"

"Could be either or both. I need to talk to Rory." Daiya addressed Gavan. "We need Mia."

"She won't leave without Max." Adam, their teammate who'd sat calmly listening, as always, spoke up.

Gavan declared, "It won't be a choice."

Ansel, his green eyes weighted, spoke. "I've been on Adam's team at the hidden realm. He's right. Mia doesn't follow orders. We've tried to get her out before. She won't leave Max."

His hair was spikier than Ashton remembered, and he had a full beard. Time was different in every realm, and Ashton's gut wrenched at the thought of everyone working overtime to help the souls.

Mason gripped the table edge with both hands. "She will if I take her place."

Ashton pried Mason's fingers from the table's edge. She made haste in the moment, his heart pounding like irregular blows in a sparring match. He was down, figuratively speaking, and the only way he could recover was taking matters into his own hands.

"Do you really believe your mom will leave either one of you there?" Ashton reasoned as the room blurred behind his eyes.

"I'll convince her so you can find whatever crystal magic you need to cover the souls." His voice was firm.

But Ashton knew his heavy heart. It was *his* parents causing the rift between realms. She'd worn the same look at his mom's human funeral when they were children…when she vowed to never let him break.

"If this works the way we believe, with Vin pulling a constant line of energy between the ley lines and Reverie, then time is of the essence." Gavan's voice was firmer.

Ashton glared at her birth father, but Mason, relieved for the snap back to reality, opened his mouth to insist. He could convince his mom to return, and at the same time, try and free his dad again.

Before he could speak, Isleen waved a veiled arm, spreading violet sparkles like stardust. Her midnight hair danced about her waist as she addressed the assembly. "Regardless of Mia's knowledge of blessed and cursed stones, her homecoming is due. Mason, we have done all we can to enable the freedom of your father. Better to have one life jeopardized than more."

"What?" His heart sank. They couldn't mean to leave his dad there.

"Mason," Nurzhen began, taking position next to Isleen. "The teams reported your father is not your father any longer. His mind is nearly gone."

"What are you talking about?"

Adam strode around the table, gripped Mason's shoulder. "I'm sorry, it's true." His breath caught. "He's confused."

"He's in shock." Mason ducked from under Adam's hand and stormed to the corner of the room.

"Mia reports daily. She's trying to help him, but..." Hannah's voice faded beyond the voiceless onlookers.

Mason waited for someone to say something...anything to set his mind at ease. How could his dad go through all he'd endured for *nothing*?

Ashton pulled him aside, pressed on his shoulders to ground him. It was a trick from their earthly human days. She knew how to take care of him and his hyper-focused tendencies, and he let it happen because once again, he needed her. His dad's mind…gone? Could he be healed?

Ashton's voice was a whisper, though he felt her heartbeat through his chest. "Do you remember what you said to me in the armory, before our mission to banish Ian?"

"What?" His mind overflowed with questions and declarations and raw, hot anger about his family falling apart. "I-I can't think now, Ash." He twisted to move away.

She leaned in with all her might, knocking him off balance against the wall. "You said I was your *everyone* and your *only*."

The pressure seized his thoughts, and he swallowed dry air. "Yeah, I said that."

"Did you mean it?"

He swore under his breath. "Of course I did. Ash, what are you doing right now?"

She pulled back, so they could each stand on their own. "I think Mia is your dad's everyone and only. I believe you are too. I know he's been through more than any human could ever process. But remember, Max chose this path because he believed he was saving the two of you." She lifted her chin, her blue eyes glossy. "We owe it to him to do everything in our power to see it through."

"Are you saying we leave my dad there?"

"I'm saying we get Mia home first. We need her help. Then we worry about getting your dad back, and how to help him regain his health."

Her last words stung, but he shook his head trying to settle their little un-private moment. She was making one of her to-do lists to check off after completion.

Hands shaking, he tucked a strand of fallen hair behind Ashton's ear. Then he turned to face the group. "Fine. I'll get my mom to come home." *First*. He took a step toward the table. He didn't need to voice his second and third items on the list. He would take care of them on his own.

He sat down, and the tense moment shattered.

Daiya cleared her throat. "Wait...I have an idea that might involve only *communication* with Mia." Mason blinked her way. "She wouldn't have to leave Max."

The room stilled.

Zander nodded for her to go on, and she looked directly at Ashton. "Your vision about lavender fields. It wasn't about streaming energy *from* a source to each soul; it was about covering the souls so demons couldn't find them. Like camouflage."

Ashton's mouth dropped. "It was a giant blanket in my mind."

"And you related it to a painting you made with your mom. The abstract irises."

Mason reached under the table, resting his hand on Ashton's leg. He could ground her right back.

"As big as trees."

"That's it. The imagery of those massive flowers is the answer."

Ashton stood, knocking Mason's hand away. "The abstract." She put a hand to her head as if the clicking in her mind had returned. "I don't need to stretch my gift to every single soul. The energy is already there. I only need to *reshape* it."

Daiya swept her hair behind an ear, the short silky strands instantly spilling across her face. "Gavan, can you set up communication between Mia and the team? We only need her *expertise* on stones and crystals, not her physical presence."

Mason stirred in his seat. The thought of putting his parents in more danger haunted, though at least they'd be together. But more, was the book done? Had anyone heard from Vin?

"The timeline? How will we know when the book comes out?" Mason's mind churned. "If my dad's mind is in question, how does he finish the project, or if he has, how can he return home and market a book launch if he isn't well?"

Isleen chimed, "Our guess is the book will release through his last publisher without notice. The unordinary, as we know here, will appear ordinary there. Just as our healers mended the minds of the Centennial's family after Ashton's transition or with the memory work conducted at the police department after Kelvin's Internet spoil, all memories of those relating to Max's book will function as naturally as if Max was the orchestrator."

The assembly room door flew opened, and a fiery red head captured the attention of the room. "My apologies for the interruption." Rory bowed to the council. "Amit made contact. The book is out, fear exaggerated. The negative soul energy is at an all-time high."

"What does that mean?" Mason's mind fluttered between his parents' possible freedom and the realm's daunting reality. No way Vin would play by the rules of Ian's contract, and he still needed to assure Hicks was safe. But what about the souls?

"It means we have work to do." Gavan held up a

hand for everyone to stop. "Ashton, Daiya, Rory, standby for connection with Mia. Ansel, Hannah, Adam, back to your posts at the hidden realm. When will Mia check in again?"

Ansel responded, "It's different each day, but about every twelve hours. We have three to go before we need to return if I'm calculating the times between realms correctly."

"I'll help retrieve my parents," Mason blurted.

Gavan paused in thought, then nodded once. "Zander will join you. I need Nigel and Bronwyn at the border again. Shunnar is battling there as we speak.

Nurzhen raised his palms, and everyone bowed their heads. He muttered prayers and blessings over the mishmash of teams, before the assembly disbanded, and Mason felt a revived energy pulsing through his veins.

He was revving to go, but he had one small to-do item to check off before he could get his parents back. He extended his arm on the way out and swooped Ashton into the corner under a blue lantern. The rest of the room emptied like water rushing down a drain.

"Thank you." He muttered into her ear, holding her tight.

Ashton gripped his vest with both hands. "One thing at a time." She buried her face in his chest, and he rested his cheek on her head. "We will bring your parents back."

He pulled her chin up to kiss her, lingering to inhale her strength and energy as he always did. "You *are* my everyone and my only. I am lucky for that."

"Go free your parents. I'll be here solving the case of the souls." She laughed as if it were a typical Friday night in their earthly high school days.

He kissed her again. "I *always* love you, Ashton Nichols."

"I *always* love you more."

Chapter 33

Charoite

Zander crouched next to Mason, behind Ansel, Hannah, and Adam. The black, inky pool of sludge, portal to the hidden realm, loomed before them.

"You're kidding, right?" Zander snarled, disgust dripping from every syllable. He scanned the dark human woods surrounding them. About an hour's hike from Mason's mom's cabin, the unknown behind them seemed a better choice than what awaited them.

Mason stretched. "It's quick."

"Thankfully," Adam added, snagging Hannah's hand.

"Off we go—" Hannah yelped before Adam pulled her with him. The two disappeared under the bog, the floating debris hardly startled by their disturbance.

Moonlight glinted off Mason's eyes, as Zander nodded for him to go first. He gulped a breath and Zander followed, hoping the experience on the other side was at least as cooling as Reverie. He'd barely registered the time passing when he dropped onto dry ground.

Gasping, he inhaled only stale, stagnant air. Coughing used more energy than it was worth. Filtering in a shallow gasp of whatever oxygen cycled in this newly created realm, he searched the pale woods until he found his team, also dry as bones, staring back at him.

Adam and Hannah pulled on matching knit hats before Hannah announced, "We always wait there." She pointed to a section of trees looking identical to the ones they stood under.

Her voice was clear, but also faint in a strange way. Zander pulled at his ears as he looked for location identifiers.

"Sound doesn't carry well here." She adjusted her cap, hiding her auburn hair.

Hannah went on as they walked. "The estate's far enough from this portal *in*, yet closer to the portal *out*. We only know of three ways to this realm, one way in and two ways out. And we're pretty sure the gateway from the library…" She looked at Mason. "That might be the only one Vin and his minions know about. If they've come that way, we've never seen it. We only know how to exit through the back bookshelf. We don't want him tracking us near the other portals Mia showed us."

Mason pulled a throwing knife from his vest.

They were on the move again when Zander stopped. Looking at his feet, he tested a footstep. Mason stopped beside him, as if understanding.

"Like Hannah said, there's hardly any noise here." Mason stomped his foot. The thud from his boot barely registered onto the strange chalky ground. "No footprints either."

Zander shook his head.

Mason walked on, and Zander followed, gulping down his questions about the atmosphere. A half mile farther, the group halted behind a denser growth of stale trees. Adam and Ansel took watch at opposite points as if a routine they'd done before. Hannah pointed beyond them, at the top of a building.

"Vin's estate?"

"The only dwelling in the realm," Mason answered without looking back. His whisper evaporated like winter mist.

"We stand in the open and wait?" Zander scrutinized their surroundings. The forest was a blank canvas of colorless trees with grayish green leaves. The bark, grayish brown. The ground, a deeper shade, grayish mahogany. All the grays melded into the ashen sky above and the chalky ground below. He found a dim light above but—could it be the sun?

"Welcome to a demon-made sliver of hell." Mason smirked, brushing past him.

"And we don't just wait." Ansel smirked at his teammate. "It's more of a *stand until you blend with the trees* type of mission." His half laugh lost, without any breeze to carry it away.

Zander noticed their dark charcoal and black seam keeper gear blended perfectly into the dim spots between trees. He was thankful Adam had loaned him and Ansel matching uniforms.

Hannah leaned against a tree. "We can't go near the estate."

"What do you mean?" Mason turned around.

Zander was surprised Mason asked before racing into action. From what he'd picked up, the mystery keeper—appearing out of nowhere and taking his place as mate to the Centennial—seemed impulsive. He surely had the temper of someone who made quick decisions.

"Vin has beasts on watch from every direction. There are only four, but they're huge. And strong." She looked at Adam, eyes like glass.

"We lost three keepers in battle when we first came to check on Max and Mia."

Mason swore. "I know how to get in. I've done it twice before."

"When it was only Ian and his servants." Hannah put a hand on Mason's shoulder. "Now, it's guarded with gargoyle giants perched at each point of entry."

"Then how does my mom report?"

"Like this." Hannah pulled a small shiny stone from her pocket, dangling on a long, silky string. It looked like a mini planet Earth, clear blue and green with little strands of burnt orange winding its way through. "It's blessed blue apatite. Our healers provided it to help reach Mia through the muted energy."

Zander exhaled whatever breath still lingered in his lungs. Claustrophobia was already setting in. "She talks through a stone?"

Mason leaned in, curious.

"Yes. Through me." Hannah sat against a tree and lifted the string around her neck. She closed her eyes. The auburn hair poking from beneath her hat was redder in this hazy environment, the brightest thing in the whole realm. Was it a sign of hope or bloodshed?

"How long does it take?" Mason grunted.

Adam answered for his mate, as she concentrated. "Each encounter is different. Sometimes minutes, sometimes hours."

"We don't have hours, especially if that book is out there."

Adam put an arm across Mason's back.

Zander stepped next to Ansel. "How are you holding up?" he whispered to his friend.

Ansel's green eyes flickered like candles snuffing out. "I won't complain about my missions under the sticky-wet aether anymore. At least it refreshes. This muck is disgusting." He waved his hand through the stodgy air. "But more importantly, how was the Human Realm?" His question came with lifted brows and a probing smile.

Zander worried about his teammate. His friend. But he couldn't stop his smile at the mention of the Human Realm, which didn't feel natural. He shut it down as quickly as it registered. "I—" How could he put his feelings into words when it would never be possible. "I wouldn't hate going back."

Ansel's face lightened. "I imagine not. You researched the human world enough in your old life, right?"

Zander felt a stab in his gut.

His old life.

The one where he'd trained for years to pair with the Centennial. With Ashton. The whole reason he'd researched human ways. But that didn't bother him anymore. It wasn't Ashton digging under his skin of what-ifs. It was the wonder of the Human world. He could only hope to see it again.

Ansel swore under his breath. "Sorry. I didn't mean to bring up your past."

Zander put a hand to his friend's shoulder. "No, you're right. I did research, and it would be amazing to see more of that world. But we all know keepers don't choose their destiny." He smirked. "Duty calls."

Mason paced between a grove of trees, pulling

Zander's attention. "Can we at least move in closer? The debt's been paid. They must know we'd show up to take my dad home. What about the terms of the oath?"

"Wait—it's Mia—shhhh." Hannah straightened, one hand cupping the stone, the other pressed her temple.

Mason halted, though he still looked ready to blow.

Zander squatted down and stared at Hannah, waiting.

And waiting.

They all gaped in her direction for some miraculous response.

Ansel shrugged at Zander. He didn't know if that meant this was a typical amount of time or too long. Should they worry? He wanted to ask what was happening, but they had to all be wondering the same thing.

The woods were eerily quiet. Mason ran a hand through his hair. Adam stretched higher, peering toward the estate. Zander stood up and faced the way of danger with Ansel at his side, readying for anything.

Finally, Hannah rose.

"Vin is alive, inside the estate. The book release paid Max's debt, but Mia said he's too weak to move."

"I'm going in." Mason stormed past Zander, toward whatever danger awaited him. He hadn't even checked in with their small group. Did he think he was fighting solo?

"Wait." Zander gritted his teeth. Mason froze but didn't look back. "What are the orders?"

"We don't have time to wait for the channel to open." Hannah stood up. "Someone must go back. Check in with the council. And we need a stone called *charoite*."

"What?" Mason turned around.

"Mia said blessed charoite could transfer the energy from Ashton's flower petals to a larger span. But the details were mumbled. Your mom sounded distracted. I don't think they're safe anymore."

"Time's up." Mason ran both palms down his face. He looked as if he could blow.

Hannah shot up a finger. "Wait—" Her other hand gripped the stone around her neck. She crouched low to the ground. Adam moved to stand over her.

Mason shifted from foot to foot. Even Ansel was on edge, his eyes scanning the dry woods. Finally, she reached for Adam to pull her up.

"It was Bethesda. With the book released, the Pacific Northwest is in jeopardy."

"Already?" Mason spit out.

"Time is different in each realm, remember? But I revealed the charoite Mia suggested. We've been ordered back to Toria. Now."

"Nope." Mason backed away. By the expression painted across his face, he didn't care about orders. Zander opened his mouth to argue, to remind him what was at stake, when the reality of what Mason was fighting for rang true.

Then the guilt of what *he* should have fought for clanged after. He'd never spoken his own mind after his reassignment. He simply followed orders and dealt with the confusion and questions on his own. *Duty.*

"Mason," Hannah pleaded. "We must go back. The souls are sinking by the thousands."

"You go. I'll get my parents out on my own." He strode up to Hannah, stopping for a moment of wordless understanding. He hugged her before turning and marching his way through the silent forest without looking at any of them.

"Is he always this angry and on edge?" Ansel shook his head.

Adam blew out a heavy breath. "He feels responsible for his demon blood. And the mess his family has created."

"We don't blame him," Hannah added. "He blames himself."

Zander could no longer hear Mason's footsteps, not that he would with the strange ground cover. "So," Zander whispered, almost afraid to break the quiet. "Where's the portal out of this hellhole?"

Chapter 34

Trap

Mason edged around a tree trunk, moving closer to the south side of the estate. The foundation of the house backed up to a chalky cliff, and from where he stood, it was a short twenty yards to the servants' door he and his mom had once entered, after Ian had abducted Ashton. She'd found a way to free herself through her gift of transference, but his parents wouldn't be so lucky.

Just as Adam had reported, four gargoyle monsters sat atop the rooftop spires, one facing each direction. While they appeared frozen in stone, Mason could imagine how dangerously alive they would become if even one of them detected his approach. His heart sank at the thought of the three keepers Hannah had mentioned, dying at their claws.

All for his family's mistakes.

No! He cracked his neck. Now was not the time to feel remorse.

He reached into the pocket holding Hannah's tiny leather pouch. It looked identical to the one Ashton kept on her weapon's belt, filled with soul spherules. All the riders carried them. Hugging Hannah had been genuine, as she'd helped keep tabs on his parents. But there had been more. He lifted the tiny bag of explosives, dangled it in the hazy light before pocketing them in his vest. He was getting past these monsters and getting *both* of his parents out.

Today.

Stepping out toward the entrance—*slam*—something pulled his shoulder. Ripped back, he landed on his rear. In a second, he flipped to his feet to face the threat, knives in both fists.

Two sets of eyes, Ansel's and Zander's, glinted back. Their arms were halfway up, as in don't attack, but both were ready to strike.

Mason's heart pounded out of his chest. "What are you doing here?"

"Helping you, mate." Ansel dropped his stance. Zander followed suit.

"What's the *plan*?" Zander smirked. "Or let me guess, you don't have one."

Mason wiped sweat from his temple and glanced across his shoulder. Had their disturbance alerted the stone demons? No movement. Exhaling, he faced the two internal keepers.

"I have a plan." *Of sorts*. He held up Hannah's leather pouch.

Ansel lifted a brow as Mason dumped the three pink marbles into his palm.

Zander nodded, perhaps remembering the weapons from his days in seam keeper training. "Soul spherules?"

"Four gargoyles. Three explosives. I figured it might cut the odds."

"Did you think about how to plant these without detection?" Zander asked. "And don't you need an—"

"Emotional connection?" Mason finished. He

342

offered a spherule to Ansel, one to Zander, then pocketed the third. "Vin *is* my uncle. And he's holding my parents here. I don't know how much more of an emotional connection I need."

"I thought…" Zander's forehead wrinkled.

Mason shook his head. The once seam keeper must be trying to remember how the spherules worked. Or maybe he knew exactly how they worked and worried about breaking rules. He seemed cautiously aware of following every instruction handed his way, including uprooting his life. Mason heaved a breath, the story sounded too familiar. In the larger scheme of things, he was relieved Zander had followed orders. He couldn't imagine his life without Ashton.

And he wasn't about to leave her or his parents. Time to get everybody back!

"It's all I have to go on." Mason stared past them at the house.

"Wait," Ansel said. "What do we do with these? What about the fourth demon?"

"We need *some* kind of real plan." Zander folded his arms.

Mason ran a hand through his hair, fingers catching in his matted mess of curls. He wasn't entirely sure how to use the spherules. "I think—I mean, I know they need an emotional charge. I know you need to whisper a name into them. What I'm wondering…" He trailed off, peering through the dull trees along the border. "The portals." He stepped farther back from the edge of the tree line, pacing. "Ashton said that once she whispered Ian's name into a spherule, all his lower demons went with him. But can we delay the explosion?"

Zander caught Mason's arm. "Do you mean to trigger them now, *then* plant them?" He shook his head. "How will you detonate?"

"The book is out. Fear is up. This—" He threw his hands into the air. "This is his new kingdom. And if it all works, then wherever these are, whatever connects to him, should *go* with him."

"Potentially…" Zander frowned, his typical stone face twisted in thought.

"We'll have to split up," Ansel slipped in, voice steady. He offered his pink spherule to Mason. "Here you go. Kiss it, whisper to it, do whatever you need to do. I can get us to the portals we entered and exited."

Zander simply nodded and held up his spherule.

Mason's mind churned at the thought of these keepers' lives in his hands. But what else could he do? Sacrifice his parents? Not an option. "Okay, I'll trigger them both. You two travel to the portal we entered, set one, then to the exit out of here. After that, go! I can do the rest."

"The rest of what?" Zander countered.

"I don't know. I'll get my parents through the portal in the library, then smash this last spherule into Vin's chest." He patted his pocket with the sphere. "Hopefully when this one meets with actual demon flesh, it will set off the others. If not, it should take down Vin and all his followers in this realm. At least I think it should." It didn't matter. He needed to act.

"How are you getting in?" Zander whispered through tight lips.

Ansel rested a hand on Mason's shoulder. "There's no way past those beasts." He angled his head at the gargoyles. "We have your extra soul spherules now."

They all stared, open mouthed as if about to suggest an idea, then closed their lips and let the silence knit them tighter in the already too-small realm.

Mason's head was about to explode when the fire they'd created at Ian's old warehouse ignited behind his eyes. "We need a distraction. Meet me on the other side once you're out. Althaia's tree." He threw himself onto the un-dusty ground, shifting awkwardly before peering up through hawk eyes. Two shocked faces stared down at him.

They wouldn't be able to read his thoughts, so he took flight, the gray sky greeting him like thick sludge. He arched his wings and soared straight up into plain sight. Before his next wing stroke, the gargoyle on the south side awoke, yellow eyes gleaming like the realm's missing moon.

Mason lowered his beak, aiming over the slanted curve of the horizon, until he was far enough away from the other entrances. In a blur he landed, shifting in one tripping motion, luckily catching himself.

Once he righted himself, he ran! Heading back in the direction of the house, he sprinted away from the spot he'd landed, zigzagging his way over small mounds of ashen nothingness, between muted trees, still somehow holding their shape in dry brittle forms. He ran, not looking back to see who or what might be following.

Finally, he latched onto a tree trunk and peered around. Any sounds he heard muffled in the atmosphere's eerie hush. Fictional gargoyles couldn't fly…only soar on puny wings. But these weren't storybook monsters. They were real.

He waited.

No sounds, as he'd hoped. They couldn't fly then. Peeking from the tree line bordering the estate, he noticed two of the statues missing. Two remained perched, awake, and on watch.

He glanced behind, nothing. To the left, nothing. To the right—

Whack!

A clawed paw struck his shoulder! The strike, meant for his head had he not ducked, ripped through the thick seams of his gear shirt. Mason tucked and rolled behind the beast.

Red blood seeped. The tingle of his healing abilities, delayed in the muggy realm, began a slow buzz. But he was back on his feet, jumping onto the demon's right haunch. Leveraging like a step, Mason thrust his body up, landing with a fisted throwing knife into the thick hide, a few inches down from its neck.

More blood. This time, the gargoyle's greenish-gray ichor spewed. Mason wiped the goo from his eyes as his opponent wobbled and groaned, toppling over.

Mason pressed on his shoulder to hold in the blood leaking from his own gash and trudged toward the back of the estate. Would the other demons smell his blood? Hopefully scents were like sound here…gone before detectable.

Looking up, he saw two demons remained. They perched at the front of the estate facing the direction the other two had disappeared. One was dead. *Where was the other?*

Mason gave another solid squeeze against his shoulder. At least the two on the roof were distracted. When he couldn't wait any longer, and pushed off the tree, ducking around the south side of the dwelling, his back against the cliff.

Still undetected.

He blew out a prayer of thanks for his ability to move swiftly, but also for the realm's inability to carry sound.

One of the gargoyles stalked toward the back of the roof. The fullness of its body was massive as if truly made of stone. Mason shuddered. It *was* stone, but from his distance, the texture appeared leatherlike or something thicker than even Vin's skin had been. The difference? Mason had been able to stab one of the gargoyle demons with his throwing knife. So, they weren't exactly like their master.

Mason held his breath, thinking about the soft spot along Vin's ear as he gripped his shoulder. He pressed his back into the mass of dirt—rock—whatever chalky substance this hidden realm was and waited for his cut to heal. Pain wasn't registering, only urgency and anger.

He thought about Bethesda, back in Toria. Then he pictured himself on her wooden floor, the eternal bright sun glowing through the tall windows, beaming across his face. He almost felt the serenity lifting his mood and inhaled a slow breath, however less cleansing.

It wasn't only his life depending on his ability to focus right now. It was his mom. His dad. His team. *Crap*! It was everyone in every realm because souls were sinking in Reverie. Because this place wasn't supposed to be.

It was *never* supposed to be real.

So…maybe it wasn't real.

He could hear, but not from a distance. He could see, though not far. He could feel, yet sluggishly. He huffed stale air from his mouth. Maybe rules *didn't* apply here. His plan—or haphazard-thrown-together-impulse-to-act—seemed more solid now.

He waited until the monster clambered to the front of the roof with its partner in crime. Wafting like wind to the estate's back entrance, Mason pushed himself against the stone wall, skating along to the kitchen window. Unlike the busyness on his last visit, the room appeared empty.

Without Ashton's gifts to break and enter, he pulled a blessed stone from his vest and traced a giant arc across the pane. The glass warbled until the arc, large enough for him to crawl under, dissolved, and he hopped through the illusion over the ledge and crouched on the marble floor inside.

Where are you, Mom?

Snuffed-out wall sconces left the room vastly dark, with only a hint of gray light falling through the window. After letting his eyes adjust, he made for the back staircase. No servants in sight. No sounds came from any of the rooms on the first floor.

He rounded up the staircase to the next level.

No one.

His parents had to be on the fifth floor, in the library. His dad had been there before, the same location with a portal exiting near Althaia's tree. But the eerie silence was *too* quiet for the loud and blaring Vin he'd encountered on his front lawn in Seattle.

Trap?

His breath released as he wound up to the next level and the one after that. Not a creak in the floor. Sconces lit the fourth floor, but still, no sign of demons, keepers, or servants.

He peered down the empty hallway. Not even a shadow flickered in the low glow. Looking back, he noticed scratches along the railing. His glare snagged on the small broken window, high above the landing. The entry had shattered from Bronwyn's entrance at their scuffle only days ago when he'd led his cast to retrieve Max. It was supposed to have been a simple mission.

Enough. He could self-loathe after he freed his parents.

Crouching, he climbed the steps with heavy caution. From his position at the top of the stairwell of the fifth and final story, he made out the two familiar doors across from each other. He knew the one on the right was the library and scanned the corridor for any shadow-hidden surprises.

The coast was as clear as it would ever be. This was it!

He took a weary step toward the library door, pushed his ear against the wood. No voices. No movement. With slow fingers, he twisted the knob, summoning every heist movie he'd ever seen. The door cracked open.

He pushed open the heavy wood and lamp light spilled across the floor. His eyes widened to the yellow radiance beaming off his parents' faces. They both stood, facing him, as if expecting—

His stomach plunged. Dad's expression was vacant, but Mom's stare held warning. One he'd never seen as a child but recognized within seconds.

Trap!

He glanced left before shifting and rolling right.

At that moment, Mom lunged to her left, hauling

Max behind a low bookshelf.

Vin stood in the center of the study—black shirt, black pants, black boots, without a stitch of heavy gear. Why wear gear when his skin *was* his armor. His dark eyes glowered over Mason as he stroked his black beard.

"Welcome, nephew," he chided.

"My dad's book is out. Ian's contract is complete."

"Max isn't your dad." He crossed his arms, seemingly unconcerned as Mia inched Max toward the back of the library. "That bargain was made with my brother, your *real* father I've learned. Perhaps this stepdad of yours made a new deal with your more persuasive uncle?"

Mason snorted at the truth of his bloodline and stormed closer, stopping only steps away. "There *is* no new deal." No way had Max been well enough to make a new pact. Seeing the man's apathetic expression proved that. Adam and Hannah had been right. He wasn't in his right frame of mind.

"Humans don't fare well living in otherworldly realms." Vin grunted. "It's taken a nasty toll on him."

"Then it shouldn't matter to you," Mason snarled. All he pictured was taking down this giant, inserting his daggered fist into his temple, and shoving the soul spherule down this throat.

But would he have the strength to do it on his own?

Would his parents have time to get out before he pounced?

Time ticked through the slush of space around them. He wouldn't look where his parents had gone, couldn't chance Vin tracking his gaze. How long could he stall? His parents had to make it through the portal.

But if there was a new deal, would he even make it through?

"Everything matters." Vin's stern voice brought him back.

It was now or never. Mason leapt with only one thought sent hastily to his parents crawling behind bookshelves. *Get through that gate!*

Chapter 35

Down, Down, Down

Ashton glanced at Daiya standing stoic on the edge of the dock. Reverie's pink skies lit up around her teammate's black hair like sprinkles on top of Sandalphon's blessing. Ashton crossed her arms, ready to jump. She wasn't happy about her original team splitting up again or being away from Mason, but she would do her part.

Daiya angled her body toward their support crew. In response, each member, wearing the realm's midnight blue uniforms, acknowledged with a heavy nod. It was a serious bunch, four females and three males. Ashton hadn't met the divers before, but she was relieved to have them despite their removal from the nest of souls. The aftereffects of violet spray misted from the waterfalls behind them, as if a final plea for resolve in their mission.

Amit strode from Nanna's central hut and stopped at the end of the dock. He pressed his palms together. "May the powers that be support your journey and the safe return of every sleeping soul." He bowed his head and stepped aside.

Daiya straightened her shoulders. "Let's do this."

Ashton tugged the strap across her chest one last time. The small backpack was situated snugly on the front of her body, lilac-colored crystals and violettia petals filled the pouches. Mia reported that charoite would transform emotions from negative to positive. And since they were blessed and used in combination with Ashton's gift of invisibility, they should negate the magnetism pulling down the souls.

Hypothetically.

Daiya dove like a blue streak of lightning before breaking the surface of aether. Their team followed suit down the line. Ashton held her breath even though there was enough oxygen and stepped off the ledge.

Their team of nine burrowed through the indigo atmosphere, daggers out to cut through the thicker aether that would come the deeper they swam. If Daiya's leg still hurt from her demon injury, she showed no signs. Ashton struggled to keep up but pushed on. She had only trained to ride on the back of Mason's hawk, to grip herself in one place and fight from her steed. This was entirely different, and her body pulsed at the strain. Slowly, the others seemed to fall back, one by one, placing themselves around her.

A new swarm of fear flushed through her system as she realized they were protecting *her*—because she was the only hope they had.

Pressure.

Before Ashton could overanalyze any further, their group stopped at the rushing watery wall that separated the nest of souls from the rest of Reverie. The iridescent pinks and blues were darker here, and she remembered they would become even gooier once she swam through the curtain-like divider.

No time for hesitation. She breathed in deeply, closed her eyes, and nudged her shoulder through the rushing force. Pressure sucked her body through, the weight of energy pressing down on her limbs. The actual minute it took to move through the wall seemed lost momentarily until she dumped out on the other side. Dizziness overwhelmed until her lungs adjusted to the heavier oxygen. The team didn't speak, only exchanged looks of determination.

Ashton *should* have been looking *up* where the buoyant soul orbs once created a miraculous light show upon her first visit. Instead, she looked *down*, her sticky breath catching in her throat.

The orbs of light had sunk deeper than she'd thought possible. Darkness enclosed as she peered below to find the souls. Dotted hues moved at a pace less relaxing and meandering than before. They now skittered with urgency, dropping and popping up again in the currents caused by the swimming teams underneath, starry night balls of light in a pinball machine.

Her team cut down along the wall of energy, their guidepost now. Deeper still, the swoosh of swimmers made their scheduled lap, keeping the souls afloat. Ashton's arms were bricks, but she forced them through the dense aether until they arrived beneath the swimming keepers.

Daiya reached out, and Ashton latched onto her offered hand allowing her new teammate to pull her closer through the current. Daiya, who she was certain hadn't liked her from the beginning, held up a harness with a rope-like contraption she'd pulled from her own strapped bag. Her glossy gray-brown gaze reached Ashton's, perhaps a peace offering. Without words, Ashton squeezed her hand.

Daiya went to work, sorting out the mechanism. It looked like a giant spider's web as she attached the center around Ashton's middle and handed the other ends to the team. Each member attached their link and pulled back in a circle, as if they were all spiders and Ashton their prey.

She shook off the creepy image.

Each of the straps was long, maybe twenty feet or more, as her teammates stretched far and away from each other. She could barely see them as they disappeared into the dark aether.

"I'm caught in a web now." Ashton voiced into her earpiece.

"Better than losing you to the depths." Daiya's voice hitched. "Nanna, report demon activity."

A moment of silence lingered as everyone pulled their ropes taut. It wasn't painful, but pressure pulsed against her middle. She had to squint to make out their shapes. Maybe the ropes were longer than she realized, or they were deeper than she thought. She threw her head back, barely able to detect the ripples from where the swimmers worked above her.

Nanna responded, "None detected, but they appear out of nowhere. Be on guard."

Ashton's heartbeat fluttered. Then she thought of Mason in that hellhole saving his parents. She pictured Hicks and Kali hiding in the woods outside Seattle and rolled her shoulders. Kali walked circles using her crystals to hide their location atop the ley lines. She double dipped, expending the energy source Vin used to hide the Pacific Northwest from his father.

Ashton's team would do the same.

If these crystals of charoite worked in conjunction

with her flowers of invisibility, they could camouflage the energy these red-eyed demons secretly sucked away. They might not be able to stop the full flow of energy. They weren't even sure how many of these unnaturally created demons were deeper than keepers could go. Ashton bit her bottom lip. She was about to use their own creativity against them…and find out.

It had to work.

I know you hear our prayers. Ashton spewed in her mind to the God she knew existed out there somewhere. *Please save these souls and all the ones coming to release their fears since Max's book has launched. I will use my Centennial gifts, bestowed upon me, but our team needs any extra strength you could offer.* She didn't take half a second to judge her terrible prayer abilities before pulling up her knees, curling over, and diving down with all her might. The pull from her tethered teammates, somewhere above, dragged in the ride.

"Far enough," Daiya called.

The tugs on her harness wrenched from every direction. Scanning above, she could vaguely make out her team's gray-hued clouds of movement through the atmosphere. They must be treading aether to hold her steady. The pressure helped her to know they were still there. She dangled below the fuss of her team's created currents, tingles starting in her toes and heels, beckoning her lower.

"Okay, you each carry charoite and petals from my violettias." She pulled a crystal from her own pouch. Then with her other hand reached into the side pocket of her gear vest. Her fingers found the dried flower petals. Gently she scooped them into her hand. "On the count of three, release the petals and move to your right until we've made one full rotation. Then we will spread another handful for the second rotation in the same direction. After three times around, we will retract and swim our laps the opposite direction. Got it?"

"Copy that." Daiya was the only one to respond, but she knew by the pull in the ropes, her team prepared to act.

Soon she dangled beneath the soul orbs, masquerading as they believed the red-eyed demons must be doing. The petals would absorb the energy extracted from the crystals causing them to work even if she wasn't holding them. Like energy repelled from another *like* source, they might react as if two positive battery ends.

She needed this to work. The petals *had* to transfer the energy waves from the crystals and her Centennial gift as her vision had appeared…lavender fields flowing like water.

"On your word," Nanna added.

Ashton imagined Rory standing before her, remembering all their training sessions, and channeled her spirited attitude. Ashton would handle the weight of her destiny. "One, two—" She inhaled a deep breath. "Three."

Every point on her harness jerked at once, but she allowed her body to drift in a slow circle as the rotation began. Turning, she released bits of violet petals. They hung in the thickness like falling feathers. The real test would be how long the ruse could hold. How many times would they have to rinse and repeat?

With any luck, far fewer than the exhausted swimmers above.

She watched the petals drift through the soupy air before they'd hitch a ride on a swirling current, ride up, then gently dip to catch another. The petals danced and floated longer than she anticipated. Sure the team's rotations were creating movement. But the aether was never still, and it was thicker down this deep. Perhaps they could float endlessly!

Excitement burst in Ashton's chest, though they hadn't even completed one rotation. *Please let this work.*

"Nanna, any changes?" Ashton's eagerness swelled.

"Not yet, sweets."

Of course, it was too soon.

"Wait—" A team member's voice called through the earpiece.

"I see it." Another voice.

"What's happening?" Panic popped Ashton's hopeful thoughts like a pin.

Daiya's voice, curious. "There's a light reflecting from *you*, a dark shade of purply-blue."

Ashton held up her hand. It was easier to see than only moments ago.

She'd focused on the flower petals before, willing her eyes to track their progress and hadn't noticed the change.

Except—a glimmer.

The crystal in her hand now smoldered indigo, like a cloud-covered moon, but more. The outline of her body *was* aglow, somehow the light knitted around her arms and legs like a glove.

Ashton's body tingled as she curled her toes in her booties and shut her eyes, a zing of warmth slipped up her legs and into her chest. The aether should feel cooler the lower she traveled. Yet she was warm. Vertigo teased her senses, but she shook it off. They were on a mission. She had to keep going.

"Nanna?" Ashton scanned her body, indigo glow blurring as she squirmed. "Is the light dangerous?"

"Aside from a slight rise in temperature and pulse, your vitals are fine, sweets. Do you see anything else?"

Ashton squinted her eyes through the glowing darkness. Nothing.

"I don't see anything. Let's keep going." She pressed her lips together, the pressure from the harnesses yanking. As she turned in a slow rhythm with her team, she focused once more on the petals scattered within the circle. But they seemed to fade out of view. Were they disappearing? The aether and indigo light played tricks in the deeper currents.

"Second rotation complete," Daiya stated. "Beginning third and final rotation this direction. Ashton, are you okay?"

"Fine." Ashton focused on her task.

"Nanna, any change with the orbs?"

"Report coming. Hold."

The group was silent in wait but kept the rotation moving. Did the midnight blue of her surroundings darken more? She tried stretching without tugging the ropes. No need to alarm anyone.

But she glanced up to where her team should be.

Their vaguely silver silhouettes were now gone completely, as if the ropes tethering them had somehow lengthened. Ashton turned her head, her braid floating up at the end. She was being silly. They were all harnessed together.

She released more petals, let the pull of the straps pivot her body. Her bag had been filled to the brim with flowers, as were the packs of each keeper. She couldn't see them floating in the aether anymore but had to trust they were there. She squeezed the charoite in her right hand and closed her eyes.

Mia hadn't given her any words to recite, only relayed to Hannah she needed to bring the charoite together with her magic violettias.

That had seemed too easy.

Her vision had come to her the night Kali completed her ritual in the woods. Movement seemed necessary then, otherwise, why all the circles. Constant swimming was keeping the souls from sinking, so their rotations seemed a requirement. Thankfully Daiya had thought of the harness idea, not wanting Ashton to fall too deep. That had settled Ashton's mind, knowing her stamina to swim might give out.

Now, alone in the dark, with only a strange glow encircling her limbs, how many times would she need to recreate this scenario to lift the souls? When would she know it had worked?

What was the backup plan if they failed?

Her mind rattled, clunkier than the usual tiny clicks at the thought of being reassigned to forever make her rounds, harnessed in the dark depths of Reverie.

Dizziness crept in. But still her body turned with the ropes suspending her.

Toss the flower petals.

Squeeze the crystal.

Her robotic movements drew lines in the dark with the strange light.

Her mind wandered again. Would Mason come

with her if this became her new post? What about her castmates? Maybe this was a ploy to reunite her with Zander...her original destined mate? Thoughts pinged from one side of her head to the other, and her chest filled with an imaginary swarm of bees, the familiar feels of her earthly anxiety blooming with angst.

"Ash—report—do you—in." Daiya's voice cut in and out through her earpiece, piercing her distractions.

She blinked, trying to make sense of where she was. Dizziness rushed again, this time behind her eyes. The rotations seemed to have stopped.

Was she sinking?

Her left palm glowed even brighter now with the same strange light buzzing around her body. But the deeper aether was like fog on a cold Seattle morning.

"Nanna?" She kicked her feet to swim upward. "Daiya?"

Her legs stroked the currents, stirring like sludge, but she wasn't gaining speed. She wasn't moving anywhere.

Although she *was* moving...down!

"Help!" Ashton screamed into the earpiece, but it was as if screaming in a dream, slow motion and silent. White noise crackled through her ears. The pulsating light flickered through her torso.

She tugged at her harness, uncaring which keeper she yanked. She needed up with the group. *Now.* "Pull me up—"

As the words pressed through gritted teeth, a new force propelled her farther down.

Down.

Down.

Chapter 36

Messy Moments

Mason grasped for Vin's shoulders, but his uncle blocked his assault, pitching his body into a bookshelf across the room. Mason tumbled with the books and broken shelves, clambering to his feet. His vision whooshed before he stepped out of the mess.

Vin leaned against the opposing wall, as if bored. "You don't need to do this."

Mason held his tongue. He had to think, wondering if the portal made noise or acknowledgement when used. Were his parents out? He wouldn't chance looking for them, but he wasn't interested in playing games with Uncle Evil either. He needed to buy them time.

"Don't I?" He had to keep the demon talking.

"You're fighting to free your earthly father, but he's gone, if you know what I mean." He shook his head, finger tapping his temple.

Mason ground his teeth. He had to believe Max could be saved. Vin was only twisting the dagger of doubt.

"And your mother? She'll do whatever it takes to protect you." He pushed off the wall. "Don't you think it's time to stop playing seam keeper and start employing your demon inside?"

362

Mason blinked. He'd never thought of an actual demon inside him before. Demon-blood, yes. That image freaked him out enough. But this monster was presenting a whole new visual. He shook it off. "No."

Vin stalked closer, still a few yards between them.

Mason glanced quickly, nothing behind him but piles of books and splintered shelves against a stone wall. He peeked in the direction of his parents. Could they be through the portal by now? Mason's heart beat in his fists.

"Are you *afraid* of the darkness running through your veins?" He scratched his chin and took a step closer. "You look more like your mother, but I can smell my brother's evil inside you. I can help you let it out." Another step. "Release the pressure."

Mason had no place to back up and stood his ground. "I can choose. And I don't choose this." He swept his arms as if to display the disturbed library, along with everything conjuring in his mind about being the grandson of Hell.

His heart tripled in speed, but his feet were cement blocks. His mind muddled more with each second either from the blow, smashing into the bookcase, or the weightiness of where he finally stood. With the sketchiest of plans, he struggled to focus on one thought long enough.

Did his ability to focus even matter right now?

He had instinct.

He had to believe Zander and Ansel had planted the spherules at each portal. He hoped even more that they'd made it out, along with his parents.

This fight could end right here. Right now. Between the two of them.

He padded his vest pocket, feeling the small round shape of a keeper's last-choice weapon. It had been the final choice for Ashton when she'd taken down Ian. It had worked because she'd had a personal connection to him. Her human side, even though she'd never been human. But they had been close enough for emotions to bloom.

Close enough.

That's all Mason needed. He cracked his neck and scanned the room.

Ashton and Ian had been *outside* this secretly created realm. Mason had to believe his blood connection would be sufficient for the soul spherule to ignite, but more, he prayed the explosion would set off the other two. And since they were all located *inside* this place that wasn't supposed to exist, he had his own bargain with the devil—his life on the line that the tripped eruptions would seal up the realm and everything in it, for good.

"You think you can choose? The calling in your blood is stronger than your weaker keeper side. And now I've acquired a chunk of the human world, flaming the fear-energy required for *my* new realm." He sidestepped to the door leading into the hallway and left.

"What the hell?" Mason uttered under his breath, but he took the opportunity to run to the back of the library, to the portal. His parents *still* huddled in the corner. His dad swiped at his mom, like a scared animal, barricading himself under a reading table.

"I can't get him out." His mom hissed. Stress radiated off her like an aura he was sure Rory might read. At least they'd been quiet. Max said nothing, staring wide-eyed and swatting the air. The eerie scene had him frozen.

Voices sounded from the door.

Mason held a finger to his lips. His mom nodded, as he slipped back into view, wishing immediately he hadn't. Not only was Vin back in the room, but he'd hauled a terrified-looking Hicks and suspiciously unreadable Kali with him.

"Hicks isn't part of this." Mason's temples pulsated against the sides of his face. He stormed forward. Nothing was falling into plan.

He almost laughed aloud. What plan?

But at least he'd gotten the fight down to him and Kelvin. Or so he'd thought. His parents were still there. And now Hicks?

Thoughts swirled behind his eyes.

"My brother left a little helper in the Human Realm, providing the insurance I need now that *stepdaddy* is incapacitated." Vin laughed. "I don't know what you thought you might accomplish coming here all alone, but it was foolish at best." He glared at Kali, and she tugged Hick's shoulder, pulling him farther into the room. As their backs turned away from the door, Mason saw movement in the hallway.

Great—more demons!

He couldn't dare react. Hick's expression caused his arm hairs to stand on end. His friend looked bewildered, mentally *and* physically.

"Hicks, it's okay." He wanted to assure him he'd be all right. But would he? Kali turned his chin her way, forcing his direct eye contact.

"Babe, everything's okay. We're stopping by my brother's place. Remember?"

Hicks's stance softened. He nodded, but still didn't speak. Mason couldn't be sure, but it seemed as if Kali's voice trembled a bit. He knew Vin wasn't her real brother, but perhaps he could end her as fast as Ian had created her. Either way, he didn't trust the fade.

"What do you want from me?" Mason peered across the room at Vin.

"Allegiance, my rebellious nephew." He chuckled as he smacked Hicks on the shoulder. Hicks looked up with an unfamiliar smile, eyes glazed over. Is that what had happened to his dad after time spent in this hellhole, secret even from Hell? Did it suck the life from humans? An invisible time bomb ticked in his chest.

He had three people to save now, with too little time, and only one soul spherule.

"You have the inside knowledge of the Human Realm. Your stepdaddy's book will bring in the negative energy needed from dreamers. And your inside connection to the keeper realms will work well in our favor. You must be bored with their rules and demands." Vin lifted Kali's chin with a finger. "Good girl, my lowly fade. You hid him well…even if, for an instant, it was out of my own range." He pushed her back, gruffly. "We'll discuss *that* later."

"Yes, brother—sir. I'm sorry. I didn't know what else to do when all those *keepers* arrived." She glared at Mason.

"Tsk, tsk, tsk." He hissed in Mason's direction. "Pesky keepers. You see? You aren't one of them, Mason. Your father had to have called for you to claim yourself. Did he not?"

Mason remembered his birth-father's voice

slithering up his spine like a whispering serpent. It had happened during keeper training when he'd almost stabbed his castmate. "I heard it. I ignored it. I am *not* a demon."

"I beg to differ. Look what's left of your so-called family." He pointed in the direction his parents had fled.

Dammit! He'd known where they hid all along.

****

Ashton blinked back into consciousness as she fell. Had she passed out? Maybe she wasn't moving at all and had only dreamed she was falling. She relaxed into the cradling aether, the quiet as heavy as her limbs. Mason's face crossed her mind. Being so adventurous, he'd get a kick out of this odd experience. Being so adventurous—wait a minute.

Mason! Where was he?

And what was she doing down here? Her hands and feet buzzed. She wiggled her fingers, dropping whatever was in her hand.

Whoops! A lavender image of charoite flickered behind her eyes.

No!

She grasped viscous air to sit up. The need to escape pulsed in her bones, but the slow pull on her equilibrium filled her with nausea. She forced her eyes to open wide against the swirling atmosphere. The only light came from the odd indigo glow around her body.

Wait. She knew this light. She shook her head, braid thumping her shoulder. She knew where Mason was—saving his parents from Vin's hidden realm. And she? She was counteracting the magnetic pull anchoring sleeping human souls.

"My crystal," she yelped too late, and thrust forward, coming face to face with a red-eyed demon.

Where was the team? No time to think. Only act.

Tucking her feet as tightly as she could, she pitched them forward, blasting off the beast's chest. Her body propelled back, though hardly gained any distance in the thick aether. The bear-sized demon barely moved.

"Daiya!" she called, pulling one of the ropes harnessed to her pack. She swam backward, pulling and pulling when the end of the severed rope fell through her hands. She felt it then, the weight of the other seven dangling cables.

She was alone.

Red-eye twitched its oblong head, black and gooey, and proceeded forward. Its movements were awkward, robotic. But Ashton didn't wait. She ripped at the clasps on her backpack. She didn't need the deadweight of empty swinging straps and had to believe her team was somehow on their way to find her.

Wait! She crooked an elbow to catch the falling pack, pressed the pouch into her chest, and kicked away through the sludge from the beast.

Still, the demon moved her way, slowly and methodically.

Jabbing a hand into a side pocket, she released all the flowers she had left. So much for rotations. She prayed Mia had been right all along.

The beast froze at the sight. Tiny, blue-tinted flowers hovered around them. The monster's glaring eyes rotated from hers to watch the petals lift and fall. Its red pupils grew and shrank as if unsuccessfully attempting to track each movement. Its head tilted oddly.

Click! Her mind filtered through panic, or at least she thought it was her gift. She couldn't tell in the chaos. But one thing she'd bet; this creature wasn't *all* real.

She thought about the other red-eyed demons and let the mental images of each previous attack reel through her mind, like a sports replay.

Computers could be shut down. And right now, this mass of made-up swine was working overtime to make sense of the cloud of petals.

Ashton looked above. No one was coming. She hadn't felt the currents of anyone passing around her, but who knew what had happened after she'd passed out. How far down had she fallen? How far was *too* far for the keepers above to call off the search?

She gulped down the thick air, her head rushing with a wave of nausea. But before she dropped the backpack all together, she fished out the remaining crystals. Holding as much charoite as her fists could hold, she let the apparatus that had one time held nine keepers together drop and used the distraction to flip up and over the demon.

The monster wasn't as distracted as she'd thought because it turned almost instinctually and moved in closer. Ashton dodged it, forcing her legs to swim in the other direction. The monster halted, releasing a strange inky residue from its snout-like nose. The murky deposit mixed with the currents, petals dancing wildly in the disturbance.

Ashton leaned sideways to avoid the muck, certain the beast was somehow locked onto her. But the creature didn't move. She kicked back, hard in the soupy air. The demon simply turned its head from side to side. Could it not see her? Was she invisible because of the petals or because of the brute's altered state?

The beast hovered in her direction again. Its giant paws cut through the atmosphere with ease. It might be some kind of half-demon, half-robot, but whatever it was, it was coming.

Channeling Mason's impulsive nature, she hoisted up and over, bringing herself closer to the demon. *You better be right!* She gave her last thought to Mason's impulsiveness before dropping down onto the beast's back. Well, almost its back.

The overly oxygenated air messed with her balance, so she landed more on its shoulder and edge of its torso. It would do. She locked one leg around its face, squeezing to keep its jaws from clamping down on her. But she only had one of its arms incapacitated with her other leg, her body thrown across the side of its round back. The demon flailed its other arm clawing in her direction, unable to penetrate her gear suit—yet.

There it was again—*click*! Her mind chimed, as if it had been all along but the deepness had blocked everything out. Visions of lavender fields finally filled her mind as the indigo light glowed from her body. The charoite glow mixed with her gift. Then she saw herself at Althaia's tree the day she'd found the violettias. The day she'd tricked those two human looking fades because she was invisible!

She willed more pressure to flood into her limbs, like a storm, pushing down on the sticky exterior of the demon, spreading her palms against its back and shoulder. The warmth in her hands ignited, just as it had that day evil threatened the borders of the Spiritual

Realm, and she'd pushed away the demon-provoked whirlwind. Rory hadn't found a safe location to assess her new gift, but Ashton had no other choice.

As the creature squirmed and bucked, she smooshed all the charoite into its oozing flesh with pulsing force. Her body shook, but she held on, forced the crystals in, some falling into the abyss, but she felt the sharp ends of other pieces lodge like gravel in an open knee wound. A flash of her childhood bike crashing into Mason flickered across her mind.

Hands empty, she gripped what had to be its neck with one hand and reached for a dagger with the other. Although her weapons had been attached to her right thigh for easy access, she was not in an easy-access position. The demon arched and spun like a rodeo bull. Its cry, a droning wail, vibrated through her abdomen. All she could do was clamp down her thighs and hold on. It might not be able to see her, but it could feel her just as Mason had felt her when she first approached him invisible.

If she could let go without getting pummeled, she may stand a chance of escape, and this half demon, half created monster, might become the beacon needed to reboot the nest. Its red-eyed energy now glowed magenta—a new conduit of the charoite's transformative frequency.

Her head pounded, arms zinging from her death grip on the thrashing creature. A tornado of energy swooshed around her, if she could only summon enough strength to swim away.

A sound filled her ears, like someone calling from underwater. Her head filled with exhaustion and vertigo. She couldn't hold on much longer.

"Hold on—hold on," the voice called louder. Though Ashton could make out the words…she was afraid to open her eyes. And she was tired.

She rested her head on the goo and held tight, fingers slipping through the ooze.

Chapter 37

Sacrifice

Mason didn't look back. He strode forward meeting Kali in his path. She'd shoved Hicks aside, drawn two daggers, and glowered with black eyes. Vin watched as if she was his trusty guard dog, and he needn't lift a finger.

"Mason, I could use your impulsive courage." He laughed, clapping his hands together. "There are no rules here that *we* don't make ourselves."

Kali jabbed him back a step.

He was double-fisting knives and used his forearms to block and tip her wrist. She dropped her blade but scooped her leg into a tight curl before extending into a strong kick, thrusting him onto his back.

Hicks ran over. "Mason, is that you?" He held up a hand to Kali. "Babe, this is my friend. You've met him, haven't you?' He dragged a hand down Mason's face, his expression pained.

"Stay back." Mason scrambled to his feet, pushing Hicks and eying Kali with Vin behind her.

"I've had my fun, fade." Vin's voice, throaty. "End them all. But leave my nephew to me. We have some catching up to do."

Kali stopped herself from lunging and caught Hicks's arm. "Time to go." She still held a blade in one hand, Mason's friend in the other, and jostled him toward the back of the library to where his parents hid.

"Not going to happen." Mason turned to attack, but Vin stepped in as if the distance between them had only been one long stride. Hicks let Kali pull him away, without even looking back, her long black hair, a curtain between them. How could he break the spell the fade had on him? Hicks was only human, but right now he could use all the help he could get.

And he thought he could do this alone!

His heartbeat boomed through his ears. It was strange how *clipped* noise was in this realm, but when sound echoed through his body, Mason could hear fine. Right now, the message was a loud, urgent cry.

Mason lifted both daggered hands and cemented his feet to the floor. Vin was much taller than him, but it didn't matter. And it didn't matter if he made it out or not. Nobody was getting out of this realm again. He hated thinking his entire family line would be wiped out in a matter of seconds, but if the soul spherules worked as he hoped they would, he'd do it to save the Dream Realm. To save the humans his monster-uncle cared so little about.

He sent his breaking heart to Ashton and vaulted toward Kelvin. Rather than attacking straight on, he dropped to his left knee, twisted his right leg around copying the same extended kick Kali had used on him.

His uncle lost his footing, but the oaf caught himself in seconds, words of an unknown language striking between barred teeth. Vin lifted an elbow, then jammed his balled fist on top of Mason's head.

Mason staggered to his knees. His eyes blurred. His mouth filled with blood. He spit, swearing in his own language, and struggled to find his feet. All he had to do was whisper the name of this demon prince into the soul spherule and jam it into his temple.

But how was he going to reach?

Mason waited for Vin to make the next move. It was a risky ploy, but if he wanted Mason to come to his side, maybe he wouldn't be in such a hurry to kill him.

"Fade!" Vin roared over Mason's head. "You're taking time I don't have." He pulled Mason up by the shoulder.

Mason drew in a breath to steady himself and stabbed Vin with the dagger in his left hand. A distraction really because the blade bounced off his armor-like skin, barely making a slice in his clothing.

Vin's fist pummeled down once more, but as fast, a blurry form flew up from behind, knocking the demon prince sideways.

This time he fell.

Mason's blurry gaze met Zander's burning brown stare. He offered a hand and Mason gripped it, letting the keeper pull him to his feet.

Ansel was behind him stabbing his dagger into Vin's shoulder. "What the—"

"His head!" Mason called out, steadying himself to get back in the fight. He needed to stop Kali. "Go for his ear."

But Vin made use of Ansel's confusion. The demon whirled Ansel's body between Mason and Zander, thudding on the other side of the library, now a heaping mess of torn books and broken furniture.

"I'm—okay." Ansel swayed to his feet.

"What are you doing here?" Mason overturned a chair and broke it across Vin's back. He had to slow him down.

Zander dusted debris from his dark hair. "Saving you." He side-kicked the back of Vin's knees, but the demon barely buckled.

"The gargoyles?" Mason kicked a chair leg out of his way. If he could get closer to Vin's head while he was down, he might be able to reach his temple.

"Dead." Zander barely got out of the way, tripping on the book-scattered floor until he crash-halted into a wall.

Vin was already up and looming. "You killed my pets?" He stormed toward Zander.

"Now!" Ansel coughed. "Do it now!"

Mason didn't understand until Vin's back was turned. He needed to stab Vin in the soft spot near his ear and shove the soul spherule into him.

Mason lunged. But before contact his dad howled from the back of the room.

Dammit! He hesitated in the distraction, and Vin twisted easily sweeping him away.

Mason crawled to his feet in mere seconds, all hesitancy gone. Ansel and Zander were also up, holding fighting stances, but nobody made a move as the freakish scene unfolded from the back of the room.

Max was like a trapped animal, desperate, practically foaming at the mouth. Mia, obviously done being gentle, fought her husband every small nudge toward the portal. Hicks was no help, obviously confused by the supernatural chaos, his girlfriend a demon.

Mason's chest tightened; his temple veins pumped at triple speed. He was losing everyone he cared about. He would never have his family back. And Ashton—

"Kill them!" Vin ordered Kali.

The fact she hadn't yet hurt his parents or Hicks registered. Mason rubbed the sweat and blood from his face as he focused on the back of the room. Slow tingles from his shifter-healing began knitting together the wound on his head and gave him a second wind.

Kali was leading his parents *to* the portal!

Mia must have deduced Kali wasn't an enemy; they were working together.

They had a chance.

"Go!" Mason ordered Zander and Ansel, pointing at his parents. But they both stood there.

"I mean it. Get them out!" He pointed at the back of the room.

"You piece of sludge!" Kelvin bellowed at Kali. "I should have known my brother could never properly raise a fade." He stormed toward Kali, as if there weren't three keepers standing ready to pounce.

By then, Mia and Kali had ushered their little group to the last bookshelf—the portal—shimmering with radiance.

His team advanced toward his family. Toward the light.

Mason ran at Vin, like a bulldozer in a storm.

Vin, moving in a blur of black smoke, now stood a mere foot from his family.

This was never going to end.

"Stop!" Mason bellowed. "I'll go with you." His relenting voice scratched the room.

Zander and Ansel both halted, eying Mason for some kind of understanding. He hated that he couldn't talk to either of them telepathically.

Vin positioned himself toward Mason.

Mason risked a glimpse at his family and friend standing behind this monster. It was long enough to see Kali's visible gulp before she shoved Hicks into Mia, who caught him, pulling him and Max onto the bookshelf as she fell. Their close contact must have triggered the opening, and the force pulled all three of them through the portal.

Hicks's call for Kali and Max's yelp were the only faint sounds before they severed.

The portal closed.

Before Kali moved an inch closer to the portal, Vin had her by the throat, squeezing the life from every human-like limb. Her wide eyes glazed over, black ichor seeping from the corners.

But that sickly stare was planted on Mason.

Now, she shaped with twisting lips.

Vin snapped her neck, the crack unable to linger in the sound-starved space, quick and insignificant, as if her heart hadn't already broken. He discarded her on the floor at his feet.

But Mason was already moving, as was his team. Ansel attacked first, assaulting from behind. He leaped onto Vin's back, pounding his fist into his shoulder, beating him down with all his might. Zander stabbed his arms. Even if his blades couldn't cut, the force deterred Vin from reaching over his head to fight off Ansel.

"Ugh!" Zander gulped.

Vin had booted him across the room. But Ansel wasn't letting go. Zander hopped up in a flash, shaking off the blow, racing to strike from the front once more.

Mason needed him lower to the ground and kicked at Vin's legs, hoping to tip his balance. But this demon was as sturdy as the possessed oak that had recently killed him…before his mom's prayer brought him back to life.

It couldn't have all been for nothing.

Zander and Ansel continued taking strikes, never letting go, and delivered them right back, wearing him down. Blood shot out from every impact, all of it keeper-red. No black ichor seeped from Uncle Evil.

Yet.

But how long could his team last?

Enough was enough. And it didn't matter how much taller Vin was than the rest of them. Mason knew what to do.

He pulled out the soul spherule and whispered Kelvin's name into the pink crystalized ball. He clasped it in his palm and called out above the brawl praying the other two understood his command. "Portal, now!"

In a flash, Mason tossed the spherule into his mouth as his feet left the ground. He'd never transformed into his hawk form so smooth, or so fast. He couldn't cry out with the tiny explosive in his mouth, so he flapped amber wings to the top of Vin's head.

Ansel, ignoring Mason's order, moved around Vin and swept him behind the knees.

Zander seized one of Vin's tree-trunk arms and suspended from it with all his weight.

With the perfectly timed distractions, Mason's hawk gripped his uncle's head, piercing talons into the soft skin around his eyes and temple.

Vin cried foreign words. But there were no other demons to call from this realm. Nobody knew it existed. The gargoyles were dead. And now, Kelvin would be too.

As Vin thrashed beneath him, overwhelm flooded Mason that these two keepers had stayed behind. But would they have time to exit before the explosion? He was ready to sacrifice his own life for the good of the cause, but he wouldn't be responsible for theirs.

Vin found his bearings and flipped Ansel over his shoulder into Zander. Mason was knocked off in the commotion. The soul spherule flew from his beak and rolled across the wood floor.

Mason cried out, *kiiiiiaaaaarrrrr!*

Chapter 38

Like the Fourth of July

Zander shoved a heavy Ansel from his chest and stumbled to his feet. "Get up!" he called down to his friend but kept his eyes on Kelvin. The demon had shaken all of them off and now worked to see through the black muck streaming down his face.

Mason had been right. Kelvin's weakness was the area by his eyes and ears; it was the only place bleeding on the beast.

Mason flapped in the small space, possibly searching for somewhere to land. If he was trying to communicate something else, Zander didn't comprehend. But Ansel wasn't getting up. He glanced at Ansel's chest. Zander's shoulders fell in relief to see it rise. Barely.

Dammit! No way he'd get that monster down on his own. He'd have to follow Mason's order instead. The thought wedged in his throat, but he had to get Ansel through the portal. His friend's heart may be beating, but only God knew what was happening internally. He needed a healer.

Vin voiced something unintelligible, staggering in his spot, *searching* for them? Was his sight compromised?

Zander couldn't chance it. Without a word, he bent

down and lifted Ansel under the shoulders, pulling him over the debris to the back of the room.

"No one's leaving this place alive." Vin either heard Zander hauling Ansel or he had enough vision to locate the scuffle of getting Ansel's dead weight across the floor.

Zander dragged hastily now, uncaring any noise it made. He dumped his friend at the back of the room, not quite to the portal when Vin ambushed them. Zander barely got a punch in before his feet left the floor, his body clutching air once again.

This time, Zander shifted as if he'd morphed into a hawk every day over the last year. So natural. So fluid. In seconds, Zander's bird of prey caught the air instead of hurling through it. He shrieked at Mason, scuttling on the ground in the corner.

Kiiiiiaaaaarrrrr!

At Zander's call, Mason scooped up something from the floor. Something round and shiny. The soul spherule.

Zander landed on a half standing bookshelf, pressing his talons into the wood. He cawed, pulling attention from Mason, but also to wake Ansel. Vin turned, heading back their way. He teetered as he walked disoriented.

Zander flew to the front of the room, pecked at the wooden door to make noise. Vin turned, making his way to the door. Zander flew as high as the ceilings allowed to the back of the room, nudging Ansel with his head, his beak, his talons.

Wake up! He urged, refusing to squawk aloud. But Vin had grabbed a chair and was swinging in the direction of Mason's hawk now. Zander took flight landing on Vin's head as Mason had done. He jabbed at Vin's already open wounds, thick ichor seeping down his bird throat in the process.

Mason cried out, but as Zander cocked his head to respond, Vin swung the chair over his head, knocking Zander to the floor. He'd barely scuttled away when Vin's boot came down.

Crack—pain exploded on his left side.

Mason was in the air, wailing in a high pitch. *Kiiiiiaaaaarrrrr—kiiiiiaaaaarrrrr!*

Zander's left wing seethed in pain. He tried shifting back, but his injured body refused. Red blood trailed behind as he willed his hawk up, hopping one legged toward Ansel. Toward the portal.

He hoped Mason's ridiculous plan to seal the realm might actually work.

He hoped Ansel would awaken and roll himself through the portal before the explosions. No way he'd make it in time.

He hoped with all his heart Daiya forgave him for leaving her.

****

Ashton woke on a dock, boards hard against her back.

Daiya, Nanna, and other faces encircled her as she coughed. Her body constricted and released as she adjusted to Reverie's surface air.

"Oh my God!" Daiya leaned back on her knees.

"Did—did it work?" Ashton forced, throat raw.

A unanimous cry assaulted. "Yes!"

She tried sitting up, but her head reeled. And her arms. She couldn't lift them on her own. Glimpses of purply-blue light blinked behind her eyes and the gooey feel of the demon still clung to her. *Yuck*. "I can't feel my arms," she muttered.

"You'll have plenty of time to recover." Daiya half laughed, something Ashton was sure she'd never heard her do. "Your magical violets worked with the crystals. And your idea to embed ol' red-eye with the crystals. Brilliant. He's hanging out down there like a beacon, incapacitated, but filled with charoite!"

"Are you thanking me?" Ashton forced through aches and pains.

Daiya laughed again, a strange sound coming from her once icy exterior. "I guess I am. You're determined. I like that. We could barely get you off that creature, you were clinging so tight."

Ashton exhaled. She couldn't remember anything past the darkness blanketing her in a place where far too much oxygen flowed. She held a thumb up, too exhausted for any kind of retort.

****

Finally! Mason hooked the sphere into his beak, tucking it under his tongue. It was tricky to sound a battle cry with an explosive under his tongue, but he had no choice. He had to believe Kelvin's name would still activate the spherule.

He had no idea how long triggers lasted?

Mason opened his wings and leaped to the only standing bookcase left. His hawk vision glimpsed every bit of broken bone protruding from Zander's wing as he hobbled to a bleeding and unmoving Ansel.

Black ichor drenched Kelvin's face. Mason heard him mumbling under his breath. It reminded him of the time Ian had done the same at Mason's beach house back in the Human Realm. With Ian, black smoke had trickled from his fingertips, providing an escape. His uncle was either too weak to call upon magic or this concocted realm didn't work like the other realms.

Mason glanced at Zander, still in hawk form. He'd somehow made it to Ansel, pecking and crying out to his friend. They'd done all they could do.

It was time.

While Vin worked frantically to call on his magic, Mason clutched the soul spherule in his beak. He lunged into the air, swooping behind Vin, and popped the tiny pink marble into an open wound behind his left eye.

Peck—peck—peck!

Vin batted the air, but Mason's wings had already lifted, soaring across the dusty room to the portal. A thud boomed behind him, hopefully Vin dropping to his knees. No time to look. Mason landed in human form atop Ansel. He scooped the unconscious keeper and lugged him toward the opening.

But where was Zander?

Mason peered out to see Vin on the ground in a heap of black mist swirling with torn book pages, broken shelves, and chair legs. The scent of rotten eggs and metal filled the air. Energy seared the hairs on his arms, but he clasped onto Ansel.

"Zander!" Mason shouted over the noise, now rising with the flailing book pages and splintered pieces of wood.

Kiiiaaarrr!

Mason barely heard the feeble cry when he saw the hawk pulling himself in their direction with one wing. Blood everywhere.

Why hadn't he shifted?

The room swirled with debris, noise bellowing like Althaia's angry oak before its possessed roots split the ground apart. They had to get out of here.

Now.

Mason heaved one more time with Ansel in tow, then leaped behind to boot him through the portal. The gateway lit up, sucking the internal keeper through in a flash.

Mason vaulted to his feet, shielding his eyes with an arm as he trudged against the dark blast of energy thrusting him back.

Time pricked behind his ears like a stopwatch.

"Zander!"

He couldn't hear Zander's hawk anymore. Squinting through the thundering darkness keeping Kelvin down. Mason ducked, arm shielding his face when he spied a lump of feathers only a few yards away. Securing each footfall to the floor, he didn't stop until he was close enough to scoop Zander into his arms.

The hawk felt all wrong—sticky, wet feathers, protruding bones. And cold.

Mason had no idea if he was alive or dead, but he gripped the downed bird against his chest and ran, storm winds whirling and whipping his back, to the portal.

The room roared its angry tornado, hurling something hard into Mason's back, but the effect actually helped push him forward. He tripped through the portal. It's clammy spider's silk engulfed him with blinding light, his body wrenching in every direction. He held his core and let the force pull him through. Swooshing sounds pulsed through his ears until he tumbled out on the other side, soft grass catching his fall, and Zander's hawk still clutched in his arms.

It was like the fourth of July.

Lights burst overhead, the blasts of red and blue garnished the sky like the sheet cake Ashton's human mom had made every year in the summer. The lights dripped from above in every color now until they drenched the horizon with pinks and grays. Thunder roared, booming in Mason's head. Maybe the lightshow only occurred in his mind. Confusion swelled. The fireworks seem to trickle through his veins as poofs of smoke and ash settled around him.

Mason glanced up to see faces…so many faces before a heavy darkness claimed his vision. Hands pulled at his body. They pulled at Zander's blood-covered form. Voices chimed, questions soaring like the storm he'd trudged through, but he couldn't make out anything intelligible. Pain in his back seized, and any magnificent light he may have seen burst seconds before disappearing to black.

Chapter 39

New Mission?

Mason stared at the massive map in the healing sanctuary. The swirling black spot in the center taunted him less than it had before.

His demon bloodline would never define him.

Bethesda cleared the teacups, leaving him in peace after their session. Their time together had already become habitual. Two weeks in a row to be exact.

Since taking down Kelvin, he'd craved his daily dose of meditation. Breathing exercises helped him accept his true self—however uncalm his true self might be. Taking time here, along with getting back to work at the Seam, had been exactly what he'd needed.

Busyness.

Routine.

Normalcy.

But he never left the sanctuary without taking a few quiet moments with the framed map. This reminder of his new world and the part *he'd* played in it had finally taken root. He'd warmed to the idea that even though he may have believed he was…an accident…he was still supposed to be there. His mom was living proof. What he once deemed a mistake was still meant to be.

Knowing what he knew to be true about the world,

about the vast size of all the worlds was still surreal. Working to meditate *and* accept his impulsive tendencies as equal parts of himself seemed even more challenging. But he would be the leader the Blessing Council assured him he could be. He would fight for that reality every day. If not for him, for his family.

He'd brought his parents home, relatively speaking. Against all odds, he and his team had rescued Mia and Max from that sliver of Hell. He would have time to reunite with his mom, to mend a bridge over their lost thirteen years, which didn't seem so long anymore after learning he would be around far longer than any human. How long? He would ask about that.

But Max.

Dad. Mason's breath hitched.

A team of healers had made him as comfortable as possible. His human mind, unable to bear the reality of other realms, retreated inwardly. He wasn't responding to anyone.

"Mas?" Ashton's voice sounded from behind.

He shook off the heavy thoughts.

"Hey." He exhaled before greeting her. She was dressed in white and khaki battle gear. "Training on our day off?"

Her nose crinkled, as if embarrassed. "Don't judge me, but..." Her blue eyes glistened before she looked down. "I finally talked with Gavan. I wanted to plan it after a training, so he could see me geared up and dedicated."

Mason laughed, relieved for the distraction from his own grief. He met her gaze. "And sweaty, in case you cried?"

Ashton threw a not-so-light punch to his gut and

headed for the door. He keeled over in jest but followed her outside. Sunshine pinned them in place, the fresh air demanding notice, as always in Toria.

"It's okay to be yourself, Ash. You're a crier."

"Am not!" She stopped on her way down the stairs. The wind ruffled her ponytail as she squinted up at him through the brightness.

He tucked a flyaway strand behind her ear and pulled her down the stairs to the path. "What did Gavan have to say?"

They walked in the direction of the garden, her strides falling into step with his, their bodies always in sync.

"Tell me." He nudged.

She slanted into his shoulder, clasping his hand.

Mason gave her time as they walked in silence down the trail to the garden gate. Leading her to their favorite spot on the stone bench, under the willow, he pulled her to sit.

"He—apologized."

When she didn't say more, he held his breath, counting the way Bethesda had taught him. He let it go, bit by bit, telling himself that silence was okay. Time passing was okay. He could be there, in the moment, with the keeper he so deeply loved. She was hurting, and it wasn't the time for jokes or even leaping into action, *yet*. His last bits of air seeped out in a gust.

"How bad does the *fix-it* in you need to act?"

His eyes popped. "I don't need to fix anything. I think you are entirely capable of handling your fath—Gavan." He pushed tangles of hair off his face. "Sorry. What did he say?"

She let the sun fall across her face again, but he

saw the slight turn of her lip. "He said he hadn't meant to mistrust my abilities when we first reunited. He hadn't intended on leaving my birth mother after the council chose me as Centennial. And after he did, he'd always meant to go back."

"But he didn't."

Ashton shook her head. "No."

She was quiet again, and this time he couldn't hold back. "He's held a grudge against Althaia for eighteen years, letting his destined mate fall away, all because—the council chose you?"

"For not being as strong as she was when it happened."

Oh.

Silence shivered down his spine. Gavan had always been stone cold. He'd been the voice barking orders in Mason's ear after his first shift into a hawk. At Blessing Council meetings, his icy blue glares were daggers from across the table.

He'd been an ass.

Now he was bowing to the strength of Ashton's birth mother. Mason blinked the irony of this incredible leader in the Spiritual Realm feeling inferior.

"He said he was overwhelmingly *sad*. He couldn't believe Althaia let me go without a word. But then he realized too late, he'd never asked her how she felt. They simply stopped communicating." She wiped a tear.

Mason pulled her closer, nestling his chin into her neck. "Maybe a good reason *not* to use the silent treatment on those you love."

Her elbow connected with his side as he muttered the last word. But then she turned to face him. "It means Gavan did what he did, good or bad, because he—"

"Loved you."

"I guess." She closed her eyes.

It had to be hard letting go of the anger she'd hoarded up for him these past weeks. He tilted his head against hers, letting the breeze lift and fall around them. Petals swirled as if their only concern was where to land. Mason rested in the moment until voices from down the path echoed their way into the garden.

"Hey," Ansel called, waving from his group of four on the path. Behind him were Amit, Daiya, and Zander.

Ashton sat up straight. "Did we forget about a BC meeting?"

Mason raised an eyebrow. "BC?"

She shrugged. "Blessing Council." She didn't wait for the roll of his eyes, instead, ascended to greet the group. "Is there a meeting or did you miss our company?"

"Definitely not your company." Daiya strode up to her but then offered a sly grin.

Zander eyed Mason, lifting his chin. Mason noticed his strange energy. They definitely weren't...buddies. Although the fact he and Ansel had come back for him and his parents had pushed his likeability up a few notches. Of course, Zander had awkwardly shared his gratitude for Mason carrying him and Ansel through the portal saving their lives.

They still had a long way to go.

"The council awaits." Amit waved them through the gate. He bobbed his head, choppy dark hair flopping to the side, in the direction of the assembly building.

Mason glanced at Ashton, who already looked

serious. He grabbed her hand, gave it a squeeze. "Whatever it is, we've got this. Okay?"

She exhaled, walking with him up the steps and down the hall to the oversized meeting room. The blue chandeliers glowed in the corners, as Mason's eyes adjusted to the dimmer light. The entire council had already arrived—all eight of them in their typical shades of ivory and violet. Gavan was at the head, also typical, with Rory and Shunnar to his right.

His and Ashton's cast were not present, and Mason crooked an eyebrow. It was strange to be there without them.

Gavan stood in greeting, motioning for them to sit. There were still vacant chairs around the enormous table and of course the one at the opposite end from Gavan, always left open for Sandalphon, even when the Angel did not attend.

"Thank you for meeting on short notice." Amit sat to Gavan's left after bowing to the three Dream Realm representatives and five Spiritual Realm representatives.

Amit called this meeting?

Mason glanced at Zander, but his dark complexion and even darker eyes hid anything he might know. Ansel wore a questionable smirk. Did they know what was going on?

"Of course." Gavan responded matter-of-factly. If he looked fatherly to Ashton now, Mason couldn't tell. The shifter had an edge he would never figure out. "Why don't you do the honors and explain our proposal?"

"Yes, yes," Amit agreed, clearing his throat and pushing his mop of hair to the other side. He scanned the room slowly. "As you know, Prince Kelvin has been banished and the hidden realm entombed. Well!" He chuckled. "If there's anything left of it after those three soul spherules erupted."

All gazes fell on Mason. He swallowed, staring straight at Amit silently urging him to go on. He was tired of explaining that his hunch had paid off because the reality of any other outcome was ridiculously frightening. And he didn't like sharing his desperation during those final moments when he'd disobeyed orders.

"A new dilemma is how to deal with the leftover fades in the Human Realm. Our healers have traced the energy of many across the northwest corner of the US. Without a leader, they are rogue and unpredictable."

"How many?" Mason interrupted, then slumped in his chair. This was still an official council meeting.

Amit looked sadly in his direction. "A fair bit. I'm afraid several escaped the fire in the Seattle warehouse. That or he had them hidden in other locations."

"Pardon me for speaking out." Ashton sat up straighter. "Kali was a fade, but she wasn't evil."

Mason stirred in his seat. She'd cried after learning Kali sacrificed herself for Hicks. For his parents. Her guise those last moments in Kelvin's library still blew him away. There was so much more to learn.

"Exactly, but we don't know which way each one will go. Lower demons given higher lifeforms take on all kinds of emotions, depending on their type, as well as their surroundings and experiences. If they've scattered, as our healers sense they have, then we're dealing with twenty to thirty, maybe more, unpredictable beings loose in the Human Realm."

"My dear Amit, you made us aware of a resolution," Nurzhen announced, his voice chiming authority down the table. "Do tell."

"Yes, of course." Amit opened his palm to the three internal keepers next to him, Ansel, Daiya, and Zander. "Gavan and I have spoken with the healers, and we believe a team is needed in the Pacific Northwest region of the US, where the energy line of invisibility was in place, to extract the fades and secure safety for the humans."

Ashton's mouth dropped. Mason pushed back in his chair. Was he indicating that the internal keepers would go? Wouldn't it make sense for Mason and Ashton to be the ones? Or maybe they were all going together. Was that why his other castmates weren't here?

Why was he so rattled? He'd get to return to Seattle.

But he was finally feeling good about his position as a seam keeper. Hadn't he been tossed around enough? He looked at Ashton, who had to be thinking the same thing.

She directed her question at Gavan. "Are we going to the Human Realm?"

Gavan put up his hands. "Let us explain." He nodded to Amit.

Amit continued, "With the Blessing Council's approval, we are petitioning to send Zander's team of three to work with a human liaison in Seattle."

"Who?" Mason blurted.

The door opened, and Bethesda led in a welcome sight.

"Hicks!" Mason bolted up, greeting his friend.

"Are you okay?" He looked over his shoulder at Shunnar and Gavan. "Won't being here make him sick, like my dad? Get him *out* of here." Images of Max in his new memory care facility back in Seattle flitted across his mind. He wouldn't lose Hicks as well.

"Um, hi?" Hicks rubbed his head, his once buzzed cut a little longer.

"Mason's right." Ashton stared straight at Gavan. "He can't be here. Why hasn't his memory been adjusted or whatever it is we do?"

Bethesda rested a hand atop Mason's arm, eyeing them both. "Hicks is fine for the short spurts of time he will be here. Please, sit down."

Hicks looked at Mason, grabbed his shoulder. "Dude, I'm okay. More than okay. I know about this place. I know what you did for me. I want to help."

Mason shook his head. "No." The thought of another human losing their chance at a normal life to an otherworldly one was out of the question. If there was any chance he might end up like Max, forget it.

"Please, everyone, sit," Shunnar and Rory spewed at the same time.

Ashton pulled Mason back and dragged Hicks around the table to sit with them.

Bethesda began, "Only so many of Michael's memories may be altered. With the mind control the fade—"

"Kali." Hicks's voice snagged.

Bethesda corrected herself. "With the mind control Kali used to protect him from Kelvin, we are unable to do any more. And with the rogue fade quandary, Hicks has agreed to help us."

"Help us how?" Mason balled his fists. All he

could see was more unforeseen danger.

Hicks stood up, glanced at the internal keepers, and then back to Mason and Ashton. "I've been asked to join forces with the Dream Realm. Your invisibility—flower petal—crystal stuff—" He scrunched his nose, not entirely sure about everything. "Ashton, it's working. The pressure on internal keepers has been eased. Keepers are getting back to their regular duties." He glanced at Shunnar, as if checking to see if his lingo was right. "I can help this team." He thumbed to Ansel, Daiya, and Zander. "In Seattle. I know the city and human ways. They can round up the demons."

Mason jumped, ready to protest, or at least complain that it wasn't his team going, when the typically stoic Zander found his feet and his voice.

"Mason, I offered to go. It was my idea."

Ashton peered up at him. "Your idea?"

Mason had a feeling there was more to the story when a look transpired between Ashton and the keeper originally destined to her.

Zander stood tall, his voice deep, as he addressed the Blessing Council. "My destiny was uprooted a year ago. I never believed I had a choice about the rest of my future. Although I appreciate all I've learned in Reverie, soaring again as the hawk I am calls to me. When I learned of the rogue fades in Seattle, I spoke with my team." He beamed at Daiya and Ansel.

Daiya wore a serious expression, sharp like the cut of her hair, but there was a spark in her eyes as she peered at Zander. Ansel grinned from ear to ear.

"We accepted his offer." Ansel slapped the table, already eager for the mission.

"With all due respect." Zander gazed at the

representatives who hadn't yet revealed their thoughts on the matter.

Mason huffed a breath. Of course, it made sense. If Hicks knew about their world, he could be the link between. And he could watch over Max too. That eased Mason's heart.

"You want this?" Ashton asked Hicks.

"I do." He rubbed his head again. "I remember everything from my time with Kali. You were all in my house. I couldn't speak around the mind control. But I don't blame her. She only controlled me after Kelvin found her." He stopped abruptly, choking back emotion. "To keep me safe."

"Dude, this is dangerous work." Mason needed him to understand the risk. If he was upset by Kali's death, then he should know the truth.

"He knows." Daiya spoke up.

Rory nodded for her to go on.

"Rory and I have been researching fades. The information Ashton shared from her time with Kali proved invaluable." Daiya nodded in Ashton's direction. If the two of them had any of the animosity Ashton had told Mason about earlier, he couldn't detect it now.

"Fades are unique and *possibly* redeemable. Kali proved that in her sacrifice." Daiya swallowed as Hicks sat down. Mason put a hand on his shoulder. "Hicks has had the most encounters with a fade and can help with recognition."

Ansel broke in. "And since the internal keeper pace has slowed down because of Ashton's demon beacon, we are the team to go. Zander has already been there and studied human behaviors and history in his prep to be—um—well—you know mated with the Centennial." His cheeks flushed.

"What he means to say is that my team is best suited to go." Zander looked at Mason. "Your time is done there. *Your cast* needs you here at the Seam."

Zander stared at Mason, as if awaiting his approval. It wasn't up to him, but Mason appreciated the gesture anyway. Zander's emphasis on the words *your cast* didn't escape him. It was as if he had surrendered himself to something holding him back for far too long.

Mason glanced at Bethesda and breathed in a deep breath.

She addressed the council. "What say you?"

Isleen stood, her indigo gown swirling as she moved. Mason wondered if the realm representatives had mind telepathy like the hawks because without verbally discussing anything with the others, she responded, "We bless this new mission and pray each rogue fade will be accounted for and…"

Nurzhen touched her hand. "And we will decide each demon's fate independently."

Ashton let out a breath, and Mason reached over to squeeze her hand. Her bracelet with the charms brushed against his wrist. He glanced down at the oak leaf sparkling on her lap. Ashton smiled. "This will be good."

A blinding blue light cascaded from the ceiling as the Angel Sandalphon strummed a song through every pore in Mason's body. He couldn't look around, as the music swept through his mind too deeply. The radiance too bright. The sense of warmth and safety and blessing too empowering.

He let the blessing run over him, through him, encircle him until it all ended as quickly as it had begun. Softly, the faint glows of illumination filtered from above and the lighting, still a soft blue from the chandeliers, adjusted back to normal.

Normal.

This word would never describe his life. Although a part of him craved to join Hicks on this new Human Realm team, he had something more pressing here at the Seam.

Epilogue

Mason was quiet as he walked back to the gardens with Ashton.

"Are you okay with Zander's team living at your dad's house? Working with one of your best friends?"

Mason drew a finger along her jawline. "Yep."

Ashton scrunched her face. "What's wrong with you?"

"Nothing's wrong." He shook his head. "For the first time in my life, things are feeling more *right*. I mean, it's potentially worrisome to have fades randomly roaming Seattle. My dad's memory loss still hurts. But I'm relieved to be back at the Seam doing what I'm supposed to be doing. Here."

He pulled her down to the stone bench. "I'm done trying to save everyone, Ash. I need to be in the moment with my cast. Present with you." He brushed back windblown pieces of her hair.

"I like *this* Mason. Focusing on one thing for now." She pulled her bag off her shoulder and reached inside. "I have something from your mom."

He lifted a brow. He hadn't received anything from his mom in over thirteen years, save the hard truth of his heritage.

"She asked me to give it to you. And she's open to answering any questions you might have when you're ready."

He eyed her sideways. "You talk to your birth father one time, and you're an expert on uniting lost families?" He grinned so she knew he was teasing. With the crisis in Reverie managed and his parents somewhat safe again, he *was* ready.

He kissed her scowl away…each eyelid, her scar, the tip of her nose, down to the corners of her lips. "Thank you."

She exhaled a long breath. "Take this before we're distracted from the matter at hand." She pushed something hard into his chest.

He caught the book in his hands, then glanced at Ashton. "Her journal." It was leather bound and worn, looking as if his mom had carried it around a lot. He opened to the middle—

I saw you today, my
sweet boy of a man
racing about, grunts
from a new language,
daring your opponent,
to take your ball,
to block your goal.
3-2 for the win. You
were spectacular.
Now I cannot wait
to see you fly.

Mason closed the book, tears his only opponent now. And he was losing.

Ashton pulled his forehead to hers. "Take your time. We have—"

"A lot of it, Centennial mate of mine." He sniffed the override of emotions and set the journal behind him on the bench. "I think our next big battle is finally settling into our new lives in Toria."

"Our new home away from home," she whispered against his skin.

He tilted to meet her lips, everything feeling as it should.

Always.

A word about the author...

Celaine Charles lives in the Pacific Northwest where she teaches elementary students, writes poetry and fantasy, and blogs about her writing journey on her site, Steps In Between. When seeking balance, CC takes long walks through the enchanting forests of Washington State and devours far too much allergy-free dark chocolate! Sign up for her newsletter at https://celainecharlesauthor.com/

Thank you for purchasing
this publication of The Wild Rose Press, Inc.

For questions or more information
contact us at
info@thewildrosepress.com.

The Wild Rose Press, Inc.
www.thewildrosepress.com